THE MUMMY OF BIRCHEN BOWER & OTHER TRUE
GHOST STORIES

THE MUMMY OF BIRCHEN BOWER
& OTHER TRUE GHOST STORIES
A Harry Ludlam Omnibus Edition

W. Foulsham & Co. Ltd.

London · New York · Toronto · Cape Town · Sydney

W. Foulsham & Company Limited
Yeovil Road, Slough, Berkshire SL1 4JH

First published by W. Foulsham as *The Mummy of Birchen Bower and other True Ghosts* (1966) *and The Restless Ghosts of Ladye Place and other True Hauntings* (1967)

This Omnibus edition published 1985

Printed at The Bath Press, Avon

CONTENTS

CONTENTS

INTRODUCTION

When I first became interested in ghost-hunting people thought I was a bit of a crank. Things have changed a lot since then. I have investigated some 300 cases of hauntings.

The question I am most asked is "How does one go about ghost-hunting?"

All I can say in reply is that it is not for the easily impressed or the easily wearied. You need to be as questioning as the most hard-nosed sceptic; and you must be prepared to get on your bicycle and go after the facts.

You need patience, too. It can take months, even years, to piece together fragmentary testimony and evidence to give the fullest possible account of a particular haunting. It is generally little use holding a one-night vigil, for ghosts are timeless and appear as they please.

The majority of ghosts are encountered not by professional "ghost-seers" but by ordinary people going about their daily lives and business. This book is mainly about such hauntings.

Unhappily, many people who see a ghost afterwards wish they had not been so favoured. Seeing an apparition is a paralysing enough experience for anyone, especially those who have never given the ghost world a second thought; but what follows can be even worse, when they are faced with suspicion and disbelief.

Small wonder that numbers of people still keep silent about what they saw. Like the patient who feels that what he is suffering from is so awful he delays telling the doctor. When he finally plucks up courage enough to do so it is to find to his relief that his condition is not unique at all. So it is with seeing or experiencing a ghost, as many of these case histories show. There can be as many as a dozen individual witnesses to one haunting; and, as will be seen, as many as a dozen apparitions or manifestations involved in others.

People who saw "things" used to be laughed at. Seldom any more. The question, "Do you believe in ghosts?" is as dated as the old idea that apparitions clanked about only in castles and stately homes. The question now is, "What do you think they are – what causes them?"

This is for the scientific researchers, and their work goes on. The wide and varying nature of these stories perhaps shows how far we still have to go to find the answers.

I would particularly like to thank Paul Lund, Robert V. Steele, Charlotte E. Tucker, Gladys Cordwell and Emma Macdonald for their invaluable help in these investigations made over a long period. My thanks also to Ernest Benn Ltd for their kind permission to retell the incidents of William Corder's skull and the leper's house at Thetford, from the late Robert Thurston Hopkin's *Adventures with Phantoms*, published by the Quality Press in 1946.

H.L.

THE RETURN OF WILLIAM TERRISS

William Terriss, forty-nine-year-old public idol of the 1890s, intrepid hero of popular melodrama at the Adelphi Theatre in the Strand, began the walk that led to his violent death shortly after seven o'clock on the evening of December 16th, 1897.

As Terriss lived out of town it was his custom to dine at the Green Room Club in Bedford Street, just off the Strand, and then walk the short distance to Maiden Lane, where he let himself into the back of the Adelphi through a pass-door to which he and other leading players had a key.

On this night Terriss, on his walk to the theatre, was accompanied by an elderly friend named John Graves. Chatting and laughing, the pair turned into narrow, gaslit Maiden Lane, and on arriving at the pass-door Terriss took leave of his friend, unbuttoned his frock coat and reached in a pocket for his key. Neither man had noticed a figure standing silently in the shadows on the opposite side of the road; a dark-eyed man with dark curled moustache, muffled in a long, shabby black Inverness cape with upturned collar, and wearing a slouch hat.

As Terriss put his key to the lock of the pass-door, the man in the cape ran the short distance across the narrow lane and swiftly plunged a knife into the actor's back. The attacker's aim was not true. The knife struck the actor's shoulder blade and glanced aside, inflicting a bad flesh wound. But as Terriss, taken completely by surprise, struggled round to face his assailant, he was struck again high up near the spine, and then, fatally, directly over the heart. He died minutes afterwards.

It was an utterly senseless murder. A tragic mistake.

The assailant was Richard Arthur Prince, an eccentric super or bit player known among the other supers at the Adelphi as "Mad Arthur". Prince, aged thirty-two, had come from Dundee to seek his fortune on the London stage, but had soon shown himself to be

totally unsuited for the profession and was lucky to get work as a
super. In the play that had been running before the present production at the Adelphi, Prince had become the butt of his colleagues,
who played cruelly on his vanity. They teased him that he was des-
tined to become one of the greatest actors of all time, that Terriss
recognised this and was determined never to let him have a chance
of succeeding. They even had him pathetically act out Terriss's role
of the hero, which by right, they said, should have been his. All this
filled the unstable man with a rabid jealousy.

Terriss remained completely unaware of what was going on, not
even knowing Prince by sight. When the play came to an end,
Prince, among others, was thrown out of work. Unable to obtain
an engagement elsewhere, he applied to the Actors' Benevolent
Fund for relief, and also approached, among other people, William
Terriss.

Terriss unhesitatingly gave the distressed man a sovereign. This
was on the evening of December 15th, 1897. Next day, a meeting of
the Benevolent Fund committee regretfully had to turn down
Prince's request for assistance. Prince asked the name of the committee's chairman, and was told that it was "Terry" (Edward Terry,
the comedian). But somehow the angry, unbalanced man confused
the name with Terriss. He went to an ironmonger's shop and, out of
the sovereign that William Terriss had given him, bought a sharp
meat knife for 1s 9d. Then, waiting till dusk, he made his way to
Maiden Lane.

Prince, after his attack on the actor, stood by and gave no resistance as he was seized and given in charge. Terriss was carried dying
through the door he had been about to open. He died twenty
minutes afterwards, his head supported by his bitterly sobbing leading lady, Jessie Millward, who had rushed to his side. The last
words he was heard to mutter were, "My God, my God."

Terriss's only near relative at hand was Seymour Hicks, his actor
son-in-law, who was taken to Bow Street police station to identify
Prince. The murderer was foaming at the mouth and looked like a
savage animal. Hicks then went to the Adelphi and knelt by the
couch on which his father-in-law lay dead, his face calm and a smile
on his lips.

"In the serenity and quiet of the room," Sir Seymour Hicks wrote
years after (in 1939), "I to this day feel sure I heard a voice say to
me, 'Are there men living such fools as to think there is no here-
after?' That night I knew beyond all shadow of doubt that William
Terriss and myself would meet again."

Prince was found guilty but insane, and committed to Broadmoor Criminal Lunatic Asylum, where he died in 1937.

The haunting of the Adelphi Theatre began very shortly after the shocking tragedy for which he was responsible. Many actors reported hearing strange tappings coming from Terriss's old dressing room, though none would openly admit the possibility of the noises being made by a ghost. In 1928, however, things came to a head.

June, the musical comedy actress, was then playing at the theatre and occupied the room which had been used by Jessie Millward at the time of Terriss's death. Terriss, every evening on entering the pass-door in Maiden Lane, had been in the habit of tapping with his walking stick on the door of this room, an affectionate signal to his leading lady as he passed by on the way to his own room.

The dressing room was a large one with three windows and an open fireplace, just like a room in a house. It was June's practice never to leave the theatre after a matinee. A light meal was brought in from a restaurant for her, after which she generally slept till seven-fifteen. It was during these hours that strange things began to happen and she described her experiences shortly afterwards.

"I had a comfortable chaise-longue on which to rest. But as soon as I had relaxed and was ready for sleep the couch would begin to vibrate, then lurch, and often it would seem as though someone were actually kicking it underneath.

"After this had happened sufficiently often to annoy me, I noticed that a pale, greenish light appeared in front of my dressing-table mirror. The first time this occurred I rose quickly, rubbing my eyes, and walked right over to the glass. The light remained until I felt I could pass my hand through it . . . then disappeared."

June's dresser then told her that often when the actress was down on the stage, a knock would come at the dressing-room door, and upon answering it she would find no one there. Eventually June told someone in the theatre of these uncanny happenings, and it was then suggested that they may be due to the haunting presence of William Terriss. A seance was held in the theatre, but without result; though after it the strange noises and lights ceased.

Inevitably many people at the time looked upon the affair as a theatre publicity stunt, but June, writing of the incident four years later, declared, "I can assure them it was no such thing. I offer no argument for or against this queer story—I can only repeat that the noises *did* occur and I *did* see strange lights, and my dresser, Ethel Rollin, *did* answer the phantom knocks at my door."

In the years since there have been, from time to time, reports of footsteps and strange noises, and the uneasy feeling of a "presence" at the Adelphi, where, although William Terriss's old dressing room no longer exists, the doorway where he was murdered is still to be seen. There is, however, only one instance of an apparition being seen, and this was outside the theatre.

The late W. J. Macqueen-Pope, the theatre historian, wrote in 1959 that a few years before, on a summer's evening, a man who did not know the story of Terriss at all was walking alone near the pass-door when "he saw coming towards him a handsome man in rather old-fashioned clothes, who passed him by. So striking was he to look at that the man in question turned his head to look again. But nobody was in sight—and there had not been time for the passer-by to get out of the alley nor is there any other entrance. The meeting had been just by that fatal door. Puzzled, he tried to dismiss it as hallucination, but he told the story to the man who writes these words—who enlightened him and drew his own conclusions."

I am told by the Adelphi management that nightwatchmen at the theatre have often reported hearing footsteps and odd noises, and confessed to a feeling that they were being watched. One uneasy watchman, in 1965, used to swear that he could sense "something" present very close at hand, as if a person was in hiding nearby, watching him. Another curious occurrence has been that lifts have started working by themselves. They have afterwards been checked and found to be mechanically sound, leaving no explanation whatever for their erratic conduct.

Meantime, since the 1950s, the actual apparition of William Terriss has in fact been seen, very many times, in perhaps one of the most unlikely places of all: Covent Garden Underground station, which is just a short walk from the Adelphi. Not for some time, however, were the uncanny events at the station linked with the murdered actor.

From about 1952 there had been rumours among some of the Underground staff that a ghostly figure had been seen, and, more frequently, footsteps heard, in a tunnel of the station after it had closed at night. This talk, chiefly among engineers and gangers at work on the line, did not spread to other quarters, probably because of a natural reluctance on the part of anyone to admit having actually heard the phantom footsteps or fleetingly glimpsed the figure. But very shortly, suddenly and frighteningly, the haunting made itself known to members of the station staff.

Just after midnight on a night of November, 1955, when the last train had gone through Covent Garden, foreman ticket collector

Jack Hayden as usual locked the front and back gates of the station and went down in one of the lifts to make a final check that the platforms were clear. While looking cursorily around he suddenly saw a tall, distinguished looking man walk up the westbound subway and, instead of entering the waiting lift, begin walking up the spiral emergency stairs.

Hayden immediately phoned up to the booking clerk—"Catch that man coming up the emergency stairs, Henry, and let him out."

Shortly afterwards Hayden surfaced in the lift, to be told by the mystified booking clerk that no one had emerged from the stairs. Together the two men then made a search, but the spiral staircase and all parts of the station were quite empty.

It was a very puzzling incident, though as yet there was no serious thought of ghosts. Jack Hayden had been at Covent Garden station since 1946 and he had not heard any suggestion of there being a ghost in the tunnel. Nor was he aware of the hauntings at the Adelphi—he had never heard of William Terriss. But confirmation that he had not been "dreaming" the platform incident came in startling fashion only days afterwards, on November 24th, 1955.

The staff messroom at Covent Garden, just below ground level, is divided into two sections, comprising a small inner room and a large outer one. It was again shortly after midnight, the last train having gone through, and Hayden was sitting at a table in the inner room with the door open, when he suddenly saw standing in the outer room, gazing at him, a tall man in an old-fashioned grey suit. Hayden noticed particularly the man's "funny looking old-style collar" and his white or yellow gloves.

Again the foreman thought the man was a straggler from the last train who had lost his way. He asked, "Looking for the cloakroom, sir?" But the man did not answer, simply shifting from view. Hayden quickly got up and went through the communicating doorway but found the large outer room now quite empty. So was the passage outside deserted, and there was not a sound of receding footsteps.

Hayden, though this time considerably shaken, did not mention to the others what he had seen. But four days later, while he was still trying to form some rational explanation for the uncanny incident, there was a further alarming occurrence. At about midday, he and station woman Rose Ring were in the inner messroom when they heard a wild scream, and next moment Victor Locker, a nineteen-year-old coloured porter, burst into the room terror-stricken. Locker gasped that he had seen a strange looking man standing in a corner of the outer room, and on halting in surprise he had felt something press down hard on his head. The figure then vanished.

Hayden, after investigating and finding the room empty, asked Locker to describe the man, but the porter was too badly shaken to say more than that he was wearing "funny clothes". Hayden then, for the first time, slowly described the figure he himself had seen four days before.

"Yes!" said the terrified Locker. "That's the one."

The situation now had become so alarming that Hayden and his colleagues decided to seek official advice, and he reported events to the nearest control point, Leicester Square, the next station up the line. The Leicester Square stationmaster sent along his foreman, Eric Davey, to investigate. Davey seemed just the man for the inquiry, for besides having the necessary authority he was also a spiritualist of many years' experience.

Locker described to Davey what he had seen, pointing out the spot in a corner of the outer messroom, near to an old-fashioned fireplace, where the apparition had appeared. To get a clear picture of the incident Davey asked the coloured boy to go outside while he took up the exact position, under the pavement lights, formerly occupied by the ghost. As he stood there he became increasingly aware of an unseen presence very close to him. Then Locker returned to the room. Greatly agitated, he cried out, "Look out—he's on you, Mr Davey—he's on you!"

Davey tried to calm Locker, telling the young porter there was nothing to worry about. Mentally Davey asked the presence to leave, on the promise that he would help it later. He afterwards wrote a detailed report which was sent to divisional headquarters.

Locker, however, could not get over his double fright. He asked for a transfer and left Covent Garden station the following week.

Some days later the ghost returned to Davey, this time at Leicester Square. It was also seen, clairvoyantly, by another staff man who was a spiritualist, and who told Davey that he believed the spirit was trying to make it understood that its name was "Terry" or something like that.

Soon afterwards, at Covent Garden station on a night of December, Eric Davey and Jack Hayden were invited to describe the features of the ghost to a third party. They did so, and Davey also produced a sketch he had made of the sad-faced, sunken cheeked spectre. Davey and Hayden were then shown photographs of William Terriss. On production of the first photograph Hayden, who still had not heard the actor's name mentioned, much less seen his picture, cried out excitedly, "That's him, that's him. That's the man I saw in here!"

Why William Terriss should haunt Covent Garden station is a puzzle. The station is only a short walk from the rear of the theatre in Maiden Lane, but it was not opened till nine years after the actor's death. The date of its opening—December 15th, 1906—is only a day before the anniversary of his murder on the 16th, but this seems to hold little significance. As for the station itself, this is built on the site of a bakery which existed in Terriss's time, and in fact the old fireplace with its tall chimney, near which the apparition was seen in the outer messroom, is a part of the old building which was retained. Again, however, this seems a very tenuous link with Terriss.

Davey, in that December of 1955, endeavoured to make renewed contact with the ghost and guide it towards its release. For a time it seemed that he had been successful in these efforts, but then the hauntings resumed and they have gone on right up to the present day.

The ghost seems to observe a regular "walk". Just inside the tunnel from Covent Garden station to Holborn is a signal cabin, ahead of which is a crossover line. The ghost's footsteps have consistently been heard on very many occasions, especially on Sundays, when Covent Garden station is closed and trains go through non-stop. One Sunday signalman who heard the footsteps repeatedly phoned Leicester Square to ask that someone be sent along to Covent Garden to "let the people out". He could not believe that the footsteps he was hearing were not real—until he also saw the apparition walk to the platform, and glimpsed it again several times. This was in 1963-4.

One Sunday at the deserted station Jack Hayden, then working in the signal cabin, heard a curious eerie rattling noise, which was also heard by another of the railway staff. Afterwards Hayden and a colleague found that a wooden passenger seat on the platform had been moved from one side of an exit to the other. It was established that no human agency could have been up to trickery in the locked and empty station. Ever afterwards, when alone in the cabin on a Sunday, Hayden kept the door locked.

Another development was the commencement of ghostly knocking on the messroom door. Two slow, measured knocks would sound at any time of the day or night, and always when Hayden quickly opened the door there would be no one outside. This phantom knocking became a joke to some of the staff who in fun used to knock in imitation of it, but the joke began to pall as the mysterious noises went on, while the atmosphere in the messroom when the ghost entered it unseen was indescribably eerie.

Hayden told me, "I would always know full well when the presence was there. My scalp would begin to creep and my hair stand on end—really up on end, rigid—and I would feel my head swelling up like a big balloon."

He actually saw the apparition on more than a dozen occasions, from his first sight of it in November, 1955 to the time he left Covent Garden station ten years later, in 1965. The apparition invariably appeared during November-December and always assumed the same appearance, that of a man in an old-fashioned grey suit wearing white or yellow gloves. What forcibly impressed Hayden was the figure's old-fashioned high collar and his "very, very sad face". Always when he saw it, it was near to a wall. On several occasions he brought himself to speak to it, asking if he could help, but there was never a reply.

The last time Jack Hayden saw the apparition was late one night of November, 1964. He was walking down the spiral emergency stairs when, at about the second landing down, he suddenly encountered the ghost *walking up* the stairs. He hurriedly ran on down past the apparition, almost falling the last few steps to the bottom in his fright.

Mr Hayden left Covent Garden station in April, 1965 after almost twenty years' service there. He told me, "It became too much for me, the knocking, the footsteps, and the feeling he was always there somewhere. I just had to ask for a transfer."

Others who have seen the continued appearances of the ghost include Stationmaster Jones, at Leicester Square, and an engineer who saw it standing in the Covent Garden messroom in 1964. Some of the engineering staff refuse to work at Covent Garden station and will not stay in the messroom there.

Meantime the footsteps from the haunted crossover in the tunnel go on at intervals. Even as this account was being written, night engineers reported hearing them follow their inevitable passage from the tunnel to the platform of Covent Garden station.

THE MUMMY OF BIRCHEN BOWER

The first report of strange happenings in the transformer department of the new Ferranti factory at Hollinwood, near Oldham, came from three men on weekend night shift who claimed to have seen a shadowy figure moving at one end of the shop. In April, 1956, when the hauntings at the factory were finally made public, there were no fewer than thirty-five night workers who claimed to have seen or heard the ghost.

Several reported seeing a shadowy figure moving at one end of the department, while others claimed to have seen an apparition hovering round the machines. When they approached to investigate, however, the intruder had vanished.

At first it was thought that the shadows might have been caused by the night watchmen on patrol, but it was established that they were nowhere in the vicinity at the time. Then it was suggested that the apparition could be a trick of light, or simply imagination.

Dubious colleagues of the ghost-seers began to refer to "the new man". But even the most sceptical among them admitted to other incidents reported to the management which could not be satisfactorily explained. No one, for instance, could give a reason why a grinding machine should start up on its own with no one to pull the lever, or why a metal sheet should suddenly crash to the ground.

But people who had lived in the district for a long time were not in the least surprised to hear of these strange upsets, for Ferranti's Avenue Works had been built on the site of an old estate known as Birchen Bower, whose former owner, Madame Hannah Beswick, was believed to have haunted the spot for most of the two hundred years since her death.

The extraordinary story of Hannah Beswick, descendant of a very old Manchester family, is one of macabre human eccentricity combined with the eerily supernatural. It is also one which, by reason of the web of legends spun around it, developed over the years into a larger mystery baffling many investigators. Examination of these legends, together with reference to family papers and numerous other sources, enables us to construct a more accurate account of the affair, if some small mysteries still remain.

The story begins quietly enough in the 1730s, when John Beswick and his half-sister, Hannah, were living a comfortable life at Birchen Bower Farm, near Hollinwood, a small village not far from Oldham and Ashton-under-Lyne. Their father had died at a very young age in 1706, when they were both infants. Hannah, born in 1702, was two years older than her half-brother, who by inheritance and industry was a wealthy man. John, however, suffered bad health and was forced into semi-retirement at Birchen Bower in an attempt to recuperate. In 1737, when his impending death became apparent, he made his will, in which he left the bulk of his substantial fortune to Hannah. He died at Birchen Bower later the same year, aged thirty-three.

Hannah Beswick, at thirty-five years old, now took over the running of Birchen Bower Farm. She was by all accounts a very active woman and managed the estate exceedingly well. It was, however, only a part of the holdings which she inherited from her brother; Birchen Bower was contained in the estate of Cheetwood-in-Cheetham which fell to her along with other local property including cottages, houses and a smithy at Bradley Bent, Hollinwood. Other assets were a valuable freehold estate at Ashton-under-Lyne and houses and land at Wakefield and Bradford.

In the years that followed Hannah seems to have lived a somewhat solitary existence at Birchen Bower, with its quaint four-gabled house built in the form of a cross. She never married, and it was probably by reason of her manorial status that she came to be popularly known as "Madame" Beswick.

She was in her forties when her peaceful life on the estate seemed gravely threatened. It was the time of the Jacobite rebellion in 1745. Reports came that "Bonnie" Prince Charles was marching south through Lancashire, and in great fear of the Highlanders looting her possessions, Hannah buried "great sums" of money and valuables around Birchen Bower. There was, of course, nothing unusual in this, safe burial of one's precious belongings being still the first thought of many people in time of unrest in that century and the next; but when the danger had passed, Hannah let her treasure lie and could never afterwards be induced by her relatives to reveal its hiding place.

She continued to farm her estate until, in her fifties, age and fast deteriorating health compelled her to give up this activity, and she withdrew to a small stone cottage on the brink of a mill-stream. Here she lived out the rest of her life in loneliness relieved only by occasional visits from her relatives and the attendances of her personal physician, Mr Charles White, of Manchester, a young surgeon of fast growing repute. According to the later memoirs of Thomas De Quincey, the author of *Confessions of an Opium Eater,* Hannah "owed much alleviation of her sufferings to White's inventive skill".

Hannah, succumbing eventually to what transpired to be her last illness, promised her relatives that if they would carry her up to Bower House she would at last disclose her secret and point out the place or places where her money and valuables were buried. But they delayed in carrying out her wish, and she became suddenly worse and died, taking her secret with her.

She was fifty-six when she died in 1758, but there was no funeral or burial. For by private arrangement with her physician, Hannah, who had a deep dread of being accidentally buried alive while in a trance, ensured that her body would be "kept above ground". Tradition says that her horror of possible burial alive arose from the fact that her brother John had once been considered dead, but that just before the coffin-lid was screwed down signs of life in him were noticed; restoratives were applied and, after having been in a trance for several days, he revived and lived on for some time. Remembering John Beswick's poor state of health this could very well have occurred. There was no other apparent cause for Hannah's morbid dread. At all events she seems to have made explicit arrangements with her physician to remain unburied, for a certain time at least.

De Quincey, born a quarter of a century later, knew Charles White very well, the surgeon being a friend of his mother, and in later years, after the surgeon's death, he wrote that he believed Hannah Beswick made a bequest of £25,000 to White on condition that he should keep her out of the ground and embalm her "as perfectly as the resources in that art of London and Paris could accomplish". But this, together with a tradition that she actually made over her Birchen Bower estate to the surgeon on the same condition, would appear to be romanticism, for in her will, made shortly before her death, Hannah left the young surgeon just £100; in those days not an inconsiderable amount, but by no means a fortune. What she did do, however, in leaving Birchen Bower expressly to her mother's relations instead of her father's, was to will the leasehold estate to a cousin, upon whose death it was to pass to the cousin's daughter—and in the event of the death of both these executrices in his lifetime, to Charles White. Rather surprisingly the surgeon did outlive both these women, so finally securing Birchen Bower. Hence a basis for the local tradition.

Hannah's will made no mention of embalmment, but a letter written in 1758 by one of the trustees makes clear that it was understood by the executrices and the physician that her body was to be embalmed. A puzzling contradiction to her believed wish to be kept "above ground", however, is her instruction that £400 be paid to the executrices "in order to defray the expenses of my funeral", any surplus to be shared among her father's relations "without giving account to any person". Whether this money was actually for her embalmment, or whether she did expect burial at some date, cannot be known. The surgeon left no records.

White, then thirty years old and a man of very forceful character, went ahead with his curious work, embalming the body with tar and swathing it with a strong bandage, leaving the face exposed. The mummy then remained at Cheetwood Old Hall, the ancestral home of the Beswicks, for two years, the same period as were the two executrices required by Hannah to stay in occupation there. Whether by Hannah's wish or by his own agreement with the executrices, White, who was a keen collector of anatomical subjects, afterwards took possession of the mummy and kept it for many years at his home in King Street, Manchester. When he retired from his profession he removed it to his country residence, The Priory, in Sale, Cheshire. There he placed it in his private museum, which contained hundreds of anatomical subjects as well as all kinds of curios.

He kept the mummy in the case of a grandfather clock from which the clock-face had been removed. The mummy's head appeared where the clock-face had once been, but was screened from view by a veil of white velvet. According to De Quincey, who as a child in the 1790s had "gazed upon the clock case with inexpressible awe", White's promise to Miss Beswick required that once a year, accompanied by two witnesses of credit, he should withdraw the veil from her silent features. De Quincey, in his teens, taking his close friend Lady Carbery on a visit to the surgeon's private collection in 1802, was sorely disappointed to find that White no longer kept the mummy prominently in sight and made no offer to show it to them. Courtesy demanded that they should not openly request to see it, but, wrote De Quincey, "Naturally on my report of the case, the whole of our party were devoured by a curiosity to see the departed fair one. Had Mr White, indeed, furnished us with the key of the museum, leaving us to our own discretion . . . great is my fear that the perfidious question would have arisen amongst us—what o'clock was it?"

Meantime, while the remains of Miss Beswick reposed incongruously in the grandfather clock, strange things had begun to happen at Birchen Bower. There were reports of Hannah being seen haunting the neighbourhood of the farm, of strange, weird noises being heard, and the inexplicable behaviour of farm animals. These odd disturbances seemed to occur most strongly on every seventh anniversary of her death.

It was also asserted locally that one of the arrangements made by Miss Beswick with her physician was that every twenty-one years her body should be brought to Birchen Bower and remain there for a week. It is quite possible that Charles White, with his evident zeal for the curious, did transport the mummy to the estate on one or more occasions. If he took it there after the first twenty-one years, in 1779, it was during the lifetime of one or both of the executrices, with whom he was patently on familiar terms. If he took it there again after another twenty-one years, in 1800, it was during the ownership of the estate by three of his children; for in 1792, when the second of the executrices had died, Birchen Bower was leased to him by the Earl of Derby in favour of the children.

So the mummy, according to villagers, was brought to Birchen Bower and put in the granary of the old farmstead. In the morning, when the corpse was fetched, the horses and cows were always found let loose, and sometimes a cow would be found up in the hayloft, though how it came there was a mystery as there was no passage large enough to admit such a big animal.

At Birchen Bower house itself Hannah Beswick's ghost appeared in more tangible form and followed no stipulated times. The old house had been divided into tenements inhabited chiefly by handloom weavers, and "Madame" Beswick's ghost was often heard by them rustling through the corridors. Then her apparition clearly appeared. One family grew so familiar with the sight of the spectre, clad in a black silken gown, that they were in no way alarmed by it. Sometimes when they were seated at supper a rustling of silk would be heard at the front entrance, and presently the lady in black would glide through the room, walk straight into the parlour, and vanish at one particular flagstone. It was a harmless spirit, annoying no one, and its appearance never caused any more excitement among the family than the remark, "Hush! The old lady comes again!"

In another part of the building one of the tenants had a treadle lathe for wood-turning, which he used after his day's work to do odd jobs for the neighbours. Sometimes when he went into his little workroom he would find the lathe working away in full motion, as if treadled by an invisible visitor.

It was not for some years afterwards that the disclosure was made by one of the weavers living at Birchen Bower house that he had found "Madame" Beswick's hidden treasure, or part of it at least. His discovery was made during the time of the severe slump at the end of the eighteenth century. The handloom weavers as a body were then desperate for want of food, but it was noticed among them that one man, "Joe at Tamer's", made large purchases and seemed to get by quite comfortably. He had a large family of small children solely dependent on his labours with the shuttle, yet in these straitened times they did not want for either food or clothing.

It began to be whispered that Joe had found "Madame" Beswick's gold; and in fact he had. Many years later he confessed how he had come upon it. He pulled up the floor of the haunted parlour, intending to put up a loom for one of his children to learn to weave, and while digging the treadle hole turned up a tin vessel filled with gold wedges. The surprised and delighted man never told anyone at the time but secretly took his find to Oliphant's, the jewellers in St Anne's Square, Manchester, where he received seventy shillings for each piece of gold. People were still living in the middle of the last century who knew "Joe at Tamer's". The tin vessel in which he found the gold was preserved by his descendants.

Despite this discovery, Hannah's ghost continued to haunt the old house and the estate. Many people claimed to have seen her spectre near the well in Bower Clough, and such was the superstitious fear in the neighbourhood that few people would use the well after dark. Nervous adults and children were known to have filled their "burn cans" from the dubious waters of the newly-built Rochdale Canal rather than go near the place.

During these years Charles White lived on in old age to survive even his three children who had taken Birchen Bower, and when they died his claim to the estate continued. In 1811 he was granted another lease of it in favour of his grandson.

Three years earlier, at the age of eighty, he had presented his anatomical collection to St Mary's Hospital, Manchester, though without the mummy of Miss Beswick, which he stowed away in the roof of The Priory. When in 1813 he died, aged eighty-four, totally blind in his last months, he left the mummy to a Dr Ollier who attended him during his last illness. In 1829, Ollier, in his turn, left it to the museum of the Manchester Natural History Society, in Peter Street, along with other specimens from Charles White's collection.

The mummy, though now without its grandfather clock casing, remained a popular attraction at the museum for many years, laid out in a glass case with a ticket briefly inscribed, "The mummy of Miss Beswick". It was kept on view in the entrance hall together with an elephant, a giraffe, and other animal exhibits including the stuffed head at Old Billy, a canal horse that had lived for sixty-one years. The mummy was insured for a mere £10 compared with £80 for the elephant. A local writer of about 1850 described Miss Beswick's appearance at this time:

"The body was well preserved but the face was shrivelled and black. The legs and trunk were wrapped in a strong cloth such as is used for bed-ticks, and the body was that of a little woman. It was in a glass coffin-shaped case."

Hannah had now been dead for nearly a century. Almost all knowledge of the mummy, on which no records were kept, had slipped so quickly into the vague past that the common answer given to inquiring visitors to the museum was that the body was that of a Manchester woman who had given a sum to charity on condition that she should never be buried.

In 1868, when the Peter Street museum was handed over to the newly-formed Owen's College, the commissioners charged with re-arrangement of the collections took an instant dislike to the mummy. They contacted Hannah Beswick's nearest descendants but no one wanted to take the body off their hands. As there was not even a death certificate to show that she was officially dead, an approach was made to the Home Secretary. Permission from him and the bishop being obtained, the remains of Hannah Beswick were finally laid to rest in Harpurhey Cemetery, Manchester, on July 22nd, 1868, one hundred and ten years after her death. A solitary paragraph in the *Manchester Guardian* reported the "curious interment".

"It may well be that her after-death wanderings have at last ceased," wrote another correspondent at the time. But if her body was at rest, Hannah's spirit was not. There were many stories of her haunting The Priory, where she had temporarily rested, while the hauntings at Birchen Bower went on. Again she was seen near the old well. A villager who went to fetch a pail of water at dusk saw standing by the well a tallish woman in a black silk gown and old-fashioned white frilled cap. Her attitude was threatening, streams of blue light seeming to dart from her eyes and flash on the terror-stricken man, who took to his heels.

This appearance occurred at a time when a descendant of the Beswick family was trying to recover the lost estate through the courts, and it was popularly considered to be a token that Hannah would get no rest until the property had been returned to her father's family. But remembering her very deliberate bequest of the estate to her mother's relations, this belief had little foundation and was possibly born of wishful thinking by supporters of the outraged Beswick descendants.

The disturbances on the farm every seventh anniversary of Hannah's death went on. Some ten years before her burial, on the fourteenth anniversary of seven years since her death, a cow belonging to the farmer then tenanting Birchen Bower was found one morning in the hay-loft. How the animal got up there was a complete mystery to everyone. Blocks had to be borrowed from Bower Mill to let it down through the hay-hole outside the barn.

Many superstitions centred around the barn, which bore the initials of the Beswick family engraved on it. Late in the last century, when all but the southern wing of Birchen Bower house had been demolished, the barn seemed to be the main source of supernatural manifestations. On dark and dreary nights the barn, it was said, appeared to be on fire, a red glare of glowing heat being seen through the holes and crevices of the building and strange, unearthly noises coming from it. Sometimes the sight was so threatening that people living round about raised the alarm and knocked up the farmer to tell him the barn was in flames. When the premises were searched, however, nothing was found wrong.

The restless ghost of Hannah Beswick also continued its wanderings on the estate. On clear, moonlight nights her apparition was seen to walk, sometimes in a headless state, between the old barn and the horsepool, always vanishing from sight when near to the pool, which gave rise to a belief that she had buried other money or valuables there during the advance of Prince Charles and was desirous of pointing out the spot to anyone courageous enough to speak to her. But no one was.

Today, with Birchen Bower vanished beneath modern factories and Hollinwood Avenue brightly lit with a steady stream of traffic, almost the only memory of the estate is perpetuated in the name of Bower Lane. All trace of Hannah Beswick and her ghost would seem to have disappeared. Unless, of course, the disturbances at the Ferranti factory in 1956 owe anything to her restlessness.

Her grave in Harpurhey Cemetery, listed as number 223, in Church of England plot number three, lies somewhere among a tangle of bushes and weeds and headstones flat on the ground covered with soil and grass. The cemetery register records, "No relations or friends were present at the burial and no stone or memorial was put over the grave."

The entry adds that some time after Hannah Beswick's death there were found, under the floor of the drawing room of Cheetwood Old Hall, human remains which were presumed to be those removed from her body when she was embalmed.

THE GREY MAN OF BEN MACDHUI

The Cairngorm mountains, situated on the borders of Inverness-shire, Banffshire and Aberdeenshire, are unlike other Scottish mountains, having characteristics all their own. There are no peaked tops as in the western hills, but great, magnificent masses of flat tops cutting down into beautiful corries with their wonderful lochs. The monarch of the Cairngorms is Ben Macdhui, at 4,296 ft. the second highest mountain in Britain.

On a misty day of early spring, in the 1880s, a lone climber continued his slow and careful way over the last few hundred feet of snow-covered ground to the flat summit of Ben Macdhui. Visibility was only a few yards and the snow was crisp and deep.

On reaching the summit the climber, a young man nearing thirty, paused for a time beside the high stone cairn set up there by an Ordnance Survey team in 1847. After his rest he was walking away from the cairn in the mist when he began to think he heard other things than merely the noise of his own footsteps in the snow. For every few steps he took he heard a big crunch, and then another crunch, as if someone was walking after him but taking steps three or four times the length of his own.

Thinking some other climber was on his track, he stopped and waited for the man to come up and join him, but the moment he stopped so did the footsteps in the mist behind. When he walked on they began again; he heard them even more clearly and they seemed to be getting closer. He again stood still, but could see nothing.

He was not a fanciful man. He was a scientist, and an experienced mountaineer. He told himself, "This is nonsense," and tried to shrug off the uneasy feeling now stealing over him. But as he walked on the pursuing footsteps began again, an eerie "crunch, crunch" close behind him. Again he looked back but could see nothing in the mist.

Suddenly he was seized with the most tremendous terror. Why, he did not know, for he had never minded being alone on the hills.

But the uncanny *something* which he now acutely sensed caused fear to grip him by the throat. He took to his heels and ran, staggering blindly among the boulders, for five miles, nearly down to Rothiemurchus Forest. Only then, close to the reassuring safety of the trees, did he manage with some effort to pull himself together.

The climber was John Norman Collie, afterwards to achieve no mean reputation as professor of organic chemistry at London University (1902-28) and a Fellow of the Royal Society. Collie, much shaken, related his strange experience to a handful of friends, but it was not until twelve years later that the story was made public for the first time. This was in New Zealand at the turn of the century, when he told the story to some mountaineering friends. His account was reported tongue-in-cheek by the local newspapers, who did not take him very seriously.

Soon afterwards, however, Collie discussed his experience with Dr A. M. Kellas, lecturer on chemistry in the medical school of the Middlesex Hospital. Kellas, also a skilled mountaineer, revealed to Collie that he too had had a weird experience at the top of the same mountain. He said that he and his brother Henry were on Ben Macdhui late one evening in June. They had spent some time chipping for crystals on the slope of a fold of the hill well below the cairn, and then parted, Henry going up to the summit.

Kellas said that later, on looking up, he saw the figure of a man come up out of the Larig Ghru or "Gloomy Pass"—the trough-like depression cutting through the centre of the range—and wander slowly round the stone cairn, near which his brother was sitting. He was surprised for it was not an ordinary thing for people to wander alone on the top of Ben Macdhui at that hour—it was then nearly midnight, but his surprise turned to astonishment when he saw that the man was practically the same height as the cairn, which was some ten feet high. As he watched, the giant figure, after circling the cairn, slowly descended into the Larig and disappeared. Kellas waited for it to bob back into view, but it never did.

He ran up and asked his brother, "What on earth was that man doing walking round the cairn?" But Henry, greatly puzzled, replied, "What man? I never saw any man at all."

There was a mist on part of the mountain but Kellas refused to believe that the figure could have been the shadow of either his brother or himself, causing an optical illusion. He asked, why not *two* figures if that had been the case?

A cold fear now possessed them both and they quickly descended the mountain.

Not long after this disclosure by Kellas a member of the Cairngorm Club of mountaineers, having heard both men's stories, made inquiries among stalkers, shepherds, and some of the older crofters in the lonely region of the mountain. He met with no luck until questioning an old man living on the edge of Rothiemurchus Forest, which stretches from Speyside up towards the Larig Ghru. This man knew the Cairngorms very well and was not the least surprised to be told the reason for the inquiry. "Oh, aye," he remarked simply, "that would have been the *Ferla Mhor* (the Big Grey Man) he would have been seeing." It was found that the tradition of the *Ferla Mhor,* the spectre of Ben Macdhui, was in fact well known and still current among the older residents on Speyside.

There the matter stood until November 28th, 1925, when at the annual dinner of the Cairngorm Club in Aberdeen, Professor Collie told again the story of his unnerving experience more than thirty-five years ago, together with an account of the apparition seen by Dr Kellas. An honorary president of the club, Collie spoke now as an accomplished scientist and a climber in the Himalayas, the Caucasus, the Rockies, the Selkirks and the Alps; he was an ex-president of the Alpine Club, the highest climbing honour any man could aspire to. He recounted his story exactly as he had told it to friends through the years, and there was no mistaking his complete belief that what had happened on the mountain summit had no answer in nature.

His speech, widely reported, brought a spirited response from those who sought to explain away the incident by the sounds of wind, falling stones or settling snow, and the apparition seen by Kellas as a trick of mist and light, or a wandering deer. There were those, too, who simply dismissed both stories as imaginative nonsense; they argued that Ben Macdhui was climbed regularly by a great many people, none of whom had noticed anything untoward, while every mountaineer well knew the high pitch of suggestiveness to which the senses could be drawn when a man was alone on the heights. But not one critic offered an explanation which Collie and Kellas, both cool and level-headed men, had not given earnest consideration to themselves, while on the other hand unexpected support came from a number of climbers who admitted that they also had experienced inexplicably eerie feelings when on the top of Ben Macdhui and had been immensely relieved to vacate the dreary summit. They had hesitated to come forward before with their stories for fear of ridicule.

And so the riddle of Ben Macdhui remains. Dr Kellas died shortly before this public controversy, collapsing on the Mount Everest Expedition of 1921 and being buried within sight of the peak. His strong belief in what he had seen had remained unshaken, as had that of his brother Henry, who described the incident many times to friends.

Professor Collie died at his home on the Isle of Skye in 1942, at the age of eighty-three. To the end he was unwavering in his conviction that it was some horrifying supernatural occurrence on the summit of the mountain which had sent him running from it for five terror-stricken miles.

He had said in 1925, "Whatever you may make out of this story I do not know, but there is something very queer about the top of Ben Macdhui, and I will not go back there again by myself, I know."

Nor did he.

THE SELF-SERVICE GHOST

When the Oxford and District Co-operative Society opened a self-service grocery branch in the village of Long Wittenham, Berkshire, strange things began to happen in the new shop, and they went on for eight unnerving days of November, 1962.

Groceries began switching about mysteriously. Packets and tins were moved off shelves, cereals turned up on the polish and detergent shelves, sweets went into levitation. Packets of bicarbonate of soda kept vanishing from their shelf and reappearing on a window ledge. Customers' order books were moved.

Then, phantom footsteps were heard. They shuffled about the shop like an old woman, said Mr Derek Bird, the shop manager. And, twice in the evening, a strange white shape streaked with blue was seen.

Mr Bird called in security officers of the Co-operative Society, who one evening covered the shop counters with powder, switched off the lights and stood by with a camera, ready to photograph anything that might appear. But nothing did.

Next day, however, the shuffling footsteps and inexplicable movement of groceries went on. Finally on the Saturday, after a week of acutely mounting tension in the shop, the chief assistant loudly challenged a clock to fall off the wall. Next Monday, when the manager and his staff walked in, they found the clock lying shattered on the floor. This same day the ghost played its twentieth supernatural trick, spiriting the bicarbonate of soda across the shop for a sixth time. At this, the fifteen-year-old junior assistant, who also heard the shuffling footsteps, fainted and had to be helped from the shop, to which she would not return.

Mr Bird, in desperation, called on the vicar of Long Wittenham, the Rev H. C. Roberts, who agreed to hold a service at the back of the premises. Mr Bird then shut the shop early and the vicar, in a short ceremony, read prayers.

The following morning, to everyone's great relief, the unsettling atmosphere in the shop had noticeably dispersed, and no further trouble was reported.

A modern shop is by no means the most unlikely place for a haunting, as cases in recent years have continued to show.

In 1965 strange noises were reported in a Territorial Army drill hall in Sandbach, Cheshire. Officers and men heard the sound of thudding boots echoing through the hall at night, the hall's iron-studded door was heard to creak and bang shut, and the passage echo with the jangle of keys. A senior officer who confirmed the haunting said that several times on hearing the noises he had gone to investigate, only to find no one there.

Members of a rifle club using the .22 range at the hall also heard the footsteps. They formed a search party, but found nothing. The stewardess at the hall for nearly twenty years said that she too had heard the mystery noises but was not frightened by them. Some of the younger recruits, however, after hearing the footsteps late one night, made sure afterwards never to stay in the hall after nine o'clock.

Local people believe the ghost to be that of an Army sergeant who died in the drill hall office many years ago.

Airfields have their ghosts. The one that appeared to night flyers at Middleton-St-George RAF station, County Durham, in 1957, was described as being tall with a slight stoop, though because of its fleeting appearances, always vanishing at the crucial moment, its features never were clearly seen. Some people, however, associated the phantom with a tall, stooping Canadian pilot called Mullen who was killed near the airfield during the war.

The first to see the Middleton-St-George ghost was Warrant-Officer William Lake. He thought he had been dreaming, until two nights later, two senior aircraftmen also reported seeing the apparition.

W.O. Lake, describing his sight of the ghost, said, "I was at my desk trying to phone a message to the operations room, but the line was engaged. I then saw someone in flying kit walking past the window. I ran to the door to give him the message, but he was nowhere in sight. I even looked into the hangar, but he wasn't there either."

The *Northern Echo* reported of the ghost, "He is a mysterious figure in overalls who never seems to want to trouble anyone, as in the small hours he takes his frequent walk past Flying Control, only to disappear by one of the nearby hangars. It's not a joke. The men of 264 Squadron, the night flyers, are very serious about him. He has never been seen close enough to determine whether he is aircrew or ground staff, but he has appeared quite recently to various responsible people going about their normal duties."

The ghost of Lindholme RAF station, near Doncaster, made its first appearance in 1947, when it was said to have been seen walking out of the nearby marshes. Several people since have reported seeing "Lindholme Willie", as the ghost has come to be known. Villagers of nearby Hatfield believe the ghost to be that of an airman killed in a crash on the marshes in the war. Every description of the ghost has been the same : a big man in aircrew dress.

In November, 1957, a corporal in Traffic Control at Lindholme reported seeing "Willie's" misty shape walk to the runway from the direction of the marshes. He radioed control, but before he could get a closer look at the figure it vanished.

Ghosts appear frequently in mines. At Glapwell No. 3 pit, near Chesterfield, in 1964, miners reported seeing ropes and lamps swinging when there was no draught to account for it, and the figure of a man in a donkey jacket appeared. It walked away, went right through a conveyor and vanished. However, the NCB declined to allow an investigator to go underground.

In 1961 a twenty-year-old bricklayer who accepted a dare to spend the night alone in Chislehurst caves was later found unconscious at the mouth of the exit by the caretaker. This is the young man's story of his experience.

"I camped down at midnight on Saturday. I had twenty cigarettes, a box of matches, and two candles. I intended to pass the time carving wood. Then I noticed a shroud of mist coming down, and the caves seemed to get darker. I had a funny feeling someone was watching me, and that whatever it was, was coming nearer.

"Then I saw it. A woman's figure. She was bound, and seemed to be slowly drowning in water which swirled round her. I remember screaming and ran towards the exit. That's when I smashed my head against the tunnel roof. I got to the door and just managed to unlock it. Then I collapsed."

The caves are reputedly haunted by the ghost of a woman murdered there in the early years of the nineteenth century. Mr James Gardner, proprietor of the caves, says that many visitors to the caves who claim to be psychic have told him a "horrible story about a woman being tied up and drowned in the nearby waterhole".

Langton House, a 200-year-old mansion at Lichfield, Staffordshire, was taken over about 1959 as a hostel for trainee priests attending Lichfield Theological College. The thirteen-roomed mansion, which housed several student priests and a member of the college staff, had a long and varied history as a private residence and was believed locally to have been haunted for many years. A murder was said to have been committed in it long ago, and an Army colonel who lived there committed suicide.

In 1962 the trainee priests began to hear "unearthly screams" echoing through the corridors of Langton House at night. Then the shadowy figure of a man was seen prowling about the house. One student who had locked his bedroom door awoke, startled, to see the shadowy figure in his room, and the door wide open.

The peak of tension was reached when one night, a student was found lying unconscious on the first-floor landing, his eyes wide open in terror. On recovering he said he had heard the most terrible screaming, as though someone was in agony or terror.

The college chaplain, who lived in Langton House with the students, held a service to lay the ghost. But the figure continued to be seen, and the noises heard, and finally in August, 1964 the Bishop of Stafford, the Rt Rev R. G. Clitherow, personally conducted a service of exorcism, during which prayers were said and holy water sprinkled over every room, door and window of the old mansion.

This service seemed to bring peace at last for the hostel's residents.

In 1958 the figure of a "White Lady" was reported to be haunting a children's home in Surrey run by sisters of the Anglican Community. The ghost was said to haunt the older part of the house, which used to be one of Cardinal Wolsey's hunting-boxes. Several members of the staff said they had seen her, usually at about two o'clock in the morning. She was described as "looking like a cloud at night".

One sister saw the White Lady in daylight. The apparition, she said, was walking along the passage to the nursery, and was dressed in a long white robe, perhaps a bridal gown, and had a white veil over her head.

Some of the children in the home, who were aged up to ten years old, told of 'a fairy" who sometimes appeared to them. They were not alarmed by the ghost as there was nothing at all frightening about her.

The same cannot be said of apparitions which appeared at a country mansion near Redditch, Worcestershire, which was once a part of the large estate of the first Earl of Plymouth. Two ghosts manifested themselves in the mansion, which had been converted to the Tardebigge country club. One apparition was that of a man dressed in a somewhat old-fashioned navy blue suit, who haunted the ballroom. The second, that of a "Lady in Grey", haunted the club lounge. When the hauntings were first reported publicly in 1962 it was stated that the ghosts appeared for fleeting moments every month or so and had been seen or sensed by staff and members.

The club's proprietor, Mr Bertram Walker, was still highly sceptical. But, he admitted, "Plenty of men who have not believed what they heard about the ghost in the ballroom have come out as white as sheets. They have heard footsteps walking immediately behind them and if it is dark they simply run. I have heard footsteps myself. New waitresses here who did not know about the ghost have heard it and refused to go back." One frightened barman did not stay at the club for long.

Mr Walker's wife, Vera, was—and still is—convinced there was something "very evil" in the ballroom. Many times on passing through it she experienced a strange, icy cold feeling and seemed to sense some hostile presence lingering there. She actually saw the apparition of the man in blue three times, twice in broad daylight. On these latter occasions the figure appeared on the verandah and, as she watched, walked away and disappeared into an oak tree.

Several members of the club also saw or sensed the man in blue in the ballroom.

Mrs Walker did not see the ghost of the lounge, the Lady in Grey, but she tells me this appeared to be perfectly harmless, the atmosphere there being nothing like the thoroughly evil aura which manifested itself in the ballroom. The Lady in Grey was seen three times by a waitress, who described her as wearing a cowl and looking "most beautiful".

As if this were not enough, the hauntings became almost unbearable with the appearance on the scene of a third uninvited guest, a destructive poltergeist. Electrical switches in the kitchen began to be turned off when no one was near. When a deep freeze stopped working it was thoroughly examined and found to be in perfect order except that the switch built *inside* it had unaccountably been turned off. Tables and chairs rocked of their own accord, glasses and ashtrays jumped from the counter and tables to smash on the floor, mirrors on the wall were seen to wobble, and decorations were pulled down as if by invisible hands.

Mr Walker's scepticism was shaken when he saw a stool rise up and wobble.

Psychical researchers who were asked to investigate found "cold spots" in the ballroom indicative of there being some psychic activity there, though they did not see either of the apparitions.

I understand that there have been no recent reports of apparitions seen at the Tardebigge, which has changed hands, but a belief still exists that the place is not altogether free of its intruders. That some mystery attends the former mansion does seem likely. Rumours in the neighbourhood concerning it go back for a number of years.

THE PHANTOM ORGANIST

Mr Henry Ditton-Newman was an accomplished organist who greatly raised the standard of the services at St John's Church, in the Devon resort of Torquay. When he died on November 19th, 1883 after only four years in the post, it was a great loss to the church. After a choral service he was buried in Torquay Cemetery.

That was when the long, extraordinary haunting of St John's began.

While the body of the organist was lying in the church before burial, the organ was heard to play entirely on its own. Months later, people were startled to hear organ music coming from the empty church at night. Then the vicar, when alone in the church one day, heard the organ suddenly start to play, and on looking up, saw the late organist sitting at the organ. The apparition also appeared to other people in the church on a number of occasions.

There had been nothing strange about the organist's death, which was from pleurisy. Yet for years the hauntings continued, the organ music being heard played by a phantom hand, and the organist's apparition being seen or his presence strongly felt by a great number of people.

The Rev R. J. E. Boggis, who became vicar of St John's in 1924, wrote a history of the church which was published in 1930. In this he referred briefly to the phantom organist, noting that "there are well authenticated accounts of apparitions of him in St John's Church". His appearances, said Mr Boggis, were recorded "even down to the present time, and he has been seen by persons who had never known him, and were unaware that St John's had a ghost".

And still, through the 1930s and the years of the last war, the hauntings went on. There was talk of one organist who would not stay in the post because he sensed someone unseen sitting beside him on the organ seat and touching the keys.

The Rev Sir Patrick Ferguson-Davie, who was vicar of St John's from 1945 to 1948, used to hear the ghost in the vicarage. Once, he said, he thought it was a burglar. He seized a riding crop and chased the footsteps down the front stairs and into the dining-room, but when he rushed into the room there was no one there. Later he was told the old front door used to be in the dining-room wall.

Sir Patrick said the ghost never worried him—it was quite a kind sort of spirit. He had a locum who saw or heard the ghost frequently, called it "Henry", and regarded it as part of the family.

In August, 1956 the Rev Anthony T. Rouse, who had then been vicar of St John's for some two years, spoke of the church's ghost when conducting a service of commemoration and thanksgiving for the organ, before it was dismantled and taken away to be reconstructed. The organ had been installed in 1873, six years before Ditton-Newman was appointed organist for his tragically short-term.

Mr Rouse disclosed at this service that former incumbents and himself had heard footsteps come down the backstairs from the vicarage, Montpelier House, which was formerly the church's resident choir school, and walk across the yard into the church.

"There are quite a number who will still vouch for the authenticity of this," the vicar said. 'I have also had many guests who have known nothing of the story, and who have spoken about the mysterious footsteps in the night."

Mr Rouse himself had heard "a heavy sort of music" coming from the organ in the empty church while he was in bed in the vicarage. On each of several occasions it played for just a few minutes. His own theory to explain the persistent ghost was that Ditton-Newman, who had died a young man leaving unfinished several pieces of music which he had composed, wanted to come back to the organ to complete them.

Mr Rouse said he had privately held two services to stop the hauntings, sprinkling holy water and saying prayers in the vicarage, and he thought they had now stopped—"unless there is some new manifestation because the organ is being taken away".

But the hauntings did not stop. Two years later, in November, 1958 Mr Rouse admitted that the phantom organist had recently returned. Members of the church's choral society had been prac-

tising "when the organ made an extraordinary noise and the ghost
appeared. He was seen by a number of people there, and his presence was felt by all."

A material link with Ditton-Newman did in fact still exist, because
although the rebuilt organ had a new console, most of the pipes
which belonged to the old organ were still in use, having been re-
voiced.

Shortly after this incident, Mr Rouse revealed that his organist,
Mr Frederick Fea, had written to the Bishop of Exeter "pointing
out that from time to time he definitely feels a presence on the organ
stool with him while he is playing, and he finds it unsettling. The
same thing has been experienced by other people while playing the
organ. We are hoping that the bishop will be able to take suitable
action."

Mr Fea himself explained, "I have never seen the ghost, but there
is a feeling of somebody watching, and one gets that very strongly at
certain times. For two years running I have noticed it on the same
Fridays and the same Sundays. It makes one feel paralysed and you
just cannot think or play normally. I have felt that I just could not
get through a hymn because of the feeling of strain. In fact, I have
always finished the hymn, but more by will-power than anything
else. The feeling also seems to paralyse the choir. They find it very
difficult to sing and the results are not what one would wish."

What now really worried the vicar was that whereas through the
years since its first appearance in 1883, the ghost had been described as a "friendly" spirit, and even a "happy" one, latterly the
pattern of the haunting had changed. A feeling of acute depression
had settled on the top floor of the vicarage, the former choir school.
Mr Rouse said he had kept this development to himself until Mr
Fea several times complained of a similar depression he had frequently experienced while sitting at the organ, and which reached
such proportions that he had even consulted his doctor. Sprinkling
the organ seat with holy water had resulted in only a temporary
respite from the "presence".

So, shortly before Christmas, 1958 Mr Rouse—"In desperation,
and because these experiences were at complete variance with the
long-standing 'friendly ghost' "—visited the College of Psychic
Science in London, where he consulted a medium. The medium,
on being acquainted with the facts, said she was conscious of a man,
an organist of the church, who had gassed himself, and had not
been given the funeral he felt he should have had, considering what
he had tried to do for music at St John's. She advised the vicar to

get someone to go to this man's grave and sprinkle it with holy water, and say prayers over it.

When Mr Rouse returned to Torquay and told Mr Fea what the medium had said, the organist said it confirmed his belief that the present haunting was not by the apparition of Ditton-Newman, but by the ghost of another organist who had gassed himself a few months before Mr Rouse became vicar. On making inquiries, Mr Rouse found that the body of the suicide had been left outside the church in a hearse while the funeral service was being held. And the man had for a short time lived in the former choir school—on the top floor.

The vicar reported all the facts to the bishop, who gave his approval for the medium's advice to be acted upon. And so on New Year's Day, 1959 Mr Rouse visited the grave of the suicide in Torquay Cemetery. He sprinkled it with holy water, prayed that the man's soul might be at rest, and recited a psalm.

After this ceremony the depression in the vicarage suddenly vanished, as did the "presence" at the organ. Both phantom organists of St John's appeared to have found peace at last.

SECRET OF THE GOLDEN GHOST

On a bright night in the early part of the last century, an old woman walked to the town of Mold, in Flintshire, to lead her husband home from a public-house. The couple were about a quarter of a mile out of town on their homeward journey, walking along the Chester road, when the woman, who was walking a little ahead of her husband, was startled to see cross the road in front of her a warrior-like figure which she later described as "of unusual size, and clothed in a coat of gold, which shone like the sun". The apparition then vanished quite suddenly into a gravel bank on the other side of the road.

When her husband came up she told him what she had seen. He laughed at her fancy, as did the many others to whom she repeated her story the next morning. There was a vague local tradition that the bank was haunted and it was commonly known by the name of *Bryn-yr Ellyllon,* or the Goblins' Hill. Despite that, however, no one took the old woman's tale of the golden ghost very seriously.

A section of the gravel bank had been cut off in making that part of the Chester road, and gravel for various purposes having been dug out of the remainder, a large pit had been made in the field adjoining the road. When, some years after the old woman's experience, farmer John Langford bought the piece of land for his farm, he employed some labourers to fill the unsightly hole by shovelling down the top of the bank to the level of the rest of the field.

As the workmen progressed, they found themselves removing much bigger stones, including several very large round ones, and at a depth of about four feet from the top of the mound—obviously the original surface of the ground—they came upon what seemed to be an outsize breastplate or corselet, some three-and-a-half feet long and eight inches wide in the centre. It lay as it might have been worn, with the breast upwards and the back parts doubled behind. Under it were discovered the bones of a man, and a little above it, as the body had been buried, a skull.

The discovery was made on October 11th, 1833. The vicar of

Mold, the Rev Charles Butler Clough, reported: "The corselet suffered considerable mutilation. Mr Langford, upon its discovery, having no idea of its value, threw it into a hedge, and told the workmen to bring it with them when they returned home to dinner. In the meantime several persons broke small pieces off it."

The corselet, richly decorated with heavily embossed work, was in fact a thin solid plate of gold. Today it is a unique and priceless exhibit in the British Museum, where also are filed the reports of the farmer and the vicar, who tells the story of the apparition seen by the old woman and testifies that it was "an undoubted fact" that she had related it at the time. The odd thing, adds the vicar, was that one of the people to whom she had told her story, years before, was farmer Langford himself, who, like all the rest, had taken little account of it.

There is a sequel. In recent years the corselet has been established as being not a portion of some rich warrior's armour, but a peytrel or breastplate for the horse on which he rode. The whereabouts of the restless soldier's own golden armour, if it still exists, remains a mystery, as does his identity. The apparition may still walk, and his armour lie, in the region of Mold, where certainly some families today include among their prized possessions gold rings and breastpins known to have been made from pieces broken off the corselet as it lay discarded in the hedge.

In a part of west Sussex there were many reports over the years of appearances made by a bearded, armour-clad Saxon warrior. All who saw the apparition gave the same description of it, adding that the wandering spectre "seemed to be searching for something". This gave rise to talk of buried treasure and caused several searches to be made in the locality favoured by the spectral warrior, close to the village of Storrington. All were fruitless. But vindication of the ghost-seers came when the phantom's hoard was eventually discovered, again by accident.

In 1865, the owner of Upper Chancton Farm, near the village of Washington, three miles from Storrington, decided to demolish an old barn which was fenced in and surrounded by a hedgerow containing some large trees. The trees were cut down and the ground ploughed up. About a year afterwards, on December 21st, 1866 one of the last remaining tree roots was dug up to allow the plough to pass. While busy on this work the farm labourers saw an old crock or earthenware pot which had been buried in the ground. Their vigorous efforts to dig up the tree stump smashed the pot into tiny fragments and disgorged its contents, more than two thousand silver pennies of the Saxon period, some coated with the green rust of centuries, but most of them as fresh as though they had just been issued from the mint.

There was a wild scramble among the labourers on the spot and many of the coins were carried away by them to be sold to people at Shoreham and Brighton, and in London. However, the bulk of the hoard, 1,611 coins, found its way to the Government, and the vicar of Storrington, the Rev James Beck, managed to retrieve another 108, though he reported that other coins were still secreted by the villagers in the hope of getting a good price for them in the future.

After the discovery of his lost treasure the Saxon warrior ceased his wanderings.

Treasure of a very different nature was discovered in 1851 in the small Northamptonshire village of Barby, a few miles from Daventry.

In the early part of that year, a comfortably off but excessively miserly widow of the name of Webb, a native of the village, was taken seriously ill. The widow, who had starved and badly neglected herself, was nursed by two neighbours, Mrs Griffin and Mrs Holding, while her nephew, a farmer in the village called Hart, supplied her with food and other needs. The widow made a will bequeathing to Hart all her possessions. At two o'clock on the morning of March 3rd, 1851 she died, aged sixty-seven.

After the funeral, all the furniture in the house was taken away and the empty house was locked up. A month later, Mrs Holding, who lived next door with her uncle, was alarmed to hear loud and heavy thumps against the partition wall, and against the door of a cupboard in the room wall. There were other strange noises, like the dragging of furniture about the empty rooms, all occurring at about two in the morning.

Then, early in April, the dead woman's house acquired new tenants. A family of the name of Accleton, much in need of somewhere to live, took the place as it was the only house in the village vacant. The husband and wife occupied the bedroom in which Mrs Webb had died, their ten-year-old daughter sleeping in a small bed in the corner. Immediately on settling in, the family began to hear violent noises in the night—"thumps, tramps and tremendous crashes, as if all the furniture had been collected together and then banged on the floor." The noises invariably occurred at about two o'clock.

One night at this time the parents were awakened by sudden

screams from their daughter. "Mother! Mother!" she cried, "there's a tall woman standing by my bed, shaking her head at me!" (Mrs Webb was a very tall woman). Her parents, who could see nothing, did their best to calm the child, but at four o'clock they were again awakened by her screams, and the cry that she had seen the tall woman.

The girl was troubled by this apparition on seven successive nights.

On another night, Mrs Accleton, during her husband's absence, got her mother to sleep with her, but she was awakened at the same hour of two o'clock by an unusual light in her room. Looking up, she saw plainly the ghost of Mrs Webb, which moved towards her with a gentle appealing manner.

The spectre was seen similarly by Mrs Griffin and Mrs Holding, also by a Mrs Radbourne. They said that luminous balls of light seemed to go up towards a trapdoor in the ceiling which led to the roof of the house, and the phenomenon was accompanied by a low moaning noise similar to that of a woman in her death agony.

Mrs Accleton then made the suggestion that the appearance of the widow's ghost might be connected with a "hoard" which she had secreted up in the roofspace. Hart, the nephew, thought there might be something in this, and together he and Mrs Accleton made a search. In the loft, by the light of a candle, they discovered a bundle of deeds and a large bag of gold and banknotes.

Still the knockings and moanings of the late Mrs Webb did not cease. They ended, however, after Hart, on finding that she had died owing certain debts, scrupulously paid them.

Tradition tells of many ghosts said to indicate the presence of buried treasure, or to be the guardians of it. Among these stories, that of the White Lady of Blenkinsopp Castle remains one of the most fascinating blends of truth and legend. The castle, which lies on the western border of Northumberland near Haltwhistle, was built 600 years ago, and though the passing centuries have taken their toll of the once magnificent building, with its seven feet thick walls, the story of the restless, plaintive phantom said to haunt it has persisted keen and strong.

Handsome Sir Bryan de Blenkinsopp, says tradition, was gallant and brave on battlefield and border raid, enjoying a very favourable reputation, but his one failing was an inordinate love of wealth. This vice he cherished in secret, until rashly disclosing himself at the marriage of a brother warrior with a lady of high rank and fortune. When, as the various toasts were made, the guests came to drink to the health of Blenkinsopp and his future lady love, he replied, "Never, never shall that be until I meet with a lady possessed of a chest of gold heavier than ten of my strongest men can carry into my castle." This statement was received in astonished silence. Blenkinsopp, ashamed of having betrayed his secret thoughts, left the castle and his country soon after.

A few years later he returned, bringing with him not only a foreign-born wife but also, as her dowry, a box of gold that took twelve of his strongest men to carry into the castle. There was a great feasting and rejoicing for the lord's return, and the fame of his new wealth spread far and wide. But the gold soon came between man and wife and after a time it began to be whispered that the life of the rich baron was anything but a happy one. Blenkinsopp and his wife quarrelled continually, and in her despair—hoping that it might bring about their reconciliation—the wife, with the help of the followers who accompanied her, hid the chest of gold in some part of the castle, during her husband's absence, and refused to give it up to him on his return. Nor was he able to extract anything from her followers, who spoke in a foreign tongue. After a further series of bitter arguments, Blenkinsopp one day rode from the castle, never to return.

His wife now broke down and was inconsolable for her loss. Vassals were sent out to all parts to discover where her husband had gone, but without success. After waiting for more than a year, the distressed woman, about whom very little was known in the neighbourhood, took her attendants and left the castle in search of him.

Neither was ever seen again, the fate of both husband and wife remaining a complete mystery. Tradition says, however, that eventually the wife did find her way back to South Tyne, and, filled with remorse at her conduct towards her husband, could not rest in her grave and wandered back to the castle to mourn over the chest of gold, the cause of their misery. This she would do until some-one with sufficient courage followed her and removed the treasure, so giving her spirit rest.

The ghost of the White Lady seen walking the castle grounds has been reported many times.

In the eighteenth century, a labourer of the estate and his family went to live in two of the more habitable rooms of the run-down castle. The parents slept in one room, their children in the other. One night, husband and wife were roused by loud screams from the other room and on rushing in found one of the children, a boy, sitting up in bed terrified. "The White Lady! The White Lady!"

he screamed. The parents examined the room but saw nothing, and tried to reassure their son.

"She is gone," replied the boy, "and she looked so angry at me because I would not go with her. She was a fine lady—and she sat down on my bedside, wrung her hands and cried sore, then she kissed me and asked me to go with her, and said she would make me a rich man, as she had buried a large box of gold, many hundred years since, down in the vault, and she would give it to me, as she could not rest as long as it was there. When I told her I durst not go, she said she would carry me, and was lifting me up when I cried out and frightened her away."

Persuading themselves that the boy had been dreaming, the parents managed to calm him and get him to sleep; but on the three following nights they were roused in the same manner, the child giving the same story with little variation. They then took him from the room to sleep elsewhere, and were no longer troubled by the spectre, though the boy would never afterwards enter any part of the old castle alone, even in daylight.

Up till 1820 some poor families continued to live in a few of the better rooms of the crumbling castle. Then all was left to ruin.

After some years, the occupier of the neighbouring farm ordered the vaults underneath the castle keep to be cleared out, so that he could winter some cattle there. When the rubbish was removed, a small door level with the bottom of the keep was revealed. The entrance to a damp passage was cleared out and the news quickly spread that the entrance to "The Lady's Vault" had been discovered, which drew many local people to the scene.

Among them, only one man was found willing to enter the passage, which was narrow and not high enough for a man to stand upright. He soon reappeared from his exploration. He said he had walked forward for a few yards, descended a flight of steps and carried on again until coming to a doorway, the door of which had fallen to pieces. At this juncture the passage took a sudden turn and there was a steep flight of steps. Opening his lantern and turning the light, he peered down the steps into the darkness. But then, encountering noisome vapours, his candle died out and he had to grope his way back to the entrance.

He entered the passage a second time, but again his light was extinguished and he was not able to descend the second flight of steps. This dampened the ardour of the treasure-seekers, and the farmer had so little curiosity about the passage that he ordered it to be closed up.

The castle now stood abandoned, a crumbling skeleton of its former splendour, but in 1875 it passed from the hands of the Blenkinsopp family to Edward Joicey, who made great efforts to restore it. In five years the castle was almost completely rebuilt, only some of the inner walls, and portions of the outer shell, being retained. During this restoration work the entrance to the secret passage was rediscovered. The passage was believed to be some one and a half miles long, linking the castle with the stronghold of Thirlwall, and somewhere along it the hidden treasure chest was thought to lie. But no more attempts were made to explore the passage.

The castle remained in the possession of the Joicey family until 1951, during which time no appearance of the White Lady was reported. In 1951 the sixteen-roomed castle, in its nineteen acres of land, was acquired by a new owner, who, it was announced, would at some later date lead an attempt to trace the treasure of the White Lady, but this never came about. In 1954 the castle was severely damaged by fire, leaving it a charred and roofless shell except for the sturdy west wing. The following year, the castle and its land was bought by Mr Charles Simpson, who restored the west wing as a home for his family and started a poultry farm and caravan site in the grounds.

Mr Simpson tells me that during his ten years at the castle he has not himself seen the White Lady, nor has he made any attempt to trace the legendary treasure.

STRANGE GUESTS AT THE INN

Dick Turpin was hanged at York in 1739, not for the many high-way robberies he committed, but, unromantically, for horse stealing. Evidence of his activities has continued to be found; as recently as 1933, jewellery and money, pistols and a mask were found in the lining of a greatcoat left by him at the Three Tuns inn, Cambridge, when he fled from the Runners in January, 1739, three months before his execution. His stay at many other inns has been well proved, if the actual total number of hostelries that claim a link with him is suspect, and there is no doubt that his ghost also has made frequent appearances.

Tradition is that Turpin gallops down Trap's Hill, near Loughton, Essex, three times in every year. He is also said to haunt the stretch of Watling Street which runs past Nuneaton and Hinckley, over the border from Warwickshire into Leicestershire. He was seen there in 1926 by a number of people, who described him as wearing a three-cornered hat and a coat with red sleeves. Early the following year some motor-cyclists saw him riding across the common land near the road.

Turpin is also said to haunt the Bedfordshire woods and Bury Lane, where he rode when striking out for Watling Street. And there have been reports of his presence being felt in or near some of the inns at which he called.

Records of the 14th-century Bell Inn, in the Huntingdonshire village of Stilton, just off the Great North Road, show that Turpin stayed there shortly before he was hanged. Many and varied stories have been told about the Bell Inn, where strange happenings were reported as recently as 1963.

Mr Malcolm Moyer became landlord of the Bell Inn in 1962. He had not been there long before he decided to leave unused one of the rooms in which the highwayman is reputed to have slept. It had, said Mr Moyer, "a strange, inexplicable atmosphere", and one evening a fire which had been laid in the grate suddenly burst into flames.

Early in 1963 Mr Moyer acquired a boxer dog which, for a joke, he called Dick Turpin, but as he said later, the joke seemed to mis-fire. The dog started howling every Wednesday soon after midnight, the time when Turpin's ghost is believed to walk the inn's winding corridors. Mr Moyer said, "The dog disturbed the neighbours, awoke my baby daughter and frightened my wife. The only solution was to give the dog tranquillisers to calm him down and make him sleep."

Mr Moyer had a second boxer dog, George, which seemed un-affected by the highwayman's presence, though it refused to go up-stairs after closing time and always slept in the bar.

The inn, a protected ancient building, was put up for sale by its brewery owners in 1964.

Early in May, 1964 two clergymen stood in the bar of another country inn, the Langstone Arms Hotel, Kingham, Oxfordshire, and prayed that a ghost which had been pestering the inhabitants of the hotel for the past eighteen months would let them in peace. The ghost had first manifested itself as a sound, something like a person coughing, said Mr James Sharp, manager of the hotel. This sound always came from an empty room. Then there were shuffling footsteps, which sometimes came from a passage in the bar and sometimes from a first floor bedroom. Mr Sharp said he often felt tense and his scalp would suddenly prickle as the ghost made its presence felt.

Then both the manager and Mrs Olive Mudford, owner of the hotel, saw a whitish shape glide past a frosted glass window lead-ing from the bar to a passage. Mr Sharp described the apparition as resembling a small, old woman. Neither of them could see any fea-tures, though Mrs Mudford said the apparition seemed to have a headdress something like that worn by a nun. After this incident they decided to call on the Rev W. Attwood Evans, rector of the nearby parish of Churchill. Then the Rev H. S. Cheales, rector of Wyck Rissington, Gloucestershire, an authority on hauntings, was asked to help.

Prayers were said in the bar and hall of the 130-year-old hotel. Mr Cheales said he had established the ghost as being quite peaceful and friendly, and not of the type that should be exorcised. Mr Att-wood Evans had gone into the history of the inn but could not trace any tragedy having taken place there.

A few days after the prayers were said, however, the ghost made another appearance. A customer at the hotel told Mr Sharp that he had seen the apparition gliding past the window.

The reports of the Langstone Arms ghost were read by Mr Duncan Stuart, a chef in a Somerset hotel. Mr Stuart then disclosed that he had had three encounters with a ghost at the Langstone Arms in 1953, when he was working there as a cellarman. He had kept silent about the incidents for ten years because he had not wanted to be a target for ridicule.

Mr Stuart said his first brush with the ghost came when he was changing a barrel of beer in the hotel cellar. He heard a female voice say, "Fred would not do it like that." The second meeting came when he returned to the hotel late one night. As he entered the kitchen, he heard her voice say, "Jock, your supper is in your room." He went to his bedroom and found a meal left for him on his bedside table.

Mr Stuart said he came face to face with the ghost on New Year's night, 1954, when he returned from a party with some Scottish friends. The kitchen door opened and he saw the figure of a good-looking woman. When he asked her what she wanted he heard her reply, "A good night's rest like you are going to have."

He left the hotel soon after this last experience.

Hauntings began at the Chequers public-house, Amersham, Buckinghamshire, in late 1963, only a few days after the new land-lord and his family moved in. They began to hear weird shrieking screams echoing through the low timbered corridors and passages of the ancient building at night. Then, one morning at about half past four, the landlord, Mr Alex Campbell-Wilson, heard the ghostly screaming and ran to the bedroom where his two ycung daughters slept. The eight-year-old daughter was crying. She told her father that she had seen a white robed and hooded figure walk round the dressing table and out of the door. The door was found open, yet the parents always kept it closed.

Mr Campbell-Wilson, a former private detective, searched the place from top to bottom but could find nothing to account for the nightly moaning and screaming noises. He and his wife were then told that a cleaner who once worked in the public-house had also seen a ghost.

When the hauntings were widely reported, in January, 1964, six weeks after he had moved into the Chequers, Mr Campbell-Wilson said, "We can't stand much more. I don't mind tackling a human being but you can't fight something you can't explain."

The Chequers, which dates back to the 12th century, has a vio-lent history. In the Middle Ages, the night before five Protestant martyrs were burned at the stake on a nearby hilltop they were chained in one of the rooms of the public-house, then a coaching inn.

Legend says that a little girl, the daughter of one of the martyrs, was forced to light the executionary fires. The martyrs' gaoler at the Chequers, a local peasant, was so shocked by the dreadful scene that he never forgave himself for keeping the men under lock and key. His guilty conscience held him a prisoner within the immediate vicinity of the inn, and he died in complete misery when in his early thirties, his grieving spirit returning to wander the stairways and passages of the Chequers.

Miss Mollie Moncrieff, the medium, read of the ghost that was haunting the Campbell-Wilsons and agreed to come to their assistance. On a day in February, 1964, she visited the public-house to give the troubled spirit its release.

Miss Moncrieff said the ghost was not hostile and would never have harmed anyone.

"I could feel his presence in the room. I spoke to him and he came and stood by my side. He was dressed in a long flowing robe with a hood and a girdle. Attached to this girdle was a long bunch of keys. He told me that his name was Auden, but I do not know whether this was a Christian or surname.

"I persuaded him that he was no longer wanted and that he must put his keys on the table and leave. Without any trouble at all he put the keys on the table in front of me, turned and left."

Since then the Chequers has been free of any manifestations.

At Brentwood, Essex, in 1963, Mrs Elizabeth Harling felt there was "something very uncanny" present in the Swan Hotel, in the High Street, the first night she took over the licence there. It was a warm August night, yet after the hotel had closed she was aware of strange and eerie pockets of cold air in the corridor, and in the saloon bar. During the night she and her daughter, Coral, were awoken by noises as if furniture was being moved across the floor below, and doors banging, though all had been fastened.

This was the prelude to seven months of almost continuous hauntings at the Swan Hotel. For the first three months of Mrs Harling's tenancy something strange happened *every night*. Religious plates on the wall tumbled down mysteriously and bar doors went crash in the early hours; lights that had been switched off were found burning in the morning. Frequently Mrs Harling and her daughter, in her twenties, were awoken by the sound of furniture being dragged across the saloon bar floor, and some mornings they found the door to the bar jammed by chairs which had been moved against it.

Mrs Harling also tells me that when busy in one bar after "time", she often heard chairs being moved in the other bar, and these noises were heard on occasion by other witnesses. Another noise frequently heard was that of plates being moved in the empty kitchen. Then began an uncanny knocking at the door. On one alarming night, at about half-past eleven, Mrs Harling, together with the barman and a friend, were clearing up in the saloon bar when they heard a "terrible knocking" at the saloon bar door. Their first thought was that it was Mrs Harling's daughter, who had gone out for the evening, trying to get in. But when the door was quickly opened there was no one there.

On one occasion Mrs Harling was roused at two o'clock in the morning by a policeman who had found the hotel doors open. On his earlier patrol, he said, he had tried them and found them locked, but now they were unfastened. There was no explanation for this.

Another time, also at two in the morning, Mrs Harling was again knocked up by police who told her they had been alerted by the telephone exchange; there had been a call from the Swan and the receiver had not been replaced, so they had called in case she was in any trouble. Mrs Harling replied that the phone in the bar could not possibly have been used as she herself had locked up the bar before going to bed. But on getting the key and unlocking the bar, she and the police found the telephone receiver lying on the floor.

At Christmas the festive decorations hung up in the Swan started behaving very oddly. Near midnight, bunches of holly leaves and other sets of hanging decorations would in turn start to rock, just as if someone was going along the line tapping them. There was not the slightest draught nor any other explanation for the strange "tapping".

One night Mrs Harling and her daughter both heard music start to play. It got steadily louder and louder, and they realised it must come from a radio but wondered where this could possibly be, as it was playing so close. Then Mrs Harling remembered that some time ago she had put out of the way in a wardrobe a portable radio for which she had no use. They went together to the wardrobe and found that this radio had switched itself on, something which was not easily done as it was of the type on which the lid had to be raised up for it to play.

Psychical investigators checked for the "cold spots" which Mrs Harling constantly experienced in the corridor and bar, and found that they indicated some psychic activity. The hauntings were linked with the spirit of William Hunter, the Brentwood martyr who was only nineteen when he was burned at the stake as a heretic in 1555. Hunter, whose memorial stands in Brentwood, spent the night before his execution locked in a room at the Swan, the original building of which dates back five hundred years. It is believed that his prison that night was a kitchen of the old building which existed where the beer is now kept.

For three months there was a disturbance of some kind every night, then the hauntings continued, at intervals, for another four months; the banging and crashing noises, movement of furniture, and unaccountable knocking on the door. Many people read of the widely reported hauntings at the Swan and asked if they also could investigate, but this interest grew out of hand and had to be discouraged. When the hauntings did finally stop it was through action taken on advice by Mrs Harling's daughter, who, unknown to her mother, placed on top of a wardrobe an open Bible and a crucifix. The disturbances immediately ceased and there followed four months of peace until the night before Mrs Harling and her daughter left the premises, when the ghost or poltergeist seemed to register itself again with one last act.

Mrs Harling had brought with her to the Swan a grandmother clock which she had hung on a wall but kept silent throughout her tenancy, as its chimes during the night could be disturbing. On the night before she left the hotel this clock was the only item left in an empty room, all the other furniture in it having been removed. At 12.30 a.m. she and her daughter were startled to hear the clock suddenly begin chiming, and its chimes continued until it was taken down from the wall.

There have been no more disturbances at the Swan since.

At a new public-house in Exeter, in 1964, an apparition was clearly seen by customers. Twice in one week, at the Cowick Barton, they saw the ghostly figure of a monk cross the nearby playing fields in the direction of the city and disappear. The figure appeared at the same time on both occasions, about quarter to eight in the evening.

The Cowick Barton was built on a site that once belonged to Cowick Priory. While digging trenches for drains on the site of the 16th-century house, workmen discovered human remains and fragments of two earthenware vessels dating from the 14th century.

In 1962, two years before the monk's appearance on the playing fields, there was a report of a woman having seen in the vicinity the ghost of a monk doing penance by laying cobbles on a footpath of the old priory. The cobbles already existed on the footpath, probably laid by the monk in his lifetime, and it is his placid spirit which is believed to haunt the spot.

THE HOUSE OF LEPERS

In 1896, thirteen-year-old Robert Thurston Hopkins, in his first term as a boarder at Thetford Grammar School, Norfolk, had a vivid dream. It came to him as he slept in the top dormitory of the school, which faced the road running from Thetford to the market town of Brandon, six miles away.

The dream began with the sight of a long stretch of heathland—gorse, heather, grass-grown holes and mounds—over which a pallid moon shone, its silver light showing up the twistings of the heath's sandy trackways. Soon Hopkins saw, in the distance, what seemed to be a patch of mist moving along a wide trackway. The dreamer watched with rather uneasy curiosity, as every now and then it flitted from sight behind clumps of gorse and thorn trees. Eventually the patch of mist disclosed itself to be a man, running, skipping and jumping over the large pieces of flint on the trackway.

There was something uncanny about the man's movements. He was coming straight for Hopkins—making great efforts to catch up with him. On he came, growing larger, forward into beams of moonlight which showed him clearly for the first time : the man of Hopkins's dream had an intensely loathsome face of silvery white and ashen grey. Continuing to advance with hurried steps, he held up a hand in which was clutched a circular wooden plate. Decayed ruffles fluttered at both his wrists.

Hopkins recalled, "My feet seemed fastened to enormous bars of lead. I was terrified, and fear of the thing catching hold of me went nigh to driving me mad—or so it seemed in my dream. The moment came when the man was hovering right over me. I was hypnotised

with fear. It was then that I could see my pursuer's face with remarkable distinctness. It was thickened and puckered, giving the
face a peculiar, heavily menacing expression. I realised that his
intention was to press his face against mine. I knew I could not have
borne that. . . ."

But the relief of waking now came, though Hopkins did not shake
off the extreme terror of the dream for hours after, nor was he
allowed to forget it for very long. At intervals of months the same
dream was repeated to him many times, with no difference in detail
except that sometimes he could see a building in the background, a
long, narrow building with a central tower capped by a pyramidal
covering of thatch.

One of the masters at the school, Dr Catt, had an interest in
hypnotism and spiritualism, and young Hopkins was rather drawn
to him. After a month or so, master and boy fell to discussing the
puzzles of local archaeology and folklore, and Hopkins then ventured to describe his strange dream.

Dr Catt at once remarked, "That man in your dreams is a leper."

The master said that he could not deduce any more from the
dream, he doubted whether either of them ever could. The best clue,
if the dream was mirroring reality, was the tower with a thatched
cap, but the boy was unlikely to trace that particular building, as
there were hundreds of curious old thatched dwellings in Norfolk
and Suffolk.

Some weeks later, however, Dr Catt, making a call on school
business at an inn on the outskirts of Thetford, happened to glance
at a photograph on the mantelpiece. To his surprise the picture was
exactly that of the building described by Hopkins as seen in his recurring dream. The master questioned the landlord about it, and
was told that the building was called Warren House. It was still
standing on Brandon Warren, about a mile out of Thetford on the
Brandon road, said the landlord. A fire had once almost destroyed
the building, but it had since been renovated. He knew nothing
about its history.

Soon after this Dr Catt and Hopkins went together to Warren
House. There it stood on its height, a hoary tower of medieval brick,
grey stone and russet walls. On all sides stretched the warren, sweeping miles of sand, furze and loneliness, with scarcely a friendly barn
or a haystack studding the whole landscape. All around, the sand-
stone mounds and hummocks had been worn smooth by countless
waves of wind-blown sands.

The master and boy were met by the warrener in charge of the house, who was unused to having visitors call. Dr Catt explained that they were interested in ancient buildings and earthworks. Had the place always been called Warren House?

No, answered the warrener, many years ago, he had forgotten how long—perhaps a hundred—it had been known as "The Lepers' House". It was then a place of seclusion for lepers; he had been shown some mounds nearby where the unfortunates were buried, and up in the top room of the tower, which was about seven hundred years old, were wooden bowls and dishes which had remained undisturbed since the time of the lepers. He said he did not use the tower as a living place because his wife was full of idle fancies about it. She had told him she always felt followed by scores of unseen eyes when she entered the place. He himself did not go there in the dark more than necessary, as there was something uncanny about it —an impression of something foul and very evil.

The warrener invited his visitors to examine the tower for themselves, and, stumbling over blocks of ancient masonry, passing a stone coffin used as a chicken trough, master and boy followed him through the tower door and began to climb the spiral stone staircase set in the thickness of the wall. The steps, once trodden by the naked feet of the lepers, were so worn as to show the marbling of the stone as clearly as layers of quartz, and the heavily oppressive air seemed thick with a sickly smell of decay. When they came to the top room the warrener pointed out the wooden platters and bowls in a corner. They were, he explained, begging bowls. The lepers used to carry them down to the Brandon road below, where they squatted to beg from wayfarers and farmers.

Picking up one of the begging bowls, young Hopkins saw at once that it was exactly like the one carried by the leper in his dream. On quickly replacing the bowl he heard a metallic clink, and saw that his boot had kicked a bell partly hidden beneath the pile of platters. He picked it up, and on taking it to the light of the arrow-shot window, saw it was not a shepherd's sheep bell or an ordinary house bell, but one of some considerable age, made of copper and about six inches high. He held it by the iron ring which served as a handle and gave it a shake. "Klonk, klonk, klonk . . ." The golden sounds which came from it startled them all a little. It was a sound that would certainly have been heard from some distance.

The warrener said he had been told, on first coming to the house, that this was a leper's bell—the leper who led a party through a town or village went a hundred or so yards ahead, ringing it to warn people to remain in their houses until the lepers had passed. Nobody since had been eager to remove it from the tower. Once, a farmer at Two-Mile-Bottom Common did take it to use as a sheep bell, and it had seemed to bring a curse with it. His cows went dry and barren, his sheep went down with rot, while his small daughter died of some horrible disease. There was no rest for the farmer until the bell was returned to the tower.

Hopkins and the master discovered that some of the older inhabitants living in the neighbourhood of Warren House retailed rumours of ghostly happenings in the old tower. People passing it at night had spoken of hearing the leper's bell ringing out across the warren, and of seeing eerie blue lights in the narrow windows.

After this visit to the old house and tower, the unmistakable pivot of his strange dreams, Hopkins was never again troubled by the nightmare. There is, however, a sequel to his story.

Forty-five years afterwards, in 1941, Hopkins, by now an author and investigator of the uncanny, revisited the house of the lepers. The long buildings which had once stood on each side of the ancient tower had now disappeared. The tower itself was rent with cracks and pierced from foundations to the top steps with holes letting in the morning sun, while the flint-faced cottage in which the warrener had lived was a mere stone heap.

Hopkins noted, "I passed under the arched doorway of the tower and found myself in a tangle of beams and fallen blocks of stone. Looking up, I found that the floor of the upper chamber was missing and that the building lay shamelessly open to the sky. The thatched roof which had been a landmark had evidently been destroyed by fire. However, the shell of the old building remained, and as I looked up at the hoary walls I paused and wondered who first lived in Warren House. Was the original building a church, a castle, or a lookout tower? No one knows."

Hoping to be able to add something to the meagre history of the house, Hopkins then called on Samuel Bull, a warrener who had occupied it during 1903-5. Bull well remembered the leper's bell and the old begging bowls which, he said, were still in the tower during his period in charge there. The warrener from whom he took over had warned him not to touch them, so he left them alone, and kept a sharp lookout for strange visitors after dark. For the place, he said, was haunted, he had had no doubt of it.

Once, said Mr Bull, he was alone on the circular stone staircase when a leper's ghost rushed right through him. "We met face to face, so to speak, and the ghost could not help but rush at me. It had a flat white face and two burning eyes, and there was a sound like hissing steam. It passed through me, making a filthy gust of hot air."

Could it not have been a white owl that he saw? Hopkins suggested.

"Mr Bull's eyes met mine without flinching. 'No sir,' he said. 'That wasn't any owl. I looked out of a circular window in the stairway and saw the leper's ghost tear out of the archway at the bottom. He went frisking over the warren at a furious speed and I heard him shouting some kind of heathen gibberish. The night air shook with his devilish voice.' "

After that, said Mr Bull, the strange disturbances in the tower became worse. Finally, unable to stand it any longer, he closed the tower door, bricked up the inner wall and left the ghost in sole occupation. From that day to the time he and his wife left the house, all was peaceful and quiet within.

THE DEATH LEAP OF CONSTANTIA

Bruce Castle, which looms surprisingly on a main road of Tottenham, North London, is not a castle at all, but a vast mansion with twin turrets and central clock tower, which for centuries was the Manor House of Tottenham. The original building on the site goes back a thousand years in history, and the manor itself is famous as being the home, at the end of the thirteenth century, of Robert the Bruce. Its ghost is, however, of much later date.

In the second half of the seventeenth century Bruce Castle was occupied by Henry, the second Baron Coleraine, who was an antiquary. His wife, Constantia, was a very beautiful woman, and Henry, then in his early forties, was a possessive and jealous husband. So jealous in fact, that he finally took to locking his wife, with her child, in a tiny room in the clock tower, away from other admiring eyes.

One bleak November night in 1680 the demented Constantia, unable to face any more of this treatment by her husband, climbed to a parapet outside the window of her prison and threw herself to her death. In the years since, says tradition, her dreadful screams have been heard on the anniversary of her death, when her ghost walks the room in which she was kept prisoner.

Constantia's ghost does not seem to have troubled her husband, who married twice more before his death in 1708, nor is there any record of the ghost having been seen by later occupiers up to the turn of the eighteenth century. Yet the legend of the haunted chamber at the castle has persisted.

In 1827 the great angular old building was bought by Sir Rowland Hill, the champion of penny postage, for use as a private school. Around this time, a master of the school seemed convinced of Constantia's appearances and wrote about the ghost.

There is at least one positive record of Constantia's screams being heard in the 1880s by people living opposite Bruce Castle. A local vicar conducted a prayer meeting to exorcise the ghost, but this apparently had only a temporary effect, for after a year or two of silence the screams were heard again.

The mansion remained a school until 1891, after which it was acquired by the Tottenham local authority as a public building and made into a museum.

In November, 1949, on the anniversary of Constantia's death, a serious attempt was made to prove or disprove the presence of the ghost, with its "ear-splitting" screams, an all-night vigil being held in the haunted chamber. It produced no result.

Another haunted building with as long a history as Bruce Castle is Penfound Manor, near Bude, Cornwall. The oldest part of this enchanting old house, which is open to the public, was built in Saxon times. Nearly a thousand years of continuous occupation have ensured its preservation and it is now the oldest inhabited manor in the country. It stands in the parish of Poundstock and takes its name from the ancient family of Penfound, who from about the fifteenth to the seventeenth centuries were classed among the chief gentry of Cornwall. The tragedy of young Kate Penfound, whose ghost is said to haunt the manor, occurred in the mid-seventeenth century, during the time of the Civil War.

Kate fell in love with John Trebarfoot, of Trebarfoot Manor, three miles from Penfound, and wanted to marry him. But as the marriage had not, in correct Stuart fashion, been arranged by her father, old Nicholas Penfound, the proposition was unthinkable. Consequently Kate and John, by a secret exchange of letters "posted" in a hollow oak tree, which still stands, made plans to elope.

On the night arranged, April 26th, after the household had gone to bed, Kate climbed out of her bedroom window and descended to the courtyard by a ladder which had been placed ready for her. John Trebarfoot waited anxiously below. Kate's father, however, had been sitting up late. He heard her on the ladder and rushed out with sword drawn. In the resulting melee Kate threw herself between her father and her lover as they fought with their swords, with the result that all three were killed.

This tragic scene, it is said, is re-enacted at midnight on April 26th each year. Kate Penfound, however, has also been seen to wander at other times through the manor, always disappearing at the head of the main staircase. On these appearances she leaves an atmosphere of great joy and tranquillity behind her.

Mr and Mrs Kenneth Tucker, the present owners of Penfound Manor, say that while they have neither seen nor heard anything

strange, they have had contact, both personal and by correspond-
ence, with many people who have told of their experience of supernatural manifestations at the manor, including in two cases the
actual sight of Kate. These witnesses have all been ordinary people
with no particular interest in psychic matters.

There is another ghost of the Penfounds. He is William Penfound
(or de Penfoun), a church clerk, who, on December 27th, 1356, was
murdered in the chancel of nearby Poundstock Church by a host of
armed men who broke into the church while he was celebrating
Mass. William's blood was spilled over vestments and church ornaments as the murderers cut him down with swords and staves. His
ghost is believed to haunt the church to this day.

Historic North Luffenham Hall, which stands in forty acres in
Rutland, is said to be visited each year by the ghost of Everard
Digby, one of the conspirators in the Gunpowder Plot. In this sixteenth century house, which was opened to the public in the 1950s,
is the Digby Parlour, where Everard used to meet his cousin, James
Digby, to try and persuade him to throw in his lot with Guy Fawkes.
Everard, only twenty-eight years old at the time of the Plot, was
the heir to large estates in Rutland, Leicestershire and Lincolnshire,
and connected with many of the most influential families in England. His part in the affair was to prepare for a rising in the Midlands when the deed was done. After the abortive attempt, he was
taken and imprisoned, and on January 30th, 1606 was executed.

Many people, including the sister of an owner in recent years,
Mr R. G. Farnham, claim to have seen the apparition of Everard
Digby at North Luffenham Hall, the ghost's last recorded appear-
ance there being in 1957.

During the last war, Polish forces billeted in dour-looking Ferntower House, near Crieff, Perthshire, swore that the eighteenth century building was haunted by the wraith-like figure of a woman.
They called her "Lady Mary". The 60 ft. high tower at the house,
with walls six feet thick, in which the ghost was seen to walk, was
blown up in 1963 by engineers of the Territorial Army.

Ferntower House was once the home of General Sir David Baird,
the hero of Seringapatam. It has no other particular history and
there is no explanation for "Lady Mary", but this is not unusual;
the hauntings of many old houses are not easily explained and very
often they remain a complete mystery. An example is the case of a
haunted seventeenth century house at Reagill, Westmorland, in
1959.

Mr William Anderson, an insurance agent, and his wife Janet, moved into School House, Reagill, in November, 1959. Soon afterwards the young couple saw the ghost of a woman in old-fashioned dress walk in their bedroom at night.

Mr Anderson was lying awake in bed at about 5 a.m. when he suddenly saw the figure of a woman materialise from between the window and the dressing table. He felt a prickly feeling at the back of his neck as he saw the figure walk round the bed and pause, gazing at the wall against which the bed stood, then turn and walk back to a point opposite the foot of the bed, where it stood for some seconds before vanishing.

The figure was in view for fully half a minute. The face was indistinct, but Mr Anderson could see it was a woman because of her dress and hairstyle. He thought at first that he must have been dreaming, or that he had merely imagined it all, but then his wife beside him suddenly remarked, "This place is haunted." She then described to him what she had just seen, which, without any prompting by him, was a description of the ghostly incident exactly as he himself had witnessed it. The figure was, she confirmed, that of a woman wearing a high stiff-necked blouse and with her hair piled upon her head.

Mrs Anderson then admitted that on another occasion, when her husband was asleep, she had seen the figure in approximately the same place, though for a shorter period.

There was no local explanation for the ghost. Nor was there an explanation for one which appeared in a seventeenth century house in Northamptonshire in 1957.

Mrs Mabel Cullen and her two daughters moved into ten-roomed Pilgrim Cottage, in the village of Wilbarston, Northamptonshire, in July, 1957. Mrs Cullen, a former nurse, thought the best bedroom, with its old beams and high ceiling, one of the nicest rooms in the house, and looked forward to a happy stay in it. But after less than a month she moved out of the room, convinced that it was haunted.

Strange things began to happen from the first night that she spent in the room. She found she could never get to sleep until three o'clock in the morning or later, and saw little lights darting about the room like forked lightning when there was no breath of a storm. Once she awoke to find herself out of bed—the first time in her life that she had walked in her sleep.

Then, one night, as she lay awake, suddenly her whole body seemed to have gone heavy and solid, and the blankets, too, seemed tremendously heavy. It was, she said, an uncanny sensation, "just like being in a tomb". The next night, as she lay awake, finding it difficult to sleep, she heard the church clock round the corner strike one o'clock, then two, and suddenly the same entombed sensation took hold of her. She then looked up and saw an apparition.

It had the head and shoulders of a man, but from the waist tapered gently away, rather like a swallow-tail coat. She saw its features quite clearly. It had a cultured, middle-aged face with a prominent chin, and was quite handsome but expressionless, taking not the slightest interest in her. She saw it both full-face and in profile as it moved quickly in a circle round the room. Once it came straight towards her, and she half expected it to touch her, but it did not.

After she had watched the figure circle the bed twice, Mrs Cullen closed her eyes and began to recite the Lord's Prayer and the Creed. She kept her eyes closed a long time, and when she looked up again the apparition had disappeared.

Mrs Cullen inquired about the history of Pilgrim Cottage, which was known in the village as "the big house". It had stood empty for some time before she took it over. No one had heard of a ghost there before, though she learned that for many years the complete right wing of the house, including the haunted bedroom, was never occupied, though there were seven children in the last family to live there.

The advent of the ghost, which Mrs Cullen and her daughters named "George", brought many callers to Pilgrim Cottage, including newspaper reporters and investigators. A medium who spent some time at the house said he believed that a man, the murderer of a baby, had lived there. The murder had been committed some two centuries ago, and the child's body was likely to be found buried under a flagstone in the cellar. But after some digging beneath the flagstone, only water was found.

Mrs Cullen asked a Methodist minister to conduct prayers with her in the haunted bedroom. It was afterwards slept in by a friend of the family, who experienced nothing unusual except for feeling peculiarly cold.

The ghost which troubled ancient Creslow Manor, in Buckinghamshire, many years ago was never positively identified. This old building, with its stone tower, vaulted timbers and oak doors with massive hinges, had in the last century a certain notoriety. Still at that time in a solid-walled dungeon, next to the old groined crypt excavated in limestone rock, lay several skulls and other human bones. The ghost of Creslow Manor, a woman in silken dress, invariably came up a staircase from the crypt to haunt a bedchamber in the oldest part of the building, entering it through a

Gothic door mounted with two sculptured heads with grotesque faces.

The restless spirit of the Lady of Creslow was seldom seen but frequently heard, very plainly, by those who ventured to sleep in the chamber or to enter it after midnight. On emerging through the Gothic door she would be heard to walk about, sometimes in a gentle, stately manner, apparently with a long silk train sweeping the floor, and at other times with quick and urgent movements, her silk dress rustling violently as if she were engaged in a desperate struggle.

Occasionally someone was found bold enough to dare the noises in the chamber, which, though still kept furnished as a bedroom, was rarely used as such. There are several stories of the experiences of those who spent a night in the room. The following, one of the more reliable accounts, is that given by a county magistrate in about 1850.

The magistrate, who lived a few miles from Creslow, rode over to a dinner party at the manor. As the night became very dark and rainy he was urged to stay overnight, if, because of the arrangements made for the other guests, he had no objection to sleeping in the haunted chamber. The offer, far from deterring him, made him accept at once, for he was a man with the strongest contempt for all ghost stories. So the room was prepared for him. He declined both a fire and a night-light, simply asking for a box of lucifers so that he could light a candle if he wished. Then, arming himself jokingly with a cutlass and a brace of pistols, he took humorous "farewell" of the family and entered the chamber.

Next morning, as the sun shone brilliantly after a night of soaking rain, the family and their guests assembled in the breakfast room. The host then noticed that the magistrate was absent. A man-servant was sent to summon him to breakfast, but returned saying that he could get no answer to his knocks, and a jug of hot water left at the door was still standing unused. Two or three of the guests then ran up to the room, and, after knocking and receiving no answer, opened the door and entered. They found the room empty. The sword and pistols were lying on the bed, which had been used, but its occupant had gone. None of the servants had seen or heard anything of the magistrate, though on first coming down in the morning they had found an outer door unfastened. It was now supposed that he must have ridden off to a board meeting held early that morning, but when the stables were checked his horse was found there as he had left it.

Just when the mystery was beginning to give rise to all sorts of wild fears the magistrate walked in on the breakfasting guests and told them the strange story of his night's experience.

"Having entered my room," he said, "I locked and bolted both doors, carefully examined the whole room, and satisfied myself that there was no living creature in it but myself, nor any entrances but those which I had secured. I got into bed and, with the conviction I should sleep as usual till six in the morning I was soon lost in a comfortable slumber.

"Suddenly I was aroused, and on raising my head to listen, I heard a sound certainly resembling the light, soft tread of a lady's footstep, accompanied with the rustling as of a silk gown. I sprang out of bed and lighted a candle. There was nothing to be seen, and nothing now to be heard. I carefully examined the whole room. I looked under the bed, into the fireplace, up the chimney and at both doors, which were fastened as I had left them. I looked at my watch, and found it was a few minutes past twelve. As all was now perfectly quiet, I extinguished the candle and entered my bed, and soon fell asleep.

"I was again aroused. The noise was now louder than before. It appeared like the violent rustling of a stiff silk dress. I sprang out of bed, darted to the spot where the noise was, and tried to grasp the intruder in my arms. My arms met together, but enclosed nothing. The noise passed to another part of the room, and I followed it, groping near the floor to prevent anything passing under my arms. It was in vain, I could feel nothing, the noise had passed away through the Gothic door, and there I saw the old monks' faces grinning at my perplexity, but the door was shut and fastened just as I had left it.

"I again examined the whole room, but could find nothing to account for the noise. I now left the candle burning, though I never sleep comfortably with a light in my room. I got into bed but felt not a little perplexed at not being able to detect the cause of the noise, nor to account for its cessation when the candle was lighted."

He then fell into a troubled sleep. On waking to find the sun shining brightly, he decided that an early morning walk would be far more refreshing than another disturbed sleep, and dressed and let himself out of the house before the servants were down.

In spite of all that had occurred, and being utterly unable to account for the noises in the haunted chamber, the magistrate still determinedly refused to believe in ghosts.

THE PROMISE OF FATHER REUBEN

When young John Chapman's parents went out to India, in the second half of the last century, he remained at school in England. Most of his holidays were spent with his Uncle John, a naturalist, in whose house, a somewhat untidy but comfortable place, the boy felt perfectly at home. From kitchen to garret, it was crammed with birds, both alive in cages and stuffed in groups in glass cases.

The boy was much attracted to his uncle's study, where he was allowed to sit and watch his uncle at work. The room was more like a workshop, being furnished with two carpenter's benches, a desk and a few chairs, and lined on three sides with shelves loaded with brown paper parcels containing the skins of birds prepared for stuffing.

Uncle John was visited by many friends, and the boy, when settled in his favourite seat by the study windows, was given early notice of a caller's arrival. The windows, which looked out on the garden, were on the left side of the front door, from which a slightly curved walk led down to the entrance gate. The gate itself was masked from view by masses of rhododendrons, but it always clanged to after being opened. It was a tiresome gate to open and shut, and people displayed their little varieties of temper as they performed the operation. The uncle, who was keen of hearing, could easily recognise his caller by the way in which the awkward gate was handled.

The boy became almost as adept as his uncle at guessing the identity of callers, his guess being confirmed when the visitor emerged from behind the shrubs into full view of the study window. One regular visitor was Father Reuben Crockford, a Catholic priest, whose easily recognisable method of using the gate was one entirely his own; his arrival was heralded by a double crash, as he always gave the gate a vicious little kick with his heel after entering, which sent it with such violence against the catch that it rebounded, and then closed again with a second clang.

Father Crockford was an active little man with a shiny head, clear blue eyes and, thought the boy, the kindest, most winning smile in the world. Crockford and his uncle had been to school together, and the priest was in the habit of coming to the house very often to stay overnight, when tired out with the duties of his pastorate. There was a room in the house always set apart ready for him, which had come to be known as "Father Reuben's room".

Uncle John had the greatest regard for the priest, although he did not agree with him in religion. One day, during a visit by Father Reuben, the boy was present when the two men entered into a discussion on the resurrection of the dead. The uncle argued that the holy resurrection had occurred too long a time ago—one wanted present evidence.

He finally told the priest, "Now, if you came back from the dead, my dear Reuben, and told me the Catholic religion was true, that would be evidence, and I would be tempted to believe it. But without some proof of that sort, I should be inclined to leave things as they are."

The priest quietly replied, "If I die first, and God permit me, I will come back and tell you, for I would do anything to see you converted to the faith."

Three years after this conversation, John Chapman, now sixteen years old, was again spending his holidays with his uncle. One morning his uncle came down late to breakfast, a most unusual occurrence for him. After opening the morning's post, he remarked, "It's very strange, there's no letter from Reuben. I felt sure there would be one by this post. I have had the strongest impression all night—a painful impression, like a nightmare—that he is coming to see us today."

His sister, who kept house for him, pointed out that the day was Friday, and Father Reuben was always too busy with his church work on Friday and Saturday to be able to visit them. But Uncle John repeated that he had the strongest presentiment that the priest was coming that day. He insisted that Father Reuben's room be made ready for him, although the carpets were up and the curtains down for cleaning, and everything in the room was in disorder.

When five o'clock—dinner time—came and the priest had not arrived on the hour, as confidently expected, Uncle John put off the meal for a quarter of an hour, thinking his friend had for some reason been held up for a few minutes. He then went out into the garden, ready to greet the priest.

John Chapman sat reading at the study window, his uncle's dog on his lap, from time to time glimpsing Uncle John as he paced to and fro between the entrance gate and the eagles' cage in the garden. Suddenly the boy heard the clanging of the gate. It was a double clang, the clang that Father Reuben alone gave, and he put down his book and watched eagerly through the window for the first glimpse of the long expected visitor. At the same time he glanced at his watch; it was just ten minutes past five.

In a few seconds Father Reuben emerged from the screen of shrubs and walked rather quickly up the curved path, carrying the small, shiny leather bag which he always brought. Uncle John also caught sight of the priest and hurried up from the farthest corner of the garden, calling a welcome and shouting loudly to him to stop until he came up to him.

To the boy's surprise, Father Reuben took no notice of his uncle's call but carried on up the path, to the front door. There he paused for a brief moment and looked in at the study window, his hand shading his eyes. The boy nodded and smiled, but the priest took no notice of his salutation.

In the boy's words : "A strange feeling of awe crept over me with no apparent cause, and I observed with concern akin to terror that his face was deathly pale, while his eyes, widely open, stared through and beyond me. The dog, awakened from his sleep by the shadow falling from outside, raised his head, and, instead of wagging his tail, as he always did at the sight of Father Reuben, gave vent to a low howl, and leaping from my lap fled into a far corner of the room.

"Then I felt a curious cold wind stir the roots of my hair, which made me shudder strangely, while I felt my cheeks suddenly blanch with inexplicable fear. I continued to gaze, as if fascinated, at Father Reuben's glassy eyes, when the sound of a deep sigh at my ear made me bound from my seat in an agony of terror and look round. I was alone in the room except for the dog, which again gave a strange, unaccountable howl. When I looked back towards the window Father Reuben was gone."

His uncle then came in and ordered the dinner bell to be rung, exclaiming delightedly, "I knew I was right—he has come!"

The dinner was served, but Father Reuben did not come down from his room, where it was assumed he had gone after the uncle saw him turn from the study window and enter the house. The bell was rung again.

"Perhaps he is finishing his prayers," said Uncle John. "I never knew such a man for saying prayers at all sorts of improper times." The maid was sent up to knock, but returned saying she could get no answer and the door was locked. The uncle then went up to Father Reuben's room, and to his amazement found no one there, the door being locked on the outside. The house was then searched from cellar to attic, but no sign of the priest could be found.

Next morning, a letter arrived which the uncle read and then handed silently to his nephew. It was from the presbytery, informing him that Father Reuben had died the previous day. It stated:

"He intended to have paid you a visit and had got as far as the railway station when, being seized with sudden failure of the heart, he fell fainting on the platform and was carried in a dying state into the waiting room. One of his brother priests was hastily summoned, who administered to him the consolation of our holy religion, and he also had the best available medical assistance. Unhappily, all efforts were useless, and he calmly expired at ten minutes past five, his last words being, 'John, there *is* a life to come'. "

The uncle, much moved, asked his nephew, "What do you think of that?"

"I think," the boy replied, "that the Catholic religion is true. Father Crockford told you he would come and tell you if it were true."

The incident affected the uncle for some time, but its influence gradually wore away and he never altered his views about religion.

But the boy joined the Catholic faith within a month. He recounted the uncanny story when himself a priest, in the magazine of Ushaw College, the Catholic seminary near Durham, in 1891. The Rev John H. Chapman explained that he had altered the names in his story, but the facts were given exactly as they had occurred.

THE GHOST OF THE UPPER CIRCLE

London has had its Theatre Royal, Drury Lane, for more than three hundred years, though the present theatre is actually the fourth, almost completely rebuilt on the original site in 1812 after a disastrous fire.

In the early 1850s, when alterations were being made to the theatre, workmen busy on the Russell Street side of the upper circle were surprised to come upon a part of the main wall which rang hollow. They reported this odd circumstance to the foreman, who decided to break through and investigate. The workmen made an opening in the brickwork and found that behind it was a small room, in which lay the skeleton of a man, a dagger stuck between its ribs.

An inquest was held on the mystery victim, at which, in the absence of evidence, an open verdict was returned. The skeleton was then quietly buried in a little graveyard on the corner of Russell Street and Drury Lane. This ceased to be a burial ground in 1853, and now lies under a small public space and children's playground known as Drury Lane Gardens.

Many theories have been offered to explain the unrecorded crime at the Theatre Royal. The most popular is that the victim was a gallant who was stabbed in a quarrel over an actress in the eighteenth century, and his body then bricked into the wall. But whatever the truth of it, it does seem highly likely that it is this murdered man's uneasy, though harmless, spirit which has haunted the theatre in the years since.

The ghost, always given the same description by the scores of people who have seen it, is that of a man of medium height, dressed in a long grey riding cloak of the eighteenth century. A sword swings under the cloak as he moves, and he wears high riding boots and a three-cornered hat. His powdered wig crowns features which, when he has passed close enough for his face to be seen, have been described as those of a handsome man with a squarish chin. He sometimes carries the tricorn hat in his hand.

The Man in Grey is always clearly visible, though sometimes

slightly misty, as if seen through a gauze curtain. He is a daytime ghost and invariably appears between nine o'clock in the morning and six in the evening, always in the same part of the building, the back of the upper circle, which he generally enters through one pass-door and disappears through another.

W. J. Macqueen-Pope, in his *Theatre Royal, Drury Lane* (W. H. Allen, 1946) describes two of the many recorded appearances of the Man in Grey.

"On one occasion a cleaner entered the upper circle to begin her work shortly after ten o'clock. A rehearsal was in progress on the stage. She saw, sitting in the end seat of the centre gangway of the fourth row, a figure of a man in grey, wearing a hat, gazing down at the stage. She thought it was one of the actors who had assumed his costume, but also thought she had better make sure. She therefore put down her pail and her broom and went to speak to the figure. As she neared it, it seemed to vanish, and then reappeared at the exit door on the right hand side of the circle, through which it passed.

"She imagined it was some trick of the eyes, this vanishing, so she did nothing about it, except to report it later. The authority on the ghost was sent for to cross-question the woman. She had never heard of the ghost before in her life, but gave a description of it which tallied accurately with all the others.

"On another occasion, during the matinee performance of a big musical play not many years before the recent war, a lady in the upper circle asked an attendant if this was the sort of play where the actors came out among the audience. The girl told her no, and asked the reason for her enquiry. The playgoer said she had seen a man in a long grey cloak, with a white wig and cocked hat, pass through the entrance door just ahead of her. The attendant assured her there was nothing like this in the play, and suggested that the figure in grey might have been a nurse in grey uniform, but the lady was sure of her story. Again the expert on the ghost scrutinised the whole house, division by division. No nurse of any kind was present. What the lady visitor had seen was a ghost."

Macqueen-Pope himself saw the Man in Grey several times before the war. The ghost was also seen by others during the war, when ENSA took over the Theatre Royal. In 1942, Mr Stephen Williams, broadcasting officer of ENSA, reported seeing the figure clearly while on the grand staircase near the upper circle entrance. Another ENSA official reported seeing it in the Green Room, which was a singular departure from the ghost's usual walk. In 1944 a visiting drama critic also saw it, this time back in the area of the upper circle.

Because some of the ghost's appearances have been made before or during a long run, the belief has become popular that its presence denotes a successful show.

The Man in Grey may not be the Theatre Royal's only ghost. It was at this theatre that Dan Leno scored his big success in pantomime, and Stanley Lupino, when playing in pantomime there years later, swore that the ghost of the great comedian appeared to him.

More recently, during the run of "Oklahoma", American comedienne Betty Jo Jones, when in difficulty in a comedy scene that did not seem to be getting across to the audience, felt unseen hands guide her to a position on the stage from which she got all her laughs successfully. This occurred again on the following night, until she got the right measure of her audience; and when the scene was going well, she felt a kindly pat on the back.

It was just the sort of thing that Dan Leno, who was completely unselfish, would have done.

Another theatre ghost, the one that haunts the Theatre Royal, Haymarket, one of London's most elegant playhouses, is of comparatively recent origin and has been identified with the famous actor-manager John Baldwin Buckstone, who was at the theatre for twenty-five years, from 1853 to 1878. He died in 1879, in his seventies.

Buckstone lived in a house at the rear of the Haymarket Theatre, as it is more popularly known, and this was later converted into the theatre's offices and dressing rooms. At the turn of the century it was often claimed that a ghost in early Victorian dress, afterwards recognised as Buckstone, had been seen or sensed in the dressing rooms and other parts of the building.

Victor Leslie, the actor, told of frequently hearing a voice in one of the dressing rooms, as if someone was going over a part in a play. Then one night, after the theatre had emptied, on going back to this same dressing room to collect a suitcase, Leslie unlocked the door and was startled to find the room occupied by a pleasant-faced elderly stranger, who was seated in an armchair. Thinking it must be an hallucination Leslie hastily picked up his case and backed out of the room, re-locking the door. He then sought the duty fireman and together they went to the room and unlocked the door. The room was empty. But, lying open on a table opposite the armchair, was a theatre account book some fifty years old, which had been stored away in a cupboard undisturbed for years. The book had not been there half an hour before. Had Leslie seen the ghost of Buckstone, returned to check over his accounts?

In the early years of the present century there were more reports of unusual happenings at the theatre. Dressing room drawers flew open, wardrobes opened and shut, and phantom footsteps were heard by many of the staff.

In 1927 Drusilla Wills, the actress, then playing at the Haymarket in the highly successful "Yellow Sands", was backstage speaking to a friend when she saw an elderly man in an old-fashioned suit pass between them. She remarked on the strange old man to her companion, but to her astonishment was told that he had not seen the man. Buckstone again, apparently.

Shortly afterwards a strange occurrence was witnessed by the theatre's manager, Horace Watson. In those days, when the theatre had a first night, the manager would sit up all night in the empty theatre doing the booking. Mr Watson was quietly busy at this work in his office together with his assistant, "Tubby" Turner, when they were startled to see the office door open wide of its own accord, *pushing back on its vacuum spring*. After a pause the door then slowly closed again—just as if someone had pushed it open, had a good look round, and then withdrawn. They searched the theatre but found no one about and nothing to account for the incident.

In the 1930s a fireman at the theatre, believed to have second sight, often saw Buckstone walking along passages in the theatre. When he followed the ghost it invariably vanished after turning a corner. Once, he and a woman cleaner both saw Buckstone cross the dress circle on a dark winter's morning. On another occasion the fireman saw Buckstone standing by a locked door. He said to the solid-looking ghost, "You can't go through there, it's locked up." But Buckstone seemed to vanish through it.

The shock of this can be imagined when considering all reports of the ghost-seers, who insist that Buckstone, unlike the sometimes misty Man in Grey, looks very real and *solid*. Mrs Sylva Stuart Watson, who runs the Haymarket today, tells me, "He is not a misty figure and you can't see through him or anything like that. When he is seen he is very real indeed—flesh and blood."

Mrs Stuart Watson admits to having no belief in ghosts, but that Buckstone revisits the theatre often she has no doubts. Through the years members of the staff, and of the companies, have seen or sensed him. Once a commissionaire who knew nothing about the haunting went to her late husband, Stuart Watson, who managed the Haymarket for a quarter of a century, and told him that he had seen a strange man in the empty theatre at night and could in no way account for the intruder. Mr Watson asked him what the man was like, and then showed him a picture of Buckstone. "Yes," said the mystified commissionaire—"that's the man."

Mr Watson had an unnerving experience about 1946, when in the theatre treasurer's office. This is now the stage director's pleasant room, but it was then much as it had been in the old days, rather dark and dismal. Suddenly all the lights in the office were switched off and Mr Watson was left in pitch darkness. He was not an imaginative man, but as he got up and crossed the room to the light switches he had a terrible feeling of cold air surrounding him which petrified him. Going quickly from the room he searched all round in the theatre but there was nobody about, and nothing to account for the strange behaviour of the lights.

In 1962 Miss Margaret Rutherford was playing at the Haymarket with her husband, Stringer Davis, in "The School for Scandal". Because of a rail strike she decided they should "camp down" for the night in her large dressing room, so as to be ready for a matinee performance the next day. The dressing room, formerly a Green Room for actors, contains a bricked up door which used to give direct access to the stage. Miss Rutherford described her strange experience that night:

"I had a vision, perhaps a very vivid dream, of something in an old cupboard in the room. The cupboard could not close because of my voluminous dresses. Among the dresses I saw a man's leg. I caught a glimpse of his face and recognised it as that of John Buckstone.

"I awoke as I was saying 'Thank you, thank you, thank you,' because he is reputed to appear only when productions are going well. My husband, who was awake in an adjoining camp bed, then told me I had been calling out in my sleep. Coincidentally with my 'dream' he had heard the creak of the door behind me and the rattle of bottles in the cupboard. It seemed to me our joint experiences set the seal of validity upon them.

"The following evening, as my dresser was helping me to prepare for the stage, we both looked up because we thought somebody had entered the room. I think it was again John Buckstone."

Another incident during the run of "The School for Scandal" was when Miss Meriel Forbes (Lady Richardson) looked up and saw Buckstone sitting in a box. The actress thought at first, quickly noticing the figure's light hair, that it was Mrs Stuart Watson seated in her customary place. But Mrs Stuart Watson was not at the theatre that night, and the box was unoccupied and could not have been entered by anyone.

Mrs Stuart Watson herself had a curious experience near the entrance to this box. She had walked along the companionway between the old and new theatre and, just before reaching the few stairs leading up to her office, passed a cleaning light on the wall. To her surprise, as she approached the stairs her shadow did not fall on them, but fell instead to the right, along the approach to the box—as if someone following close behind had proceeded in that direction. Next time she passed the light her shadow fell properly before her on the stairs.

In late 1963 Miss Olga Bennett, assistant stage manager for "At the Drop of Another Hat", then playing at the theatre, was astonished to see, during a performance, a man standing on the stage behind Michael Flanders' wheelchair while he was singing. It seemed to her that she had no other course of action than to ring down the curtain. Then the figure moved, showing that it was not, as she had supposed, a negligent stagehand, but a man clad in a long black frock coat. At the same instant it vanished. Miss Bennett, greatly relieved, and no believer in ghosts, then forgot about the incident until speaking later to an authority on the theatre's history. It was then found that her description of the frock-coated figure exactly fitted John Baldwin Buckstone.

Mrs Stuart Watson, in her office charged with the fascinating air of the Haymarket, past and present, told me, "My husband and father-in-law never liked being in this office but I don't mind it at all. In fact I find it a very friendly room to be in. Buckstone may play tricks at times but he is a kind and gentle ghost and I am sure his last wish would be to frighten anyone. He is a darling and we all love him. If a door rattles or there are odd noises we may say it's a draught, or we may say it's Buckstone. We know he does come and that he can be here at any time. There is no doubt that he loved this theatre so much he does not want to leave it."

The ghost of the old Royalty Theatre, in Dean Street, Soho, now seems to have vanished along with the theatre. The Royalty opened in 1840 under the management of Fanny Kelly, an actress of Drury Lane who lived at 73, Dean Street. The theatre was built at the back of her house by Fanny's patron, the then Duke of Devonshire, and was known as Miss Kelly's Theatre. One of those who played there was Charles Dickens, who in September, 1845 took the part of Bobadil in Ben Jonson's comedy "Every Man in His Humour".

But Fanny Kelly's venture was not a successful one, and after the close of her management the theatre underwent several changes; it became the Soho Theatre, and then, in 1906, the New Royalty

Theatre. But Miss Kelly's presence seems never to have left the building while it was in use. The ghost of a woman in grey was seen to walk down the staircase of what was once Fanny Kelly's house, afterwards part of the theatre, and cross to the centre of the vestibule, where it vanished. Many people also saw the same woman in grey sitting quietly in the stage box.

Mr Charles Landstone, who was manager of the theatre from 1931 to 1934 tells me, "A number of the staff claimed to have seen the ghost, which generally appeared in the stage box about 1 a.m., if a dress rehearsal was in progress. It was reputed to be the ghost of the proprietress in the mid-1840s (Fanny Kelly) who is said to have committed suicide."

With the closure of her theatre Fanny Kelly seems to be at rest.

Mr Landstone later managed the Theatre Royal, Bristol, where the ghost of Mrs Sarah Siddons continues to be reported. The Bristol theatre, the oldest theatre building in the country, celebrated its 200th anniversary in 1966. It was some twelve years after its opening in 1766 that Sarah Siddons, after failing at Drury Lane, went there to play for four happy years before her triumphal return to London. Her dressing room remains still.

Mr Landstone, who managed the theatre from 1942 to 1961, tells me that during that time many actors and staff at the theatre swore to him that they had seen Mrs Siddons' ghost, which is said to be a kindly spirit. One who has written of her experience is Yvonne Mitchell.

In her autobiographical book *Actress* (1957) Miss Mitchell says, "In 'Macbeth' I played the second witch, and the lily-livered boy. Passing behind the stage one night, in my chain-mail as the boy, I thought I saw a ghost. A tall, sand-coloured draped figure, standing in the scene-dock. I looked again, and there was nothing there. I was assured by other actors that I had seen the ghost of Sarah Siddons, who had played Lady Macbeth on that stage. I hope it was she."

THE UNQUIET ARMIES

On the hill of Echt, in Aberdeenshire, famous for its ancient fortification called the Barmkyn of Echt, almost every night during the winter of 1637-38 there was heard "a prodigious beating of phantom drums". The drumming was afterwards supposed to have presaged the bloody Civil War which shortly followed.

"The parade and retiring of guards, their tattoos, their reveilles and marches, were all heard distinctly by multitudes of people," wrote Gordon of Rothiemay. "Eye-witnesses, soldiers of credit, have told me that when the parade was beating, they could discern when the drummer walked towards them, or when he turned about, as the fashion is for drummers, to walk to and again, upon the head or front of a company drawn up.

"At such times, also, they could distinguish the marches of several nations. The first march that was heard was the Scottish March; afterwards the Irish March was heard, then the English March. But before these noises ceased, those who had been trained up much of their lives abroad in the German Wars, affirmed that they could perfectly, by their hearing, discern the marches upon the drum of several foreign nations of Europe—such as the French, Dutch and Danish."

The phantom drums were so constantly heard that all the country people living in the region of the hill became familiar with them. Sometimes the drums moved from the hill and were heard beating in places two or three miles from it.

"Some people in the night, travelling near by the Loch of Skene, within three miles of that hill, were frightened with the loud noise of drums, struck hard by them, which did convoy them along the way, but saw nothing; as I had it often from such as heard these noises, from the Laird of Skene and his lady, from the Laird of Echt, and my own wife then living in Skene, almost immediately after the people thus terrified had come and told it.

"Some gentlemen of known integrity and truth affirmed that, near their places, they heard a perfect shot of cannon go off as ever they heard at the battle of Nordlingen, where themselves some years before had been present."

Five years later, when the first engagements of the Civil War were in progress, further strange happenings were reported in Scotland. The vision of a furious battle was seen on the hill of Manderlee, four miles from Banff. The warring armies looked so real to those who saw them that many ran to bury their valuables in the earth, safe from the invaders.

At Bankafair and Drum, in Aberdeenshire, the "tonking" of phantom drums was heard. The minister of Ellon in the same county, Andrew Leitch, reported that while sitting at supper one night he also heard "tonking of drums, vively, sometimes appearing near at hand and sometimes far off".

On February 12th, 1643 a vision was seen on the hill of Brimmond, four miles from Aberdeen, by William Anderson, a tenant of Craibstone. Anderson testified that he had seen "a great army, both of horse and foot", appear on the hill at about eight o'clock on a misty morning. The phantom host, with accompanying noises, remained visible till the sun rose above the mist, when they vanished.

Five days earlier, says a chronicler, "it was written here to Aberdeen that Kentoun battle at Banbury (Battle of Edgehill, October 23rd, 1642) wherein His Majesty was victorious, has in vision been seen seven sundry times sin-syne".

News of the strange vision seen at Edgehill—of the battle there, the first and fiercest encounter between the Roundheads and the Royalists, being re-enacted over and over again by spectral armies —had quickly spread to many other parts of Britain. The uncanny contest of the ghost armies was seen by many reliable witnesses, including investigators sent to the spot by Charles I. The whole story of the events was recorded in a pamphlet published immediately afterwards.

The bloody battle at Edgehill, on the Warwickshire border three miles from Kineton, had been fought between opposing armies each 20,000 strong. The Parliamentarians had failed to stand up to the charge of the Royalist cavalry led by flamboyant Prince Rupert, but because the victorious horsemen did not quickly return to the field and regroup for a second charge, the Parliamentarians were able to rally and crush the King's foot soldiers. Hours of hard fighting resulted in 4,000 dead. Both sides claimed victory but the advantage rested with the Royalists, who were not prevented from continuing their march on London.

The battle was fought on a Sunday. The first report of spectral armies continuing the fight exactly as it had occurred, on the field of the 4,000 dead, came two months after the event, on the Saturday morning before Christmas, 1642. The pamphlet testified:

"Between twelve and one o'clock in the morning was heard by some shepherds, and other countrymen, and travellers, first the sound of drums afar off, and the noise of soldiers, as it were, giving out their last groans." Astonished, they all stood still to listen. The noises began to come closer, and taking sudden fright, they were just about to run away when "there appeared in the air the same incorporeal soldiers that made these clamours, and immediately, with ensigns displayed, drums beating, muskets going off, cannons discharging and horses neighing—which also to these men were visible—the alarum or entrance to this game of death was one army, which gave the first charge, having the King's colours, and the other the Parliament's, at their head or front of the battle, and so pell-mell to it they went.

"Till two or three in the morning in equal scale continued this dreadful fight, the clattering of arms, noise of cannons, cries of soldiers, so amazing and terrifying the poor men that they could not believe they were mortal or give credit to their eyes and ears. Run away they durst not, for fear of being made a prey to these infernal soldiers, and so they, with much fear and affright, stayed to behold the success of the business. After some three hours' fight, that army which carried the King's colours withdrew, or rather, appeared to fly; the other remaining, as it were, masters of the field, stayed a good space triumphing, and expressing all the signs of joys and conquest, and then, with all their drums, trumpets, ordnance and soldiers, vanished."

The terrified spectators immediately hurried to Kineton, where they knocked up William Wood, a magistrate. He called up Samuel Marshall, the Kineton minister, and together they heard the men tell their incredible story on oath.

Wood and Marshall, knowing some of the men to be of proved integrity, suspended judgment until they themselves had visited the spot the next night. This was Sunday—Christmas night—and the magistrate and the minister, together with their informants and "all the substantial inhabitants of that and neighbouring parishes" went in a body to Edgehill field, where half an hour after their arrival "there appeared in the same tumultuous warlike manner the same two adverse armies fighting with as much spite and spleen as formerly; and so departed the gentlemen and all the spectators, much terrified with these visions of horror, who withdrew themselves to their houses, beseeching God to defend them from those hellish and prodigious enemies".

Nothing was seen the next night, nor for the rest of that week, so that all were hopeful that the spectres had departed. But on the Saturday night following, at the same time, the phantom armies reappeared, fighting with even greater force for nearly four hours before vanishing; and on the Sunday night the fantastic sight was repeated again.

This was too much for Mr Marshall, the minister, and several of his friends, who "forsook their habitations thereabout and retired themselves to other more secure dwellings". But the magistrate and others stayed—to see the spectral battle fought out yet again on the next Saturday and Sunday nights.

Reports of the phenomenon reached King Charles, then at Oxford, and he immediately sent Colonel Lewis Kirke, Captain Dudley, Captain Wainman and "three other gentlemen of credit" to conduct an investigation. Their journey was made both to satisfy the King's curiosity and to quieten the mounting terror among the inhabitants of Kineton and the surrounding districts.

After hearing the accounts of the magistrate and other eye-witnesses the six men stayed, and on the following Saturday and Sunday nights not only saw the ghostly battle fought out again exactly as described, but were able to recognise on the Royalist side several of their personal friends who had been slain, including Sir Edmund Verney, the King's standard bearer.

The six investigators returned to the King and testified on oath as to the remarkable sight they had seen. The pamphlet giving the whole story was published within days of their report.

The phantoms of Edgehill have remained unquiet throughout the centuries. There have been persistent reports of apparitions and noises of battle, of phantom riders seen—messengers for the armies, perhaps—and the noise of hard galloping horses. But in recent years the battlefield has lain inside the barbed wire surrounding an Army ammunition dump set up on the site, which has not made for easy investigations.

The ghost of ill-fated Sir Edmund Verney has also been seen far from the battlefield. In the fighting, the Buckinghamshire squire was hacked down until all that was recognisable was his hand still clutching the King's standard. He was buried in a common grave, but the severed hand was eventually returned to the Verney family at Claydon House, ten miles north-west of Aylesbury; the ring it bore is still the family's most treasured heirloom. Sir Edmund is said to roam the house which he built, looking for his lost hand. In recent years several people have experienced his "presence", including a member of the family and pupils of a girls' school evacuated there in the last war.

Three years after Edgehill, and not many miles from that battlefield, King Charles himself was visited by a ghost. This was in June, 1645 at Daventry, Northamptonshire, where the King had marched his army of less than 10,000 men, intending to do battle with the Parliamentary army then quartered at Northampton.

About two hours after the King had gone to bed in the Wheatsheaf Hotel, in Sheep Street, some of his attendants, hearing an "uncommon noise" in his chamber, went into it and found Charles sitting up in bed greatly agitated. The King told them he had been disturbed by an apparition of Lord Strafford (whom he had had beheaded on Tower Hill four years before). The apparition, after upbraiding him for his cruelty, told the King he had come to return him good for evil, and advised him not to meet the Parliamentary army at Northampton for he could never conquer it by arms.

Next morning Prince Rupert talked the worried King out of his fears, but the following night the apparition appeared to Charles a second time, and told the King angrily that this was the last advice he would be permitted to give, and if Charles kept to his resolution of fighting it would be his undoing.

The King wasted another precious day at Daventry "fluctuating between the apprehensions of his imagination and the reproaches of his courage", but was again persuaded by Prince Rupert to disregard the warning, and the Royalist army marched on northward. There followed, on June 14th, 1645 the disastrous Battle of Naseby. The defeat put a finishing touch to the King's affairs, for after it he could never get together an army strong enough to look the enemy in the face. It was the decisive battle of the Civil War.

Charles was often heard to say that he wished he had taken *the warning* and not fought at Naseby, the meaning of which nobody knew except those to whom he had spoken of the apparition, and whom he had charged to keep the affair secret.

Forty years after Naseby, the ambitious young Duke of Monmouth met his defeat at the Battle of Sedgemoor, near Bridgwater in Somerset. His ghost has many times been seen riding the moor and is said to appear on July 6th, the anniversary of the battle fought in 1685; but the duke's phantom has also been seen across the border in Dorset, where he was captured after fleeing the battlefield.

Monmouth rode from Sedgemoor before the fighting was over, leaving more than a thousand of his soldiery to be cut to pieces and many others taken prisoner and hanged on a long line of gibbets on the road from Weston Zoyland to Bridgwater. He fled with Lord Grey and a party of horse, and when their horses failed they disguised themselves as rustics and went their own ways on foot. Grey and others were soon picked up by search parties of Royalist troops, and Monmouth himself was discovered hiding in a ditch at Shags Heath, a spot between the villages of Horton and Woodlands, in east Dorset. Gaunt, dirtied and ragged, the handsome rebel was identified with difficulty.

Monmouth was executed on July 15th, the executioner taking five blows to sever his head from his body, and his remains were buried under the communion table of St Peter's Church in the Tower; but through the years the duke's bedraggled ghost, carrying his hacked head, has been said to haunt the ditch where he was found, especially on July 16th, the night following his execution. The exact spot where he was seized is marked by a tree known as Monmouth's Ash.

A phantom army which appeared near Keswick, Cumberland in the next century had no connection with an actual battle, but, like Edgehill, it appeared several times and was seen by a host of witnesses together, and the events were recorded very soon after they occurred. The spectral army appeared on Souter Fell, a precipitous mountain with sheer north and west sides rising to 900 feet.

On Midsummer Eve, 1735 a farmhand at Blakehills, about half a mile from the mountain, looked up to see the eastern side of its summit covered with marching troops. They came in distinct bodies from an eminence on the north end and disappeared in a cleft in the summit, the spectral march continuing for a full hour.

No one believed the farmhand's story, but two years later, also on Midsummer Eve, the farmer himself, William Lancaster, saw the phantoms. On looking up at Souter Fell he saw a few men following their horses on the mountain and took them to be returning huntsmen. But when he looked up again, ten minutes later, he saw to his astonishment the same figures now mounted and followed by a great array of troops, marching five abreast and following exactly the same path as that described by the farmhand two years before. Each company of soldiers was kept in order by a mounted officer, but as evening came on discipline seemed to be relaxed and the various sections of troops intermingled, moving at unequal speeds, until all were finally swallowed up by darkness.

All the Lancaster family saw the phenomenon, but their story was no more believed than that of the farmhand. However, on Midsummer Eve eight years later—June 23rd, 1745—the Lancasters gathered together twenty-six people to keep watch on Souter Fell with them, and all witnessed the same spectacle as before—and more besides. For this time, carriages were interspersed with the troops, a "multitude beyond imagination" who filled a space of half a mile. They marched on quickly till darkness fell and hid them —still marching. There was nothing vaporous or indistinct about the soldiers, who looked so real that some of the watchers went up next morning to look for the hoofmarks of the horses. They found nothing.

The witnesses attested their story on oath before a magistrate. It then came out that two other people had seen strange things on Souter Fell, but had kept silent to escape ridicule. On a summer evening in 1743, two years earlier, Mr Wren of Wilton Hall, and his farm-servant, had looked up and seen a man and a dog pursuing some horses along a ridge of the mountain so steep that a horse could hardly by any possibility keep a footing on it. The figures moved with great speed, and their disappearance at the south end of the Fell was so sudden that Wren and his servant went up the next morning to find the body of the man, whom they were convinced must have fallen to his death.

But of man, horses and dog they found no trace.

THE RED MONK AND HIGHWAY HORRORS

At about four o'clock on a dark winter's morning in January, 1964, two young women cleaners cycling home after their night shift at a recently opened car factory near Basildon New Town, Essex, suddenly saw walk, or float, across the road in front of them the ghostly figure of a monk. They rode on, speechless and considerably shaken, until well past ancient Holy Cross Church, near which the apparition had appeared.

It was a frightening incident which they did not expect to have repeated. But at the same time on another morning the same ghostly figure, seemingly robed in a crimson gown, again appeared on the road, this time directly in the path of Mrs Rita Tobin's cycle. She rang her bell but the figure did not move and she cycled on right through it.

"The air was cold and clammy," Mrs Tobin said. "I went numb all over and could not speak. It was terrible." Her companion, Mrs Sylvia Smith, described the monk's appearance as ghastly and "just like a transparent rainbow".

Within the next few days, and before anything was made public, all ten women engaged on the night-cleaning shift at the new Ford factory had seen the phantom monk while cycling home in the early hours. They saw it individually and in pairs. The figure, one woman explained, was "just floating, in deathly quiet".

The monk was seen to come out of the bushes, shuffle silently across the road and disappear among the graves in the 600-year-old churchyard of Holy Cross. The ten women saw the monk more than a dozen times between them, and were terrified. They decided they would only use the road from the factory in gangs, though this was hard on those among them who wished to get home early to their young children, as it meant they had to wait for the others to finish before they could leave.

All the ghost's appearances were made between four o'clock and six o'clock in the morning. Mrs Kay Bull, supervisor of the cleaners, saw the figure twice, and her theory was that it might be a lost soul who wanted release. She thought it was, perhaps, the apparition of one who had been forced against his will to go into the monastery which once existed at the spot; he was always seen at the early hours when the monks used to hold their meditations at the monastery, and might be trying to escape it.

Mrs Bull disclosed that prior to the monk's several appearances the cleaners had once been startled by a man's sudden appearance on the lonely road as they were going to work, and they told him, jokingly, that they thought he was a ghost. He replied, "Not me, lady, but there is one because I've seen it. And I wish someone would do something, because the shock of seeing him could kill anyone with a weak heart."

The cleaners, on the ghost's first appearances, did not at once ask the local vicar for help because they thought they would be laughed at, but the persistent haunting of the road brought matters to a head. Their story, widely reported by the newspapers, found support from many old residents who were convinced that Holy Cross churchyard was haunted.

The Rev Bernard Lloyd, curate in charge of Holy Cross Church, said he had often been at the church late on dark winter's nights and on some occasions had heard odd noises, like footsteps in the church porch without anyone being there, but he believed so many things like bats or mice could be responsible for this. He had not seen anything strange. If there was a ghost, Mr Lloyd said, from the description given by the cleaners it could be that of a former Basildon rector who became dean of a London church. This would account for the crimson gown. Or it could be the apparition of one of the two Basildon rectors who were deposed at the time of the Reformation. But, said Mr Lloyd, whatever the identity of the apparition, as it was said to cross the road into the churchyard there was no question of an exorcism as such a ceremony could not be performed on consecrated ground.

Mr Lloyd took part in a special vigil kept outside the church, but nothing strange was seen or heard.

The newspaper reports of the Red Monk brought a constant stream of sightseers to the haunted spot. One local clergyman, meantime, wrote in a local newspaper urging the cleaners "to have faith". The monk, however, was not seen again and there have been no reports of him since.

A report of a glowing figure in monk's clothing being seen walking the woods at Oxney Bottom, Kent, early in 1962, reopened the mystery of the hauntings at ruined Oxney Court, formerly a monastery. The Court, standing in fourteen acres bordering the main Dover Road near Deal, was habited until 1936. It was badly damaged during the last war.

In 1962 the hollow shell of the old abbey was still to be seen in Oxney Woods, with the graves of members of the d'Auberville family, the original owners of Oxney Court, laid beside it. The report of the "glowing monk" came from three young men who took part in a ghost-hunting expedition in the woods one night. The figure was said by one of them to have appeared out of the blackness "brightly lit, in the habit of a monk, with its arms outstretched". Though they had gone out purposely to seek anything unusual, the phantom monk gave them a shock.

Their seeing the monk's apparition was unusual, but only because the ghost most commonly claimed to have been seen in the vicinity of the old house has been that of a woman known as the Grey Lady of Oxney Court. Why the monk should wander in the woods no one knows, nor whose wraith he might be; but apart from this most recent appearance, on which his figure was said to be "glowing", all who have seen him describe him in exactly the same way: a monk wearing a grey habit with a hood, and with no sign of a face or hands.

There is an explanation for the Grey Lady. In fact, several. The most common is that she is the spirit of a prioress of the abbey who was murdered by a person unknown, and who returns to search the area for her assailant. She walks through the woods, across the Dover Road, and into the fields in the direction of Eastry.

Dozens of people claim to have seen either the monk or the Grey Lady, as the *East Kent Mercury* discovered following reports of the "glowing" monk's appearance in January, 1962. Once a motorist saw a woman in the middle of the road and was unable to avoid running her down; but when he got out of his car to find out the extent of her injuries, there was no sign of a body. On another occasion a couple on a motor-cycle also ran into a "woman in grey" in the road at the same spot, but could see nothing when they stopped.

Miss O. Pittock, of Walmer, told the *Mercury* of the strange experience she had had about four years earlier while driving her car, with three passengers, along the road past Oxney Bottom. She was near Eastry when she saw in the moonlight what appeared to be a clump of grass growing in the hedge at the side of the road, but in no time at all it detached itself from the hedge and came on to the running board, next to the driver's window.

Miss Pittock continued, "Naturally, I swerved, and we ended up with the car stopped on the wrong side of the road. What I had seen, without any doubt whatsoever, was a person in a monk's habit, although there was no face, and the arms appeared to be crossed." She stressed that she had seen the apparition quite clearly, and was positive of its shape and appearance; in the moonlight she could see that the monk's habit was grey in colour. A woman passenger in the car also saw the apparition and gave exactly the same description of it. One of the other passengers suggested they should go back and look around, but Miss Pittock did not much like the idea and drove on.

Miss Pittock said that when she described this uncanny incident to an elderly acquaintance who lived in Deal, he told her that as a young man he was driving a horse-drawn van along the road not far from the spot where she had seen the ghost, when a figure in monk's clothing jumped on to the cart and rode with him a short distance before disappearing.

A recent appearance of the Grey Lady occurred in 1956. On an autumn evening a man was in the woods picking blackberries when soon after dusk he saw a woman walking down the track towards the road. She seemed "somewhat transparent", and he hid behind a tree as she walked, or rather drifted along. At first he thought it was not necessarily a ghost, but he was perfectly convinced when he next saw her walk through a bush, which did not even waver as she went through it.

Unfortunately the publication in 1962 of these reports of the phantoms of Oxney Court prompted some young boys to set out on a ghost-hunting expedition which ended in tragedy. One boy, only twelve years old, fell to his death down a deep well after he and a companion had succeeded in removing a heavy cover placed over the well-mouth. Shortly afterwards the owner of Oxney Court said he had at last obtained permission to demolish the building, which had earlier been claimed as of historical interest.

In Huntingdonshire the haunting of a lonely stretch of road is believed to have persisted for some forty years. Many motorists have had to brake sharply on seeing the figure of a young nun loom out of the darkness directly in their path near the bridge over Alconbury Brook, Huntingdon. Several cars have swerved and hit the side of the bridge. There have also been fatal accidents at the spot, which rumour has blamed on the nun.

Not far from the bridge lies Hinchingbrooke House, former home of the Earls of Sandwich, and it is thought that here the explanation for the wandering nun may lie. Hinchingbrooke, a sixty-roomed mansion on an estate of 1,700 acres, was originally a Benedictine nunnery believed to have been founded by William the Conqueror and suppressed at the Dissolution in 1536. The present mansion, opened to the public in the 1940s, stands on the same site and portions of the old nunnery survive in the entrance hall, library, billiard room, and a concert hall built over the cloisters.

The nunnery, always small and poor, took in paying guests, and at the time of its dissolution there were only three nuns there besides the prioress. Centuries afterwards, in January, 1830, a disastrous fire broke out in the Great Bow Room of Hinchingbrooke House and demolished the floor and ceiling. The north and part of the east side of the house, the halls and drawing rooms were burnt out, the great carved staircase destroyed, and many of the archives, papers and records burnt. During the rebuilding, two skeletons of prioresses, in their thirteenth century stone coffins, were found buried beneath the floor at the foot of the stairs outside the library. The actual burial ground of the nunnery was in the garden on the east side of the house.

And so it seems that the spectral nun haunting the road at Alconbury Brook, and seen on the bridge by many people, may be the restless, and to motorists highly dangerous, spirit of one of that last small band of sisters in 1536, returned to haunt the vicinity of the cloistered home from which she was ejected.

Another phantom of the open road which has made a number of appearances in recent years is the ghost of Castle Hill, on the boundaries of Golborne and Newton-le-Willows, Lancashire. In tradition the Castle Hill ghost, which, according to popular belief, has haunted the woods of Newton-le-Willows for centuries, is known as the White Lady; but its appearances in recent years have certainly not been in that romantic image.

In 1947 it was seen as a white shape in the woods by Mrs E. Waywell, wife of a Newton butcher, and Mrs P. Hardman, wife of the Newton librarian, while they were out walking. Two years later Mr and Mrs Cyril Ball, also of Newton, were walking in the woods when Mrs Ball pointed to a figure motionless among the trees. About 6 feet tall it stood with arms folded and appeared to be wearing a monk's habit. When the couple approached it vanished into the trees. Then it suddenly reappeared and they began to run towards it, but after a time they had to give up the chase, being out of breath. They then saw it vanish into the trees again.

In August, 1960, nineteen-year-old John Swift, of Golborne, reported seeing the ghost as he was cycling home shortly before midnight through the Hollows, near Castle Hill. He was completely unaware that the area was reputed to be haunted and was terrified.

His description of the encounter was brief and vivid. "I picked up in the beam of my cycle light a huge figure, double the size of any normal man, dressed in white about the top part of the body. The figure remained for some seconds. Then I cycled as fast as I could go to the East Lancashire Road, half a mile away. . . ."

THE MURDERED PRIME MINISTER

Early on the night of Monday, May 11th, 1812, John Williams, a Cornish mine manager, awoke his wife in great agitation and described to her a startling dream he had just had.

He said he had dreamed he was in the lobby of the House of Commons and saw a small man enter, dressed in a blue coat and a white waistcoat. Immediately after, a man wearing a brown greatcoat with yellow basket buttons drew a pistol from under his coat and discharged it at the small man, who fell almost instantly.

Williams told his wife that he clearly heard the report of the pistol and saw the blood fly out and stain the white waistcoat a little below the left breast; he even saw the change of colour in the small man's face. The man in brown, whose face he also saw in detail, was seized by some men who were present. He (Williams) then asked one of the men close by who had been shot, and was told, "The Chancellor".

Mrs Williams very naturally told her husband it was only a dream, and calmed him, telling him to try and get some rest. He did fall asleep again, but shortly afterwards awoke his wife and told her he had had the very same dream a second time. She suggested that he had been so disturbed the first time that it had probably dwelt on his mind, and urged him to try and forget it and settle down for the night. But again, for the third time, Williams experienced the same haunting dream—the entrance of the small man, the shot from the man in brown, and he himself asking the name of the victim, and being told, "The Chancellor".

At this, although it was only between one and two o'clock in the morning, Williams knew he could not possibly settle himself to sleep any more, so he got up and dressed.

At breakfast in his house at Scorrier, near Redruth, Cornwall, Williams' sole topic of conversation was the strange dream that had come to him three times in the early part of the night, each time explicit in every detail. In the afternoon, when he drove in his carriage to Falmouth on business, he repeated the events of the vivid dream to every acquaintance he met.

About dusk the following day, May 13th, the mine manager was visited by his daughter and son-in-law, named Tucker, who lived at Trematon Castle. No sooner had the pair set foot in the house than Williams told them of his odd dream. In fact he was so full of it that he kept them standing till he had finished. Tucker at first commented light-heartedly that it might do very well in a dream to have the Lord Chancellor, the Speaker of the House of Lords, in the lobby of the House of Commons, but that he would never be found there in reality. Then, seeing that his father-in-law was in earnest over the matter, Tucker asked him to describe the man he had "seen" shot, which Williams did. Short, thin and pale, in a blue coat and white waistcoat. Tucker replied that this description was not at all that of the Lord Chancellor, but was exactly that of Spencer Perceval, the Prime Minister and Chancellor of the Exchequer. Had he (Williams) ever seen the Prime Minister?

Williams replied that he had not, nor had he ever written to Perceval, either on public or private matters. And he had certainly never been near the lobby of the House of Commons in his life. But the dream of the assassination had seemed so real that he wondered should he send warning of it to London? He frankly did not know what to do.

While the two men were still talking they heard a horse gallop up to the front door of the house, and immediately afterwards, Williams' son Michael, who lived at Trevince, entered the room. Michael said he had galloped the seven miles from Truro after hearing the sensational news brought by a man who had come with that evening's mail coach from London. This man had said he was in the Commons lobby on the evening of May 11th when a man called Bellingham had shot dead the Prime Minister.

Michael Williams' haste in bringing the news was to tell his brother-in-law, whom he had learned in Truro had gone to visit his father, so that Tucker could alert his political friends, who might be affected by ministerial changes. The two men were more than shocked at the news and when Michael was told of his father's dream he understood how they felt.

Perceval had been shot down at about five o'clock on the evening of May 11th, the man from London had said. The extraordinary fact now before them was that within a few hours of the assassination, John Williams, nearly three hundred miles away in Cornwall, had in his dream seen the event re-enacted *exactly as it had hap-*

pened. There were of course in those days no means of communication by which Williams could have gained early knowledge of the tragedy.

Again John Williams described to his family the appearances of the men he had seen in the dream, and whom he had never met in real life, and the place where he had never been. The details he gave matched absolutely to the real thing.

In London at this time the assassin, John Bellingham, was in custody. Aged about forty-two, he was an English merchant in Russia who had suffered business injuries there and had sought redress from the British government, only to have his petitions rejected. On the evening of the 11th, Bellingham had stationed himself in the recess of a doorway inside the Commons lobby, where a number of people were standing. On the entrance of the forty-nine-year-old Prime Minister, who had walked there from his house in Downing Street, Bellingham had committed the murder precisely as in Williams' dream. He drew out a small pistol and shot Perceval in the lower part of the left breast. Perceval took a few faltering steps forward, and fell. He was carried to the room of the Speaker's secretary, where he died after twelve minutes.

Bellingham had been seized, offering no resistance. His trial was held at the Old Bailey four days after the murder, and was over in eight hours. The following Monday, May 18th, a week to the day from his firing of the fatal shot, a vast crowd watched his execution. A witness observed, "He was hurried as it were out of the world, not being allowed above two minutes to remain on the scaffold after he came out of Newgate." He was hanged, and his body anatomised.

Six weeks after the murder, John Williams, having business to transact in London, took the opportunity to make his first visit, with a friend, to the House of Commons. As soon as he came to the steps at the entrance of the lobby, he stopped, and said, "This place is as distinctly within my recollection in my dream as any room in my house." Inside the lobby he pointed out the exact spot where Bellingham had stood when he fired, and where Spencer Perceval had reached when he was struck by the ball, and where and how he fell.

John Williams, all through the years till his death in 1841, freely related every particular of his remarkable dream, supported as it was by the many witnesses who had heard it from him at the time. An authentic report of it appeared in *The Times* in 1828.

THE GHOST THAT MOVED NEXT DOOR

Newly married Mr and Mrs John Durston moved into their flat in an old country house near Newton Abbot, Devon, at the end of August, 1963. Aller House, in the tiny hamlet of Aller, had been converted into three flats, and the Durstons' was on the ground floor. Strange, frightening things began to happen only days after their arrival.

Mr Durston, a young apprentice fitter, and his wife Carol, began to hear loud, measured footsteps tramping up and down the passage outside their flat at night, but on looking out found no one there. Ornaments began to move by themselves along the mantelpiece. Then, several times they both saw a white, misty figure of a man pass through their living room.

One night, after a fortnight of these eerie disturbances, Mr Durston and his wife saw the heavy wardrobe in their bedroom violently shaken and moved away from the wall. They decided they could stand no more, and although it was then one o'clock in the morning, the couple got their things together and walked a mile to the home of Mr Durston's mother, in Kingskerswell, where they stayed. Twice they tried to convince themselves that there must be an explanation for the strange happenings, and went back to the flat at Aller House for a night, but each time something else strange happened. It seemed to them that a presence had taken over their home, one that was becoming increasingly more violent and noisy.

Even in their absence from the flat the disturbances went on. The neighbouring flat, separated by an adjoining corridor, was occupied by Mr Leonard Culley and his wife, and their two schoolgirl daughters. Both Mr Culley and his wife were woken up at night by noises coming from the Duttons' empty flat. Mr Culley reported hearing furniture being moved around and crockery rattling; there was also the sound of footsteps, and the wireless was unaccountably switched on and off.

The Durstons asked the vicar of Abbotskerswell, the Rev Gordon Langford, for help. Mr Langford made a thorough investigation, and after tracing the case back through earlier tenants and a former owner of Aller House, became convinced there was a ghostly presence in the Durstons' flat. The haunting appeared very likely to be connected with the death in 1915 of Mr Victor Judd, manager of a knackers yard, who lived at Aller House. He committed suicide with a humane killer in the yard, which at that time adjoined the house, and the vicar found there had been complaints of unusual happenings ever since.

Mr Langford reported the matter to the Bishop of Exeter, Dr Robert Mortimer, who then sent his chaplain to make an investigation. As a result of these inquiries the bishop decided to exorcise the ghost.

On a Sunday in November, 1963, when the bishop conducted a special thirty-five minute service in the haunted flat, everyone there sensed the ghostly presence. Mr Langford said, "The room temperature suddenly dropped alarmingly, and we all shivered as though we were standing in an icy blast. Even the bishop commented on the icy blast as he came into the room."

A few minutes before the service began the misty figure of the ghost was seen again by Mr Durston's mother, and during the service itself, in which the bishop said prayers and sprinkled holy water, Mr Durston and his wife vividly sensed the presence standing right behind them. They felt it go from the room part-way through the service.

The following day the young couple had breakfast in their flat after sleeping there for the first time that month. Mr Langford celebrated Holy Communion at the house, and all were aware of a totally different, wholesome atmosphere about the place.

But the peace at Aller House was short-lived. Three weeks after the exorcism, Mr Culley, in the flat across the corridor, reported that the ghost had now invaded *his* flat. Both he and his wife had seen it. He was not at all frightened of the ghost, he said, but exasperated because it made so much noise.

Mr Culley, a painter and decorator, said he suddenly felt the ghost behind him while he was doing some accounts one morning, and on looking over his shoulder he saw the figure of a man aged forty to forty-five, dressed in Edwardian clothes. The figure was quite plain for some seconds, and then vanished. Mrs Culley said she saw the ghost in the kitchen. A kind of mist appeared in front of an airing cupboard, and she then saw a shadowy figure. The ghost also turned off the gas while she was in the living room.

Through all this, from the start of the hauntings, the tenant of the third flat in the house had neither heard nor seen anything strange.

Mr Culley received letters from a number of spiritualist societies and four Newton Abbot mediums agreed to hold an all-night vigil at Aller House shortly before Christmas, in a further attempt to lay the ghost. However, the occupants of the house suddenly changed their minds about this. The spirit, they said, had not done them any actual harm and it would be unkind to try to eject it from the house before Christmas.

So nothing more was done, and it appears that peace did eventually come to Aller House.

A suicide was also believed to be responsible for the sudden haunting of a house in Nottingham, which was let off in flats. This occurred in the autumn of 1961. Two distressed young mothers who saw the ghost, that of a tall woman with her dark hair tied in a pigtail, were driven to seek the help of the local vicar. One of the two wives was in the bathroom one day when she thought she saw a pair of hands reaching out. After that, no one dared go to the bathroom, for it was there, the families occupying the flats learned, that a woman had killed herself some years before. A third young mother, who had only been in the house a week, twice saw the pigtailed ghost. She spoke to the apparition and asked if she could do anything to help it, but it just drifted away in silence.

There were other incidents in this persistent haunting, which decided two of the families to leave. One night a baby asleep in its cot suddenly started to laugh. In the morning a little girl asked if the "strange woman" would be coming back; she had seen the apparition tickling the baby during the night. It was also seen by another little girl, and in a series of other incidents a pram was rocked by invisible hands, clothing moved, and knives and cotton reels shifted mysteriously from cupboards to a table.

The apparition was seen only by the women and children, but the husbands of the three families all said they were strongly aware of there being something uncanny in the house. Even on a warm September night they had felt rooms go suddenly cold and draughty, and there was an acute feeling among them that they were being watched.

Members of a sectarian church prayed in the house in the room where the ghost had been seen with the baby. This seemed to have some effect.

A similar ghostly figure, described as having the appearance of a woman more than six feet tall, troubled a family of seven in their council house at Meltham, Huddersfield, in the same year. This haunting persisted for several months.

Mrs Betty Horn first saw the ghost in her bedroom on the night of Good Friday, March 31st, 1961. It was "big and horrid", and touched her on the face with its hands, which were like a cold mist. She saw the figure three more times during the Easter period and described it as being that of a very tall woman.

The ghost returned again in the middle of August, and, sleeping alone as her husband was on night work, Mrs Horn was terrified. Her husband, however, still could not believe that what she had seen was actually a ghost. But on a Sunday night of October, when Mr Arnold Horn was home, it reappeared and he saw it for the first time. He said, "I lashed out at it and it backed through the bedroom wall into the children's room. At the very point where it disappeared my six-year-old daughter was sleeping. She screamed and ran frightened through the house."

The ghost was seen again five nights later by a neighbour and a youth. The parents then learned from their eight-year-old son that, night after night, the ghost had sat on his bed talking to him and massaging his legs; he was not afraid of it. The parents had often heard their son talking aloud at night about what he had been doing at school, but thought he was talking in his sleep. Now they were not so sure.

This evidence of the boy seemed to provide the key to the haunting. While the children slept, spiritualists held a seance in the bedroom where Mr and Mrs Horn had seen the figure manifest itself. A representative of the *Huddersfield Daily Examiner* was present at the seance and saw and heard nothing out of the ordinary; but the medium claimed afterwards to have seen the distinct form of a castle and to have heard a voice whisper the name "Annie". The medium also said that she had been subjected to a strong desire to open one of the drawers in a dressing table behind her, in which she believed a photograph of the ghost was kept. Another of those present at the seance said she had seen the face of a woman aged about sixty, with her hair tied in a bun.

Mr and Mrs Horn then said this description of the ghost fitted that of Mr Horn's aunt, Annie, who had died some nine years previously. It now seemed likely that it was the apparition of this relative which had returned to help heal one of their children, for the boy to whom it had constantly appeared was stricken with meningitis when two years old, following which doctors had said he might never walk again. Two years later, however, he began to regain the use of his legs and was now a normal healthy child. It seemed that he had the attention of the persistent spirit to thank for his recovery as well as the doctors.

This strange story of the friendly healing spirit attracted a stream of visitors to the house at Meltham, and unfortunately many people even stood in a field late at night watching the bedroom and waiting for the ghost to appear. Mr Horn also received a large number of letters. As far as the family were concerned, however, the explanation advanced by the seance released the tension in the house and brought them their first peaceful night for months. They had no more fear of the ghost and Mr Horn declined offers by spiritualists to try and make further contact with it.

At her cottage in Oxfordshire in 1962, Mrs Frances Lovell also came to terms with the ghost which she said had troubled her since she had moved there eighteen months before.

Mrs Lovell said that when she was redecorating Brook Cottage, Moreton, near Thame, someone used to knock on the door every five minutes, but when she got to it there was never any one there. Then, one night as she was putting out the milk bottles, she saw the figure of a tall, whey-faced man, aged between fifty and sixty, wearing a black cape and black top hat. "He just looked at me, never saying a word. I realised that if I was going to live here somebody had got to be the boss, so I walked straight past him and did not let him bother me."

Mrs Lovell, a hairdresser, next saw the whey-faced man in daylight, standing by her garage. He walked across to the house, but still did not say anything before disappearing. On another occasion she also felt the ghost's presence very strongly while watching television. She said she was not frightened of it and it was free to ramble about the house as it liked, so long as it did not interfere with the family's comfort. Her husband and grown-up son and daughter did not take any notice of it.

When Mrs Lovell reported the ghost, which she came to call "Archibald", Mr Robert Quartly, the owner of the old cottage, disclosed that he also had been visited by it. Mr Quartly, who had moved from the cottage ten years before, after his wife's death, said that a farmer had hanged himself in the garage of the cottage at the turn of the century. While living there, said Mr Quartly, he had often heard the ghost about the house. One night he and his wife were home when she felt the ghost touch her leg. Then the lights and the radio were switched off. They waited, and suddenly both were switched on again. They did not see anything, but they always knew when the ghost was there.

"He always wore heavy boots. We could hear him clumping up to the door and he would give it a hard bang. Sometimes I was able to open the door immediately, but there was no one there. We were never bothered by the ghost. If he started throwing things about I would then try to do something, but generally we just lived with him. I never attempted to have the ghost exorcised."

A family in the mining village of Thornley, County Durham, were haunted intermittently by a "black ghost" for no less than sixteen years. Their worrying secret was disclosed when, in 1963, they sought the help of a vicar; they had kept silent for so long about the haunting for fear of ridicule.

The Moody family moved into their newly built, five-roomed council house at Thornley in 1947. Then Mrs Evelyn Moody saw a "floating black shape" in the house. The shock was all the greater to her because the possibility of a ghost in a brand new house seemed completely out of the question. But she saw the black shape distinctly and, as she said long afterwards, "I felt as if I was just going to die. It was an awful sensation."

This was the first of many occasions during the next sixteen years on which Mrs Moody saw the black shape. Sometimes it did not render itself visible but she could sense that it was there. Always, whether visible or not, it brought "a terrible sensation". At times the ghost looked like a black shirt floating past, seemingly suspended in mid-air, said Mrs Moody. Her terrier dog was with her on one occasion when the black shape appeared. The dog pricked up its ears and looked up, but it did not seem to be in any way affected by the apparition and did not even bark.

The ghost would vanish for months on end, but just when the Moody family were hoping they had seen the last of it, it would return. It visited the house at all times of the day and night and was experienced by all three of the couple's daughters. In 1963 one of the two daughters still living at home said that once she was in a bedroom with her sister when they sensed the presence of the ghost there. They got out of the room right away. "It seemed to take every bit of our will-power to get out, even with all the lights on. The ghost is overpowering and very strong when you realise it is there."

This daughter did not see the apparition but felt its presence on many more occasions. "It is difficult to describe it, but when it makes its visitation you *know* it is there. It is all very horrible. Its power seems to reach a peak and then fade away."

The other daughter living at home actually saw the black ghost, as did her boy friend, and her brother-in-law.

The father, Mr John Moody, a medical attendant at a colliery, was sceptical about the ghost till one day he saw it himself. He was downstairs at about half-past six in the morning when he was suddenly confronted in the passage of the house by a hovering black shape, "like a human body without limbs or head". He saw it distinctly, then it vanished.

Mrs Moody, who saw the black ghost more times than anyone else in the family, lost three stone through worry and had to be given treatment by her doctor. Her husband finally sought the help of the vicar of Thornley, who prayed in the house. After that, things seemed more peaceful for the family.

There was no local explanation whatever for this long, persistent haunting of a brand new house in which the Moodys were the first tenants.

THE BROTHERS' FOOTSTEPS

The editor of the *Arminian Magazine,* in 1780, received an intriguing letter from a friend. This told him of "wonderful marks" known as The Brothers' Steps, which were still to be seen in the fields about a third of a mile north of Montague House, in Bloomsbury (now the British Museum).

The tradition concerning these footprints, said the correspondent, was that two brothers who quarrelled over a worthless woman had fought a duel there with sword and pistol, killing each other in the fight.

"The prints of their feet are about the depth of three inches, and nothing will vegetate so much as to disfigure them. The number is only eighty-three, but probably some are at present filled up. For I think there were formerly more in the centre, where each unhappy combatant wounded the other to death. And a bank on which the first who fell, died, retains the form of his agonising crouch, by the curse of barrenness, while grass flourishes all about it.

"Mr George Hall, who was the librarian of Lincoln's Inn, first showed me those steps twenty-eight years ago, when I think, they were not quite so deep as now. He remembered them about thirty years, and the man who first showed them him, about thirty years more, which goes back to the year 1692; but I suppose they originated in King Charles the Second's reign.

"My mother well remembered their being ploughed up, and corn sown to deface them, about fifty years ago. But all was labour in vain, for the prints returned in a while to their pristine form, as probably will those that are now filled up."

The magazine editor did not know what to make of this extraordinary story. He knew the correspondent, a Mr John Walsh, to be perfectly reliable, and Walsh was clearly describing what he had seen with his own eyes, but still the editor felt that before publishing the story he should have the testimony of more witnesses. This was not long forthcoming.

"Being at Mr Cary's, in Copthall Buildings," the editor wrote, "I occasionally mentioned The Brothers' Footsteps and asked the company if they had heard anything of them. 'Sir,' said Mr Cary, 'sixteen years ago I saw and counted them myself.' Another added, 'And I saw them four years ago.' I could then no longer doubt but they had been. And a week or two after, I went with Mr Cary and another person to seek them.

"We sought for near half an hour in vain. We could find no steps at all within a quarter of a mile, no, nor half a mile, north of Montague House. We were almost out of hope when an honest man, who was at work, directed us to the next ground, adjoining to a pond. There we found what we sought for, about three-quarters of a mile north of Montague House and about 500 yards east of Tottenham Court Road. The steps answer Mr Walsh's description. They are the size of a large human foot, about three inches deep, and lie nearly from north-east to south-west.

"We counted only seventy-six, but we were not exact in counting. The place where one or both the brothers are supposed to have fallen is still bare of grass. The labourer showed us also the bank where, the tradition is, the wretched woman sat to see the combat."

So with all the accumulated evidence of eye-witnesses, the haunting footprints had been seen to exist for a hundred years successively after the senseless duel.

Today, armed with these facts and a street map, the interested reader can strike north from the British Museum, the former Montague House, and pin-point for himself the likely spot where the brothers' footsteps once existed for all to see; and where, for all that is known, they might exist still, buried beneath the weight of modern London.

THE FATE OF CAPTAIN WHEATCROFT

In September, 1857, Captain German Wheatcroft, of the 6th (Inniskilling) Dragoons, went out to India to join his regiment. His wife remained in England, living in Cambridge. Two months afterwards, on the night of November 14th, she dreamed that she saw her husband. He looked anxious and ill, and she awoke feeling very distressed.

She then looked up and saw, in the bright moonlight, the same figure of her husband now standing by her bedside. He was in uniform, his hands pressed across his breast, his hair dishevelled, and his face very pale. In his large dark eyes, fixed full upon her, was an expression of "great excitement" and she noticed the peculiar contraction of his mouth, which was habitual to him when agitated.

Mrs Wheatcroft saw her husband very distinctly, down to the smallest detail of his dress. She even noticed between his hands the white of his shirt-front. He seemed to bend forward, as if in pain, and make an effort to speak, but there was no sound. He remained visible for about a minute, then disappeared.

Mrs Wheatcroft's first thought was to make sure that she was actually awake. She rubbed her eyes with the sheet and felt that the touch was real. Then, her small nephew being in the bed with her, she bent over the sleeping child and listened to his breathing. The sound was distinct. This convinced her that what she had seen was no dream, and there was no more sleep for her that night.

In the morning she described the strange experience to her mother, saying that although she had seen no marks of blood on her husband's uniform she had the strongest feeling that he must be either killed or severely wounded. She was so convinced of this that during the next few weeks she refused all social invitations, saying that, uncertain as she was whether she was not already a widow, she would never enter a place of amusement until she received a letter from her husband—if he still lived—dated later than November 14th.

In the following month of December, 1857, her fears were confirmed by publication in London of the fateful telegram which she had fully anticipated. This stated that Captain German Wheatcroft had been killed in action at Lucknow—but gave the date of his death as the *fifteenth* of November. When Mr Wilkinson, a London solicitor who had charge of Captain Wheatcroft's affairs, met the widow, she repeated to him that she had been quite prepared for the bad news, but she felt sure that her husband's death could not possibly have occurred on November 15th, as it was during the previous night of the 14th that he had appeared to her. There must have been some mistake. She persisted in this belief, in spite of the War Office certificate later obtained by Mr Wilkinson, which repeated that the captain had been killed in action on November 15th, 1857.

The solicitor, puzzled by the widow's story, called at the office of the Army agents to see if there could have been a mistake made in the certificate. But he was shown that the captain's death was mentioned in two separate despatches of the commander-in-chief, and in both these instances the date given was the 15th, as in the first published telegram.

There the matter rested for three months. Then in March, 1858, Captain Wheatcroft's family received a letter from a colleague of their son, written near Lucknow in mid-December, 1857. This officer told the family that Captain Wheatcroft had been killed at Lucknow while gallantly leading the squadron, on the afternoon of *November the fourteenth*. The officer said he was riding close by Wheatcroft's side and saw him fall, struck by a fragment of shell in the breast. Wheatcroft never spoke again after he was hit. He was buried at Dilkoosha, and on a wooden cross erected by a friend at the head of his grave were cut the initials "G.W." and the date of his death, "14th November, 1857".

Such was the turn of events that eventually proved the widow right, and offered at the same time the most conclusive proof of the apparition she had seen. The War Office finally corrected the date of Captain Wheatcroft's death to the fourteenth, though not until more than a year after he had appeared at his wife's bedside.

The story of Captain Wheatcroft is one of the more outstanding cases affording proof of a person's apparition being seen elsewhere at, or soon after, the time of death. These appearances are not, of course, uncommon, as has been more widely recognised in later years, though cases where two or more persons together have seen such an apparition are less usual. A graphic example of the dual sighting of a passing spirit is the experience, in 1785, of Captain John Cope Sherbroke and Lieutenant George Wynyard, of the 33rd Regiment.

The regiment at this time was stationed on Cape Breton Island, off Nova Scotia. The two officers, having very similar tastes and preferring study to idle pleasure, spent much of their free time together busy at their books.

On the evening of October 15th, 1785, between eight and nine o'clock, they were sitting in Wynyard's apartment, to which they had retired from the mess to continue their studies. The apartment consisted of a sitting-room and a bedroom, and was entered by a door from the passage, with a door in the sitting-room giving access through to the bedroom. There was no other means of entrance to, or exit from, the bedroom, the window of which was fastened against the icy weather.

Sherbroke, happening to glance up from his book to the passage door, saw a tall youth aged about twenty, pale and very emaciated, standing beside it. Surprised, he turned to Wynyard, who was seated near him, and drew his friend's attention to their strange visitor, who was dressed in light indoor clothes in contrast to the heavy garments which they themselves wore against the severe weather. Wynyard turned his eyes to the youth, and his shocked reaction to what he saw astonished his colleague.

"I have heard of a man's being as pale as death," Sherbroke said afterwards, "but I never saw a living face assume the appearance of a corpse, except Wynyard's at that moment."

As they both looked intently and silently at the figure before them, for Wynyard seemed incapable of speech, which also silenced Sherbroke, the pale youth moved slowly across to the bedroom. As he passed the two men, he cast his eyes with an expression of melancholy affection on the petrified Wynyard.

Wynyard, struggling to recover himself, seized Sherbroke's arm and muttered almost inaudibly, "Great God—my brother!"

"Your brother?" repeated Sherbroke. "What can you mean? There must be some deception—follow me!" Taking his friend by the arm he led him into the bedroom, which the youth had entered. It was quite empty. As they looked around, baffled, another officer coming in joined in the search, but the mysterious youth had vanished, though there was no possible way out of the bedroom other than by the communicating door.

Wynyard was convinced that what he had seen was the spirit of his young brother, John Otway Wynyard, a lieutenant in the 3rd

Regiment of Foot Guards, who had come to some harm. Sherbroke, however, firmly believed that some trick had been played on them, though he could not guess how. At the suggestion of the officer who had joined them, they took note of the day and hour at which the strange incident had occurred, and agreed not to mention it to the others in the mess.

But, much as his friend tried to persuade him that the "apparition" must have been a skilful illusion engineered by some of their colleagues, Wynyard remained full of fears for the safety of his brother. His worried state eventually roused the curiosity of the other officers, so that he was finally obliged to confess to them all that had happened. This brought everyone to a fever of suspense, and they waited impatiently for letters from England—in particular, letters for Wynyard—which might give an answer to the mystery.

The next ships to arrive at Cape Breton Island had all left England before the day of the apparition's appearance. The letters which they carried, therefore, could not be expected to give a clue to the event. But at last, on June 6th, 1786, nearly eight months after the inexplicable incident, the long wished for ship arrived. The mail was distributed in the messroom at suppertime. All the officers except Wynyard had letters, which they read avidly but found no mention of Wynyard's family. They then examined the several newspapers which had been brought, but these contained no mention of any death, or of any other circumstance connected with Wynyard's family which could account for the "ghost".

There remained a solitary letter for Sherbroke. The mess watched in silence as he broke the seal and glanced at its contents. He looked up, beckoned to Wynyard, and they left the room together.

The other officers now waited tensely for their return, certain that Sherbroke's letter must contain the long expected news. After about an hour Sherbroke rejoined them, obviously full of emotion. He drew near to the fireplace, and, leaning his head against the high mantelpiece, said in a low voice to the man nearest to him, "Wynyard's brother is no more . . ."

The first line of Sherbroke's letter was, "Dear John, break to your friend Wynyard the death of his favourite brother . . ." John Otway Wynyard, the letter disclosed, had died on the day, and the hour, on which the two friends had seen his spirit pass through the apartment.

In spite of this corroboration of the testimony of his own eyes, Captain Sherbroke found it extremely difficult to accept that he had in fact seen a ghost. Some years later, having returned to England, he was walking with two companions in Piccadilly, when on the opposite side of the road he saw, to his excitement, a man passing who bore a striking resemblance to the figure which he and Wynyard had seen. He immediately pointed out the man to his companions, who knew of the incident on Cape Breton Island, and hurriedly crossed over and spoke to the man. The man listened to his urgent questions and answered them understandingly. It transpired that he was another brother of the dead youth and had never been out of the country.

There is, on record, another version of this encounter. A surviving colleague of Wynyard and Sherbroke—the officer who joined them in the apartment minutes after the appearance of the apparition—said in later years that he believed the man Sherbroke approached in Piccadilly was not a brother of the dead man, but someone noted for having a strong likeness to him, and dressing like him.

The outcome, however, was the same : Sherbroke must have been convinced at last that he had, unquestionably, seen a ghost.

In some cases, corroboration of an apparition seen near to the time of death has come from an independent party unaccompanied by a member of the family. An example is the following incident told to me by my friend Richard South.

"During World War I, my cousins, Madge and Jean Telfer, were living with their mother at a house in Hornsey, North London. Jean was engaged to a young soldier who was away fighting in France, and had been corresponding with him, but because of his unit being moved about at the front, his letters were very often a long time catching up with him.

"Then came a time when he was lucky enough to get leave, and of course on his arrival in London he came straightaway to visit Jean. On arriving at the house he was shown into the front room by the maid, who said that Jean was out but would not be long. He was seated there when Jean's mother (my aunt) appeared in the doorway. She did not speak, which he thought rather strange, but simply smiled at him, then turned and left the room.

"When Jean arrived home he mentioned having seen her mother, and remarked how odd it was that she had merely smiled at him without speaking, for he was certainly no stranger in the house. He asked if anything was wrong. Jean then told him that her mother had died three weeks before. Madge, the younger daughter, had found her one morning on taking her a cup of tea. She was sitting up in bed, dead, having choked to death with asthma.

"Later, when all three were talking things over, Madge admitted that she also had seen the apparition of her mother, several times, but had not said anything for fear of it being thought she was going out of her mind. She was very relieved to find that others could see the apparition of her mother besides herself.

"Jean's young man stayed for about a week at the house, and he saw my aunt's apparition on three more occasions. The last time was as he was putting on his tie, when he caught a view of her *in the mirror*. She was standing in the doorway of the bedroom and again smiling at him.

"Eventually her spirit did seem to find rest."

A further unusual and poignant example of the lingering ghost is the experience in the 1920s of Mr and Mrs Frank Davies. There seemed nothing unusual about the furnished flat in Westbourne Grove, Bayswater, which Mr and Mrs Davies went to view one day. Reasonably decorated and comfortably furnished, it looked ideal for their purpose, and they decided to rent it. Immediately they moved in, however, it became clear there was something strange about the place.

The morning after their first night there, on coming into the parlour the couple found that the two big armchairs in the room had both been moved closer to the fire. Puzzled, they moved the chairs back to their former positions. But the next morning when they entered the parlour the chairs had again been moved closer to the fire; and this odd behaviour of the furniture went on for several days. The couple noticed, too, that newspapers and a book were in a different place to where they had been left the previous night.

This strange movement of the furniture so worried his wife that Frank Davies promised her the next night he would stay up and keep a vigil. They both went off to their bedroom as usual, but when his wife was in bed Davies returned to the parlour. He found to his astonishment that the chairs had already been moved beside the fire, and sitting in one was an old man reading a newspaper, while in the other was an old woman resting with her hands folded on a book in her lap. Neither of the figures seemed to heed him.

He returned immediately to his wife and told her what he had seen. Both then went to the parlour, but the apparitions had vanished—though the chairs remained where they had been moved.

The following morning Millie and Frank Davies made inquiries in the neighbourhood. They discovered that the previous occupants of the flat had been an elderly couple who were very close to each other. The old man had died suddenly, and his wife had not lived long afterwards; she was found, one day, dead in her chair by the fire.

It seemed to the Davies' that the spirits of the old couple were returning each night to be together where they had been happiest. From that day onward they made a practice of themselves moving the armchairs closer to the fire before they went to bed, and leaving magazines, newspapers and books handy beside them. They then, on one or two occasions, peeped in to catch a further glimpse of their ghostly visitors, but never saw them. The old couple apparently ceased to visit the flat, probably because they knew they had been discovered when the chairs were moved in readiness by the fire for them. When eventually the Davies' stopped repositioning the chairs at night they were never moved again.

WILLIAM CORDER'S SKULL

The body of Maria Marten, stabbed, shot and possibly strangled, was found buried in the Red Barn at Polstead, Suffolk, in April, 1828. Four months later her lover and murderer, twenty-three-year-old William Corder, was publicly executed at Bury St. Edmunds Jail, watched by a crowd of more than 20,000.

Corder's body hung on the scaffold for an hour. It was then taken down and three surgeons made an incision along the chest, folding back the skin to display the chest muscles, after which the body was exhibited on a trestle in one of the courtrooms, sightseers filing past. Finally, as directed by the sentence of the times, the body was dissected and anatomised, for the benefit of medical students at the West Suffolk General Hospital.

This operation was performed by Mr George Creed, surgeon to the hospital, who also tanned the murderer's skin, part of which was used to bind an account of the crime, and pickled the scalp. When all this was done, the skeleton that remained was put on public view at the hospital, after which it came into use for teaching anatomy to the students.

Creed, on his death, bequeathed Corder's skin and scalp to his friend Dr John Kilner, a medical officer at the hospital and a well-known practitioner in Bury. In the late 1870s, by which time the skeleton had been in use at the hospital for some fifty years, Dr Kilner began to look at it with more than a professional eye. Corder's skull, he thought, would make an interesting addition to his collection—he could easily remove it and put a spare anatomical skull in its place. He resolved to make this change.

The doctor naturally did not want to be disturbed at his task and planned to switch the skulls late one night. Arrived at the room containing the skeleton he lighted three candles, but no sooner were they all lit than one snuffed itself out. He turned to relight it, but as he did so, the flames of the other two candles died. This strange behaviour of the candles went on all the time he was busy removing the murderer's skull and wiring the spare one to the skeleton in its place; first one and then another candle would flicker and snuff out. But he managed to keep at least one candle alight while he was working.

It was an uncanny incident, and Dr Kilner said afterwards that from the first moment he removed Corder's skull he felt very uncomfortable about "something". However, he was a man entirely free of superstitions and scornful of "all this mumbo-jumbo nonsense about ghosts". To the close friend in whom he confided, he remarked that even if the skeleton had possessed some kind of supernatural quality, it must have had most of that nonsense knocked out of it during the half a century it had been handled by doctors and students at the hospital.

Dr Kilner now had Corder's skull polished, mounted and enclosed in a square ebony box, which he placed in a cabinet in the drawing-room of his home. A few days later, just after he had finished evening surgery, a maid came in to the doctor and said a gentleman had called to see him. Kilner, irritated by this unwarranted interruption of his leisure hours, asked if the caller was anyone she had seen before. No, said the maid. She added that the man was "proper old-fashioned looking, wearing a furry top hat and a blue overcoat with silver buttons".

Telling the maid to bring a lamp, Kilner reluctantly went to meet the caller, whom she had left waiting in the surgery in the twilight. The doctor said afterwards that when he looked into the room it was rather dark; there *might* have been someone waiting by the window, he was not sure. However, he experienced the strong feeling, independent of sight and hearing, that he was not alone in the room. Then the maid came behind him with the lamp, and when its light crossed the doorway it was to show a totally empty room.

The puzzled doctor chaffed the maid, saying she must have been dreaming. But she remained quite positive that a gentleman had called. Perhaps, she suggested, it was a patient with toothache who had made off when the pain stopped. She recalled that a man with toothache had changed his mind and rushed out like that only a few months back.

After a few days the doctor had nearly forgotten about the mysterious visitor. Then, one evening on looking out of the drawing-room window, he caught sight of somebody lurking near the summerhouse at the end of the lawn. He could just see that the figure was that of a man in a beaver hat and a greatcoat of antique cut. The doctor quickly stepped out into the garden, but the figure vanished.

Kilner was now thoroughly uneasy, and, suffering the pangs of a guilty conscience for having disturbed the murderer's remains to gratify a personal whim, he became convinced that there was some-one dogging his footsteps. The someone, whoever it was, seemed very anxious to communicate with him but its presence did not seem quite strong enough to accomplish this.

Tension now rose in the doctor's house as things began to happen at night. "It" opened doors, walked about through the house, and stood breathing heavily and muttering outside bedroom doors. Occasionally the members of the household heard a frantic hammering and sobbing below in the drawing-room. And all this time, through a maze of dreams, the doctor felt sure that someone was pleading and begging him to listen and attend to his needs.

The doctor had little sleep for some three weeks. There seemed no doubt that Corder's ghost, if such it was, would go on making things very unpleasant until the skull was returned. But this was an impossible thing to do: the skull, which now had a highly polished tortoise-shell gloss, would attract attention immediately it was restored, and it would be very difficult to explain away the sudden change in its appearance. So Kilner decided to wait a few more days, and if the ghostly visitor did not cease its wanderings, he would have to think of some other way of disposing of the skull.

The next night, Kilner left his bedroom door wide open, so that he would know immediately of any disturbance. He then got into bed and drifted off to sleep. An hour or two later he awoke suddenly, some noise having disturbed him.

He listened. The sound came from downstairs. He debated whether to call out and rouse the household, and decided against it. He did not want to appear an alarmist. So he stayed in bed for some minutes, watching and waiting. He then got cautiously out of bed, lighted a candle and walked out on the landing. Holding the candle over the stair-rail, he could just see, below, the glass handle of the drawing-room door, as it reflected the candlelight from its many facets. Suddenly, as he looked, the glass knob was blotted out. A white hand was on the knob, he could see it distinctly. But apparently the hand belonged to no one, for he could not see any figure near it.

As he watched, the handle was slowly and softly turned by the phantom hand; he could just hear the faint squeak of the bolt as it turned in the lock-case. The door was gradually and stealthily opening, there was no doubt of it.

Kilner was gazing in wonderment at this phenomenon when he was startled by a loud explosion, which sounded like the report of a blunderbuss. Filled with a sudden anger, and a great loathing for the skull he had so foolishly "acquired", he dashed downstairs, pausing only to pick up the heavy plated candlestick as a weapon before rushing to the drawing-room. At the doorway he was met with a tremendous gust of wind which extinguished his candle. But was it wind? It seemed like a powerful, menacing form which enveloped rather than touched him.

He thrust forward into the darkness of the room, agitatedly striking a match. As the match flamed, his attention was caught by a litter of black splinters on the pale carpet. After his first puzzlement he quickly realised what had happened: the box which had held the skull was broken into fragments. His eyes went to the cabinet which had contained the box. The door was open, and there, exposed on a shelf, was the grinning skull.

Dr Kilner now lost no time in ridding himself of the ghostly trophy. Thinking, no doubt, that once the skull was out of his house its supernatural qualities would cease, he insisted that his close friend, Frederick Hopkins, a local builder, should accept it as a gift. Hopkins, a former prison official, was now the owner of Bury Jail, where Corder was executed. He had bought the property when it was vacated as a prison and moved his family into the governor's residence, Gyves House, within the walls of the jail. Kilner told him, "As you are the owner of Corder's condemned cell and the gallows on which he was hanged, perhaps it won't hurt you to take care of his skull."

But misfortune visited Hopkins from the start, even as he was on his way back to Gyves House with the skull, wrapped in a silk handkerchief. While coming down the steps of an hotel he twisted his foot and fell heavily, the skull rolling to the feet of a shocked member of the local gentry, Lady Gage, who sprang back with a cry of alarm.

The twisted foot kept Hopkins in bed for a week, but a further blow followed only the next day, when his best mare rolled over the side of a chalk pit and broke her back.

In the next few months Hopkins knew illness, sorrow and financial disaster. With Dr Kilner he had embarked on several very successful land and property deals, but suddenly the tide turned and, overtaken by heavy losses, both men were swept to the verge of bankruptcy.

Hopkins, in desperation, resolved to break the skull's evil spell once and for all. He took it, one day, to a country churchyard near Bury St. Edmunds, and bribed a gravedigger to give the thing a Christian burial. After some weeks of peace and one or two strokes of good fortune, he thanked heaven that he had cast the troublesome relic out of his house.

This was the uncanny story which young Robert Thurston Hopkins, one of five children, heard his father and Dr Kilner tell and retell many times afterwards in the family circle, a story frankly and openly told, and verifiable to the smallest detail.

THE LADY OF THE CRINOLINES

On an August night in 1955, two workmen in south Wales, being unable to find lodgings, entered a bare and derelict mansion, where they settled down in a room high in the west wing, away from the rats in the lower quarters. What followed was, in the words of a judge, a "ghostly and ghastly experience" for both men.

The mansion, 300-year-old Bush House, Pembroke, was without lighting; there were no locks on the doors, which groaned at a touch, and the oak panelled staircases creaked to each tread. Bats flew in the upper rooms and passages.

The old mansion was due for conversion to quarters for students of a new school being built close by. The workmen, a father and son from Manchester, had come to lay flooring in the school. They had expected to be provided with lodgings, but as none were available they went to the lonely mansion to sleep, at the suggestion of the clerk of the works. What happened next was told later to Mr Justice Salmon at Glamorgan Assizes.

The workmen, Mr George Hesketh and his son, Roy, said that after bedding down in a room at the mansion they heard queer tapping noises on the walls, and the sounds of someone walking about in a corridor. On looking out of a window, at an hour well after midnight, they were startled to see the apparition of a woman, attired in a crinoline gown, walking in the grounds. The son watched her for half an hour, as she walked elegantly up and down a path immediately opposite before disappearing through the built-in door of an old stable.

On their second night in the mansion the paraffin lamp they had with them was mysteriously turned down four times, and both men had their mackintoshes plucked off their shoulders, as if by invisible hands. On the third night, bedded down in a room on the third floor, having barricaded the lockless door, they were kept awake by constant knocking noises and a tap, tap, tapping at the windows. About one o'clock in the morning they decided they had had enough, and hurriedly quit the mansion and went back to the partly-finished school to sleep.

Mr Hesketh and his son told their story at Glamorgan Assizes in March, 1958, when the father claimed damages for injuries received when he fell down some unlit steps at the school. Their frightening experience at Bush House had previously been reported at length in a local newspaper a week or two after the event.

Mr F. Elwyn Jones, Q.C. (later Sir Elwyn Jones, the Attorney-General), who appeared for the father, said that both men were certain they had seen a ghost at the mansion, which had a reputation locally as a haunted house. "A ghost in a crinoline—but a ghost she was, nevertheless," said Mr Jones. Later, when the clerk of the works, a man who had lived all his life in the district, learned what the Heskeths had seen, he told them that he personally would not have slept in the mansion for a gold clock.

Mr Justice Salmon, in his summing up in the action for damages, commented on the Heskeths' "somewhat eerie experience" in the mansion. He said, "They heard or thought they heard supernatural noises, and saw or thought they saw a ghost. The house was unlit, extremely dirty, and infested with rats. Their experiences on each of the following nights were much the same as on the first night. They were ghostly and ghastly."

This appearance of the Lady of the Crinolines at Bush House was not an isolated incident. Eighteen months before, a night watchman on the Bush House site had reported seeing the strange appearance there of "a gentleman with three dogs, a gun under his arm". And only days after the Lady's appearance to the Heskeths, there was a report of a locally stationed National Serviceman and his girl friend, who, on going close to the house during an after-dark stroll, saw to their amazement what appeared to be an illuminated figure approaching. They hurriedly left the spot.

There is, however, no explanation for the ghost or ghosts of Bush House. The centuries-old building was rebuilt in 1905 after being destroyed by fire, and remained the home of the Meyrick family for half a century. Neither the family nor any member of the staff reported anything unusual during that time.

In recent years, residents at the newly converted mansion have heard nothing more disturbing at night than the noises of the bats.

The "lovesick ghost" of Jarman, believed to haunt the Manor House at Little Gaddesden, a picturesque village in Hertfordshire, was described to an inspector of the Ministry of Housing in 1963, when he heard an appeal by a man who had been refused permission by Berkhamsted rural council to build a new house on land adjoining the 16th-century manor. The council's solicitor, who described the old manor as "a bit of a gem", told the inspector that it was reputed to have been haunted by the ghost of Jarman since the 18th-century. "He is still there today. That's the sort of place it is, and it should not be allowed to be jostled and huddled by houses of a suburban kind."

Jarman was a member of one of two generations of Jarmans who lived at the Manor House. Local tradition is that he hanged himself "for the love of the heiress of Ashridge", a nearby estate. Often afterwards Jarman was seen at night watering his white horses at the village pond.

Miss Dorothy Erhart, the occupant of the manor, said at the time of the inquiry that the previous owner had told her that at night, she and her child always ran past the village pond.

Once a year, Jarman is supposed to make his presence known by dimming the lamps and candles in the Manor House, though he has never actually been seen inside the building. Miss Erhart recalled two occasions when it was thought Jarman was to blame. "Both were some years ago—once when a standard lamp was switched off for no reason at all, and the other when the house was plunged into sudden darkness as guests arrived for a music concert."

In the village, one of the large chimneys of the Manor House, because of its shape, is known as "Jarman's coffin".

The Minister of Housing upheld the decision of Berkhamsted council not to allow the modern house to be built next door, the inspector in his report stating that the proposed building "would be a step towards depriving the adjoining Manor House of its proper setting".

Ghosts have also figured in rating appeals. In 1957 the spectre of the Manor House at Buriton, Hampshire, was put forward at a Petersfield valuation court as one of the reasons for Lieutenant-Colonel A. L. Bonham-Carter's appeal for a reduction in the rates of his 15th-century home, the place where Gibbon wrote much of his *The Decline and Fall of the Roman Empire*.

There is a local belief in Buriton that a young woman hanged herself from an oak beam in the manor. The colonel's agent told the court that there were four bedrooms on the first floor and one of the two main ones was reputed to be haunted. The colonel had told him that he had seen the ghost some years ago.

A member of the panel asked, "Does that bring up, or does it reduce, the assessment?"

"I suggest it would reduce it," said the agent.

The colonel obtained a reduction in his rates.

In 1956 a valuation court at Upton-on-Severn was asked to consider, as one of the reasons for a rating appeal, the troublesome ghost of the Grey Lady of Priors Court, a 16th-century house in the Worcestershire hamlet of Callow End.

Mrs I. M. Hopkins, the occupier, told the rating panel that she could not keep staff because of the ghost. Some weeks before, she had been about to engage a very nice couple but unfortunately they went into the village, heard about the ghost, and would not stay. She added that local people would not stay in the house after dark.

The chairman said he regretted no allowance could be made for ghosts. The rates were, however, reduced for other reasons which had been put forward.

Mrs Hopkins said afterwards that she understood one ghost at the house had been laid by a clergyman in 1906, but a second ghost had not. She had not seen it, but had felt its presence.

The tradition in Callow End is that Priors Court, once the home of the late Lord Monckton of Brenchley, is haunted not only by the Grey Lady, but by monks from Malvern Priory church. The story goes back to the 17th-century, when two women, a mother and daughter, sought refuge in the Court, where a prior and some of the monks then lived. In the night monks murdered the women. Ever since, it is said, the daughter, in her long grey cloak, and her murderers, have returned to haunt the precincts of the house.

'I'LL TRY TO GET IN TOUCH'

In the early 1950s, Mrs Amy W. Kingdon was working as a home help, specialising in nursing chronic cases. One patient she attended was a woman in her late fifties suffering from cancer.

The patient, whom we must call Mrs L., was a gentle, kindly little woman devoted to her husband. Her older sister, however, who often stayed with them for two or three days at a time, was of a totally different nature, a very forceful and domineering woman who was convinced that "One could get well if one really had a mind to." The sister's unkind attitude to Mrs L. and her husband was explained by the fact that the two women, when their parents died, had been left a considerable sum of money, and the sister was worried that Mrs L. would leave her share of the money to her husband when she died. The sister felt that Mrs L. should leave the money to her; that it should be hers by right.

The sister constantly harped on the subject and was really unpleasant to Mrs L. at times, making her very unhappy. Mrs Kingdon continues the story:

"The sister's domineering attitude often upset my gentle little patient, of whom I grew very fond, but if I read to her for a while or drew her out to talk about her early life, she would relax and be able to turn a deaf ear to her sister. She liked our talks together over 'elevenses'; it was almost the signal for our conversation when, at these times, I went to open the oblong-shaped brown biscuit tin which she used, and took out the biscuits for the mid-morning tea. One day, as her conversation turned to thoughts of a possible 'after life' she suddenly said to me very earnestly, 'I'll try to get in touch with you, my dear.'

"I was taken off that case after a few months and sent elsewhere. There was no thought at all in mind regarding my former patient when, one day on returning home, I walked in and saw on my dining table that same oblong-shaped brown biscuit tin. It was *so real* that I reached out for it, but as my hand neared it the tin vanished.

"Next morning I phoned the husband of my former patient and asked how she was. He replied, 'My wife died yesterday morning.' "

Many people at some time during their lives have an experience which, if the word "psychic" is disliked, can only be described as strange or unusual; like a flash of "second sight", a compelling dream with more than a basis of truth, or the sense or sight of a supernormal presence. Others particularly sensitive may have several such experiences, as in the case of Amy Kingdon, and it is when these incidents are compared that the regularity of their occurrences becomes evident, if their nature at present remains wrapped in argument. For example, the tie of blood and intimate relationship. Mrs Kingdon tells me:

"My mother and I were very close to each other, and especially after my marriage, we would each have that sixth sense when anything was really wrong with either of us. She lived in Paddington, and I in Perivale, Middlesex, and on one occasion she knocked at my door at 8.30 a.m., as she knew without being told that I was ill.

"In January, 1944 I was sitting alone one Saturday evening. My small son was in bed and my husband far away in India. I had a fleeting vision of my grandmother, and though she did not speak, I knew that I had to go to my mother. Next morning my son and I set off for mother's home and when we arrived, in answer to my knock at the door, my sister appeared.

"I asked, 'How is mother?' My sister in astonishment replied, 'How on earth did you know she was ill?' I said, 'I just knew.' "

Much is said about personal "projection" and there is not a scrap of doubt that it does occur, sometimes rather frighteningly. Here again is an example from Mrs Kingdon:

"Two months after my daughter's fifth birthday she was ill with measles, and during the night I got up to go into her room to see if she was all right.

"As I went in I *distinctly saw myself* seated by her bed, but by the side where the bed touched the wall. As quickly as the other 'me' faded, my small daughter said, 'Mummy, why are you over there, you were here just now,' patting the place where I had just seen myself."

Is natural sensitiveness, or psychic ability, inherited, or in some cases at least handed down from parent to child? The following strange incident told me by Mrs Kingdon, again involving her daughter Jane, would seem to suggest that it could be. The story is of such a deeply tragic nature that the names of the family are changed but the facts are as they occurred.

"Elsie and Don Andrews came to live in the house opposite us a few months after their second child, a daughter, Sarah, was born in November 1937. We met at the pre-natal clinic; I was then expecting a child, my son, who was born the following January.

"Elsie and I became good friends and as our children grew, they were equally at home in either house and we women were 'Auntie' to each other's children. Sarah often slept at our house.

"They were a very happy family, but tragedy struck on the night of December 23rd, 1942. Don, an electrician, was killed in an accident caused by a drunken van driver, who collided with Don's motor-cycle. Elsie was heroic. Though grief-stricken she did not tell the children of their father's death until after Christmas, but made excuses for his absence—'he wasn't very well after working hard, so grandma was making him rest at her home for a day or two.'

"About ten days after Don's death, Elsie came to me and said that she had had a shock. A teaset which her husband had given her recently, and which had never been in use, had quite suddenly fallen from the glass cabinet in which it was kept, and two cups, saucers and plates were smashed, and others cracked. No one had been near it. A day or two later she vowed that she had seen bloodstains on the bathroom wall, and what appeared to be the imprint of a hand with the small finger missing. Elsie could not have known about this injury to her husband but I did. The friend who had identified Don's body had told me that when Don's motor-cycling gloves had been handed over to him, the little finger was in the glove.

"Elsie was by now getting very nervy and almost on the verge of a nervous breakdown. The shoe repair man who used to call at the door for his orders, suggested that she should go to a spiritualist meeting where she possibly would find help and enlightenment. We both went a number of times in the following year or so. She was told that her husband had tried to contact her and the family.

"She worked hard to support her children, and I looked after them during the day. Just before Sarah's eighth birthday my own daughter, Jane, was born. Four years later—that is, eight years after Don's death—Jane came to me one day and said 'Mummy, I've been talking to Sarah's daddy and he sends his love to her.'

"Jane could not possibly have known what Sarah's father was like, as she had not seen any photograph of him. I said to her, 'How nice of Uncle Don to come and see you. What was he like?' My daughter then described him accurately—'He is big like my daddy, and has lovely black curly hair and brown eyes that crinkle when he smiles'; and other details of which I am not certain now.

"Don Andrews appeared to Jane in the very room in which his own daughter sometimes slept, and we wonder still if perhaps it was she whom he had really tried to contact."

THE HOUSE ON THE CORNER

It is difficult enough for a family suddenly visited by an apparition, having to cope not only with the inexplicable and often very frightening haunting, but also with the scepticism of those unwilling to believe anything they have not seen with their own eyes. It can be equally distressing for a family visited by an unseen spirit or poltergeist, with the resultant noises and physical disturbances. But a great many other uncanny incidents that occur are more puzzling still, offering as they do no certain evidence to include them in either of these categories, yet making life fully as unbearable.

It is small wonder that people are extremely reluctant to admit these incidents, some fleeting but others experienced over a long period, as they can never be sure themselves that the answer really lies in the supernatural.

An example of a case of this nature, fortunately noted in detail as it occurred, is the following told to me by my friend Noel Thompson. In this case, involving a family in which no one was a more than usually sensitive or impressionable person, nothing was seen that by any stretch of imagination could be called a ghost, yet the strange events were sufficient to drive them out of their house within less than a year of moving into it. Mr Thompson relates the story :

We were a family of five. I was the eldest of three boys, barely in my teens. My brother Louis was two years younger, and my brother Bernard eight years younger; so young as not to have been affected by anything which occurred.

The house in question to which we moved, in the 1930s, was in Portswood, a good middle-class district of Southampton, and had been built about twenty years. It was a long, single-fronted house standing fully detached on the corner of a road, and in one respect this physical feature is rather important.

I think we might first have suspected that something was quaint about the house on the day we moved into it, from the house only about half a mile away, where we were then living. On this warm and calm day in August, I walked from the old house to the new with Bruce, my dog, an Irish terrier, and to everyone's surprise he could not under any circumstances be persuaded into the house of his own accord. He finally had to be dragged in. Looking back, it would seem that the dog was possibly aware of more than we and had an uncanny instinct for what was about to occur.

The house, to which we had moved because it was larger than our old one, had four bedrooms, and there was a very long upstairs landing. This became a continual source of worry, to my mother especially, because of the sound of footsteps at night, which were heard to progress backwards and forwards the length of this landing. At first it was thought that these sounds might have been made by people walking on the pavement outside, but—at the same time as the footsteps were pursuing their course up and down the landing—it was possible to look from my parents' bedroom down on to the long pavement and see no one there. The fact of it being a detached house, well removed from its neighbour, eliminated any possibility that the footsteps were from the people next door. To add to the mystery, the footsteps were never heard from any other room than that of my parents, the main bedroom.

My dog again seemed to have some instinct about these strange noises, for he could never be persuaded to go upstairs in the house, day or night.

Confirmation that the phantom footsteps were not imagined by us all came on the one and only notable Christmas that we spent in the house, when my parents entertained some very old family friends. My parents very deliberately decided not to tell the visitors anything at all about what had been bothering us, and instead of putting them in the guest room, "gave up" their own bedroom for the visitors' use.

After Christmas the visitors were then asked if they had heard anything strange, and they confessed that, yes, they had been rather concerned at footsteps which they had heard going up and down the passage each night they had slept in the bedroom. They had not liked to mention this until asked.

There was one night when the couple did not sleep in the bedroom at all, for the very simple reason that there had been a card game which went on until about half-past five in the morning. During this long game my mother visited the upstairs toilet two or three times, and on each occasion found to her consternation that the guillotine-type window was being flung wide open despite the fact that she kept closing it. In exasperation she accused the guests of playing a trick on her, but they denied all responsibility; expressing surprise, in fact, that on going to the toilet themselves on one or two occasions they had seen the window thrown open on such a very cold night.

It was ultimately established that no human agency within the household on that particular night had been responsible for persistently opening the window.

There followed several other strange occurrences which defied explanation. The downstairs morning room, in which Louis and I did our homework at night, had in it an ideal boiler. Many times my brother and I heard and saw the boiler being poked although there was no visible poker in use; we heard the metallic clank of poker on bars and the shaking of fuel, and could see the gradual settling down afterwards of the red hot embers. This phenomenon we reported to my parents, and they on occasions were able to see it for themselves. This naturally enough left us all completely mystified.

The morning room had abutting on to it from the outside a conservatory in which my father kept quite a substantial collection of geraniums, and to prevent them gumming up the window between the morning room and the conservatory, a characteristic of geraniums placed too near to glass, a curtain was hung on the conservatory side of the window. On two or three eerie occasions Louis and I, while doing our homework, saw the curtain *lifted upwards* and heard a persistent tap, tap, tap at the window. We thought at first that possibly the ventilating panes in the conservatory had been left open, and that some strange trick of the wind, or a draught, had caused the curtain to defy the laws of gravity. This, of course, would have made no explanation for the tapping noise, for there was nothing whatever to be seen tapping against the glass. But in any event, each time we saw the curtain lift up and heard the tapping, Louis, being the braver of we two, would check in the conservatory that the door to the garden and the ventilating panes were closed; and they always were.

In the same room, too, the light frequently switched itself off. My father, who was then, and still is, highly sceptical of the supernatural, insisted that the cause must be a faulty circuit, until my brother and I explained to him that it was the tumbler switch itself which was clicking off—we would hear the tumbler click as the room went into darkness, and hurriedly dash over and put the light on again for ourselves. There was no question of an intermittent break in the circuit.

My father then suggested that it must be a weak switch spring that was responsible for the switch clicking to the "off" position. But what rather shattered his rationalisation was the fact that we even went so far as to tie a thread on the switch and fasten a weight on the end of the thread to hold the switch down; yet still it was clicked off. On one very frightening occasion, having so weighted the switch, my father stood back and said to it, "Now let's see you switch yourself off!" And it immediately did so.

One of our downstairs rooms was used as a library-cum-lounge, and because of some structural defect in the floorboards had to be emptied of furniture while workmen replaced the faulty boarding. In one corner of the room where it had not been necessary to move the floorboards a large brass tray was left standing against the wall. One day, while we were lunching in the adjoining room, the whole family heard a sudden metallic clanking from the library-lounge, for all the world as if a large brass tray were being thrown violently around inside it. We rushed in to find the tray no longer in the corner where it had been left, while on the wallpaper round about were newly-made scars and indentations caused as if by its damaging rim. This, too, defied all explanation.

One of the strangest occurrences of all in these months of increasing uneasiness—during which time the footsteps on the landing kept up their continuous tramping—was in a bedroom in which the hot water tank was kept in a cupboard. Below the hot water tank were stored books and toys. One night my brother and I were woken by a cascade of water which, investigation showed, had poured in a torrent into the toy cupboard below the tank and out into the bedroom itself. A plumber was called in, and despite his extensive examination of the entire water system, the very puzzled man was unable to give any reason whatever for the flood of many, many gallons of water below the tank, which was in perfect order.

By this time, after some eight months in the house, my mother had become quite adamant that we would have to move out of it. My father insisted that if only our mortal minds knew in which direction to look it should be possible to give a plain, simple, earthly explanation for everything that had occurred, but that was not enough to satisfy my mother. And so ultimately my parents searched for elsewhere to live.

Finally, just as we were about to move out of the house, a letter arrived addressed to the previous occupants, two unmarried sisters who had lived there for some considerable time after the death of their parents. My mother, for some unknown reason, examined the contents of this letter and found that it was a demand for some small fee for the maintenance of the grave of the dead parents. She made inquiries locally to discover the whereabouts of the two sisters, and managed to forward the letter to them.

One day, weeks later, she made a special visit to this grave, and was able to satisfy herself that it had been freshly attended to. By this time we were living elsewhere in Southampton, and more discreet inquiries, because my parents certainly did not want to upset the new tenants of the house, revealed that nothing untoward had happened in it since.

To this day there is not a member of my family who will say that the house was haunted; none of us will say there was a ghost there. But despite the scepticism of my father, there is still an awful lot of doubt in our minds as to precisely what was responsible for all that occurred in that particular house.

THE GRASSLESS GRAVE

The job-hunting stranger who was introduced to widowed Mrs Morris, at her house and farm at Chirbury, on the Shropshire border three miles from Montgomery, said his name was John Newton and that he came from Staffordshire. Apart from these facts and a few comments which showed him to be an intelligent man, with obvious experience of running a farm, he was reticent about his personal history. But to Mrs Morris he seemed eminently reliable, on this introduction to her by her brother, and his opportune arrival seemed to offer her new hope for the future.

Mrs Morris was the owner of Oakfield, a house which in better days had been a manor house, but her late husband, a dissolute and idle man, had left her and their only child, a young daughter, in straightened circumstances. For some time it had seemed she would have to part with the property and let it to a Thomas Pearce, whose family had formerly owned Oakfield but had squandered it away. But she now, in this year of 1818, took a chance on young John Newton and engaged him as a bailiff.

Newton succeeded far beyond her expectations. He managed the farm with such industry and skill that in a short time it became prosperous and flourishing, and the widow put aside all thoughts of resigning it to Pearce.

Newton remained non-committal about his past and did not appear willing to make any acquaintances beyond those he encountered in the business of running the farm. He had to go to the neighbouring fairs and markets, and was a regular member of the congregation at Chirbury Church, but he kept his own company and counsel, in spite of the efforts of the clergyman of the parish to draw him out of his reserve. He seemed for the most part, "a melancholy, grief-haunted man", though he was contented and happy enough in his work at Oakfield. His behaviour towards the widow and her daughter Jane was at all times respectful, and even cheerful. He seemed to consider it a part of his duties to make their rather lonely domestic life as comfortable and pleasant as possible. Occasionally, at the end of the long working day, he would read to them. But even in their close company he studiously avoided all reference to his past life and was grateful to them both for their unquestioning acceptance of his silence on these matters.

This happy state of affairs at Oakfield lasted for more than two years, and the widow was not displeased when Jane's growing affection for the young bailiff became evident. Elsewhere, however, Newton's success with the farm and his bond with the family caused disappointment and jealousy. Thomas Pearce had had the farm that once belonged to his family almost within his grasp before Newton arrived. Now his chance of regaining it seemed lost. He was intensely disappointed, yet apparently managed to live down his regrets.

But Robert Parker, a young farmer and neighbour of Pearce, looked on Newton with a bitter hatred, for he saw in the stranger a successful rival for the affections of Jane Morris, of whom he had long been fond though without declaring himself. Parker fired the disappointed Pearce with some of his own hatred and desire for revenge on Newton, and the two men met frequently to discuss the situation. Eventually they devised a plan which would rid them of Newton, their one wish being to see him far removed from their lives. They watched and waited, then sprang their trap.

One day Newton went to a fair at Welshpool, a few miles to the north. He was kept late on farm business and it was six o'clock on a dark November evening when he left Welshpool to walk home. Parker, who had been stealthily keeping an eye on his movements, followed after him with Pearce, a short distance behind on the road. Not long afterwards Newton was brought back to Welshpool by the two men, who accused him of highway robbery with violence. He was taken before a magistrate, charged with the offence and committed for trial.

The crime of which Parker and Pearce, men of known respectability, accused Newton, was punishable by death. But at his subsequent trial Newton employed no counsel and asked no questions of the two witnesses, simply protesting his innocence of the charge. He was found guilty by the jury. When the judge asked if he had anything to say why sentence of death should not be passed upon him, he replied in a firm voice that he forgave the two men on whose false testimony he had been convicted.

"But, my lord," he declared, "I protest most solemnly, before the God in whose presence I must shortly appear, I am entirely guiltless of the crime for which I am about to suffer. I do not say that

I am an innocent man. I have committed a crime, but it is known only to my Creator and myself. I have endeavoured to atone for it by all the means in my power, and I humbly believe I have been forgiven.

"I protest once more, I am entirely innocent of this charge. It is my devout and earnest desire that the stain of this crime may not rest upon my name. I have, therefore, in humble devotion, offered a prayer to heaven, and I believe it has been heard and accepted. I venture to assert that if I am innocent of the crime for which I suffer, *the grass, for one generation at least, will not cover my grave.*"

Newton was sentenced to be hanged. On the day fixed, in 1821, no sooner did the bell begin to toll for the public execution at Montgomery than the sky became heavily overcast. Newton had scarcely set foot on the scaffold when "a fearful darkness spread around, and the moment the fatal bolt was withdrawn, the lightnings flashed with terrific vividness, the thunders rolled in awful majesty, until the town hill seemed shaken to its base; the rain poured down in torrents, the multitude dispersed, horror-stricken and appalled, some crying out, 'The end of all things is come.' "

*   *   *

This was the story, couched rather differently in the flamboyant language of historical romance, told by the Rev Richard Mostyn Pryce, in a pamphlet which he published at Newtown, Montgomeryshire, in 1852. It was, as we shall see, heavily fictionalised. All the names were fictitious and it would seem that Mr Pryce had a gay regard for fact, inventing a number of aspects to heighten his moral tale. Yet some thanks are due to him for first bringing to light a haunting story which, even when shorn of the cleric's embellishments, provides one of the most intriguing mysteries of recent history.

To continue Mr Pryce's account, he tells us that he inspected the solitary grave in a remote corner of Montgomery Churchyard where the remains of John Newton were buried. He found it was not a raised mound but simply a bare space level with the surrounding ground, with no stone or marker to give its identity. And still, thirty years after Newton's burial, the grass had not covered the grave.

Mr Pryce wrote, "Numerous attempts have, from time to time, been made by some who are still alive, and others who have passed away, to bring grass upon that bare spot. Fresh soil has been frequently spread upon it and seeds of various kinds have been sown; but not a blade has ever been known to spring from them, and the soil has soon become a smooth, and cold, and stubborn clay."

In the same year that Mr Pryce wrote his strange story someone covered the "Robber's Grave" with turf, tending it so carefully
that it grew all over the grave except at the head, which remained
bare, with withered grass around it. But in a month or so all the
grass again died away, leaving the grave bare once more.

And the allegedly false witnesses who sent John Newton to his
death? Robert Parker, declared Mr Pryce, became a drunkard, and
was killed during the blasting of some rocks in a lime-works at
Llanymynech. His confederate, Thomas Pearce, became dispirited
and "wasted away from the earth". As for the widow Morris and
her daughter, they left Oakfield for ever.

Mr Pryce's chief informant for his story, especially regarding the
grave, was William Weeks, who was the Montgomery parish clerk
at the time of the execution. Weeks died five years after publication
of the pamphlet and Pryce killed himself a year later, in 1858. So
the two principals were gone.

Confirmation of some parts of the story, however, came long
afterwards from someone who was actually on the spot in Montgomery some two years before Pryce published his pamphlet. Young
Elias Owen, in about 1850, got to talking to an old blind carpenter
in Montgomery who at the time of the execution was in his early
forties. Not until 1884 did the Rev Elias Owen, as he became, describe in print the conversation he then had with this man, but this
was his memory of it :

"My informant . . . told me that a stranger came to reside in the
neighbourhood of Montgomery—I think he said at a farm. No one
knew whence he came, nor what he had been, and he was reticent
upon all personal matters. This caused the man to be spoken of
and suspected, but there was nothing in his conduct, excepting this
silence as to his own matters, that anyone could blame; on the contrary he was most exemplary, and by his assiduity and trustworthy
behaviour he gained the full confidence of his master and family. It
was said he loved his employer's daughter, and that this love was
reciprocal. But something had been stolen—I think my informant
said sheep—and the silent man was suspected. He was arrested and
condemned to death. He pleaded innocence of that offence for
which he was to be hung, but in a general way he spoke of being
in other matters not guiltless. The judge, however, pronounced his
doom, and the man then invoked the Great Ruler of all things to
vindicate his innocence to that generation by not permitting grass
to grow on his grave.

"This solemn appeal was without effect, and the day for the execution came. It was a shocking day; the storm was terrific. At the time fixed for the sad event no one dare move for the storm; the procession was in consequence delayed. But at last it cleared up, and the man was hung. When he was suspended, a beautiful white dove rested above his head. This was seen by people, and they said it was a proof of his innocence. The man was buried in the churchyard, and, singularly enough, no grass grew on his grave."

Mr Owen, after hearing the old carpenter's story, went to the churchyard and had no difficulty in finding the "Robber's Grave".

"It was a long strip of ground, longer than the length of the body of an ordinary-sized man, with no grass on it, and, by the place where the neck would be, the grass approached to a point, but did not come in contact. The first generation had then gone by; still there was no grass on the grave."

In fact in the grave lay not John Newton, as styled by Mostyn Pryce, but, to give him his real name, John Davies, who indeed had been executed as described (Pryce must have known the real name but for some reason changed it). But before examining these stories of John Davies we must move on to a discovery of much more recent years. In 1937 Mrs Mary Jones, a lifelong resident of Montgomery, died at the age of ninety, and among her effects was found a narrative of John Davies which she had written in 1893 from an account by her father, who at the age of eighteen had seen Davies executed.

Mrs Jones's story, published in the *Montgomeryshire County Times* in 1946, confirmed many points made by Mostyn Pryce in 1852 and by Elias Owen in 1884, including Davies's impassioned speech and the storm on the day of execution. "It was," said Mrs Jones, "a morning of beautiful sunshine, but as the time of the execution drew near it became very dark; the lightning and thunder were dreadful; it seemed almost impossible to hang the man; women and children were too terrified to leave their homes. The storm was general, and the damage done upon the Welsh Coast and in the interior of the county was appalling."

After the execution, wrote Mrs Jones, the body was given to "two respectable men" who had asked for it. One was a carpenter, who made a coffin for it, and the two men buried the body in unconsecrated ground in the north of the churchyard.

Mrs Jones gave the real name of the fictional "Oakfield", which was Heightley Hall, and she told also of how Davies's two accusers had actually picked a fight with the unfortunate man and hidden a watch on him, which they afterwards charged him with stealing.

She repeated that one of these false witnesses was killed during rock-blasting, and said the other was found, some years later, by the sexton, weeping beside Davies's grave and proclaiming the "robber's" innocence. He died shortly afterwards.

From these three tales we come now to the facts, which are few enough and were unearthed only recently through the researches of Mr J. D. K. Lloyd.

From a deposition which still exists, we learn that on April 20th, 1821, John Davies, who described himself as a plasterer and slaterer, born at Wrexham and lately working at Oswestry, appeared before two magistrates at Welshpool, accused by William Jones of assaulting him on the highway and robbing him of a watch worth thirty shillings, and fivepence in coppers. In his deposition to the magistrates this William Jones, a labourer employed near Welshpool, testified that at eleven o'clock the previous night he was on the road from Welshpool returning to his master's house when Davies accosted him, beat him with a stick and threw him into a ditch, demanding, "Damn your eyes, deliver your money or I will kill you in a minute." Davies then, after going through his pockets, made off, somewhat disgusted, with the watch and fivepence in half-pennies, all that Jones possessed.

Jones said he then walked back to Welshpool and at the first public-house he came to found William Jones (another man of the same name) and his brother Thomas, to whom he told his story. All three then set out and when only a quarter of a mile from town met Davies, whom he recognised as his attacker. They set upon Davies and found the watch in a knee of his breeches, Davies himself returning the fivepence of his own accord. They then brought him into town.

Davies, on the testimony of the three men, was committed to the autumn sessions. Four months later a paragraph in the *Salopian Journal* of August 29th, 1821, recorded that at the Great Sessions for Montgomeryshire, at Welshpool, "John Davies for stopping William Jones on the highway and robbing him of a watch and some money, was found guilty, and had sentence of death passed on him in a very solemn and impressive manner". A fortnight later, on September 12th, 1821, the same newspaper briefly reported that Davies had been executed at Montgomery. Elsewhere in the paper, however, appeared a weather report which confirms absolutely the sudden storm which overtook the area on the day of execution.

Whether Davies was innocent and "framed" is unlikely ever to be known, but of the singular behaviour of the surface of his grave there are no doubts at all. Before his death in 1857 William Weeks, the parish clerk, made a written statement in which he said he was responsible for making the grave and burying John Davies. He testified that attempts had been made by various people to make grass grow on the grave by spreading soil over it and sowing seed, but without success. The grave, he said, had always returned, a short time after each experiment, to its original bare state.

Right up to the turn of the century the grave of John Davies retained its bare patch, though with the passing generations it grew fractionally smaller. Today, I am told by the Rev C. Michael Semper, there is still a barren patch of earth around the rose bush which now marks the "Robber's Grave". The bare patch, sunk in the ground amid the surrounding grass, is in the distinct form of a cross.

A PRICE ON ITS HEAD

A house in the village of Sampford Peverell, a few miles from Tiverton, Devon, first gave rise to gossip when a terrified boy apprentice claimed to have heard peculiar sounds there and seen the apparition of a woman during the night. Little credence was placed on his tale. However, beginning in April, 1810 and lasting over the next two years and more, the house was the scene of one of the most striking cases of continual haunting on record.

The house was tenanted by John Chave, with his wife and several servants. In the April they were alarmed by loud noises heard in every room, even during the day. It was found that if anyone went to an upstairs room and stamped on the floor a few times, he was immediately answered by the same number of sounds—and more, making the floorboards vibrate and throw up dust. At noon, loud knockings in one room or other were often heard by more than a dozen people at once. The noises sometimes followed people through the upper rooms, repeating their footsteps wherever they went. If two people went to different rooms, and one stamped with his foot in his room, the sound was instantly repeated in the other.

This disturbing but harmless haunting went on for five weeks, when suddenly there was a new and vicious development. The six women servants, who slept in two rooms of the house, were attacked and beaten by an invisible force as they lay in their beds.

The events were recorded in a detailed account of the case by the Rev Charles Caleb Colton, who was present during some of the manifestations. He said that he himself heard more than two hundred blows given in the course of one night, sounds which he likened to a strong man striking violently with his clenched fist on the bed.

The invisible blows left real marks. The cleric saw a large swelling on the cheek of Ann Mills, one of the maids, who testified that she was alone in bed when she received the blows from an invisible hand. Two other servants, Mrs Mary Dennis and Martha Woodbury, swore before the parson, Mr Sully, an exciseman, and Mr Govett, a surgeon, that they were beaten so severely they were sore for several days afterwards. It was confirmed that the shrieks they had given while being beaten were too real to have been faked.

Chave, the tenant, said that on one night the two maids were so terrified they refused to sleep in their own room and he allowed them, in the middle of the night, to bring their bed and bedclothes into the room occupied by him and his wife. After the candles had been put out all was quiet for half an hour, but then a large iron candlestick began to move rapidly about the room of its own accord. He had got up to ring the bell for assistance when the candlestick was thrown violently at him, narrowly missing his head.

One night, Mr Searle, keeper of the county gaol, together with a friend, kept watch in the servants' room. The two men saw a sword, which they had placed near them on the foot of a bed, with a large folio Bible placed on it, thrown violently against the wall, seven feet away. Another witness testified that when he rushed to the room, on hearing the shrieks of the women, he saw the sword still in the air and pointing towards him, after which it fell to the floor.

Ann Mills suffered a further attack. She said that one night, while striking a light, she received a very severe blow on the back, and the tinder-box was forcibly wrenched out of her hands and thrown into the centre of the room.

Colton himself, during his investigations at the house, often saw the bed-curtains violently shaken, "accompanied with a loud and almost indescribable motion of the rings". The four curtains were each tied up in a large knot to prevent their being moved, but the knots were then "thrown and whirled about with such rapidity that it would have been unpleasant to be within the sphere of their action".

On one occasion, together with Chave and another witness, Colton saw the knotted curtains flung about for a full two minutes, ending with the sound of tearing linen. The three men then discovered that a strong new cotton curtain had been rent across the grain.

Colton also heard, in the presence of other witnesses, footsteps walking by him and round him; and he was conscious of candles burning near him, but could see nothing.

A Mr Quick heard *something*, like a man's slippered feet, come downstairs and seem to pass through the wall. He testified, "I have been in the act of opening a door which was already half open when a violent rapping was produced on the opposite side of the same door. I paused a moment, and the rapping continued. I suddenly opened the door with a candle in my hand, yet I can swear I could see nothing.

"I have been in one of the rooms that has a large modern window, when, from the noises, knocking blows on the bed, and rattling of the curtains, I did really begin to think the whole chamber was falling in. Mr Taylor was sitting in the chair the whole time; the females were so terrified that large drops stood on their foreheads.

"When the act of beating has appeared, from the sound of the blows, near the foot of one bed, I have rushed to the spot, but it has been instantly heard near the head of the other bed."

Colton swore an affidavit in the presence of Mr B. Wood, Master-in-Chancery, Tiverton, in which he declared that after six nights of investigation at Chave's house, during which time he had rigorously questioned the servants and used every means to discover the cause of the disturbances, even to placing a seal with a crest to every door and cavity in the house through which any communications might be carried on, he was still utterly unable to account for the things which he had seen and heard.

But the owner of the house, Mr Talley, refused to believe there was anything supernatural about the disturbances. He alleged that the noises were made by a cooper banging tubs with a broomstick and bludgeon, and seemingly ignored the beating of the maids and the torn bed-curtains. He insisted that the whole affair was engineered by Chave, the tenant, in order to lower the value of the property so that he could buy it cheaply. The locals accepted this "exposure" and took Talley's side in the affair—and poor Chave was attacked and severely assaulted by those who believed him guilty of fraud.

However, despite Talley's statements to the contrary, the disturbances continued.

A reward of £250 was offered to anyone who could give information leading to a solution to the mystery. Colton, who himself was abused as a dupe in the affair—some even accused him of being its instigator—personally offered a reward of £100, depositing a document to that effect with the mayor of Tiverton. But two years afterwards the money was still unclaimed.

Colton then wrote, "The real truth is that the slightest shadow of an explanation has not yet been given, and that there exists no good grounds even for suspecting anyone. The public were given to understand that the disturbances had ceased, whereas it is well known to all in the neighbourhood that they continue, with unabating influence to this hour.

"We were told, by way of explanation, that the whole affair was a trick of the tenant, who wished to purchase the house cheap—the stale solution of all haunted houses. But such an idea never entered his thoughts, even if the present proprietors were able to sell the house, but it happens to be entailed. And at the very time when this was said, all the neighbourhood knew that Mr Chave was unremitting in his exertions to procure another habitation in Sampford on any terms. And, to confirm this, these disturbances have at length obliged the whole family to make up their minds to quit the premises, at a very great loss and inconvenience.

"If these nocturnal and diurnal visitations are the effects of a plot, the agents are marvellously secret and indefatigable. It has been going on more than three years, and if it be the result of human machination, there must be more than sixty persons concerned in it."

There never was a claimant to the price on the head of the Sampford ghost. The hauntings, undoubtedly by poltergeists, eventually ceased as mysteriously as they began, and in later years the house was quite free from all supernatural phenomena.

FLIGHT FROM THE PHANTOMS

Mr and Mrs Albert Barker, in 1958, bought a large, rambling house in Macclesfield, Cheshire, with the purpose of inviting Mrs Barker's mother and two brothers, who lived in Wales, to come and stay with them. The twelve-roomed house overlooked a church graveyard, the boundary wall of which was only a few yards away.

Six weeks after the purchase, the brothers and their mother arrived from Cefn Forest, in Monmouthshire. Ivor and Clifford Packermoore, both miners, were aged thirty-eight and forty-eight respectively. Their mother, Mrs Nellie Packermoore, was in her seventies.

The brothers were given a bedroom on the second floor, overlooking the open space at the back of the house, while their mother had a room on the same landing. The Barkers slept on the ground floor, the third floor being as yet unfurnished.

Soon after their arrival the brothers told of seeing a "white figure" in their room between one and two o'clock on a Tuesday night. They became so nervous of sleeping in the room that Mr Barker decided on the Friday night to keep a vigil outside the bedroom door, sleeping on a mattress. He gave up at about 1.30 a.m. when nothing occurred, and went down to his own room. But at 2 a.m. the brothers claimed to have been visited by the ghostly figure again.

The brothers were now thoroughly uneasy, especially as a worker in the graveyard had told Clifford, "I wouldn't live in that house for a fortune."

On the Saturday night all retired to bed after playing cards for most of the evening. In the early hours of Sunday morning the Barkers were awakened by a loud yelling and banging from one of the upstairs bedrooms. They jumped out of bed, Mrs Barker falling over the bedstead in her haste and gashing her shin. On the landing they found the two brothers and their mother, ashen-faced and shaking with fear. The mother was in such a nervous state that Mr Barker had to carry her downstairs, and he also had to carry down his wife, who was completely shocked by the sight of her terrified brothers, and especially her mother. The situation seemed so desperate that Mr Barker called the police, who arrived to find the three frightened people in the kitchen and Mrs Barker nursing her injured leg. Upstairs, in the brothers' room, was chaos; part of the skirting board had been smashed and there were two gaping holes where the door panels had been. The two brothers then told their story.

Ivor said he saw a figure "dressed in white, with staring eyes" near the window. He yelled in fright to Clifford.

Clifford said he looked across the room and in one corner saw something white with "a horrible looking face". As he leapt out of bed, Ivor kicked at the figure with his metal left leg and hit the skirting board. After that all was confusion as they both rushed to get out of the room. Clifford said he felt something dragging him back from behind, and in their panic they did not stop to open the bedroom door but smashed out the door panels and clambered through. On the landing they were joined by their terrified mother, who said that she had seen the door knob of her own room turn twice though no one was there.

The police were satisfied that something, whatever it was, had really frightened the Packermoores. With Mr Barker they searched the house from cellar to attic and examined windows, but found nothing. They also spent some twenty minutes in the brothers' bedroom, waiting in pitch blackness, but nothing untoward occurred. The brothers and their mother, however, were so convinced that there was something supernatural in the house that they left it to return to Wales later that same day.

There was, so far as could be discovered, no history of anything strange in the house, though a previous occupant was said to have left because of "bad nerves". Two years earlier, in 1956, workmen digging up the road nearby had unearthed skeletons that were believed to have formed part of a paupers' grave in the days when the graveyard extended beyond its present bounds, a bare twenty feet from the house.

The ghostly incident attracted nation-wide attention and Mr Barker, who refused to believe the house was haunted, received many offers from people to sleep in the room. Shortly afterwards an all-night vigil was kept there, but nothing more unusual was seen or heard.

At Bolton, Lancashire, in 1963, a family fled their council house after a haunting which they said had been going on for more than five years.

Not long after the Smith family moved into the house, on the

Hunger Hill estate at Bolton, Mr Harry Smith, a crane driver, and his wife began to hear bumping downstairs during the night. Mr Smith many times went down to investigate the noises but could never discover the source of them. At first the Smiths did not think too much of the disturbances, but in time the thumping and banging began to get unbearable.

Other strange things began happening. At times a "bony figure" clambered into the Smiths' bed. Mrs Smith said, "You could really feel its bones sticking into you, but when you put out your hands there was nothing there." When they switched on the bedroom light they would hear the ghost banging on the floor under the bed.

Elsewhere in the house lights were turned off and on, cups and other objects strewn on the floor, and the ghost began to walk about the house even in broad daylight, stamping up and down the stairs and touching people. At least one neighbour hurriedly left the house after "something" walked past her and brushed her shoulder.

In spite of all these unnerving experiences the Smiths and a few close friends managed to keep the haunting a secret for more than five years, being careful not to mention anything about it to the four children. But then, in October, 1963, as if determined to get the family out of the house, the ghost began attacking the children. The two boys, aged seven and eight, and their sisters, aged eleven and seventeen, began to complain of noises in the night and a presence getting into bed with them. The mother then suspected that the ghost had been tormenting them in their sleep for some time. The boys said they were pinched by an invisible force, and had their hair pulled.

One night the parents, hearing moans coming from their seventeen-year-old daughter's bedroom, rushed in to find her struggling to push something invisible away from her. Afterwards the distressed girl said that a strange force had had her in a stranglehold.

The family had scarcely any sleep in their last few weeks at the house. Finally, one night of November, 1963, the thumping and banging so worsened that Mr Smith called a taxi and the family left for the house of a married daughter.

Mr Smith told Bolton Corporation that his family could never go back to the house as there was something intensely malignant there. Two women officers of the Salvation Army spent a night in the house. They heard bumpings and growlings, and while not prepared to say that there was a ghost, they could not say definitely that there was not. And they testified that the Smiths were very, very frightened.

Bolton Corporation, treating the matter as an emergency, moved the family to another council house a mile away.

No one was able to trace anything in the haunted house that could have caused the family's alarm. A next-door neighbour, however, said that once she had heard banging on the party wall and later discovered there was nobody in the Smith family home at the time, which gave her quite a shock.

Mrs Smith revealed that when her family moved in they had been told there was a case of suicide in the house about thirty years previously, shortly after it was built.

A newspaper reporter and photographer kept a night's vigil in the house but saw nothing. The house, after redecoration, was relet to other tenants, and no more disturbances were reported.

In 1962 a family of seven, the parents and five children, who had lived for a year in a council house at Rumney, Cardiff, packed up one night and left it for the home of a relative, claiming the house to be haunted by a "White Lady". The ghost, said Mr Ernest Lewis, a building worker, and his wife, took the form of a young girl dressed in white who appeared generally at night, peering around doorways and at windows in the upstairs rooms. She would beckon to them, then vanish.

Mrs Lewis said the haunting started from the day they moved into the house, when they had heard sounds of digging, "as if someone was making a grave". More incidents followed: icy blasts on still, warm nights, and the sound of footsteps at midnight; the ghost eventually came so close that she and her husband could hear the rustle of a dress and the smell of perfume. Then the White Lady became visible. Mrs Lewis said she saw the apparition twice. The first time it gazed at her from the bedroom doorway; next time it appeared as a vague misty figure by the window. Her husband also saw it.

Mrs Lewis tried to get rid of the ghost herself. "We called in a priest, but he said he could only get rid of her in the daytime. But he did give me a Bible and a cross. We had to go round each room and say, 'Begone with thee, and be cast out of my home.' Then we had to say the Lord's Prayer."

She and her husband were, however, too nervous to do this. Mrs Lewis went to her doctor, who found she was in a state of acute anxiety and advised her to move. So the couple packed up and left, and asked Cardiff Corporation to rehouse them.

The previous tenants at the house, which was built in 1947, were there for thirteen years and said they had seen nothing strange during this time.

In January, 1963 three people walked out of an eighty-year-old house in Isleworth, Middlesex, because of the uncanny things which they said had occurred there. Rather than return to the house they stayed out in the winter cold and slept "rough" in a railway waiting room.

Earlier, police who were called to the ten-roomed house found Mr Ronald Bush, his wife Ann, and mother-in-law Mrs Barbara Basted, "in a genuine state of distress". Mrs Basted said she had seen the figure of an elderly, white-bearded naval man, and also smelled strong pipe tobacco in the house although nobody had been smoking. There had also been many strange noises.

Mrs Bush told of hearing the sound of a baby crying in an empty room, and footsteps on the stairs.

The police searched the whole of the house, pulling up floorboards and examining walls and cupboards, but found nothing to account for the noises. After their search, Mrs Basted returned to the house alone, only to leave it again hurriedly after hearing a groaning noise and a sound like that of crockery being smashed.

Neighbours whom Mrs Basted knocked up at three o'clock in the morning, after she had felt the ghost push her down the stairs, said they understood the house had been built eighty years ago to the design of a Captain Auden, who had been a sea captain.

An investigator held a vigil in the house but saw nothing. Mrs Basted afterwards returned home, the ghost seeming to have vanished from the premises as abruptly as it had invaded them.

At a farm worker's cottage in Faringdon, Berkshire, in 1963, it was not an apparition that frightened the Wheeler family but a relentless succession of mysterious noises. Police, local architects and villagers all tried to discover the source of them. Floorboards were taken up and the walls examined for flaws that might be producing some freak echo, but nothing was found.

The noises began suddenly with tappings on the windows and persistent knocking on the walls, which caused the Wheelers, who had lived there for eighteen years, to abandon the upstairs bedrooms and sleep with their children in the ground floor living room. The bangings and knockings brought Mrs Dorothy Wheeler to the edge of a nervous breakdown, and the three girls among the four children, aged from five to nineteen, were given sedatives. The noises, an unearthly banging, rumbling and howling, continued for several weeks into January, 1964 and finally drove the family out, Mr

Norman Wheeler taking his wife and children to stay with in-laws. But to their horror the noises followed them to their temporary home, emanating from the walls and furniture there. Mr Wheeler, not wanting anyone else to be frightened, decided to return to the cottage with his family. The banging and howling noises pursued them, continuing in the car as they were on their way back to the cottage, and resuming in the cottage the moment they opened the door.

Mr Wheeler was then told by a medium that the vengeful spirit was that of an old man who had lodged at the cottage seventeen years before, and who had afterwards committed suicide. Mr Wheeler recalled that they had only let the man stop with them for a week because he was a trouble-maker. The same night he left the cottage the man had lain down in front of a train outside Uffington station and killed himself.

Mr Wheeler now sought the help of Faringdon's acting vicar, Canon Christopher Harman, who, after visiting the cottage, said he was conscious of an oppressive atmosphere inside it and there was "something uncanny about the place". He agreed to carry out a service of exorcism.

The ceremony took place one night of February, 1964. Canon Harman conducted a thirty-minute service at the cottage during which he said prayers and sprinkled holy water in each room. After this the noises stopped, giving the family their first peace in weeks.

THE HEADLESS LADY OF WATTON

On a night of June, 1956, seven workmen settled down to sleep in makeshift beds set up on the ground floor of Watton Abbey, near Driffield, Yorkshire, whose owner was selling up after a tenancy of more than thirty years. A fierce June wind howled round the reputedly haunted building as they slept. Then, above the wind, at one o'clock in the morning, there sounded the eerie tolling of a bell.

The workmen sat bolt upright in their beds, spines tingling. They knew that nowhere in the abbey was there a bell.

One frightened man dived head first through an open window, landing in a flower bed. The auctioneer's foreman, who was in charge, grabbed a sporting gun, loaded it and fired two shots skywards. The bell ceased to toll. But the workmen, who had come up from Retford, Nottinghamshire, to help with the three-day sale at the abbey, picked up their beds and spent the rest of the night in a large marquee put up in the abbey grounds. They were taking no chances. The ringing, they thought, could have been the work of the Watton ghost.

The haunting of twenty-roomed Watton Abbey, or at least the presence of its more commonly believed ghost, dates from the time of the Civil War. The Tudor mansion, built on the site of an ancient priory, was then the home of a devoted Royalist. In 1644 he was away fighting in the ranks of King Charles, leaving the lady of Watton at home with only a handful of servants for protection. After the battle of Marston Moor, near York, in which the Royalists were defeated and the Parliamentarians gained complete control of the north, a band of fanatical Roundheads began a trail of persecution and plunder across east Yorkshire. They eventually arrived at Driffield, five miles from Watton. News then reached the abbey that the marauding Puritans were on their way there to loot "the home of a Royalist malignant", at which the lady of Watton shut herself and her baby in an oak pannelled room with a secret door. She hoped, in extreme danger, to escape through the secret door, formed by one of the wood panels, down a concealed stone stairway to the moat.

The Roundheads, on their arrival at the house, hammered at the door, demanding admittance. On getting no response from the terrified household they searched around for some implement with which to break down the door. During their search they caught sight of a low archway opening into the moat, which they guessed to be a side entrance to the house, and, crossing the moat, they found the stone stairway. Climbing this they came to the disguised door and broke through.

They found the lady of Watton prostrate before a crucifix. Rising up and taking her baby close in her arms, she demanded to know the reason for their violent entry. They answered that they had come to despoil the mansion of "a worshipper of idols"—and to kill him if he were there. The strong-minded lady spiritedly lashed the raiders with her tongue for their vandalism, but they roughly demanded the plate and other valuables of the house. These she scornfully refused to give up. She continued to upbraid them until, provoked by her bitter tongue, they suddenly pulled the baby from her arms and dashed its head against the wall. They then cut down the screaming woman and struck off her head.

After stripping the house of its valuables the marauders then made off.

From that time, the headless ghost of the lady of Watton, her baby in her arms, has haunted the room in which they were both murdered. The tradition sprang up that she returned to the room nightly to rest, for constantly in the morning, the bedclothes were found disarranged, as if someone had slept in them. To anyone bold enough to sleep in the room, the headless ghost would appear dressed in her bloodstained garments, the baby in her arms. She would stand motionless at the foot of the bed for a time, then vanish.

On one occasion a visitor who knew nothing of the legend was put to sleep in the wainscotted room. In the morning he said that his sleep had been disturbed by the spectre of a woman in bloody dress, carrying an infant in her arms. Her features, he said, bore a strange resemblance to those of a woman whose portrait hung in the room.

This is the only recorded appearance of the spectre *with* her head.

Other hauntings reported at the abbey may have their explanation in much earlier violent events at Watton, for the abbey has another ghost story. This goes back in time to when Watton, once a nunnery but destroyed by the Danes, was refounded in the twelfth century as a Gilbertine Priory. The priory housed thirteen monks and thirty-six nuns of the new Gilbertine Order, all quartered in the same block but separated by a party wall. It was the monks' duty to serve the nuns "in terrene, as well as in divine matters", which brought them into regular though silent contact.

Murdac, Archbishop of York, who was instrumental in setting up the new priory, placed in it a four-year-old girl, Elfrida, to be educated for taking the veil. Elfrida was a vivacious and merry girl who, as she grew older, came in for constant correction by the nuns for her spirited behaviour. She also grew to be quite a beauty, which excited the jealousy of the sisters, who were mostly elderly and middle-aged spinsters. When she began to express doubts about the worth of convent life, even going so far as to satirise the ways of the nuns, they subjected her to stiff penances, but this only increased her desire to escape and mingle with the outer world.

The monks of Watton, being responsible for the secular affairs of the community, often entered the nunnery to hold conference with the prioress. On these visits Elfrida found herself particularly attracted to one young brother, and he quickly responded to her surreptitious glances. After maintaining this silent but eloquent liaison for some time they managed to find ways of meeting at night.

Elfrida became pregnant, and in time concealment was impossible. Summoned before her scandalised superiors she boldly confessed her fault, saying she had no heart for a convent life and asking to be banished from the community. The angry sisters, however, would not consider this for a moment. Various terrible punishments, such as execution by fire or being walled up alive, were suggested, but the more prudent nuns averted these extreme measures. Elfrida was stripped and beaten with rods till the blood ran down her lacerated back. She was then chained in a dungeon without light and fed only bread and water, which was handed in to her with bitter taunts and reproaches.

Her lover, meantime, had left the priory. The nuns, by falsely promising Elfrida that she would be released to go to him, got from her the information that he was still in the neighbourhood in disguise, and, not knowing their secret was discovered, would come as usual to visit her, signalling his arrival by throwing a stone on the roof above her sleeping cell.

The prioress alerted the monks, who were waiting the following night when Elfrida's paramour appeared. After looking cautiously around, he threw his signal stone, at which the monks rushed out of hiding, cudgelled him and took him prisoner into the house. The younger nuns demanded that the man should be handed over to them for questioning. Their request, which seemed reasonable enough, was granted, but taking him to an unfrequented part of the convent, and bringing Elfrida up from her dungeon to witness the scene, they then handled him with savagery.

Afterwards Elfrida, still chained in her dungeon, became penitent. One night, as she was sleeping in her fetters, an apparition of the dead Archbishop Murdac, her patron, appeared before her and charged her with having cursed him for placing her within the harsh confines of the convent.

"Rather curse yourself," said the apparition, "for having given way to temptation."

Elfrida answered contritely and Murdac exhorted her to repentance and the daily recitation of certain psalms, then vanished.

The nuns at this time were worried as to what they should do when Elfrida's baby arrived. But this problem was solved when Elfrida was again visited in the night by the ghost of Murdac, accompanied by two women, "who, with the holy aid of the archbishop, safely delivered her of the infant, which they bore away in their arms, covered with a fair white cloth".

When the nuns came to the dungeon the next morning they were astonished to find Elfrida now slim and bright. She told them what had happened in the night, but this was too much for them to believe. They accused her of murdering the infant, though how she could have done this, being chained to the floor, was problematical. But there was a second shock to come. On the morning of the next day, the nuns found Elfrida standing free of her chains, which were nowhere to be seen in the locked dungeon. She told them that the fetters were removed from her by a mysterious agency during the night.

Alured, Abbot of Rievaulx Abbey, north of York, was called in to investigate the strange affair. He decided after careful questioning that it was a miraculous intervention, and cautioned the community, "What God hath cleansed call not thou common or unclean, and whom He hath loosed thou mayest not bind."

What afterwards became of the penitent Elfrida is not known, for Alured, from whose chronicles this account is taken, does not say. But it may be safely assumed that her critics were silenced and she achieved considerable status among the Gilbertines.

Alured concluded, "Let no one doubt the truth of this account for I was an eyewitness to many of the facts, and the remainder were related to me by persons of such mature age and distinguished position that I cannot doubt the accuracy of their statement."

Whether Elfrida herself, after death, returned to haunt Watton Abbey has never been clear. In later years her penitent spirit seems to have been confused by many with the headless phantom of the Cavalier's lady murdered by the Roundhead fanatics.

HANGED BY A GHOST

Gossip soon sprang up around John Walker, a widower of comfortable means, when he took in a young relation of his, Anne Walker, to keep house for him in the village of Lumley, near Chester-le-Street, Durham. Late in the year 1630 the scandalised neighbours were convinced that he had made the girl pregnant, and their suspicions were correct.

A few weeks before the child was due, Walker took young Anne to her aunt, Dame Cave, who lived in Chester-le-Street, promising the aunt that he would provide both for the girl and her future baby. But one evening towards the end of November, he returned in company with an acquaintance of his, a Lancashire coal miner named Mark Sharp, from Blackburn, and told Dame Cave that he had made other arrangements for the girl. Sharp, he said, would take Anne to Lancashire, to a place where she could remain in peace and safety till her confinement was over.

Walker would not say where this place was, but the aunt, knowing him to have an excellent character apart from his recent indiscretion, allowed him to take the girl away.

Fourteen days after Anne had left the district with Sharp, James Graham, a fuller who lived about six miles from Walker's house in Lumley, as was his practice stayed on working late in his cloth mill, the doors of which he had closed up. It was past midnight when he came down the stairs from the upper to the lower floor of the mill and was horrified to see standing before him, in the centre of the ground floor, a woman with dishevelled and bloodied hair hanging down about her head, on which were several large wounds. Graham halted, appalled, and quickly blessed himself. Gradually he recovered sufficiently to ask the poor woman who she was, and what she wanted.

The apparition said, "I am the spirit of Anne Walker, who lived with Walker, and, being got child with him, he promised to send me to a private place, where I should be well looked to till I was

148

brought to bed, and well again, and then I should come again to keep his house.

"Accordingly I was one night late sent away with one Mark Sharp, who, upon a moor (naming a place known to the fuller) slew me with a pick, such as men dig coals withal, and gave me these five wounds, and after threw my body into a coal-pit hard by and hid the pick under a bank; and his shoes and stockings being bloody, he endeavoured to wash them, but seeing the blood would not forth, he hid them there."

The spectre told the fuller that he must be the man to reveal the crime and have her murderers punished, or she would appear again and haunt him.

Graham returned home "very sad and heavy" but did not say a word to anyone about what he had seen, nor did he act on the ghost's startling information. Instead he took care to leave his mill early in future, and when kept there till late in the day, never to be without company. But one night, just as darkness fell, the apparition appeared to him again, this time seeming "very fierce and cruel", and warned him that if he did not reveal the murder she would continually pursue him and haunt him. Still Graham did not act, hoping that it was the last he would see of the ghost, but night after night, the urgent spectre pulled the clothes from his bed and on December 20th, as he was walking in his garden soon after sunset, it reappeared and threatened him so strongly that he finally promised to obey its wishes. The next morning he went to a magistrate and told the whole extraordinary story.

A search was made and Anne Walker's body was found in the coal-pit exactly as directed by the apparition, with five wounds on the head. The pickaxe, and the bloody shoes and stockings, were also found at the spot she had named.

A warrant was issued and John Walker and Mark Sharp were both arrested, but would confess nothing. The fact of Sharp's bloodstained clothing, and the pick, being found at the scene of the murder was strong evidence against the collier, but no evidence could be brought against Walker other than the account given Graham by the ghost, which charged his complicity. Both men were allowed bail, and in August, 1631 their case came before Judge Davenport at Durham Assizes. In the meantime the circumstances of the murder, and the nature of its discovery became known all over the north of England, producing much excitement at the trial.

During the hearing the judge appeared "much troubled". He summed up strongly against the prisoners, and when the jury found them guilty, he pronounced sentence that night, a thing which was unknown in Durham, either before or after.

Walker and Sharp were executed, protesting their innocence to the last. The foreman of the jury, named Fairbair, said afterwards that during the trial he had seen the likeness of a child standing on Walker's shoulders. It was believed that the agitated judge, too, had seen it, or the spectre of Anne Walker herself, which had appeared "as if to supply in his mind the want of legal evidence".

In the next century, a murder trial in Scotland of two men denounced by the ghost of the victim did not have such conclusive results, though their guilt was widely believed and, it later transpired, not the least by their own agent or solicitor.

Events leading up to the trial began one night of 1751 in the remote Highland district of Braemar, in Aberdeenshire. Alexander Macpherson, a twenty-six-year-old farm servant living in the hamlet of Inverey, was in bed in his cottage when someone came to his bedside and commanded him to get up and follow him out of doors. Macpherson, believing the visitor to be Donald Farquharson, a neighbour and friend, did as he was asked, but when they were outside the cottage to his amazement he saw that the night caller was not his neighbour but an apparition.

The spectre told him it was the ghost of a murdered English soldier, Sergeant Arthur Davis, and asked him to go and bury the sergeant's mortal remains, which, it said, lay concealed in a certain place in a moorland tract called the hill of Christie; he was to take Donald Farquharson along to help with the burial.

Macpherson solemnly agreed to do as he was bid.

Next day, however, he went alone to the place described by his ghostly caller. He found the remains of a human body, much decayed, but he did not bury them.

A few nights later, the sergeant's ghost came again and upbraided him with breaking his promise. Macpherson asked the spectre who was his murderer, and it replied that the killers were two Highlanders, Duncan Terig and Alexander Bain Macdonald. After this second plea by the ghost Macpherson went for Farquharson and told his friend the story of his night visitor, and they went off together to bury the sergeant's bones.

This, for the two men, was an end of the affair, but their evidence was to form a vital part of the case for the Crown when proceedings were taken against the men named by the ghost.

Davis, a sergeant in General Guise's regiment of foot, had disappeared in September, 1749. This was not long after the Civil War, and with passions still smouldering there was ample reason why a stray English soldier might meet his fate in that lonely region of Scotland. It was not until after long, determined efforts by a retired Army officer named Small that Duncan Terig and Alexander Macdonald stood trial on June 10th, 1754, three years following the appearance of the apparition and Macpherson's burial of the bones.

Terig and Macdonald were tried before the High Court of Justiciary in Edinburgh, accused of the murder of Sergeant Arthur Davis on September 28th, 1749. Davis, when he disappeared, was known to have had a fowling-piece and money and rings in his possession, and some of his valuables had afterwards been seen in the hands of the two Highlanders. Robbery appeared to have been the sole object of the murder.

Alexander Macpherson, who spoke no language but Gaelic and gave his evidence to the court through an interpreter, told of the visits of the sergeant's ghost, and his directed burial of the remains. His account was supported by Donald Farquharson, who had assisted him, while further evidence of the apparition was given by a woman named Isabel Machardie, who slept at the same communal house as Macpherson in one of the beds that ran along the wall in the Highland dwelling. She said that on the night when Macpherson said he saw the ghost, she had seen a naked man enter the house and go towards Macpherson's bed.

Her recorded evidence was that "she saw something naked come in at the door, which frightened her so much that she drew the clothes over her head; that when it appeared, it came in a bowing posture; that she cannot tell what it was; that next morning she asked Macpherson what it was that had troubled them the night before, and he answered that she might be easy, for it would not trouble her any more."

In spite of this added testimony to the appearance of the sergeant's ghost, the whole incident was cleverly ridiculed by the defence and, in fact, was so discredited as to sway the case in the prisoners' favour, even though there were other strong presumptions against them.

Defence counsel, cross-examining Macpherson, asked the farm servant, "What language did the ghost speak in?"

Macpherson, who was entirely ignorant of the English language, replied, "As good Gaelic as I ever heard in Lochaber."

"Pretty well for the ghost of an English sergeant," commented counsel.

It was a remark which registered with the jury, who found no flaw in this inference that ghosts might reasonably be expected to make themselves understood only in the language they had known in life. The jury found the two Highlanders not guilty, though most of the court had little doubt they had committed the murder.

Years afterwards, when both Terig and Macdonald had died, their solicitor disclosed that he was fully persuaded of their guilt.

THE FACTORY SPECTRES

There had been several unexplained happenings at a Lancashire mill over a period of about four years. They culminated in a bizarre incident one night of October, 1963 which caused a nineteen-year-old cloth roller at the mill, at Standish, near Wigan, to faint over his machine while working on the night shift.

When he recovered he said that on looking up from his machine, he had seen a figure in a long coat. It floated in the air about two feet from the floor, and seemed to be wearing knickerbockers. There was something white near its neck.

Though he did not know it, the frightened worker's description exactly fitted the Rev Charles William Newton Hutton, rector of Standish for fifty years, who died in 1938. Older villagers of Standish remembered Mr Hutton as wearing gaiters. He was short-necked and had a light beard, which accounted for the "something white" seen near the neck of the apparition.

It is widely believed in the district that the old rector's ghost, which is quite harmless, still haunts the vicinity. The mill was erected on glebe land belonging to the rectory and Mr Hutton had a financial interest in it when it was first built. He frequently visited the premises during his lifetime.

By an odd coincidence the apparition's appearance to the mill machinist occurred the day before Rector Hutton's widow died.

In the spring of 1963 workers at the Vickers-Armstrong plant at Weybridge, Surrey, on the old Brooklands racing track, reported several appearances by a figure clad in the dress of a racing driver, which was seen to walk through the new VC 10 jet-airliner hangar and vanish into a wall.

The apparition was seen by a number of workmen, who described it as wearing a flying helmet and a brown leather coat, in the style of the drivers who competed on the famous old track in the nineteen-twenties. One workman in the hangar said he spoke to the ghost as it appeared suddenly and walked across the building. He called after it, "Hey, mate, you mustn't go in there!" But the apparition walked on until it came to the wall, into which it vanished.

The ghost's fleeting appearances were disturbing at first, but the men in the flight shed got used to them.

Several drivers and mechanics were killed during races at Brooklands, which was bought by Vickers-Armstrong in 1945. Not all the workmen, however, believed the apparition to be that of a racing driver, as that part of Brooklands was not closely associated with the actual racing track. More likely, it was suggested, the ghost was that of a pioneer aviator. In the early days it was not unusual for planes to crash into the old sewage farm which once occupied the area. Several pilots were killed in such accidents.

It was not the first time that a ghost had been seen in the vicinity of Brooklands; reports had been made in earlier years of similar apparitions, or a hazy presence. A bailiff on the Brooklands Estate, when it was privately owned, claimed to have clearly seen the ghost of an old-time aviator.

Again in industry, in 1961, an apparition appeared in the Vauxhall car factory at Luton, Bedfordshire. Three men on night shift at the factory said they saw the ghost twice, and recognised it as being that of an inspector at the factory who had collapsed and died at work nearly a year previously. The men were cleaning out the spray booths in a block in the factory when they first saw the apparition. They said it came into view walking only a few yards away. The inspector appeared quite real to them until they saw him walk through a component box and then vanish into a brick wall.

Other men reported seeing the factory inspector's ghost, and the upshot was that one man quit his job and two others asked for a transfer from the block.

Another case of a recently dead employee believed to have returned to haunt his place of work was reported the same year at Bracknell New Town, Berkshire. The ghost of the modern engineering works of Fluidrive was thought to be that of a nightwatchman who had died the previous year. Because of it the firm had three new nightwatchmen come and go in three months.

The dead watchman, with his Alsatian dog, had been with the firm for many years. The first watchman engaged after his death resigned after taking alarm at unaccountable sounds of coughing and the barking of a dog which he heard coming from inside the factory when he was alone. The next watchman who undertook the job failed to turn up one night, giving no reason but simply refusing to spend another night in the factory. The third watchman engaged soon gave in his notice too. He also said he had heard coughing and the barking of a dog, and on going to investigate in the silent factory had sensed something indescribably eerie.

One of the watchmen, at midnight, heard the checking-out machine being operated, and on going to inspect it found that a workman's card had been stamped at exactly midnight.

A tape recorder was set up in the factory one night, but it did not register any unusual noises. A local newspaper reporter then held a night vigil, but this also proved fruitless.

THE LAST HOURS OF LORD LYTTELTON

Thomas, the second Lord Lyttelton, was as noted for his loose life as his father had been for his upright one. Even after seemingly repenting and marrying, in his twenties, he soon deserted his wife for a barmaid whom he took off to Paris. In 1779, at the age of thirty-five, not the least of the scandals current against him was his association with three sisters named Amphlett, who lived near to his country residence.

In November, 1779, Lord Lyttelton had just returned from Ireland, where he had left one of the sisters, when, at his home in Hill Street, Berkeley Square, he suffered a number of suffocating fits.

One night he had an appalling vision. As he lay in bed he was wakened out of his sleep by the noise of a bird fluttering at the window. The room then seemed to fill with light, and he saw in the recess of the window a female figure robed in white. It was an apparition of the mother of the girl he had seduced, Mrs Amphlett, who had recently died.

Badly shocked, he called out, "What do you want?"

"I have come to warn you of your death," the apparition replied.

She pointed to the clock on the mantelpiece, which showed the time as midnight, and said solemnly that on this hour, three days later, he would die. Then she vanished, leaving the room again in darkness.

Lord Lyttelton immediately called his manservant, and in a sweat of fear, told the astonished man in detail what he had just seen. In the morning he was noticeably agitated, and to several people who asked the cause, he similarly described the visit of the apparition.

By the third day—Saturday, November 27th—Lyttelton was seen to have grown very thoughtful, and although the matter was obviously still weighing heavily on his mind he attempted to make light of it. At breakfast, to which he entertained several guests, including the other two sisters with whom his name had been linked, he remarked that he felt very well and, "If I live over tonight I shall have jockeyed the ghost, for this is the third day." Afterwards, while out walking with a cousin who was also a guest, they passed a graveyard, and, running his eye over the gravestones, Lyttelton suddenly commented on the number of "vulgar fellows" who died at thirty-five, his own age, adding, "But you and I, who are gentlemen, shall live to a good old age."

Later that morning Lord Lyttelton and his guests set out for his country house, Pitt Place, near Epsom, where they had not long arrived before he had another of his suffocating fits. But he was well enough to dine with his friends at five o'clock, and again he joked about the apparition, asking why they looked so grave and assuring them, "I am as well as ever I was in my life, and I shall bilk the ghost!"

By a friendly trick, the clocks throughout the house, and the watches of the whole party, including Lyttelton's own, were put forward half an hour. The evening passed agreeably, no further mention being made of the ghostly warning, and Lyttelton seemed to have recovered his usual gaiety. Around eleven o'clock he retired to his bedroom, and soon afterwards undressed and got into bed.

His uneasiness had now very plainly returned. He kept looking at his watch, and ordered his valet to close the curtains at the foot of his bed. When it was within a minute or two of midnight by his watch he asked to look at the valet's watch, and seemed pleased to find that it nearly kept time with his own. He then put both watches to his ear, to satisfy himself that they were going. As the minutes ticked by he waited, and when it had gone a quarter-past twelve by the watches, he said in a matter-of-fact voice to his valet, "This mysterious lady is not a true prophetess, I find."

When it was close to twelve-thirty—the real hour of midnight—he told his valet, "Come, I'll wait no longer. Get me my medicine. I'll take it and try to sleep."

The valet duly brought his lordship's dose of rhubarb and mint-water, which, not having a spoon at hand, he began to stir with a toothpick. Lyttelton, seeing this, scolded him and sent him away for a teaspoon. The valet returned after a minute or two with a spoon to find Lyttelton in a fit, with his chin, because of the elevation of the pillow, resting hard on his neck. Instead of trying to relieve him the valet ran for help, and when he returned with an alarmed party of guests, Lord Lyttelton was dead.

Among the company at Pitt Place earlier that day was Miles Peter Andrews, a close friend of Lord Lyttelton. Andrews, having business at the Dartford powder-mills, some thirty miles away, in which he was a partner, left Pitt Place early, though not before he was satisfied that his friend was restored to his usual good spirits. Andrews had given such little thought to the "ghostly warning" that he did not even remember the time it was predicted the event would take place. He had been half an hour in bed at the house of his partner at the mills, when suddenly the curtains at the foot of the bed were pulled open to disclose Lord Lyttelton standing there, dressed in nightclothes and nightcap.

Andrews, bewildered at Lyttelton's unexpected appearance, looked at him scarcely believing his eyes. Then, recovering, he began to reproach the peer for coming down to Dartford Mills without warning, as there was no accommodation for him. "However," said Andrews, "I'll get up and see what can be done." He turned to the other side of the bed and rang the bell.

On turning back he found that Lyttelton had left the room. When his servant came in, he asked, "Where is Lord Lyttelton?" The puzzled servant replied that he had not seen anything of his lordship since they had left Pitt Place earlier that day.

"You fool!" said Andrews angrily. "He was here this very moment at my bedside."

The servant, however, persisted that it was not possible. Andrews, convinced now that Lyttelton must be up to some trickery, dressed himself and with the servants searched every part of the house and garden, but no Lord Lyttelton could be found.

Still Andrews believed that Lyttelton had played a trick on him, until at four o'clock on that same day, a message arrived informing him of the peer's death, and the circumstances of it. It was plain now that the figure he had seen at the foot of the bed could not have been of flesh and blood. The shock of this was so great that he fell into a dead faint.

Lord Lyttelton's death, on November 27th, 1779, was attributed to a fit. There was no post-mortem examination of his body, which lay in state for some days at Hill Street before burial. Throughout the years since many attempts have been made to explain away the whole uncanny story, even to a suggestion that Lyttelton took poison, and invented the story of the ghostly warning to deceive his

friends. However, though accounts of the coming of the apparition
have differed a little in the retelling (and also gathered some embellishments along the way) they agree in all essential particulars.
The family, and Lyttelton's many friends, who heard the story personally from him, never doubted it in the least. Nor could any of the
circumstantial evidence be broken, or the testimony of immediate
witnesses, including the valet who was present with Lyttelton in the
last hours of his life. Also beyond doubt was the story of Mr
Andrews, always told by him "reluctantly and with an evidently
solemn conviction of the truth". This friend of Lyttelton's, after his
dreadful shock, "was not his own man again for three years".

In 1780, the year following her son's death, there hung in a prominent position in the drawing-room of the Dowager Lady Lyttelton, at her house in Portugal Street, Grosvenor Square, a picture
she herself executed. It showed a bird, a dove, at a window, while
a woman in white stood at the foot of the bed giving warning to
Lord Lyttelton of his coming death. Every part of the picture was
faithfully designed by the dowager after the description given by
her son's valet, to whom he had told all the circumstances of his
grim night visitor immediately after the ghost had appeared.

THE GHOST OF SARAH THORNE

On a July day in 1874 the rebuilt Theatre Royal, Margate, opened its doors under the new management of a woman. She was Sarah Thorne, a well known actress in her thirties, who gave the century-old theatre a busy and colourful new lease of life. She had been, as *The Times* later observed, "a useful member of various companies, her talents being rather of the 'sound' than the brilliant order". For some time on assuming the management she took leading parts in plays presented at the Theatre Royal, but she then found the ideal outlet for her talents in setting up a training school for young would-be actors and actresses.

Sarah Thorne reigned at the theatre for twenty years, living for much of this time just across the square in a home built by Nelson for Lady Hamilton. Her school of acting became famous. She put her pupils through an intensive course of tuition and practice on the old "stock system" principle, also sending out companies on tour throughout the southern counties. From her school came many leading actors and actresses of later years, among them the Vanbrugh sisters, Irene and Violet, George Arliss and his wife, and Sir Seymour Hicks and his wife.

The late Dame Irene Vanbrugh, who made her debut at the Theatre Royal at the age of fifteen, recalled, "What a teacher Sarah Thorne was. She was not a good actress and her appearance did not help her, but the ability to teach others—that was a real gift."

Sarah died tragically on February 27, 1899 from a severe attack of influenza, just as leading theatre personalities were about to celebrate her stage jubilee with a special performance at the St James's Theatre, London. She died, aged 62, at her home in Chatham, where in later years she had also acquired the lease of the Chatham Opera House; but her heart remained in Margate. When dying she was heard to declare, "So long as the Theatre Royal is there, I shall be there."

During the following years there were a number of strange incidents at the theatre which led some people to believe that

Sarah had indeed kept her vow and returned to haunt the place she loved. The witnesses of various unaccountable noises and, from time to time, a "filmy form", included theatre staff, actors, and Sarah Thorne's son (she was married to Mr Thomas MacKnight, a journalist). He told several people of his seeing the wraith of his mother, among them N. V. Norman, who in the 1930s recalled: "I used to send companies to Margate and play there a great deal, and I remember Mr MacKnight emphatically telling me that he had many times seen the ghost of his mother. My wife (Miss Beatrice Withers) who as a young girl was a pupil of Sarah Thorne, has heard Mr MacKnight say the same thing."

That there should be such firm evidence about the existence of Sarah's ghost was doubly surprising because the theatre had already received the attentions of one ghostly figure. This was believed to be the spirit of a demented actor of the last century, who, on being summarily dismissed, bought himself a box for the next night's performance and during the course of the play leapt from the box to the orchestra pit, breaking his neck. After the turn of the century this actor's ghost was seen to appear sitting motionless in the box on so many occasions that the management eventually had to withdraw it from sale and leave it always curtained. Even then the actor's apparition was seen to continue to draw aside the curtains during a performance, one of the many witnesses of this phenomenon being the late W. J. Macqueen-Pope, the theatre historian. The haunting ceased when the boxes were finally bricked up as part of new fire precautions in the theatre, when an escape tower with spiral staircase was built at that side of the stage; but this work was only done in recent years.

In the 1920s and early 1930s, however, Sarah Thorne's ghost provided the more poignant haunting at the theatre, though few people at the time cared to speak openly about it, which was why in April, 1934 when Mr Caspar Middleton took over the lease of the Theatre Royal, he knew nothing at all of its ghostly background. He was, in any case, strongly sceptical of such matters. Yet within weeks he had seen the ghost, not once but three times. This was his later testimony:

"Twice on coming out of the circle buffet some time after the performance I saw it walk though the doorway from the stairs leading to the boxes and gallery on one side, and go slowly round the back of the circle and disappear through a wall on the other side. At one time there was an opening in this wall with stairs leading down to the stage, and I am told that Sarah Thorne had a small office on the side of the stage which could be approached from these stairs.

"On one occasion the ghost passed so close that I could almost have reached it with my hand. On another night I was standing in the circle, when I saw it by the door in the stalls leading to the boxes."

The ghost, according to Mr Middleton, wore clothes similar to the accepted sleep-walking dress of the stage Lady Macbeth—bluish-grey draperies, flowing and transparent. He did not immediately say anything about what he had seen but asked a few patrons of the theatre about its history, and made inquiries among several old residents of Margate. Even when he had established that the threatre was strongly believed to be haunted, he kept silent. What finally made the whole affair public was the alarming experience of two unsuspecting actresses very shortly afterwards.

On the night of August 22, 1934 members of the theatre's new repertory company were rehearsing at midnight for their opening performance of "The Naughty Lady", and as the stage was laid out for use by the company appearing that week, the rehearsal was being held in the circle buffet. One of the actresses, Miss Peggy Ford-Carrington, left the buffet and stood under a small gaslight at the side of the circle, reading her part. The rest of the theatre was in darkness, with the fireproof curtain down on the silent stage. In her own words: "Suddenly I was startled by a gentle moan or cry which broke the stillness, and glancing up I saw something leaning over the box on the other side, waving its arms about. It was terrifying and I could not stop myself from screaming. Chic (Miss Chic Elliott, another actress) came rushing out, and immediately she saw it she fainted. I could not take my eyes off it. . . ."

Next out of the buffet on hearing the scream was Mr Middleton. "I immediately looked across the theatre, and, in the circle box, saw something swaying and waving over the edge. Despite what I had previously seen I tried to think it was some practical joke, yet I could not understand how anyone could have entered the place to carry it out, and the door to the stage itself was locked. I immediately ran round the circle, through the door from which I had previously seen the ghost appear, and into the box. No one was there and nothing had been disturbed."

While Mr Middleton was running round to the box Miss Ford-Carrington was held transfixed by the apparition—a bluish-grey transparent figure of a woman—and to her continued amazement saw it gradually rise into the air over the front of the box and disappear into the theatre roof.

Now that the haunting was made public other evidence in support was forthcoming, and it seemed clear that the ghost's practice was to make a tour of the circle, just as Sarah Thorne had done after every evening performance, disappearing at the spot where her office had been. Investigators who held a night's vigil, however, saw nothing.

There was an unexpected development when Sister E. Thorne of Harrow, a niece of Sarah Thorne, on hearing of the renewed ghostly activity at the Theatre Royal called and told the lessee that it might not, after all, be her famous aunt who was responsible for the haunting. Many people had believed in the ghost as far back as the 1890s, said Sister Thorne, and Sarah herself had often described how she encountered a supernatural figure wearing a grey habit, in a vault beneath the theatre. The vault, formed by a subterranean passage which then ran under the street, was believed to date from a Catholic retreat that stood on the site long before the theatre was built. Sister Thorne said that her aunt, using this passageway one day, came face to face with the apparition and promptly fainted, lying helpless in the vault for some three or four hours before being found.

So this posed the question, *was* the apparition recently seen that of Sarah Thorne? Wearing, perhaps, the dress she had used when playing Lady Macbeth? Or was it the figure the actress herself had seen, gowned in a blue-grey costume like that of a nun? The evidence was not at all conclusive.

During the following years there were more reports of inexplicable happenings at the theatre; mainly strange noises and half-seen ghostly shapes. The ghosts remained with the theatre through a chequered career which saw it used for repertory. twice-nightly revue, wrestling, and even as a cinema. The theatre closed during World War II when badly damaged by a bomb that fell nearby. In 1948, the year of its reopening—and the year in which Dame Irene Vanbrugh, celebrating her diamond jubilee on the stage, returned to tread the boards where her apprenticeship had begun—manifestations were seen again. Late one night just before the reopening in July, phenomena occurred of which the chief features were the prolonged screams of a terrified woman and the sound of footsteps hurrying across the empty stage. Mr Robert G. Butler, the theatre's managing director, and no fewer than thirteen other people testified to this weird occurrence.

Another phenomenon reported at the theatre was a mysterious orange ball of light. This, first seen in the auditorium and scarcely bigger than a marble, travelled over the footlights and across the stage, growing to the size of a football before disappearing through the passage to the stage door.

Later, in 1954, two frightened workmen who stayed on late one night doing repairs at the theatre, said that just as they were preparing to leave they heard, in the circle overhead, the sound of agitated pacing. The ghost, however, was not visible. Early the following year the assistant stage manager told of the theatre's heavy front doors being unbolted twice in the early hours, and of the foyer lights blazing on hours after they had been put out. There was, he said, a general feeling of eeriness about the place. The caretaker at the time supported this, adding that frequently after turning out the gaslights backstage he found them on again some time later. Often, he said, the sensation of uneasiness in the theatre at night was almost overwhelming.

So the theatre hauntings persisted through several changes of management into the 1960s, when, after a period of quiet, the ghost or ghosts became suddenly very active once more.

In January, 1966 Mr Alfred Tanner, who was not a local man and knew nothing about the theatre's history, undertook to paint the auditorium for the lessee, Mr Harry Jacobs. He began work at 10 pm. on a Sunday night, working through alone in the theatre till 6.30 am., and several times during the night thought he heard "coughing and whispering". Puzzled, he searched the building but could find nothing to account for the noises. The following night, as he later told the *Isle of Thanet Gazette:* "At about 1.30 am. I heard the booking office door slam. When I investigated the door was wide open. A few minutes later I heard a backstage door slam heavily. I went to look and found it was closed and bolted, as it was when I started work."

Then, as he was standing by the entrance to the auditorium, there suddenly came into his startled view what seemed to be a disembodied female head.

"It came round the curtains on the left of the stage. It was just a head and neck, with a lot of frizzy hair, two slits for eyes and a thin, receding chin. It was the head and shoulders of a woman. I watched it for a few seconds moving across the stage before it disappeared."

His eyes were then drawn to another door of the auditorium, where a set of heavy curtains had been lifted clear of the wall and folded on a large semi-circular wooden pelmet.

"I saw the curtains lift up and then slowly drop down as if someone was lifting them down from the pelmet. I went to the door, and as I lifted the curtains I felt an odd sensation at the back of my neck, as if someone was staring at me, and my hair started to bristle."

It was then that Mr Tanner decided he had had enough. He

locked up the theatre and went home, but was so shaken that he could not sleep and sat up the rest of the night reading.

On returning to the theatre next morning Mr Tanner, as he was going upstairs with a colleague, stopped suddenly by an old photograph of Sarah Thorne dressed in her sleep-walking costume for "Macbeth".

"That's the face I saw last night!" he exclaimed.

Mr Tanner refused on any account to work alone again in the theatre at night. Mr Jacobs, the lessee, told me, "I did not know what to make of his story; after all, one might expect a very old theatre to be full of noises at night. The main thing was that the painting should be finished, so I suggested to Mr Tanner that he took someone with him for company on the third night, and he finally agreed to this."

The man who accompanied Mr Tanner was Mr Lawrence John Rodgers, of Margate, who, like his companion, knew nothing of the theatre's ghostly history. Mr Rodgers afterwards described how, when they were both in the auditorium, strange noises culminated in "a terrific crash, as if something very heavy had been thrown into the stalls from the balcony. We went to the spot where the noise came from but could find nothing."

At this Mr Tanner gave up and went home, but Mr Rodgers went along to the police station to report the strange happenings, with the result that at 2 am. eight policemen searched the theatre from top to bottom but failed to find anything that would account for the noises.

Mr Tanner, summing up his alarming three nights in the building, told the *Isle of Thanet Gazette:* "All the time I was in the theatre I experienced the same feeling I had during the war when I used to go out on night patrol in the desert in the Eighth Army—a feeling that someone or something was always behind you and that something awful was going to happen."

An interested reader of the *Gazette* report of these most recent hauntings, published on the morning of Friday, January 28, 1966 was Mr James H. Chell, a Margate teacher who had for some years studied psychical research. Mr Chell immediately sought and was given permission to keep observation in the theatre that night. He duly arrived at the theatre with his dog to be told that there was now another man who wished to keep a vigil—would he agree to them keeping watch in company? Mr Chell agreed to this, and so he and Mr Thomas Redshaw of Margate, who had not met before, prepared for their vigil. After the bingo sessions were finished for the day the two men searched the building thoroughly to make sure that no practical jokers had been at work. Then, after ensuring that all external doors were secure and not capable of being opened from the outside, they turned off the electric lights at the big switches situated on a high platform behind the stage back-cloth. This left the theatre in darkness except for two small gas-lights, one on each side of the auditorium.

Mr Chell now gives his concise record of what followed:

"We began our vigil at about 12.30 am. After half an hour there was a sudden coldness and a noise sounded behind the stage back-cloth, as though several large pieces of furniture were being dragged about. My dog, which had been silent till then, began to howl; her hackles went up, something which I had not seen in her before, nor have I since.

"I investigated the noises but found nothing at all behind the backcloth; no furniture, boxes or anything. Returning to my seat I began to eat the sandwiches I had brought. At about 1.35 it again went intensely cold; then there was a loud explosion and all the lights in the auditorium came on. I immediately went with Mr Redshaw to the platform behind the backcloth, climbed the ladder and saw that the heavy iron-clad light switches, which we had switched off, were now back in the 'ON' position. Human hands could never have switched on *all three* of these switches simultaneously; even were a man to find the strength to do so, he would need three hands to operate them all at once.

"We searched all through the building again, going up the spiral stairs ascending a tower at the side of the stage where formerly three boxes existed. At the top of this staircase we noticed a smell as though there were dead leaves present, and after a few minutes this smell changed to one of roses. Again we experienced a wave of intense cold, which despite the fact that the building was centrally-heated was very unpleasant. As before, the cold disappeared with the passing of the event.

"At about 2.30 there was another explosion and all the lights went out again. On re-inspecting the light switches I found they had now been returned to the 'OFF' position. Returning to my seat in the front stalls I began to make a note of what had occurred and was suddenly aware of the ticking of a large clock, which lasted for exactly four minutes. I knew there was no clock in the theatre and later found that none had existed in the build-ing within living memory.

"Nothing more occurred until about 3.15, when I became aware of a large patch on the wall where, years ago, there had existed a box, which was now bricked in and the wall painted blue. The patch, which was dirty brown in colour, moved slightly, then disappeared. I thought it might be my imagination at first, but when the 'thing' appeared a second time I knew it to be a fact. It remained for about 30 seconds and then vanished.

"During all this time there were various shufflings and scratchings in the theatre but I knew it was hopeless to try and track the source of them.

"At 3.55 I thought I would try and have a nap, as our vigil had been rather a strain, so I took a blanket from the organ in front of the stage, put my bag under my head and settled down. It was then two minutes to four. I awoke suddenly to find Mr Redshaw absent. Hearing a noise from the first gallery, I looked up and saw him trying to light a match and walking slowly forward. On seeing I had woken up he came down and asked if I had heard a bump. I said I had not, but that something had woken me. It was three minutes past four; I had fallen asleep immediately and slept for only five minutes.

"Mr Redshaw asked for my torch, but as I handed it to him I thought I could 'feel' something in the vicinity of the first gallery, so I turned and shone the torch towards the gallery, where, in the beam of light, I saw the same brown shape as before. It hung around near one of the slim pillars supporting the gallery and then glided towards the next pillar where it suddenly disappeared, again accompanied by the wave of intense cold. We searched the building together, and when we came to the spot where we had seen the brown shape, the place felt evil.

"It was now about 4.30 and we decided to leave. We locked the door quietly as we left and walked up the road towards the main road. We had been walking for some time, well out of earshot of the theatre, when we were suddenly caught up with by a policeman on a motor-cycle. He asked us our business and, when we told him, what time we had left the theatre. He then said that only fifteen minutes ago someone living near the theatre had heard a loud explosion coming from the building and telephoned the police station. We had heard nothing, so the explosion must have taken place *after* we had left the building."

The ghost of Sarah Thorne, it appears, is scarcely alone in her beloved theatre.

THE RESTLESS GHOSTS OF LADYE PLACE

When he retired from the Royal Engineers in his late thirties, wealthy Lieutenant-Colonel Charles Noel Rivers-Moore looked around for a small country estate on which he and his wife could settle. He eventually found the ideal place at Hurley, East Berkshire, in the valley of the River Thames; Ladye Place, an historic building standing in twenty acres of land.

The year was 1924. The grey pile of Ladye Place, girdled by its silver moat, rose through the trees at the end of a quiet lane set well away from the roads around Maidenhead. Though the big house was scarcely a century old, its foundations and other buildings and remains close by went back many hundreds of years.

Colonel Rivers-Moore had in fact come as near as any man to owning a piece of English history, for Ladye Place had begun life shortly after the Norman Conquest as a small Benedictine priory. The Colonel had of course learned something of its background; a handful of histories of Hurley and Ladye Place had been written in recent years, and the previous owner had even put up some explanatory tablets on different parts of the buildings, and published a little guidebook. On moving in the Colonel and his wife, Barbara, keenly read up every account of the place they could lay hands on, and this same year the Colonel, who had developed a great interest in archaeology, joined the Berkshire Archaeological Society.

Ghosts? Yes, there were many hints locally of phantoms reputed to haunt Ladye Place, but the Colonel was not concerned with these. His studies over the next few years were conducted exclusively into the historical past of the fascinating old property he had acquired.

Ladye Place, when he bought it, could be summarized in the dull language of the estate agent as comprising twenty acres of land with long river and road frontages, and containing a main residence with thirteen bedrooms, five bathrooms and four reception rooms; also two secondary residences and two cottages. But this bald description took no account of the living history there which included, among several ancient buildings and ruins, the old parish church of Hurley.

The Colonel found in his enthusiastic researches that the Domesday Book contained first mention of the estate, referring to a one-time Hurley Manor which had belonged to Easgar, Master of the Horse to King Edward the Confessor. A church had existed on the site even then. On the Norman Conquest, Easgar's lands were given to Geoffrey de Mandeville, who founded St Mary's Priory there in 1086. Some of the existing buildings, and most of the church, dated from this time.

After Henry VIII swept the monks out of St Mary's Priory in the dissolution of 1536 the land eventually was bought by the Lovelace family. In 1600 Richard Lovelace, first Baron of Hurley, built a great Elizabethan mansion—Ladye Place—on the site of the Priory, converting the monks' refectory or dining hall into stables and a hayloft for his horses. This mansion stood for more than two centuries, falling eventually into such decay that in 1837 it was demolished, and the present house built in its place.

Colonel Rivers-Moore was eager to commence digging right away in an attempt to uncover the various mysteries of Ladye Place, which, although written about, was archaeologically almost completely untouched. He hoped to disclose the early foundation work and chart the ancient buildings as they had once existed: also to retrieve whatever archaeological treasures may lie buried under the rebuildings and restorations of centuries. He was particularly intrigued by a charter dated the 15th year of Richard II, which mentioned that Editha, sister of Edward the Confessor, was buried there. One of his cherished objects was to try and find the grave of Editha, for it was her ghost—the Grey Lady—that was locally claimed to haunt Ladye Place, along with the spectre of William Rufus, who was once known there, and the sombre spirits of the monks who had prayed in the cloisters of the old Priory.

But where was he to begin excavations? The buildings of Ladye Place were grouped round a courtyard partly occupying the site of the original cloister yard. On the south side of this quadrangle was the old parish church, and on the north side the converted refectory and a large Tudor barn, to which had recently been added a garage and schoolroom.

On the eastern side of the courtyard was a building which had always been known as "Paradise". This was a secondary house believed to have been rebuilt in the 17th century on the actual cloister foundations. Its upper windows at each end, now blocked, had once looked respectively into the church and the refectory.

Detached from this group of buildings and shaded by a great cedar said to have been planted in the days of the Crusaders, was the remaining portion of the old crypt which Lovelace had used as the cellar of his mansion, while other buildings still standing included a tythe barn and dove-cote both erected in 1306.

The present main residence of Ladye Place had been rebuilt round the old farmhouse of the Priory, and parts of it still dated from the 16th century. One stroke of luck for the Colonel was the advent of an exceptionally dry season, which caused the foundation outline of Lovelace's vanished mansion to appear through the turf of the lawn and allow him accurately to trace its dimensions. Between 1924 and 1930, however, being unsure of where to start, he attempted no serious excavation beyond digging a trial pit against a corner of the church, to see if the walls had once extended at that point. It was his first move in the search for Editha's grave. But three feet down he struck a flat floor or pavement of hard chalk, and gave up. What made it so much harder to find the early walls of the church was that at the last restoration both the ground around the church and the church floor itself had been raised some three feet because of flood trouble.

It was shortly after this abortive effort that the slowly awakening ghosts of Ladye Place seemed to take a hand.

The strange sequence of events began in the early spring of 1930, when Mrs Rivers-Moore's brother, a doctor on the staff of a London hospital, came to stay. One day he told them he had had a surprising "vision" in which he seemed to be in the dining room of "Paradise", talking to a monk dressed in a brown habit. He remarked to the monk that it was a pity about the fireplace in the room as it was not in keeping with the house. The monk, by way of reply, said three times, "Sweep it away," making a sweeping motion with his hand—and to the doctor the fireplace then seemed to fade away, revealing behind it a semi-circular fireplace surmounted by a big oak beam.

Next day, out of curiosity Mrs Rivers-Moore asked some builders who were then working in the house to remove the offending fireplace. To everyone's astonishment, when they took it out there was disclosed behind it a much older fireplace exactly as described by her brother.

From this time on the ghostly incidents at Ladye Place rapidly gathered momentum. A woman visitor who stayed at "Paradise" had some strange experiences in the house which, she felt sure, indicated the presence of unseen forces. She decided to take some instruction on psychic research in London, and on returning to "Paradise" tried experimenting with automatic writing. One day she came to the Colonel and his wife with a paper on which was written "Empty well". As they did not know of any well about the place, however, this puzzling "message" meant little. Then, shortly afterwards, their guest brought another scrawl produced by automatic writing which seemed to be a drawing of a well and three arches of the old Priory.

Feeling that there might be something to this allegedly psychic phenomena after all, Colonel Rivers-Moore and his wife, together with a few friends, decided to try a table-rapping seance in the hope of gaining information. The seance was conducted with perfectly open mind and with no medium or spiritualist present, the simple procedure being that the table should give one rap for "No" and two raps for "Yes". They found the table very quickly responsive and were soon obtaining answers from a spirit or entity who gave his name as "King" and said he had lived 400 years ago. The sitters asked "King" about the mysterious well, and he replied that there was such a well 13 feet south from a corner of the church and six feet east, and that it was filled with rubbish.

The Colonel, after six somewhat impatient years at Ladye Place, was willing to take a gamble, and so on April 23, 1930 he began digging where instructed; but all he found was the remains of an old flint wall. Another table-rapping seance was held and "King" then told him that he should dig two feet farther south. He did this, and then found the well exactly as described, filled with building debris. After clearing it for some depth he struck water and work was suspended, though he had now, under guidance, uncovered the foundation of the Tudor mansion and unearthed a few relics including the foot of a skeleton.

There were more table-rapping seances and Mrs Rivers-Moore, seeking a special test for "King", asked the spirit, "Can you tell me something we can find in the morning that nobody knows is there?" The answer came "Look for the rust line." Next morning her husband quite easily found a rust line just under the surface of the ground where they had been excavating, at the precise spot indicated.

The messages received by table-rapping continued to be so explicit that relics were unearthed within a few hours of a seance. The well, two old fireplaces and hidden foundations were all discovered by this means. The Colonel pressed on for two years with the work, amassing little treasures as he went: 13th-century floor tiling from the church and Priory, old church carvings, pottery, 17th-century smoking pipes, a skull and other remains. He began a unique museum in the old musicians' gallery of the ancient refectory.

The Colonel also rediscovered and cleared out a "secret passage" leading from the moat to the cellar of Ladye Place. The cellar had been constructed over the monks' burial ground, and skeletons had since been dug from its floor. It was here in this cellar, in the bloodless revolution of 1688, that the Whig plotters against James II had met at the request of the third Lord Lovelace and decided to invite William of Orange to the English throne. Through the "secret passage" from the moat, which was in fact a sewer to the mansion, had crept the revolutionaries gathering for their midnight conferences.

So far as the Colonel and his friends were able to make out at the seances, "King", who had lived at the time of the dissolution of the monastery, had stolen some jewels and thrown them down the well which he had directed them to find. The Colonel, however, having by the spring of 1932 got down to river level, working up to his waist in water in the old well, had little hopes of ever probing the bottom of it, even though the table-messages urged that it should be emptied so that the spirit of the Grey Lady could find peace. There had also been conversations, meantime, with a monk named Edipus, who had lived about the year 1200. In fact the phantoms of Ladye Place had really become alive, for several guests who stayed there, some among them the strongest of sceptics, confessed to psychic experiences including the sight of spectral monks. All this made the Colonel and his wife more inclined to give credit to the reports of people who, in the past, had claimed to have seen the apparitions of William Rufus and the Grey Lady.

In April, 1932 Colonel Rivers-Moore and his wife, at the invitation of friends, described at a drawing-room meeting in Reading the remarkable psychic guidance they had been given in their excavations so far at Ladye Place. The Colonel, not for the first time, stressed, "We have had no so-called mediums or spiritualists at all, but have conducted proceedings entirely on our own. We are not spiritualists but have quite open minds on the subject." A former vicar of Hurley who was present at the little gathering said there must be some great good to come out of what was happening and there was no knowing what would be the end of it.

Indeed, as the years went by there seemed no end. Throughout the 1930s the Colonel, freely enlisting the help of friends, fellow members of the Berkshire Archaeological Society and others interested to help dig or research and classify his mounting collection, pursued his investigations of the old Priory with singular dedication, having a devoted helpmate in his wife. A second old well was discovered, though after much effort to drain the water from both wells nothing of interest was found. No jewels. The wells had obviously been cleaned out when Lovelace's mansion was built. Editha's grave, too, upon the discovery of which the Colonel had placed so much hope, eluded him. He had vowed he would search for the Grey Lady's resting place if it meant ruining the grounds, but although many graves were struck and some mixed bones and other grisly relics uncovered, all that came to light that could possibly be connected with Editha was a base of hard core surrounded by traces of tile flooring, in the centre of the north transept of the church. This may well have formed the base of some early shrine.

The Colonel did succeed in laying bare other secrets of the Priory. He uncovered almost all the foundations of the monastic church, chapter house, part of the cloister, and a range of buildings north of the church. His discoveries brought such new light on the buildings that he had to take down some of the tablets put up by the previous occupier as they were so obviously incorrect. The contents of his museum swelled. And during all this work the ghosts of Ladye Place grew steadily more restless.

A woman who for a time occupied "Paradise" with her child became convinced there was an evil influence in the building. She was advised to sprinkle holy water in the rooms. But just as she was about to do this, the warning apparition of a monk appeared to her and said, "You must not do it—you will stop my work." A medium was brought in, but as soon as he went into a trance the monk took possession and became violent, trying to attack the sitters. Through the medium the monk declared that he had practised black magic, and ever since had tried to keep his persecutors out of the house. He was assured by the circle that he had been forgiven by his Father Prior, whereupon he promised not to cause further difficulty in the house.

Other shades, however, began to appear. Spectral monks of the old Priory were seen by friends and visitors to Ladye Place many dozens of times during the 1930s. Commonly a visitor walking in the cloisters in the early evening would see a man dressed in monk's habit, with arms crossed, pass him and then vanish before his eyes. Colonel Rivers-Moore and his wife compiled a dossier of the weird happenings, each story being signed by the witnesses. The signatures included those of an architect, a doctor, and prosaic-minded officers of the Navy, Army and Air Force.

For nine years the Colonel and various helpers were busy digging at Ladye Place; he then finished the remaining work alone or with an occasional companion. In the 1940s, when he had been more than twenty years on the estate, he had wrested from it practically every archaeological secret—except the last resting place of the Grey Lady. In the spring of 1947 he took members of Berkshire Archaeological Society on a last excursion to Ladye Place, and in the autumn he put it up for auction, "A Small Country Estate of Great Historical Interest. . . ."

His work was there for all to see. The prospective buyer could walk the haunted grounds, peer into secret passages and climb the creaking stairs to look into the cloisters of the old monastery. He could, the *Maidenhead Advertiser* reported, walk "lawns full of mystery. On the one leading to the old monks' fish pond is the wooden lid of a vault. Lift it and you will see a skeleton. Buried near the crypt is the body of a man, accidentally disinterred, wearing the robes of a monastic order. Near him lies a local giant. Under the lawn is a subterranean passage approached through a trapdoor. The foundations of the chapel built in 1086 can be traced and you can walk on pieces of the original floor. There is a glass case round the foundations of the chapter house so that the historical features may be seen. A reconstruction of the old Priory is in the museum reached from the gallery in the magnificent refectory hall. . . ."

Museum, furniture and effects were all included in the sale, but Ladye Place did not reach its reserve price and was sold shortly afterwards in pieces; the cloisters, chapter house, monks' parlour and refectory together; the land for farming as a market garden; the mansion itself for conversion into three homes.

Colonel Rivers-Moore moved to Wargrave, Berkshire, where he remained for some years and joined in other local archaeological work. Following the death of his wife, and remarriage, he moved to Scotland, where he died at Elgin in 1965.

The restless ghosts of Ladye Place had quietened long before.

GO AWAY SAMUEL GREATREX

Widowed Mrs Kathleen Keogh noticed something strange about her Corporation-owned home in the Small Heath district of Birmingham, immediately she moved into it, in the summer of 1963. It was an old back-to-back house in Garrison Lane, set among rows of similar houses eventually to disappear under city clearance schemes, and had one bedroom, with an attic above. Mrs Keogh, on going up into the bedroom found it to be abnormally cold.

There was, however, little she could do about this, so she prepared the room for sleeping in with her five-year-old son in a double bed. Within a week she received a tremendous shock, awaking one night to hear an eerie noise like a man finding it difficult to breathe, and a voice saying "My God, my God. . . ". The ghostly sounds seemed to issue from the exact spot in the bed where she lay—*coming from and through herself.*

This experience so frightened her that she never slept upstairs again, using instead a bed settee downstairs, with her young son. But it was only the start of her ordeal. A mirror hung by a chain on the bedroom wall began to rattle at night; she constantly heard the chain rapping against the wall. Then came sounds of footsteps on the stairs, usually at night, and a series of uncanny knockings, both upstairs in the bedroom and downstairs in the living room. It was just as if someone was rapping sharply with the knuckles, mainly on the furniture.

Mrs Keogh had no belief in ghosts and had seldom even thought about them. She was a devout Catholic and had many religious ornaments about the house. She tried to make the best of her accommodation, working hard to make the little house comfortable, but the brooding atmosphere, the mysterious footsteps and the knockings persisted. On more than one occasion they so terrified her that she left the house at night and walked the streets with her son asleep in her arms; she was afraid to tell the neighbours about the noises in case they should think she was losing her mind.

One day she was visited by her sister from Bristol, who brought
with her a friend, Miss Roberts. Both women were concerned to
find Mrs Keogh obviously distressed, but she still did not reveal
what was troubling her; they were left with the impression that
she was frightened of something. Miss Roberts offered to stay and
keep her company for a few days, an offer which was very gladly
accepted.

Miss Roberts had been in the house for three days, with nothing
untoward happening, when Mrs Keogh went as usual to collect
her son from school at 3.30 in the afternoon. Mrs Keogh returned
to find her guest collapsed in the front room in a state of hysteria.
Eventually Miss Roberts was able to tell her what had occurred.
She said she suddenly heard footsteps coming down the stairs and
turned to the doorway where the stairs descended to the living
room, expecting the door to open; but it did not. She then felt the
room go strangely cold. She was close to the sideboard smoking a
cigarette, and to her horror became aware that the smoke from
the cigarette, instead of spiralling up in the normal way, kept down
to one level, *moving in a wavy line horizontally along the top of the sideboard*. She reached hurriedly for her coat, put it on and turned to
the front door, but as she tried to open the door there was a
sudden pressure on her shoulders like hands seeking to press her to
the floor. She struggled up and again tried to open the door, but
this time had the feeling of restraining hands round her ankles. At
this she collapsed completely, slumping to the floor near the front
door, which was how Mrs Keogh found her.

Miss Roberts went back to Bristol that same day.

The noises in Mrs Keogh's house continued all that summer and
into the winter. One night after midnight, when they were
particularly bad, she went in desperation to the public-house
directly opposite and knocked up the licensee, telling him that
there was "someone" in her house and she was afraid to stay in it.
The licensee found a policeman and together they went to the
house. The constable made a thorough search but found and
heard nothing; yet as soon as Mrs Keogh was alone again the
ominous knocking restarted.

Caught in a nightmare that seemed never-ending, Mrs Keogh
was now forced to tell others about the ghostly noises, and found
that her next-door neighbour, Mrs P. Butler, had also heard the
sound of the chain on the bedroom mirror being rattled. Mrs
Keogh finally sought the help of Birmingham psychical research
workers, and a seance was held in the house. At this, in the
presence of several witnesses, Mr A. T. Steadman, a medium from
Solihull, made contact with the ghost, which said it was that of

Samuel Greatrex, a man who had lived in Mrs Keogh's house in the 1920s. Speaking through the medium, "Greatrex" said he had been jailed for a knifing incident in the house, and had died at Dudley Road Hospital after being transferred there from Winson Green Prison, where he was serving his sentence. At a second seance held shortly afterwards "Greatrex" repeated the information about himself, and at a third seance his "voice" coming through Mr Steadman was tape-recorded and pictures taken of the medium in trance. Again "Greatrex" talked of the stabbing incident in April, 1927.

Mr Steadman told me, "I saw him so clearly that I was able to make a sketch of him. He was wearing a white robe and carried a knife in his hand. He said he had hidden it in the pantry of the house."

In describing his arrest "Greatrex" gave the name of the police inspector who dealt with him, an Inspector Dixon. He said he was taken to Small Heath police station, and when he got there the police were having their sandwiches. He also mentioned two priests who visited him in hospital. The hospital and prison records were later checked and the ghost's information found to be perfectly correct, as were all the names given at the seance. In addition a retired policeman, PC James, was found who was on duty the night Greatrex was arrested, and who remembered the incident well.

Why had Greatrex haunted Mrs Keogh and not any of the previous tenants of the house in Garrison Lane? Because, the medium found, Greatrex was a Catholic, and as Mrs Keogh was a devout member of the same faith and furnished her home with religious ornaments, it was this which had brought him back. Through the medium "Greatrex" told Mrs Keogh, or "Kate" as he referred to her, that he was sorry for what he had done and would try not to bother her in future.

Mrs Keogh, however, left the haunted house and refused to go back. For three months she lived at a Corporation hostel, until another suitable house was found for her at Upper Thomas Street, Aston, a short distance from her former home. This was early in 1964—almost a year from the start of the hauntings.

Mrs Keogh's first day at her new house was peaceful, but on the second day, to her utter despair the familiar knockings and footsteps on the stairs began all over again. There was also on one occasion a loud bang from the storage cupboard, and on looking inside she found that her son's rocking horse, which she had put there, had for no reason been thrown to one side. Appalled, she sent for the medium, and a seance was held in her new home. After this the widow removed from the house all her religious ornaments except a single plaster statue. But still the knocking on the furniture continued.

A further seance was held, and at this Mrs Keogh herself broke in and appealed to "Greatrex", saying, "Why are you making my life a misery? Go away—why don't you leave me alone?" The ghost's reply through the medium was "I'm sorry, Kate, but I like the atmosphere here." The voice added, however, that it did not want to make her unhappy and promised not to be a nuisance.

But the promise did not hold good. The knockings continued intermittently; as, I am told by Mrs Keogh, they still do. But there are no more violent noises and Samuel Greatrex knocks unheeded, for she just isn't frightened of the ghost any more.

THE MONKS OF ST DUNSTAN'S

In East Acton, London, the spire of St Dunstan's rises in an area of sudden near-quiet reached surprisingly on turning out of the heavy traffic stream of Western Avenue. Built of dull red brick, the big church stands solid in its grassy and leafy square of ground in Friar's Place Lane, closely flanked by modern semi-detached houses. The footpath leading back from the pavement to the church door continues on to give access from one road to another, and the church's stained glass windows are protected by wire guards against the stones of young vandals.

The scene was vastly different in the 1870s, when the church was built. Then, not far away was the stately mansion of Friar's Place, which, with its magnificent grounds, hothouses and fountains, was one of the showplaces of Middlesex. The mansion fell into decay at the turn of the century and was demolished; now an ice-cream plant stands on the site, renamed The Friary. A persistent local tradition says that in the Middle Ages the old Friar's Place estate, on the edge of which St Dunstan's church stands, formerly belonged to St Bartholomew's, Smithfield, and that a "cell" or outpost of the St Bartholomew's friars existed there. If this tradition holds true, and it seems to be historically well supported, then there seems little doubt as to the identity of the phantom visitors to St Dunstan's.

The strange story of the haunting of St Dunstan's begins one Sunday morning early in the 1930s, when the then curate, the Rev Philip Boustead, was walking home with the assistant organist after the service. Mr Boustead, a much liked elderly priest who had taken holy orders late in life, had then been curate at St Dunstan's for many years, and on this Sunday morning his companion casually remarked on the history of the church. Mr

Boustead appeared to be lost in thought for a short time. Then he said, very earnestly and impulsively, "I must tell you something. I cannot tell anyone else, because they will laugh at me. There is something strange about our church. I have seen things when I've been alone in there. Some of these old monks who used to live round here. No, no—I don't want to say any more, but I know there is something there. Now please don't tell anyone else what I have been saying. They'll think I'm mad".

His surprised companion never did divulge this conversation; not until this account came to be written. But as will be seen later, Mr Boustead did confide in at least one other person.

A few years afterwards, in the winter of 1937-38, there came news of hauntings in the neighbourhood; not at St Dunstan's, but at the northern edge of the old Friar's Place estate, scarely more than half a mile away. Here, at the junction of Horn Lane and Western Avenue, an old world building which had preserved its ancient air in a changing neighbourhood, was said to be troubled by the spectre of a monk. This former farmhouse, which had become St Gabriel's Vicarage, with its cell-like cellars, cobbled paths, and what was thought to be the remains of a medieval courtyard, was then up for sale as it was too big for the vicar's needs. The vicar, the Rev C. V. Camplin-Cogan, though himself highly sceptical about the haunting, admitted that people who stayed in the house had heard uncanny noises, and that these were supposed to be caused by the ghost of an old monk buried under a cobbled path just outside the house. The vicar's wife said that she had often heard noises like padded footsteps on the stairs and in the hall, but on going to look had seen nothing. Then the apparition had appeared. A bedroom in one of the older parts of the house had a marble floor—it was thought to have been used as an oratory—and a startled guest who slept in the room described to the vicar and his wife how he had seen the shadowy figure of a monk suddenly appear in it. The harmless spirit, it seemed, had returned to wander about its former home.

The haunting of St Gabriel's Vicarage was looked upon as a fleeting wonder, more arguments being raised over the actual age of some old parts of the building rather than over the ghost, though it was generally agreed that if the monks of long ago had not actually lived on the vicarage site they had certainly lived close by to it, on the old St Bartholomew's land.

Six years later, in December, 1944 a new vicar came to St Dunstan's. The Rev Hugh Harold Anton-Stephens, who was in his fifties, had held two long ministries in Cheshire and London, and in his younger days had served as an Army chaplain. He was a widower, his wife having died only that year. Mr Anton-Stephens had not been many months at St Dunstan's before, like the late Mr Boustead, he found there was something very strange about the church; but he kept his own counsel about this, until one day he chanced to hear of the recent haunting of St Gabriel's Vicarage. After checking back carefully on the circumstances of this, he decided it was time to make public his own extraordinary findings at St Dunstan's, and accepted an invitiation to write an article for the local newspaper, the *Acton Gazette*. The article was published in November, 1946, and in it, after noting "the familiar attitude of respectable scepticism" at the time of the vicarage haunting, and recalling that the ghostly figure seen was that of a monk, Mr Anton-Stephens revealed:

"About a dozen such monks can be seen on most evenings walking in procession up the centre aisle and into the chancel of St Dunstan's church. They wear golden brown habits and are hooded. Another monk attired in eucharistic vestments occasionally celebrates Mass in the memorial chapel. Four of us, unknown to each other, have witnessed these phenomena, from time to time. We are all truthful folk and it is impossible for four people to suffer from the same hallucination at the same time.

"More interesting is a solitary monk, wearing a violet hood, with whom we hold conversation.

"The procession of monks probably belonged in some past age to a religious foundation in the locality. They are attracted to the nearest consecrated building. Their deepest satisfaction is to repeat what was their greatest happiness during earth-existence.

"My violet-hooded friend belongs to a different class. He is a ministering spirit, sent to inspire and instruct. I am indebted to him, as to many others, for much help." This monk, said the vicar, had recently given him advice regarding confirmation classes at the church.

Mr Anton-Stephens, after firmly establishing the appearance of the apparitions, went on to suggest in his article how such spirits could inspire, encourage and guide those who saw them. He invited debate on the subject. He was, I am told by a parishioner of the time, far more concerned with the religious aspect of the phenomena than the ghostly one. This parishioner, who was one of those who saw the monks prior to the vicar's disclosures, tells me, "I saw them three or four times on evenings when a discussion group was being held in the vestry. Because of the warm weather the vestry door leading into the body of the church was kept open, and I saw exactly the same thing on each occasion: a body of monks in brown habits walking in procession up the central aisle towards and into the chancel. Seen out of the corner of the eye they were clear, but disappeared when looked at directly.

"I knew nothing of any previous sightings or of the history of the church. The experience had no emotional impact on me—they were just monks walking up the aisle. When I mentioned the occurrence to the vicar he was quite matter of fact about it."

Not so the newspapers which immediately took up the vicar's story. They were intrigued by the unusual spectacle of twelve ghosts appearing together, and found from the vicar that those who had seen the manifestations included another parishioner who helped as his secretary.

As dusk set in on the cold and rainy November evening following Mr Anton-Stephens' disclosures, a reporter of the *Daily Graphic* made his way to St Dunstan's with the declared intention of either confirming or disproving the curious story. The vigil, however, produced more than he had bargained for.

The reporter, Kenneth Mason, wrote that he took a seat up in the far left-hand corner of the darkened nave. He was tired and cold, and wet; and the silence of the deserted church and the heaviness of the atmosphere combined to force him into sleep. It was with the thought of the monks that he closed his eyes. What it was that wakened him he did not know, but as his eyes opened he saw the phantom monks, six of them, in grey gowns, hooded, with heads bowed.

"Slowly but happily they came towards me. I took my courage in both hands and barred their way. I faced them. Then quickly I had to turn and look back at them. They had passed right through me."

The monks, who were walking to the altar, passed through Mr Mason two-by-two—"slightly below my neck and to the left of my collar bone". The time was ten minutes past seven. As they walked on he was aware of a voice speaking to him.

"'Near here, 500 years ago,' the quiet voice told me, 'stood a monastery. We were its occupants. This is our past, this is our future.' Reverently the monks genuflected to the altar. Then at the back of the church a light snapped on. A human voice spoke and the spell was broken. From the tower came the mournful toll of the service bell. As its sound the monks vanished, while I was left, uncomfortable, wide awake, wondering.

"That is all. I cannot explain it; that is not my function. But these things I saw last night."

A footnote to this surprising report in the newspaper stated: "Kenneth Mason is a quiet, sober-minded, reliable reporter who has never dabbled in the occult. He was a lieutenant in the Royal Navy during the war."

Mr Mason held his vigil on a Friday night. During the weekend he returned to St Dunstan's with a photographer, in the hope of obtaining a picture of the manifestations. By the vestry door, one of the twelve ghost monks, plainly visible to Mr Anton-Stephens, his secretary, and a parishioner, stood looking on as the cameraman tried vainly to snap him; but Mr Mason saw nothing. He reported, "The distraction of children trying to peer inside, and the babel of people wanting to see the ghost, upset the atmosphere of my previous vigil."

St Dunstan's now became an attraction for many curious sightseers. The way in which the ghost monks had caught the popular imagination, to the exclusion of the more serious examination of such phenomena which he had tried to encourage, greatly disappointed the vicar. He wrote in the parish magazine a few weeks later:

"I was rather afraid that the popular Press would vulgarize the manifestations I described, but I was not prepared for the avalanche of letters which reached me from all parts of the world. Apparently every newspaper in the USA published a third-hand account. I was interested to hear from a former Sister here that the curate of her day (Mr Boustead) saw similar phenomena, and from the Psychic Research Society to the effect that they have had St Dunstan's monks on their records for over 12 years. They tell me that the manifestations occur in four-year cycles. As I suspected, more people have witnessed the phenomena than I knew."

The vicar continued: "May I repeat that, apart from the congregations, there are no spirits in the church. These visions are merely thought-pictures, televised by subtle rays, the nature of which are as yet unknown to scientists, but of course somewhere there is a personality responsible, consciously or unconsciously, for the vision. Please dissuade curious sightseers from visiting the church. The whole business is really very trivial and commonplace, and was only mentioned as an introduction to the more serious matter of my original article. . . ."

And he added, just by the way: "You may be interested to know that the 'radiation' was almost overpowering during the midnight Eucharist." (Christmas, 1946).

The vicar declined to allow more vigils in the church and did not refer to the monks again publicly for many months. When at last he did so the result only added to his disappointment and annoyance. In the January 1948 parish magazine he told how he had been telephoned by a most friendly newspaperman "who asked if he might trespass on my valuable time for a chat. He came, and we talked for hours on the most fascinating subject of psychic phenomena, especially as related to religion and philosophy. At times we ascended into the heights of metaphysics and fourth dimensional thought, and both thoroughly enjoyed ourselves. . . ." The reporter was shown over the church, and, said the vicar, "I made one stipulation about anything he might write, and he willingly agreed. It was that the subject should be kept a sacred subject and not written about lightly or sensationally. Some of you saw last Wednesday's paper and know how horribly the promise was broken. Not one so-called fact is true. There was no owl in the churchyard, no hand on a doorknob, no conversation with the organist, no mention about a 'violet monk' in church last Sunday, no stumbling, and no command from me to be quiet. There was no wind and no strange noises. . . ."

In spite of this unfortunate experience Mr Anton-Stephens went ahead and published in the parish magazine some weeks later an article on confirmation headed "Supernatural", which he said had been dictated to him by the violet-hooded monk. It concerned the Te Deum and suggested how it might be altruistically expressed.

The vicar said he believed the violet-hooded figure to be the spirit of a monk who died in the ninth century. The monk had continued to appear and converse with him generally through the medium of his secretary, who conversed with the monk while he wrote down the conversations. The monk, who had promised other contributions when he had time to take them down, always appeared at confirmation classes. The other monks had made no verbal communication, though they had now been seen by a number of parishioners.

There were also many sceptics among the parishioners; yet there were further incidents that could not be explained. One of those extremely sceptical about the ghosts was Mr F. H. Harris, who as a churchwarden and, during staffing troubles, a sort of voluntary verger, was much about the church with no one else present. Mr Harris often said in a scoffing way that he had been locked up in the church alone hundreds of times, but the only noises he had heard were those of the pigeons pattering and fluttering about in the belfry. But very shortly before his death in 1948, he one day said to his wife, quite out of the blue, "You know, the vicar is right after all. There *is* something in that church—I've seen the monk." He also spoke of the incident to a local shopkeeper with whom he had been friendly for many years.

There were other incidents. Mr R. N. G. Rowland, the St

Dunstan's organist, tells me: "One Sunday evening after service, I was leaning over the back pew side-by-side with another chorister, discussing music (not a word or thought about ghosts), and we were staring vaguely down the church towards the chancel. The only others in the church were the vicar, the verger and a warden, who were in the vicar's vestry. The nave was fairly well lit, the chancel in darkness. Quite suddenly, for no apparent reason, we stopped talking (we had been having an animated conversation) and stood silent gazing up into the chancel. I was aware of unseen activity there, and in a low voice said to my friend, 'Do you see anything?' He answered 'No, but there's something going on in the chancel.' I said, 'The vicar says that they hold services there.' 'Oh, the monks,' he replied. 'Yes, I believe it now. I didn't before, but I know they're there now.'"

On another occasion, with the vicar present, Mr Rowland was conducting choir practice with his assistant at the organ. "We were rehearsing Stanford's 'And I saw another angel' for All Saints' tide. In one of the more lush, full passages, looking a few bars ahead, I saw a typical 'horn cue' in the organ accompaniment. I said to myself, 'Oh, for an orchestra to do this full justice.' At that moment we reached the 'horn cue' and I distinctly heard the two horns—an effect quite impossible to reproduce on the organ—singing out their parts above everybody else. After we had finished the anthem I said to the vicar, 'Well, if it goes like that on Sunday, we shan't have anything to worry about.' 'Yes, very good,' he replied, 'but you might not have the orchestra with you on Sunday.' 'What orchestra?' I asked, deliberately. 'Come off it,' he said, 'you know as well as I do that you had a full spirit symphony orchestra out there in the chancel, playing along with you. Didn't you see them? I did.' 'No,' I replied, 'I did not see them.' 'Ah, but you knew they were there, didn't you?' he said. And somehow I could not deny it."

A former chorister tells me that Mr Anton-Stephens continued to take the church phenomena so much as a matter of course that in the years following, most of his parishioners became quite as cool about it all, the non-believers because of their distaste for the subject and the others because they were quite prepared to believe, from the vicar's casual statements made from time to time, that he did indeed "see ghosts". He explained the four-year cycle of the twelve monks very simply as a build-up of spirit-energy in the church over this period which then manifested itself in a fairly rapid series of appearances, and then lapsed to begin the build-up all over again. The violet-hooded monk, on the other hand, obeyed no definite cycle.

At all times during the remainder of his seventeen years' ministry at St Dunstan's the vicar was perfectly open about the church phenomena and the subject as a whole, whether joining in a discussion with the Over-21 Club and giving his views on the "spirit" causes and interpretation of some dreams, or by putting constant emphasis on spirit influences in life and on the ministry of angels. He did not, however, publish anything more ascribed to the violet-hooded monk, nor did he encourage further investigation of the church ghosts, because of the sensationalism which he so disliked. Retiring in 1961, he died shortly afterwards without publicly mentioning the subject again.

Do the monks of St Dunstan's still walk?

Mr Rowland, the organist, tells me of an incident late in 1966:

"I went into church one evening, about half an hour before the boys' choir practice, to play the organ. The church door was open to allow the boys to enter as they arrived. After playing for some ten minutes I felt a movement behind me, as if someone had stepped into the choir-stall and was standing behind my left shoulder. For a split second I assumed that one of the boys had arrived early, and I looked over my shoulder. There was no one to be seen—but there was certainly someone standing there. I had not stopped playing, and I just carried on, projecting a thought of 'Good evening—it's nice of you to come and listen to me.' I had no sense of fear or discomfort, rather a sense of elation. And until a boy came in a few minutes later, and broke the spell, I know that whoever was standing there was emanating a feeling of pleasure and approval, and wanting me to go on playing because he was enjoying it so much."

It was only the moment after setting down this account of the incident for me that Mr Rowland, to his own surprise, heard from a third party that two years earlier his son, an organ student, had had a similar experience when playing the organ alone in St Dunstan's.

"Avoiding leading questions, I asked my son about this at the next opportunity. He told me that on one occasion only, he sensed that someone was standing in the choir-stall immediately behind his left shoulder. However, not liking the experience he immediately switched on all the chancel lights—to that moment only the organ lights were on—and the feeling passed."

St Dunstan's, it would seem, might have its monks yet.

FOUR KNOCKS AND NO MORE

The King family moved into the Manor House, a typical old-fashioned farmhouse in Sussex, during the early autumn of 1933. In a few weeks they were happily installed in their new home, which stood in the charming hamlet of Denton, situated in a hollow of the Downs near Newhaven.

The house, which adjoined the churchyard and lay about 150 yards from the old rectory, was a sturdy building which had withstood the test of two centuries. A stone over the front door bore the inscription "P.M. Esq., 1724". It was a house of character, most of its fourteen rooms being reached by winding passages. One of its less attractive features was a dismal, dark and dungeon-like cellar, in which could be seen the doorway of a secret passage believed to lead under the churchyard to the church. This entrance, however, had long been bricked up, and the door of the cellar itself, reached through a room to the left of the front door, was kept bolted.

For the next seven weeks Mr and Mrs Sydney King, their twelve-year-old daughter, and Mr King's mother, Mrs Heasman, who was in her seventies, had perfect peace. Then, at intervals over about a week, Mrs Heasman heard strange, unaccountable noises in the house. Once there was such a loud bang from one room that she thought a wardrobe had fallen over, but on investigation this was found to be undisturbed.

The family were more puzzled than alarmed by these odd noises and it was not until a few days later, on a Sunday night in November, that the incident occurred which plunged them into terror.

On this night Mrs King was walking in a passageway leading to two bedrooms when she was suddenly confronted by a ghostly figure. Her shrieks brought her husband running to her. He grabbed a stick and beat at the apparition, but the stick only cut through it and struck the wall, breaking under the force. The ghost, which was of indeterminate appearance, melted away.

There then followed a series of terrifying thunderous knocks—one, two, three, four at a time. There were never more than four knocks and, repeated at intervals, they could be heard right through the house.

For the next three days the occupants of the Manor House were haunted by the eerie knocking, which played havoc with their nerves. It followed Mrs King to the scullery and other parts of the house to which she went alone, yet nearly always seemed to emanate from the centre of the house. The knocks seemed to follow a regular cycle, generally being heard at either twenty minutes to or twenty minutes after the hour, at intervals of five or six hours.

All the family heard the weird banging, as did two visitors to the house. Besides this, the cellar door started playing tricks, frequently being found open after it had been left firmly bolted.

The rector of Denton, the Rev E. Pinnix and his wife, were told of the ghost noises and on the Wednesday, with the family's nerves now stretched to breaking point, they stood in the house at different times and clearly heard the banging—one, two, three, four knocks at a time. Mrs Pinnix afterwards declared she would never forget the terrible shriek which they caused Mrs Heasman to give.

The rector offered a prayer in the house, in case the ghost should be an earthbound spirit in need of release. But it did little good, the noises continuing just as strongly as before.

Mr King decided that his family had suffered enough, and they packed up and left the house that night for a new home a quarter of a mile away. The empty Manor House was securely locked up but not abandoned, a policeman and several men keeping vigil outside. At about 10.20 pm. the stillness of the night was broken by the sound of heavy knocking coming loud and clear from inside—one, two, three, four knocks and no more. At once the front door was unlocked and the constable and his helpers rushed in with their torches, but though they searched the house thoroughly from roof to cellar, they found nothing.

One of the searchers had an unenviable experience. He said that while alone in a darkened room he distinctly heard a rustle as of someone rushing along the wall for about two yards. He immediately flashed his torch on the spot, but the room was empty.

Next day a reporter from the Brighton *Evening Argus* arrived to find the family packing up the last of their belongings for removal from the haunted house. He wrote in astonishment: "I heard the noises myself. I was standing in one of the rooms talking to the rector when suddenly, from the direction of the scullery, there came the sound of four distinct knockings, followed by a loud shriek from Mrs King, who had shortly before gone in that direction. She almost collapsed and had to be assisted into another room."

These knocks followed only forty minutes after identical bangings heard by the King family and two helpers. There was further evidence, too, of the peculiar behaviour of the cellar door. As the reporter entered the room, one of the visitors suddenly noticed that the cellar door was open again, though it had been securely bolted only a short time before.

The Kings now lost no time in vacating the premises for good.

What was behind the mysterious knocking? Many people locally were convinced that the haunting sprang from a former occupant of the house, long since dead, who had planted some trees in the front garden and declared that they should never be cut. They never had been until the previous Saturday—the day before Mrs King saw the apparition—when her husband cut them down.

When the disturbances at the house were revealed, two young girls who lived some distance from it told of a weird experience they had had one night three weeks earlier. They had gone out together to post some letters and when passing the old rectory heard a rustling in the trees. They turned to see a figure in white standing on the wall, and ran terrified from the spot. The apparition, they said, had no visible features; it was transparent and they could see right through it.

Whether this was the same nebulous figure which Mr King had tried ineffectually to beat off with his stick there was no means of confirming, but on the Saturday, at the end of the week of excitement, there came final proof from the Manor House of its noisy intruder. That night, in pitch darkness, as a knot of sightseers stood close together outside the padlocked gate of the old farmhouse, suddenly from inside the deserted building came a loud bang, followed by a second, a third and a fourth. Then silence.

It was the ghost's last fling.

The frightening bumps in the night that suddenly haunted a Lancashire family not long ago occurred in an ordinary terraced house, and were so loud that they could be heard at the end of the street, 200 yards away.

It was on Christmas Eve, 1959 that mysterious banging sounds began in the house in Tully Street, Salford, occupied by Mrs Clive Hill and her husband, and their twelve-year-old son. The noises started at about eleven o'clock, in the living room ceiling, and went on until 2 am.—"like an iron ball bounding on the ceiling". They continued over Christmas and into the New Year, hardly missing a night, resounding along and across the street, and disrupting the sleep of neighbours.

Mrs Hill and her husband searched under the floorboards and in the rafters for some physical explanation for the weird noises, but found nothing. To the house then came a procession of water board men, gas men, town hall officials and police, all of whom examined the premises thoroughly and left baffled.

Psychic research experts from Manchester University also searched the house and studied the noises. They were found to represent a code: one bump for "A", two for "B" and twenty-six for "Z". The bumps seemed to be spelling out messages to a neighbour, Mrs Freda Roberts, from her father-in-law, who had died some time ago, some of the later messages containing very personal things which only "Teddy", the father-in-law, could possibly have known. An investigator told the family that it seemed their son was being used by the spirit to communicate, for the boy remained quite oblivious to the noises at all times.

Further confirmation of the fantastic noises came from the Rev Edward Dimond, rector of St James's Church, Broughton, who came to the aid of the distressed family as the bumps continued for weeks on end, right through January and into February, 1960. Mr Dimond was sceptical when first told, but after hearing the noises himself on two nights he was convinced they came from something supernatural. No one, he said, could have made a noise quite like the persistent knocking, which was very loud and "just like a sledgehammer". He agreed that the spirit seemed to be answering questions by knocking a certain number of times to represent the letters of the alphabet.

Mr Dimond acted promptly. After consulting the Bishop of Manchester he decided to hold a special service in the house to drive the disturbing influence away. The twenty-five minute service was held on a night of February, 1960 while the Hills' son was upstairs in bed, Mr Dimond being assisted by a Manchester vicar. During the service police had to be sent for to move a crowd that collected in the street.

There was not a single noise after the service. The ghost seemed to have gone for good, and the thankful residents of Tully Street settled down once again to peaceful nights.

THE HEREFORD SENSATION

The first report of ghostly happenings in the ancient cathedral city of Hereford came, seasonably enough, just before Christmas 1932, when the news spread that two city policemen had encountered a phantom monk outside St Peter's Church.

It was shortly after midnight, the report went, when the two constables met in deserted St Peter's Square. At least, they had believed the square to be deserted, until one of them noticed a figure seated on or leaning against the War Memorial, wearing a long, dark, flowing robe. There had been a fancy dress dance that night so that the policeman promptly assumed that he had to deal with a stray reveller, and approached the man to ask him to move on. But as he got near to the robed figure it rose in silence and walked slowly towards the main porch of St Peter's Church, then, without pausing, melted through the massive iron gates of the outer porch, which were securely locked. As the other policeman hurried up to his astonished colleague, the monkish figure proceeded on its uncanny journey to the heavy oaken door of the church, also closed and locked, through which it vanished.

There could scarcely have been a more ideal setting for a ghostly visitation. St Peter's was built shortly after the Norman Conquest by Walter de Lacey as a priory for his monks, and its founder fell to his death from the battlements. Later, the provost of the little community of monks was murdered at the altar by the Welsh.

The present vicar, however, said he did not believe in ghosts and had never heard that his church was haunted, while the Hereford police proved very evasive and would not confirm the story.

This was a challenge to the *Hereford Times*, which determined to get to the bottom of the affair. The newspaper finally managed to question the policemen said to be involved in the incident, with the result that one of the officers denied having ever seen a ghost, but the other admitted that six years previously—in 1926—he and a constable no longer in Hereford had indeed seen the monk one night, exactly as had been described. Why had the incident only now come to light? Because, the newspaper discovered, a group of Hereford policemen had recently been discussing ghosts and the disclosure about the phantom of St Peter's was then made, and had leaked out in gossip.

It could all have ended there, a belated ghost story unsatisfactorily resolved, but as so often happens, corroboration came unexpectedly from another source. The son of the late Mr William Mason, who was organist at St Peter's for twenty-six years, revealed that his father claimed to have seen the spectral monk on a number of occasions. The first time, he saw the figure on the chancel steps, and, thinking it to be the verger, took no notice—until it suddenly disappeared. Two years later he again saw the figure, which he then described as "wearing a long dress, like a woman's".

Another time, said the son, his father told of seeing the same figure in the aisle. When he walked up to it, it vanished into the darkness. On yet another occasion he got quite close to the figure and saw clearly that it was garbed in a monastic robe. It walked noiselessly away and glided through the closed vestry door.

The son added that his father often confided to him that there was something uncanny about the church during the month of December, and in later years he would not go into the church alone after dark during that month.

In spite of these disclosures no investigation was made at St Peter's and the episode faded from the public mind. Two years later, however, the city was again the scene of ghostly activity, this time of much more sensational proportions; and oddly enough it was again two policemen who had first sight of the phantom.

The two officers, soon after midnight on an October night of 1934, saw a dark figure moving through the close of Hereford Cathedral. Because of its dark appearance one of the constables, mistaking it for a colleague, called out a greeting, at which the figure, which had been approaching him, immediately vanished. It was then realised that it had been wearing a cassock and cowl.

Not many days afterwards Mr W. E. Henner, a Hereford printer, also encountered the ghost. He was walking through the close at about 2.30 am. when he saw a sudden ray of light move across a corner of the Deanery, and when he had walked on a few more yards, another light quickly followed it. There was nothing to account for the strange lights and he was still puzzling over them when he saw a figure glide from behind a wall near the Deanery. Glued to the spot, he numbly registered every movement of the ghost. First the upper part of the body became visible, as if it were peering round the corner, then the whole figure appeared on the path, walking rigidly with hands at its sides. It was clothed in cowl and cassock of dirty white, but no face was visible. Mr Henner watched as it walked towards the Cathedral school and vanished behind the wall.

Only ten days after this, the ghostly monk was seen again by a young man returning to his rooms after walking his fiancée home. Mr S. H. Bach said he was passing through the close at about the same time, 2.30 am., when he saw the apparition, "swathed in a robe of dirty white and with its arms folded across the breast, gliding across the close with the air of one in deep contemplation".

These reports now decided a number of people to keep watch, and so on the night of Sunday, November 12 a party of eleven men and women made their way to the close to keep a vigil into the early hours. They took up their positions shortly after midnight and waited quietly opposite the cathedral entrance. At about two o'clock their patience was rewarded. According to all the witnesses, strange rays of light were seen to play upon one of the windows of the cathedral, then, within a few yards of them, there emerged from the wall on one side of the close the bent figure of a monk enveloped in cassock and cowl.

The watchers were perfectly ordinary people, not investigators, not experts, and not all believers in ghosts. What happened is described by one of them, Mrs Weaver, herself a sceptic until that night.

"I heard someone shout, 'Oh, there it is'. I turned round, and only a few yards away was the figure of a monk emerging, apparently, from the wall. It seemed to be crouching as if under a heavy load, and it walked silently across the close.

"I could see everything quite plainly—the cowl, and the dirty white robe with a lace fringe, covering a black garment. It stood out against the blackness of the night. I could not see any face. I was fascinated by the vision.

"I had heard that ghosts were troubled spirits, and, carried away by the desire to find out what was troubling the monk, I began walking towards it. I was not afraid of it then. As I walked, I recited the Lord's Prayer, and when I was within a few feet of the spectre I started to recite the Rosary. The figure of the monk vanished quite suddenly, and as it disappeared Miss Miles (another member of the party) pulled me away. The figure did not appear again."

Miss Violet Miles corroborated Mrs Weaver's story. She said the sudden appearance of the spectre gave her such a severe fright that she stumbled backwards, catching her leg on one of the chains that bordered the green. Her brother, Mr R. Miles, another member of the group and a decided sceptic, also testified to the strange scene, as did the rest of the eleven people, the younger ones among them not being fully recovered from the shock of their experience when interviewed the next day.

Excitement now ran high in the city and many people came to stare curiously in the close. They also came by night, alone and in crowds. One night, most of the passengers alighting in Hereford from a 2 am. train made for the close—"just as if they were going to a football match, there were so many on the same errand", one passenger said—while a noisy crowd of some 200 flocked there on another night in the hope of seeing the ghost. There was, in fact, such a constant traffic to the close, with some damage being done to the grass enclosures, that the clergy complained to the chief constable and the police took action to dampen the ardour of the ghost-hunters. The clergy did not accept that there was a ghost and maintained throughout that someone was playing a joke on the public. They were supported by others who suggested that the eleven people who together saw the ghost had been hoaxed by one of their members putting a handkerchief over his face and taking on the role of a spectre, though how he managed to make himself disappear into thin air was not explained.

With the police keeping a keen eye on visitors to the close the situation quietened, and the ghost itself made no further appearance during the next few days. But, just when all the excitement seemed to have died down there came another report of the monk being seen, this time in a different part of the cathedral grounds. Mr P. Thomas and his wife, Hereford residents, claimed to have seen the spectre near the library at the west end of the cathedral, some distance from the Deanery. First, they saw a strange light flash across a library window, and this was followed a second later by the ghost, a cowled figure walking slowly with its head down, as if looking for something or in deep contemplation. The startled couple were convinced that it was not a human figure and called to two soldiers, who came and also saw the monk before it vanished.

The controversy flared again, to be answered a few days later by the Dean, Dr Waterfield. In reply to suggestions that the monk might be trying to deliver a message, and that the clergy should keep a vigil and allow it an opportunity to speak, he said it was not likely that his clergy would "prowl about the close at midnight". Only that morning at two o'clock, the Dean added, "the 'ghost' was seen—but the person who saw it was in such an admirable position that it was possible to see that the figure was very much too solid for a ghost. It is obviously some hoaxer, and I am going to see the chief constable about it."

It seemed the last word on the subject, for after this the phantom figure was never seen again. But had the score of eye-witnesses all been mistaken? In spite of the Dean's conviction, many Hereford people remained unshaken in their belief that the thoughtful monk was a real ghost; and certainly nothing ever was found to prove them wrong.

LITTLE CHARLIE AND OTHERS

"I never believed in ghosts until these things happened to me and my family. I would have laughed if anyone had suggested to me before that a house could be haunted."

Time and again this same statement occurs in testimony given by eye-witnesses to police, clergy, reporters, investigators and others, and the strong feeling with which it is said can only be imagined. One who said it, in the summer of 1948, was the mother of two teenage boys, when describing their harrowing experience in the basement flat of a house in Swiss Cottage, London, which had been requisitioned during the war by Hampstead borough council.

The mother and her sons moved into the flat in 1946, and had been there only a short time when the uncanny incidents began.

Strange marks appeared on the doors and walls, and the mother began missing things. She thought her younger boy, aged fourteen, was responsible for this, and he was soundly spanked. But the incidents continued, knives and pokers mysteriously disappearing.

"One evening," she told the *Hampstead and Highgate Express*, "my curling irons vanished in front of my eyes. Six weeks later I saw them sticking out of the garden.

"Books flew in the air and landed on my son's head. None of our pets would live in the basement and had to be looked after by relatives.

"One night I came home and found my younger son hysterical with terror. He told me that hearing a noise in one of the cupboards, he opened the door and saw the figure of a crippled man standing before him. At first he thought it was a burglar and threw a milk bottle at the figure; but when the bottle passed right through and hit the wall, he rushed out into the street, where I found him sobbing his heart out.

"For months we endured lights being switched on and off, midnight tappings on the wall, and the room suddenly turning icy cold. One night I saw the ghost myself. It was so small and looked so ugly that I thought it was a monkey. I was even about to phone the Zoo and tell them that an animal had escaped, when the apparition vanished.

"I read up the history of the district to see if there was any reason for these manifestations. Then I called in some psychic research people and a number of seances were held in the flat. I learned that the house was haunted by an ugly hunchback murderer, and also a poltergeist."

The hunchback, apparently, had lived a hundred years ago, said the mother. At the seances she spoke to him and found that he was "very friendly." He told her he was sorry for his previous crimes and wanted to repent, and promised to leave the basement. She added, "We all call him 'Little Charlie.' He said that he murdered because of his ugliness."

Some further extraordinary evidence was now given by a woman who had lived in the flat from 1937 to 1939. There was definitely something strange about it, she said—"We used to find the lights being switched out or the curtains drawn, or even knives and scissors vanishing. We had no pets; they would not stay in the flat.

"I was cooking fried fish in the kitchen one evening when the room suddenly went cold. I turned for a moment to see if someone had opened the window. When I looked back at the stove the plate of fried fish had vanished. I never found it again."

The mother and her sons, when the haunting by "Little Charlie" was made public, were moved to a new council flat, though not on account of the ghost but "because of their domestic needs". The basement flat was renovated and let by the council to another tenant, when the hauntings by ghost and poltergeist apparently ceased.

The reactions of local authorities to complaints of ghosts are as unpredictable and varied as the hauntings that are so often brought to their notice.

In the same months as the Hampstead haunting, a family of five living in a flat in Bristol, suffered a haunting which kept them awake for sixty-three nights, and they finally had a recording made of the ghostly sounds, after which the city's assistant medical officer acted promptly to find the family other accommodation.

The noises that troubled Mr and Mrs J. Britton and their three children in their flat at Horsefair were mainly those of padding footsteps and eerie tappings; the only person who actually saw the ghost was Mrs Britton, who described the figure as that of a little old woman in brown with "a terribly evil face", whom she saw crossing the room towards her baby daughter's cot.

A psychic investigator was called in and a vigil was kept in the

flat one night, with representatives of a sound recording firm
standing by with their equipment. Just after 2 am. the sound of
padding footsteps and irregular tapping began. Then suddenly
Mrs Britton stood up rigid in the room, turned towards the cot
and shrieked "My baby, my baby!" As a woman helping with the
recording switched on the light and rushed into the room, Mrs
Britton fainted and fell. She was unconscious for fifteen minutes,
and on recovering said she had seen the apparition of the old
woman come through the door and go towards the cot.

When the record was played over the noises and screams were
reproduced, but there was also an unaccountable metallic vibration throughout the recording, which was one of the first to be
made in a haunted house. The record was played over to Dr
Irving Bell, the assistant medical officer, who said the noises
seemed very genuine and he believed they might do harm to Mrs
Britton's health, so he would look for other accommodation for
the family.

There was no such swift help from authority for a young couple
in Chorley, Lancashire, in 1954 whose little terraced house
seemed plagued by ghostly footsteps, shrieks and scratchings, and
the appearance of a grey figure. Mr Alan Mather and his wife had
lived in the house since their marriage eighteen months before,
and because they had decorated and furnished the house, in
which they were tenants, they decided to say nothing about the
manifestations but to try and put up with the grey, flitting shape,
the size of a small man, which they both saw often in the house
near the fireplace, and hearing the sounds of scratching, and
a noise which they described "like a moan rising to a scream".

A priest blessed the house, but to no effect.

The climax came when the couple went out for an evening
leaving the wife's eighteen-year-old sister sitting in with their ten-
week-old baby. When they returned the frightened girl told them
how, while reading, she had heard slow, deliberate footsteps overhead, and the footsteps then descended the stairs. The Mathers'
dog, which was in the room with her, rushed to the stairs, but
immediately turned round, its hairs bristling in fear, and hid under
a chair. When Mr Mather went upstairs he found all the bedclothes had been thrown on to the floor.

It was the last straw, and the couple moved out to live temporarily with relations. There was no explanation for the haunting, and no record of previous ghostly activity in the house. The
ghost did not deter desperate house hunters who sought the first
chance to rent the property should the couple finally give it up.

There was no lack of prospective tenants, either, for a council house in Boston Spa, Yorkshire, which had been claimed by a succession of occupants to be haunted. In 1965 the housing committee of Wetherby rural council decided not to accept a vicar's offer to lay the ghost, or to act on letters that flooded in asking to be allowed to investigate the case, but simply to make repairs to the house to rectify a "peculiar smell", and then relet it for the fourth time in three years.

The three-bedroomed house, only fifty years old and modernised, was said to be haunted by the ghost of a young man dressed in tennis clothes and carrying a racket. One who thought his council colleagues had made the wrong decision was their Boston Spa member, Mr William Hill, who had had many complaints from successive tenants of the house. He said afterwards, "The last tenant was particularly disappointed. He was a young man who thought he couldn't be frightened, but after meeting the ghost in tennis kit he left the next day, saying 'Noises in the night are one thing, but meeting something face to face is totally different'."

The housing committee's view was put by its chairman, who said that if anything regarding a ghost needed to be done it was the tenant's job to organise it, not the council's. So after standing empty for three months, the house was let to a strong-minded young couple who said that as the ghost, if it existed, seemed not unfriendly, they should get along with it very well.

Birmingham Corporation in 1955 quickly received many hopeful applications for the tenancy of a house in the Ladywood district, which was vacated by a haunted family after only four weeks. In this instance, too, after some repairs the house was briskly relet, apparently without any resumption of the haunting. Yet the experience in the house of Mr Frank Pell, his wife and five children, is among the most strange.

The family, after having lived for two years in a condemned house, moved into the three-bedroomed house in Coxwell Road in June. It was newly decorated and a most comfortable home, and Mr Pell, an ex-paratrooper, and his wife had the house blessed for them by Father Francis Etherington, a local Catholic priest. But the hauntings began the weekend of their arrival. They were woken by the sound of banging doors, and there were loud thuddings on the kitchen ceiling at night which Mr Pell likened to blows from a twelve-pound hammer. There were also eerie whisperings and strange smells, like garlic, turning to the smell of burning rubber.

Three weeks after the Pells moved in, their month-old baby girl, who was sleeping with them, died during the night. At the inquest

evidence was given that the baby, who was unmarked, had died
from accidental suffocation, yet the parents, who on a hot night
had thrown back the bedclothes, could not understand how the
tragedy could have occurred.

The hauntings continued each night, with tapping on the ceiling above the kitchen, doors banging unaccountably, and the
strange smells lingering in different parts of the house.

A few days after the baby's death, their four-year-old son asked
his parents, "Did the baby go with the little white dog?" He then
explained, "It comes and sits on my bed sometimes. I saw him
sitting on baby's face the night baby left us."

The Pells had never had a dog.

Police searched the house and found nothing. Father Etherington, who came to hold a service in the house, stood with a relation
in the upstairs room and heard the tappings and mysterious
whisperings, which he afterwards described as like someone talking
close to a microphone. The priest told Mr Pell that he had done
all that was possible, and for the sake of their health the family
should leave the house.

One morning Mr Pell was shaving downstairs when he heard
the whispering again, just behind him. He knew that only his wife
was in the house, and rushed to the stairs to see if it was her.

"She was standing at the top of the stairs, mouth open as if
screaming, but I could hear no sound. I started to climb the stairs,
then I stopped dead. There was some kind of invisible barrier I
could not break. I caught hold of the banister and heaved.
Suddenly I broke through. At once I could hear my wife's sobs
and screams. She said the voices had been whispering to her as
well."

The Pells resolutely quit the house and went to stay with
relations living not far away. But still the strange tappings went on;
two people who went to the house to collect some of the family's
belongings heard them.

Council officials and workmen checked the house and found
nothing wrong, and psychical research workers held a fruitless
night's vigil in it. The family of eight to whom the house was then
relet experienced no further trouble.

The Ladywood haunting had lasted only a month. A council-
owned property in Dudley, Worcestershire, which became
haunted shortly before the Pell's distressing experience, was all the
more inexplicable because the family had been in occupation for
nearly three years before the strange incidents began. The property
itself was also vastly different. The Jolly Collier, at Holly Hall,
Dudley, was a lonely century-old building at the bottom of a steep

bank in Low Town, which had been a public-house until shortly before the outbreak of World War II. It had since been converted as an ordinary house, though its nine rooms were still gas-lit.

After two peaceful years in the old building, Mr Edward Westwood and his wife and five grown-up sons and daughter heard strange noises for a period of some six months, but took little notice of them until shortly after Christmas, 1953 the various phenomena intensified and two apparitions suddenly appeared, one the figure of a young blonde woman wearing lipstick and other make-up, and the other that of a bald-headed man. The two ghosts appeared singly and in company.

The intense activity of the ghosts began, according to the family, when an eighteen-year-old son suddenly felt his bed move and was tipped on to the floor. He heard footsteps and uncanny knocking, but could see no one. He got back into bed and about half an hour later an alarm clock began ringing; yet there was no alarm clock in the house.

Then, footsteps were heard when there was no one about, and invisible hands touched shoulders and heads. Spiders' webs grew under water. There were shining lights at the windows, and the ghosts were seen often.

Mr Westwood called in the police, and while an officer was up-stairs investigating the room in which the blonde ghost first appeared, and which the family said was permeated with "the smell of death", the ghost of a young woman in a white shroud appeared at the window of a room below where Mrs Sarah Burton, sister-in-law of Mr Westwood, was sitting alone.

"The curtains parted and there she was," said Mrs Burton. "I screamed. I put my hands to my face and I was pulled from the chair by my hair. Before the policeman could reach me she disappeared through the window."

The almost daily ghostly incidents were too much for the family of eight, who in July, 1954 after reporting the strange happenings to the police, left the Jolly Collier to stay with neighbours.

The uncommon aspect of the lipsticked female ghost being seen in colour, when apparitions generally appear in monochrome, particularly interested psychical research investigators and two mediums, who kept night long vigils. The research investigators after a night at the inn came away without any evidence, but one medium said she contacted the blonde ghost who gave her name as "Martha", and appeared to have been involved in a murder.

The other woman medium, Mrs M. A. Brooks, from Birming-ham, who investigated independently during two successive nights, claimed to have contacted both spectres while in trance. She said she saw the two phantoms emerge at the foot of the winding stair-case. "I saw them vividly, a man with a yellow dahlia and a peroxide-blonde young woman in a white and forget-me-not coloured blouse. There was also a child and another woman. I understood that among them there had been an illicit love affair."

Others sitting with Mrs Brooks in a downstairs room where a fire blazed, felt the temperature fall, and listened to the sounds of knocks and footsteps in the unoccupied room above.

Mrs Brooks and an assistant broke down two sealed doors and drained a stone well in the cellar in further unsuccessful efforts to clear up the mystery, as well as searching the dust-laden upstairs rooms.

For want of other accommodation, Mr and Mrs Westwood and four of their grown-up sons returned to the Jolly Collier, but, afraid to go into the haunted room upstairs, slept for a week together in the parlour, the parents in a double bed and the four sons huddled on the floor in the light of an old-fashioned fire. A week of further manifestations, during which they saw the ghostly blonde and her companion nearly every day, forced them again to leave and stay with a relative, but they had to return once more to the Jolly Collier, the whole family sleeping in one downstairs room, and Mr Westwood said that two of his sons lost their jobs through lack of sleep.

In the early months of 1954 the Westwoods had their second application to be rehoused rejected by the Dudley housing com-mittee. The Jolly Collier was considered suitable for the family and ghosts, said the committee chairman, were not a reasonable excuse for wanting to move house.

So the Westwoods had to continue living with the spectres of the old inn until the haunting subsided.

SIR GEOFFREY WALKS

The puzzle of why Geoffrey de Mandeville, the rebel Earl of Essex, should return to walk the ancient parish of East Barnet, Hertfordshire, is as intriguing as his phantom itself. For the earl died in Suffolk and was buried in London, and as far as is known he had not the slightest connection with East Barnet except that at one time it formed a tiny part of his vast administration. Yet for more than 800 years his ghost has been linked with the old village.

Strong-headed "Sir Geoffrey", as the earl is more popularly remembered, played a dangerous game when Stephen and Matilda were contesting for the crown of England, blatantly taking honours from both. Pardoned in 1141 for treason against King Stephen, he then became sheriff and justice of Hertfordshire, and of London and Middlesex, as well as of Essex, wielding complete power over the capital and the three counties. He outmatched all other nobles in wealth and importance and acted everywhere as king; and was eagerly listened to. It was an intolerable situation for Stephen, who, in 1143, having again the ascendancy from Matilda and suspecting Sir Geoffrey of negotiating with her, sent officers to arrest him. The great earl, who was attending his court at St Albans, was seized after a sharp struggle and taken to London. There, under threat of being hanged, he was made to surrender his strongholds in Essex and the Tower of London, the principal sources of his might. He was then released.

But Geoffrey, though shorn of his more dangerous powers, was by no means defeated. Bursting into open revolt he quickly set himself up as master of the fenlands, forcing Stephen to march against him. His inglorious death soon afterwards came as an anticlimax, for the noble earl, while attacking a heavily fortified post, carelessly removed his headpiece and was shot in the head by a humble bowman. He lingered on for a few weeks before dying at

Mildenhall in September, 1144; excommunicated, because of his plunder of Church property, though he was later given absolution.

Such was the man, who, it was claimed, returned to haunt the old village of East Barnet. Through the years, tradition firmly linked his wraith with the village, while a further legend grew up that his ghost, clad in armour, red cloak and spurs, was also to be seen at Christmastime in Trent Park, Cockfosters, not very far away. This story, however, was bound up with hints of a hidden chest of gold, and told of outlawed Sir Geoffrey drowning in a well at Trent Park, which strayed a long way indeed from the historical facts. There might have been some confusion between two different apparitions, as does happen, but there was no doubting the link between Sir Geoffrey and East Barnet. And, not many years ago, there were dozens of people to testify that he walked the parish several times this century.

New prominence was given to the centuries-old haunting in 1925, when rumours spread of strange things being heard and seen at a stables at East Barnet, belonging to the local authority. It was the ghost of Sir Geoffrey, active once more, said those mindful of village tradition. The following year, the district council decided to pull down the stable and use its bricks in making a new road. Scarcely had this road work begun, however, than "Sir Geoffrey" was heard clanking his spurs as he walked across the floor of an old house in the locality. The same phenomenon was heard a second time in the house, and a third; while on another occasion, when it was again firmly established there could have been no human person about, there were impatient knocks at the front door and a rattling of the letter-box, which frightened the family and their dog. Odd noises were heard, too, near the road works, and finally a man walking past the haunted stables at midnight also heard the phantom spurs and, on looking round, caught a brief, startled glimpse of an apparition in a red cloak.

All this, occurring early in December, 1926 brought many reporters from London papers to the spot in search of a good ghost story, and a number of colourful reports of the East Barnet spectre, seemingly disturbed by the road works, were written but later denied, which served to make the whole affair highly suspect. Undaunted, a small group of interested local people gathered in the valley one night later on in the month to wait for the phantom and, according to their evidence, had a clear sight of the armoured earl in the moonlight. Because of the earlier events, however, their story was little believed and it was not until 1932, six years later, that the phantom of Sir Geoffrey was finally admitted to have been reliably and definitely seen by dozens of witnesses.

It came about through the efforts of a group of people actively interested in psychic matters, who, making careful inquiries in the East Barnet area, found that over the past twenty years, before which no records of any kind had been kept, the alleged visitations by the ghost had seemed to occur every sixth year—the last being the contested appearance in 1926. Older residents in the East Barnet valley said that at recurring intervals when the ghost appeared in the period between the full moon and the last quarter in the month of December, a strange, uncanny disturbance of the atmosphere developed as midnight approached. Acting on this information the group decided to hold a vigil, which was arranged for the night of Saturday, December 17, 1932.

In a freshening wind the group took up their position in the valley. They had waited patiently for some time when, just before the rising of the moon, they heard an uncanny noise like the clanking of spurs. It sounded first in the distance, and a moment later was heard around them at close quarters. The noise was repeated again and again, then became fainter. The watchers started walking slowly towards the fading sounds, making their way southward along the valley from East Barnet village on to land at Oak Hill recently acquired for an open space by the district council. And here their cold vigil was rewarded. On rising ground towards the east, with a woodland copse as a background, a sudden break in the clouds enabled the astonished group to see very distinctly in the faint moonlight the phantom of Sir Geoffrey, accoutred in his old-time armour. Their report of the incident stated, "The glance was a fleeting one, but very distinct, and the sight is fixed in the minds of those who saw it as plainly as if it had been revealed in midday sunlight".

The success of this vigil produced a great deal of excitement and hopes were high that the phenomenon would repeat itself on the following Tuesday night, St Thomas's Eve (the vigil of St Thomas, the apostle who doubted the existence of the spirit state) or on Christmas Eve, both days being especially favourable for ghostly manifestations. It was eventually decided to hold a second vigil on the Christmas Eve, and a general invitation was extended to anyone seriously interested to come along on that night and keep watch for themselves.

An hour before midnight on the Christmas Eve a crowd of curious sightseers gathered at the junction of Brookside and Cat Hill, at East Barnet. They drifted off in various directions while the group of investigators and others moved on a quarter of a mile southwards from the village to take up their position beside a small wooden bridge spanning the stream known as Pymms Brook. The bridge allowed wayfarers using the old church path to cross over on their way to Cockfosters.

As midnight approached this main group became aware of unusual sounds coming from the south. The sounds produced an uncanny feeling among them and they walked slowly on to investigate. After following the line of the stream through the recreation ground, they paused for a moment opposite Oak Hill, but all was quiet again. Continuing on in the direction of the cemetery they again paused opposite the locality of Monk Frith, when suddenly a long-drawn, wailing howl of distress was heard. As they stood and listened, highly tensed, the sound was repeated *among* the watchers. The night was very dark but they did not use their torches in case the spell should be broken. Then they heard, intermingled with this soulful howl of a dog, the clanking of armour. In a few moments they were conscious of movement and quite suddenly saw the shadowy form of a long-legged, headless hound slowly fading into the rising mist; without doubt, they thought, the phantom dog which legend had said often accompanied Sir Geoffrey, but which had not been seen by anyone within living memory. Next moment the clanking noise of armour seemed to surround the group, and they then saw the phantom of Sir Geoffrey clearly revealed. It vanished again into the mist as they watched.

The group made a detailed report of the incident which was placed on record with a psychic research society. There was, however, great disappointment and not a little scepticism among the many other people who had waited at other points in the valley and seen and heard little or nothing. But among those who had stayed close to the research group and could confirm what they had seen was a reporter of the *Sunday Dispatch*. Noting how some ghosts were most obliging, Sir Geoffrey appearing promptly on schedule, he wrote, "I, with many others, gathered in the old village to await the arrival of the ghostly visitor. The night was cold and cloudy. There was a woodland copse in the background. As we stood, staring, there was a sudden break in the clouds and there could be seen clearly a figure in armour—Sir Geoffrey de Mandeville.

"I made careful inquiries in East Barnet and found at least a dozen people willing to testify that they have seen the same phenomenon three times in the last twenty years."

Whether Sir Geoffrey appeared on the next of the six-yearly cycles we do not know, as there are no authentic records; understandably, as war was imminent and minds were on other things, while at the next cycle, war was in progress. So the phantom earl lapsed again into history.

Whether he continues his periodic return to modern East Barnet remains to be confirmed. Though the old village has seen the spread of red-bricked housing, its ancient history perpetuated only in the names of such pleasant residential roads as Monkfrith Way and Friars Walk, the open space of Oak Hill exists much as it was yesterday. And in the little valley, the December mists still gather.

THE MURDER STONE

Towards the end of the summer of 1821 Margaret Williams, an attractive Carmarthen girl, went into service at a small farm near the village of Cadoxton, in the neighbouring county of Glamorganshire, South Wales. She was a level-headed girl in her twenties, a hard worker whose industry and cheerfulness soon made her well liked in the district. Her charms also quickly registered with the farmer's son, and in time the two came to be seen together often.

It then became evident that their association was not faring too well and that the girl was troubled; but she asked no one's help and settled matters herself, giving notice to the farmer and leaving to care for an old man who occupied a small house not far away, near Neath. Here again her capacity for hard work was quickly noticed and approved by the neighbours, together with the cheerfulness she had now regained; but in this new community she made no secret of the fact that the farmer's son had made her pregnant. She was heard frequently to declare the wrong he had done her, openly giving his name.

Margaret Williams began her new job with her kindly old employer in May, 1822. Ten weeks later, on the morning of Sunday, July 14 her pathetically beaten body was found in a ditch on the marsh adjoining the village of Cadoxton. There was only sixteen inches of water in the ditch and though she lay on her left side with her head submerged, the ditch was too narrow to allow the rest of her body to sink into it. Both her arms were bruised, as well as her throat and neck, and clearly her attacker had used considerable force to overcome and strangle her.

Near her on the marsh lay the basket she had carried, containing her hat and a sheep's head which she had bought at Neath on the Saturday night.

The brutal murder aroused the intense anger of the entire district, all eyes looking in a certain direction for the killer. An inquest attended by several magistrates and landed gentlemen was opened on the Tuesday morning, and no sooner had the doctors confirmed that the girl had been violently attacked and strangled, and that she had indeed been pregnant, than a warrant was issued for the arrest of the farmer's son. He was taken at once and held prisoner to await the inquest verdict.

For two days the inquest went on, the jury themselves being locked up together on the Tuesday during the necessary overnight adjournment; but although the strongest suspicions existed against the prisoner, in all the evidence threshed out by the coroner there was nothing to establish the young man's guilt. The verdict of the jury therefore had to be one of "wilful murder by some person or persons unknown", and the suspect was discharged.

The deep feelings of the local people, which had been roused further by the heart-breaking scene when the girl's parents, summoned from Carmarthenshire, identified their murdered child, were well mirrored by *The Cambrian* which reported, "The magistrates have declared their resolution to seek out fresh evidence with unremitting scrutiny, and it is devoutly to be wished that the inhuman monster who perpetrated this foul and horrid deed may yet be brought to justice. The eye of Providence is upon him, and we trust the hand of Providence also will be with those who endeavour to find the clue of the discovery, which human wickedness and cunning have for the present concealed."

The strenuous inquiries, both official and unofficial, went on for months, but in spite of all these efforts the servant girl's killer remained at large. There was, however, little doubt that, as *The Cambrian* forcefully put it, "the unfortunate girl was murdered in a moment of confiding affection by a monster—rather a demon— in the form of a man, by whom she had become pregnant". The villagers were incensed by what they considered to be the escape of a callous murderer, and the local gentry no less. It was decided to punish him in the only way open to them, by striking at his conscience.

One of the local gentlemen, Mr George Tennant of Cadoxton Lodge, undertook to foot the entire expense of a memorial to Margaret Williams to be put up in Cadoxton churchyard. This was to be "a massive stone, extremely simple but of conspicuous form and dimensions", and Elijah Waring, brother of Letitia Waring, the hymn writer, was asked to compose an inscription for it which would convey the feeling of the community.

The "Murder Stone" was set up in Cadoxton churchyard on an April day in 1823, nine months after the discovery of the girl's body. For many Sundays afterwards people from miles around walked to the churchyard to see the ominous memorial, and those who could to read the damning inscription. This is what Elijah Waring wrote, as it appeared on the stone:

1823
To record
MURDER
This stone was erected
over the Body
of
MARGARET WILLIAMS
Aged 26
A native of Carmarthenshire
Living in service in this parish
who was found dead
With marks of violence upon her person
In a ditch on the Marsh
Below this Church Yard
on the Morning
of Sunday the fourteenth of July
1822

Although
THE SAVAGE MURDERER
Escape for a season the detection of man
Yet
GOD HATH SET HIS MARK UPON HIM
Either for Time or Eternity
and
THE CRY OF BLOOD
Will assuredly pursue him
To a certain and terrible, but righteous
JUDGMENT.
Canys nyni a adwaenom y neb a ddywedodd, MYFI
BIAU DIAL, MYFI A DALAF, MEDD YR ARGLWYDD
Hebreiad x..30

It was too much for the farmer's son, who vanished from the community and then from the country, never to be seen again. In after years the stone became the focal point of eerie ghost stories, and in winter, when night fell early and the wind whipped across the marsh and the churchyard, many people were afraid to pass by it. Several villagers swore they had seen two ghostly figures gliding near the stone, and it was firmly believed that these apparitions were those of the murdered girl and her lover, returned to the memorial which cried out for her revenge.

Stories of the ghosts being seen continued right up to the 1920s, a hundred years after the tragedy, when it was suggested that the stone, an embarrassing reminder of community hate, should be removed. The arguments for and against this went on for a number of years, but no direct request was made to the church for the stone's removal and so it remained in its position in the church-yard, near and facing the main road; and it is there still.

Though there have been no recent reports of the gliding ghosts, the cry of the outraged populace still seems to echo from the grim monument, ever strong.

Violence provides the background to many ghosts, and few hauntings are so weird as that following a murder in the Forest of Dean, Gloucestershire, in about the year 1840.

It became noticed that there was missing from the neighbour-hood of Ruardean Hill a stonemason known by the nickname of "Get-it-to-go." He was last seen at a drinking-house and there was a whispered report of a quarrel and some blows being struck. It was thought that the stonemason had received what the foresters called "an unlucky blow"—and there were no police around to investigate.

Twelve months afterwards word got about that a strange ghostly noise was to be heard coming from the depths of a disused pit. A family living in a cabin nearby said the noise sounded like a man boring a hole with a hammer and drill. Rumour spread, quickly connecting the ghostly sound with the stonemason's dis-appearance, and the parish constables were ordered to make a search. A windlass was put up and the pit examined, but no body was found. The eerie noise, however, continued at intervals, until about a year later it was so loud and insistent that another wheel was put up and a second search made; and this time, when the bottom of the pit was cleared of debris, the searchers found the stonemason's body, or what was left of it after the attention of the rats.

A large crowd collected at the pithead as the body was brought up. The clothes helped to keep the remains together as they were shovelled into a coffin, which was afterwards laid down in the open for all to see. Timothy Mountjoy, from whose eye-witness account this record is taken, noted, "The wonder was that scores did not die from the horrid stench; it was reported that one person died from blood-poison."

Why was the body not found on the first search? Because, it was strongly believed, some of the men employed then to search the pit were those who had thrown the stonemason into it. On the discovery of the body the ghostly noise from the old pit ceased.

A particularly shocking accident was believed to be the reason for a macabre haunting of the railway track running through the little colliery village of Burnopfield, Durham, during the autumn of 1932. Here is the account of one man who encountered the ghost:

"I was coming down beside the line to get to Burnopfield, when I was stopped by hearing several metallic clangs, just like those a platelayer makes when laying or repairing rails. After stopping for a few moments I walked on, but my progress was again arrested by seeing a face hanging in mid-air. It was horribly twisted and scarred, and the eyes blazed in a terrible and eerie way.

"I saw the face for a second, then I heard a thunderous roar like hundreds of coal wagons out of control on the line. I did not stop for any more but turned and ran."

Several other people claimed to see on different occasions the twisted face, its head covered with a shock of white hair, and always the ghost's appearance on the colliery wagon-way was heralded by a number of clangs like a sledgehammer striking metal. Older people in the village recalled a distressing accident in 1879, when a platelayer on the railway was killed when the wire rope connecting a line of moving coal wagons suddenly parted. It seemed that the unfortunate man's agonised spirit had returned for a time to haunt the spot.

At Lydney Docks, on the River Severn in Gloucestershire, a man hanged for murder in the last century was thought responsible for a persistent haunting in the neighbourhood of the mortuary. At intervals through the years following his execution the ghostly figure of the murderer, who killed a woman on the marshes, was seen, though not too much notice was taken of the witnesses' stories. Then, in the autumn of 1934, a quick succession of incidents seemed to offer conclusive proof of the ghost's existence.

Among the first to report its appearance was a terrified young girl who said she was walking up the lock bank one night when something seemed to appear out of nothing in front of her. "Then I could see the misty outline of a man with a slouch hat and raincoat. I could not see his legs. I was terribly frightened and took to my heels and ran away as fast as I could. I am sure it was not a human being."

Another Lydney resident testified, "I knew nothing of the 'ghost' before I went down to the lock one evening. When I rounded a corner I was surprised to see something in front of me. It appeared to be a very tall man. I said 'Good night' but there was no reply and the figure vanished before I went further."

If there was still doubt that the raincoated figure was really that of a ghost, the frightening experience one night of another man seemed enough to dispel it. He stated, "I was riding my bicycle when suddenly, near the mortuary, I saw a figure surrounded by a halo of mist in front of me. I rang my bell because I thought it was a man. The figure did not move an inch, and I kept on ringing my bell. Just as I was about to jump off my machine to avoid a collision the figure vanished—just evaporated into nothing."

Other people, men and women, reported seeing the ghost, which always took the form of a light raincoated figure in a slouch hat, its legs not visible, standing immobile in the half light. All the witnesses vowed that when disturbed, it dissolved into thin-air. One old sailor admitted that he had seen the figure on several occasions over the past twenty years; it never made any sound, he said, and seemed just to stand or hover for some moments, gazing at passers-by.

Following this most recent spate of appearances by the ghost several attempts were made to lay it, but all the vigils were unrewarded.

Murder was also thought to be behind a haunting at St Mary's Barracks, Chatham, the Navy's oldest barracks, though in this case it was the ghost of the victim that seemed to have returned. Unrest at the barracks, then in use as a naval gunnery school, became public in the spring of 1946, when young naval ratings protested at having to do sentry duty on their own at dead of night. They said that during the middle watch from midnight to four o'clock, while patrolling a long stretch of ramparts overlooking an old moat, they had heard, individually, mysterious footsteps padding along behind, and an incessant tap, tap, as of somebody walking with the aid of a stick. So alarmed was one rating that he ran off to the guardroom in a panic, the mysterious footsteps following him until he was off the ramparts.

It was on a night shortly after this that a startled rating, by the light of the moon, saw to his horror the figure of a man dressed in the uniform of Nelson's days, hobbling along the ramparts on a crutch. The man wore his hair in a pigtail as was then the fashion. The apparition eventually vanished into the moat which was twenty feet deep.

The rating, scarcely able to believe his eyes, reported the incident to the guardroom and it was entered in the logbook: "Ghost reported seen by sentry during the middle watch."

The barracks, built in 1787 by French prisoners-of-war and convict labour, was honeycombed by underground passages and an official theory now put forward was that when the wind was blowing in a certain direction, footsteps reverberated through the passages beneath the ramparts, producing an echo immediately behind the rating on lone patrol. It was suggested that on hearing such "footsteps", the ghost-seeing sentry may have mistaken a bush moving in the wind for the figure.

Only two years later, however, the ghost of St Mary's seemed to return again. In Room 34 of the Cumberland block strange things began happening: sudden gusts of hot and cold air, unaccountable footsteps, chairs moving, and blankets being tugged from beds. Petty Officer Mechanic Joseph Dickson, of Newcastle, was told about these things by his four room-mates on returning from Christmas leave in 1948. He scoffed; but his scepticism received a sudden jolt when some days later he was roused from sleep at 2 am. by a mysterious jerk at his bedclothes. Three days later the same thing happened, and on both occasions everyone in the room with him was asleep.

The following day Dickson's colleagues went on leave, leaving him alone in the room. Now the ghostly incidents became more pronounced. He testified, "Again I felt someone touch me. I sat up and heard footsteps, as though whatever it was was wearing great nails in its boots. I put on the light, still hearing the footsteps, and searched the room, but there was no one there. I went back to bed and was just going off to sleep again when I heard the sound of someone poking the fire in the next room. I got up and went to the room, but it was empty. Then, perfectly clearly, I heard someone coughing in the room and I knew no living person was there."

It was what occurred the following night that finally convinced him of the ghost. Awakened by a cold draught of air, he sat up in bed to see the wardrobe door swing open before him. He got up and closed the door and tried to make it swing open by shaking it, but found that he could not. As soon as he got back into bed, however, the door swung open again; and then a chair moved about three feet across the floor.

Though the ghost was not actually seen on these occasions it was thought to be the same spirit as had haunted the ramparts two years before, and was commonly believed to be that of a sentry murdered by escaping French prisoners during the Napoleonic wars. The sentry's relief had been late and he was apparently following a ghostly errand to Room 34 to shake the relief from bed.

The old Royal Marine Barracks at Chatham, which were even older than St Mary's, also had their ghost officially logged not many years ago. Over a long period several Marines had reported seeing the ghost, which was believed to be that of a Marine who shot himself. When, after 167 years at Chatham, the Royal Marines left the barracks and the town in 1950, it might be thought that the ghost, too, would vacate the premises, but this was not to be.

Four years later, in 1954, the Naval Patrol which policed the streets of Chatham had made its headquarters in the former guardroom section of the otherwise deserted barracks in Dock Road. The area was fenced off from the rest of the barracks. At 6.30 one November evening, Leading Patrolman David Fell, a sturdy, level-headed man and among the biggest and heaviest members of the patrol, went up to his locker in a top-storey room to get some tobacco. The room, which overlooked the graveyard of St Mary's Church, was empty but for a few lockers and lit by a single 100-watt bulb. Suddenly out of the corner of his eye, Fell saw what appeared to be a solid figure standing near one of the windows. He swung round and the figure vanished before he could make out any details of its dress or appearance. Badly shaken he rushed down two gloomy flights of stairs to the patrol-room and told his incredible story. Even the strongest sceptics were impressed by his belief in what he had seen. The Master-at-Arms confirmed, "He is one of the best lads to have around in a tight corner and is not easily disturbed, but there was no doubt when he came rushing down here something had given him a really bad shaking."

No amount of ragging by other members of the patrol or official questioning by his superiors shook Leading Patrolman Fell's belief that he had seen a ghost, and the Provost Marshal was convinced of the reality of his experience. Accordingly a report on the incident went through official channels and finally reached the Commander-in-Chief Nore. Inquiries then made among Royal Marines formerly stationed at Chatham disclosed that this section of the barracks had reputedly been haunted for years by the ghost of a Marine who killed himself in the room now containing the lockers. Many times a mystery figure had been reported in this same room or nearby; and so strong had been the feeling about the supposed hauntings that one well known sergeant major had flatly refused to go near the room unless it was absolutely unavoidable.

The ghost's brief appearance in 1954 was the last recorded before the barracks was demolished a few years later.

The Congress Hall in Clapton, East London, used for fifty years as the training school for Salvation Army officers, would seem an unlikely place for a haunting resulting from sudden death, but a ghost walked there and was seen by many. The Army trainees called her "Maria" and she was still walking in the hall in the 1930s.

Maria was a nurse when the Congress Hall was a home for

foundlings in the last century. She murdered her own baby, hiding the body in a dark nook occupied in later years by the baker's oven; and, bitter-faced, she returned after her own death to pace the corridors.

A woman major just before the outbreak of World War II told how, when she was a cadet at the training school, Maria was frequently seen on a regular "walk".

"She went from the kitchens along the downstairs corridor, up the front stairs and past what we used to call Scotch Corner. I used to have to conduct a prayer meeting there when I was in training, and once I'm sure, if I had opened my eyes, I would have seen her. I did not dare look that time. But I have personal friends who swear they have seen her. She wears a grey nurse's uniform and does not look misty and ghostlike. One of my friends was reading in the library when we were cadets, and looked up to see Maria sitting opposite her. The ghost then just faded away."

Maria ceased her travels as war began.

THE HAUNTED HOSTEL

The early wartime case of the haunted hostel for girls really began for Miss G. Methvea Brownlee, a well known photographer in the West Country, when a bomb fell on her home in Charlotte Street, Bristol, on a November evening in 1940. In her own words, "That bomb destroyed all I had, and I felt that my one salvation would be to find a job."

She found one at Oldbury House, St Michael's Hill, Bristol, which the BBC had taken over as a hostel for girls on the staff. It was a very old house, reputed to have been used by Prince Rupert as his headquarters when Bristol was besieged in the days of Cromwell. Underground tunnels were believed to run from the house to the centre of the city, and to the old Bristol Fort.

Miss Brownlee's job was to look after the general well-being of the BBC girls. There were twenty-eight of them, all in their late teens and twenties, and there was a hostel staff of seven.

Miss Brownlee and her charges soon found that the old house also had seven other "residents". This is how she described the eerie experiences of herself and some of the girls soon afterwards.

"I slept on the ground floor by the front door, and was awakened frequently by thuds, by heavy dragging sounds, and by the sobbing of a child. Then, I saw the ghosts.

"There was a very tall, thin man, dressed like a monk, in long dark robes, with a bunch of keys hanging from a girdle at his waist. There was also a little old woman, dressed rather like a housekeeper of the same period; and finally there were five ladies, always together, dressed alike in clinging robes with high head-dresses.

"I discovered that there had been at one time an opening from my room to the stables beyond. It was here that I first saw the monk. After that, at frequent intervals, I saw not only the monk but the housekeeper also, and the five women together. The women seemed to stand on a balcony, as if in a vision. They talked agitatedly among themselves, and in the background there was the monk again, seemingly pleading for something.

"I said nothing about this to the girls as I did not think it would be good to arouse their imaginations. But one day several girls came to me and told me of things they had seen. Their experiences corresponded exactly with my own. Eight girls saw these presences in the house exactly as I did. The other twenty experienced nothing at all.

"Often two or three of the girls saw the figures simultaneously. On other occasions one girl would see a figure coming through the door, and a minute or so later another girl would see it at the end of the passage, and later still yet another girl would see it at the foot of the stairs."

In the space of three months the persistent hauntings so got on everyone's nerves that in March, 1941 the girls were moved away and the hostel closed. After that no one stayed overnight at Oldbury House, which was taken over by a Ministry and afterwards became the Bristol Inland Revenue tax office.

Seven ghosts together were also claimed to be seen in the late 1940s at Rye, Sussex, only in this case all of them were monks. Several people testified to seeing the phantoms at the Monastery Hall, a fourteenth-century Augustine Friars' chapel, walking in single file across the garden and through a ten-foot high brick wall.

Disclosure of the hauntings early in 1950 brought many sightseers to the chapel. The caretaker there, Mr Fred Parris, had become convinced some years before that it was haunted, but had said nothing so as to avoid publicity. He now admitted:

"I have seen the ghost of a cowled monk several times. He is tall, over six feet, and can walk through walls.

"Once, when I went to open the garden gate I stretched out my arm and it went cold and stiff, as if suddenly frozen. Then a few feet away I saw the monk looking at me. Another time I was chopping wood, when suddenly I began to grow colder and colder, and could not stop shivering. Then something tapped my head three times, and the coldness vanished."

Even indoors, said Mr Parris, he and his wife had felt a breath of cold air as if someone was walking through the room. No pets would stay with them. "We have had dogs, but they ran away or seemed to go mad. We have tried cats, but they became crazed and aged. We no longer keep pets." All the ghostly events, he said, occurred not at midnight but between tea time and dusk.

Part of the monastery's garden was excavated during World War II for an air-raid shelter, and a few feet underground a row of skeletons was discovered, all but one standing upright, and the other kneeling. Experts said the bodies had been buried alive. Mr Parris himself found skeletons in other parts of the garden.

One of the local theories for the haunting was that the monks of long ago resented the Monastery Hall now being used for entertainments, auctions and public meetings.

Among other cases of monks of the past returning to haunt their former homes, the incidents on Caldy Island in the 1920s are somewhat unique; for on this tiny island off the coast of Pembrokeshire, a spectral monk appeared among a community of monks still very active there.

The island, with its monastery and white-robed Benedictine monks, its Celtic church and twelfth-century priory, was owned by the Benedictines; there were thirty-six of them among the island's total population of ninety-eight. It was an almost self-supporting community, with no public-houses, no policeman, and no rates; and in complete silence the monks went about their tasks of praying and ploughing, spinning and weaving.

During the day the only sounds that broke the stillness were the lappings of the waves and the occasional chimes from the monastery tower; but sometimes at night the peace of the little "island of saints" was, according to the islanders, disturbed by ghostly shrieks, and villagers saw a ghostly figure. Some felt "something" brush them, while others spoke of an uncanny presence.

A strange black-robed monk more than six feet tall, with cowl drawn over his head, was reputed to wander round the ancient priory. It was said that his wraith rose from the burial ground, where monks had been laid to rest since the fifth century. On one occasion, after a dinner at the monastery, a woman who had been helping with the cooking found her path barred by the black monk. She turned and fled.

Several other of the islanders, who were given to no special flights of imagination regarding the monks with whom they lived daily, told of their encounters with the eerie black monk. One was Mrs McHardy, wife of the island bailiff, who said, "One evening, at dusk, I was sitting in our parlour at the old Priory Farm when I heard footsteps descending the stairs, and, going into the hall, I saw it was my son Jo. Then I shrieked, for behind him on the stairs I saw the gaunt figure of a monk in black robes with a face like death—grey and pallid—peering from beneath his cowl.

"As I gazed, the spectre faded and disappeared."

Mrs Stiles, another of the islanders, told how when she was walking down a lane one evening she came upon a ghostly black figure sitting or leaning on a fence. She could not see its face but said it was wearing a hat "like a mushroom". She took to her heels.

A white lady, and the ghost of a madman who buried himself alive were also said to have haunted the island in the past. There was a belief, too, that an enormous sapphire of great value, thought to have been brought to the island from Glastonbury Abbey at the dissolution of the monasteries, was hidden in the walls of the priory; at times what some islanders described as "a pointing hand" and others as a "luminous glow" was claimed to be seen on the walls, indicating, as it were, the position of the hidden treasure.

But in 1927 it was the intensified haunting by the black monk that worried the lay population. The Benedictines, who had then been on the island for some twenty years, made no comment on the apparition, which, oddly enough, seemed to end its startling appearances two years later, when the Benedictines left the island for Gloucestershire. Monks of the Cistercian order then took over Caldy's hillside monastery, continuing the silent work of their predecessors in the island's floral valley; and the black spectre was seen no more.

A less alarming sight than the Caldy Island spectre, and in fact an eagerly looked for visitation, were the five phantom monks or friars claimed to have appeared at regular intervals through very many years at Braughing, in Hertfordshire. Hundreds of years ago there was a monastery at Braughing and, according to local tradition, five monks from it died one day in May, poisoned by some trout they had fished from a local stream which the abbot had placed out of bounds. "The hand of God" was the verdict in the village—a punishment for poaching; and as if retribution had fallen upon the whole community, the village then fell on hard times. Cattle did not thrive, lambs were eaten by the fox, and crops suffered the blight. This hapless situation lasted for five years.

Then, one night in May, the fifth anniversary of the death of the five monks, their ghosts were seen to walk at Horse Cross; and from that day forward the village prospered.

Every five years afterwards the ghosts of the Braughing Friars seemed to expiate their misdeeds by following this "penance" of a ghostly revisit to the scene of their misdeeds. Right up to the early years of the present century, people of Braughing parish firmly believed that the results of harvests and the village prosperity generally depended on the appearance or otherwise of the ghosts. In the 1920s there were still living older villagers who swore that they had seen the ghosts appear every five years for some fifty years.

But the last time the beneficial phantoms were seen was in 1921. In 1926 they did not reappear, and during the long interval till 1931, manorial lands and farms which formerly were fat and prosperous, failed, and passed into other hands. All the old squires died, and people who were merely wealthy and had no root interest in the locality took their places.

When in 1931 the Braughing Friars still did not reappear it was thought that these changes in the old neighbourhood had had much to do with it; that the penitents' affinity with the district had faded once and for all. Certainly there have been no reports of them being seen since.

THE MUMMY OF MARBURY

Marbury Hall is one of those forlorn old country mansions which one feels at sight must have its ghost—or ought to have. In fact, the haunting attached to this building, tangled in local legend as it is, provides one of the more grotesque of ghost stories.

The ancient manor of Marbury Hall, near Northwich, Cheshire, was largely rebuilt in the 1840s in French style, and was obviously magnificent in its day. Now it has a blighted look, with windows broken, though shuttered from the inside, ornamental stonework missing from the roof, statues lying flat and broken around the garden, and terraced steps overgrown with weeds and grass. A far cry from the time when the mansion's two pointed towers, each topped by a golden ball, rose in elegance over a rich scene.

The house was built on three sides of a large courtyard, with another courtyard at the back approached through a stone archway with a large impressive clock over it. A rose garden flourished on the slope down to the water of Marbury Mere. But the garden now is overgrown, and the Mere, surrounded with reeds, seems attended by sorrowing mists. All that still keep faith with the old house are "Lord Barrymore's pigeons", as the crows, which for countless years have nested at the Hall, are called locally.

Marbury Hall takes its name from the Merbury or Marbury family who formerly owned it, but from the early eighteenth century it became a seat of the Earls of Barrymore, afterwards passing on to the Smith-Barry family, descendants in line, in whose hands it remained until the 1930s.

The ghost of Marbury Hall is a White Lady, whose appearances over many years frightened people living in the locality. Late travellers hurried past the imposing gates of the mansion, never stopping on moonlight nights to look down the long red shale drive to the Hall, for fear of seeing the spectre of a woman on a white horse pass silently by. Right up until recent years there were people returning late at night along lonely Marston Lane or the old Warrington Road who ran home terrified to tell of their encounter with the phantom.

The hauntings by the mysterious White Lady appear to have started some years after the untimely death at the Hall of a lovely, dark-haired French or Egyptian woman. It is said that one of the early Lords Barrymore, an extensive traveller, met the woman during a sojourn in Egypt, and promptly brought her home, rather to the dismay of his family. Whether she remained there as mistress or housekeeper is uncertain. However, when dying, she made a will expressing a wish that her body should be embalmed —a practice then being experimented with by some French and English surgeons—and her body kept at Marbury Hall, of which she had grown very fond. Her wishes were followed, and the mummy was kept in its coffin under the stairboards at the foot of the spiral staircase. The next generation, however, so disliked having it in the house that they had it removed to the family vault at the church of St Mary's and All Saints, at Great Budworth, three miles away.

Soon after this belated "funeral" the hauntings began. Frightened villagers told of seeing the ghost of a lady riding by on a white horse, while at Marbury Hall itself there were many strange incidents, including service bells in the servants' quarters ringing for no apparent reason. The upshot was that the mummy was taken out of the vault and brought back one night through the dark Cheshire lanes to the Hall. The hauntings stopped. Some time later, however, and for the same reason of distaste, the mummy was again taken to the churchyard and "reburied"; but again the hauntings began, and the mummy was brought back to Marbury once more. It was put in a narrow, lead-lined box similar to a monk's chest, which remained in its place under the spiral staircase, near the servants' quarters, until the 1930s.

In 1959, when the *Northwich Guardian* investigated the stories of the White Lady, it found two people at least who remembered seeing the strange coffin. One was Mrs Fanny Weedall, daughter of a maid to the Barrymore family, who as a young child had crept in through the servants' door to see the coffin. Another was Mr Alfred Hayes, in his seventies, who as a young man had seen the bones and wrapping of the mummy.

When, shortly before World War II, the Smith-Barry family vacated the Hall and it was converted into a country club, the head gardener took the coffin and buried it in the rose garden. This might have re-activated the White Lady for a time, for during the war she is said to have been seen by German prisoners at Marbury.

Earlier there had been reports of a "black lady" being seen at Marbury. This is partially explained by the fact that for a long time a housekeeper who always dressed in black lived alone at the Hall and was seen about the grounds at night, which gave rise to some of these stories; yet one man who said he saw the ghost on a number of occasions, and that she definitely was black, was an old villager who worked at the Hall and died not long ago, in his nineties. Whether the Lady did vary her appearances, or whether she became confused with another apparition, cannot be known.

After the war, Marbury Hall was taken over by Imperial Chemical Industries Ltd, who housed some of their workers in the park and Hall. No one reported seeing the ghost from that day forward. The mansion became empty once more in the early 1960s.

Tradition suggests that the horse ridden by the White Lady may be the phantom of Marbury Dunne, the famous mare which belonged to the Smith-Barry family and whose grave is still to be seen in Marbury Park.

Marbury Dunne formed the stake in a wager, and had to run from London to Marbury in the hours between sunrise and sunset. The plucky horse accomplished this, galloping in with time to spare, but during the excitement and confusion, quenched her heavy thirst at a water trough, and the shock killed her. On her grave was placed a stone recording her gallant effort. It bore the words:

> *Here lies Marbury Dunne,*
> *The finest horse that ever run,*
> *Clothed in a linen sheet,*
> *With silver hoofs upon her feet.*

There are, however, some discrepancies in the dates regarding the phantom lady and her supposed steed. The first hauntings appear to have occurred long before Marbury Dunne was alive. So the phantom horse remains as much a mystery as the White Lady of Marbury herself, for there are no records to tell us of the Lady's true identity.

To walk all round the Hall and through the darkest shrubberies on a dark and stormy night, and sit in the abandoned courtyard, causes one to wonder not so much at the ghostly phenomenon as at the vibrant personality of the woman whose wraith it is.

THE ELUSIVE LADIES

There are other elusive ladies. One among them is the Grey Lady said to have haunted Hill Hall, a lonely Elizabethan mansion in Essex, until recent years.

The Grey Lady was active to the end of the 1940s, with a then unbroken history of 350 years of haunting. Very many local people claimed to have seen her sad, gentle figure. She even haunted the nurses' bedrooms when the London Hospital's maternity section was evacuated to Hill Hall during the war. As the mansion's lodge-keeper, Mrs Bingham, said shortly afterwards, "The matron saw her time and again, and if she sees a ghost there is a ghost."

Mrs Bingham's husband was among those villagers who saw the Grey Lady. She said, "Something forced him out of bed one night, and made him walk to a window in a far away part of the mansion to light a cigarette. The ghost walked by. Next morning there was a half-smoked cigarette on the window ledge to show it was not a dream."

The Grey Lady seemed to retreat when plans were made to turn Hill Hall into an open prison. Tradition says that she walked for centuries round bloodstains on the floor of a room in which seven men, all brothers, died in a fight with daggers to win her favours; the brothers were the sons of Sir Thomas Smyth, Secretary of State to Queen Elizabeth, who owned the house in the sixteenth century.

But Sir Thomas had no children except an illegitimate son, who was killed before his own death, while the "bloodstains" have been explained away as damp. Only the continued appearances of the ghost of the Grey Lady have been real enough, though her background remains a complete mystery.

At Winnington, in Cheshire, the last recorded appearance of the ghost of the Winnington Lady was in the 1870s, about a hundred years after her death. In local tradition much is claimed to be known about this beautiful wraith, though there are several versions of the circumstances of her death. The following is considered the most reliable.

In the late 1770s a niece of Lord Penrhyn, the tenant, was preparing to attend a party and ball given in magnificent old Winnington Hall. She was excited, for among the guests being received by her uncle, MP for Liverpool, in the Long Gallery below, was a young man of whom she was very fond.

Her excitement and haste had given her a high colour which was not at all fashionable, and, determined to look her best, she took her lancet to bleed herself a little; it was a method of regaining composure then popular among the ladies. The lancet slipped, and she cut an artery instead of a vein. Frightened by the sight of the spurting blood she dashed out of the room crying for help. She reached the stairs rapidly weakening, and, still moaning for help, collapsed at the foot of the main staircase with helpless guests looking on. She bled to death.

Local people claim that the unfortunate girl afterwards returned to look for her lover, and the tales of Winnington's ghost persist up to the present day. Children are still told of the phantom lady who walks near Winnington Hall, though the last known appearance was so long ago. On this occasion an Irish labourer, finding his way through the new chemical works of Brunner and Mond, was caught up in a mist that swirled into the valley, and suddenly, as he peered into the murky shadows, saw before him a figure of a young woman dressed in white. He turned and fled.

The mysterious lady of Repton Manor, a very old mansion near Ashford, Kent, which was mentioned in the Domesday Book, seemed to continue her hauntings all through the early part of this century and intensify her activities in the late 1940s, when the manor was taken over for a REME Depot, and became the officers' mess.

Shortly after Christmas, 1948 the news leaked out about officers having the lights mysteriously switched on in their rooms at night, and seeing the ghostly figure of a woman bearing a candle pass up the stairs in their quarters. A REME craftsman on guard duty one night also saw the White Lady flitting across a field, and was more frightened by the fact that she appeared to have no feet than by her eerie gliding motion. The guard was turned out to investigate, but the ghost vanished.

Other soldiers and civilians told of seeing strange visions in the gardens.

Local tradition was that centuries ago, a former owner of Repton Manor murdered his wife, and it was her ghost that returned at intervals to haunt the house. On this occasion, however, "Ashford Mary", as the soldiers came to call her, seemed not to be alone, for one officer described the apparition he had seen as dark and cowled, like a monk.

Mr Eric Shepherd, gardener at the manor, was convinced there were two ghosts. He said he had twice seen the ghostly monk in the walled kitchen garden; once at about 5 pm., when it vanished through the wall, and again when, noticing a movement at the end of the garden, he pursued a figure which disappeared into the wall, beyond which there was a 14ft drop. Later, after dark, he and another gardener watched the spot, but saw nothing.

Often in broad daylight, Mr Shepherd said, he and others had been working along the paths and plainly heard approaching footsteps, though nothing whatever was visible.

Sometimes while in the garden he was acutely conscious of a steady, malevolent stare directed on his back, but on looking over his shoulder saw nothing.

Mr H. B. Amos, the previous resident of Repton Manor, said that although he personally had never seen anything uncanny, a friend of his was sure he had seen a ghostly "something" one night as he came up the drive.

Mr Amos's daughter was fully convinced that her old home was haunted. She said that her mother, who had died recently, always assured her that the ghost was harmless, that it liked the occupants and should be accepted as part of the manor and its history. Miss Amos said she had often felt a touch as she went to her room, and had heard rappings, as though of knuckles being struck on the panels of the wall opposite her bed. She had also felt a presence brushing against her.

"Once," she added, "I was sitting at dusk in the same room, with my terrier, when suddenly it gazed at the doorway, its hair stood on end and it leapt in terror through the window. Another time a cat was frightened, apparently by an apparition visible only to itself, but this time in the attic, and it, too, sought escape by the window."

It seemed that Repton Manor might well have two ghosts, one kindly and the other decidedly not.

The phantom lady of Gwrych Castle, near Abergele, North Wales, also walks as the result of a tragedy, according to local belief, and again her true identity is unknown. She is said to be the ghost of a young woman who was thrown from her horse and killed while out riding; she was buried in unconsecrated ground, and is trying to get to consecrated ground. Alternatively, she had been so happy in the castle that she wanted to be buried there, but this was not done as the ground was not consecrated, and so her unhappy ghost has roamed the grounds ever since.

This haunting only dates from the last century, as the castle, with its embattled towers, is not really a very old building. It was built in 1819 in the style of ancient castles, to satisfy a whim of Robert Bamford Hesketh, member of a rich Lancashire family of land proprietors, when he married into the Lloyd family who had squired at Gwrych for generations. The castle, built at great expense, replaced the old Gwrych mansion, a solitary building lying close to the seashore.

Just where the Gwrych Lady fits into the castle's history is obscure, but the more recent accounts of her hauntings date from just after World War II, when the Gwrych Castle estate of some 1,500 acres was sold off in lots by the Earl of Dundonald, into whose hands it had passed.

In 1948 the castle and its furnishings, together with several hundred acres, was bought by Mr Leslie T. Salts, a Liverpool businessman, who went to live there with his wife and two children and converted the building into the popular off-beat holiday and day-trip centre which it is today.

In the spring of 1950 Bruce Woodcock, the British heavyweight boxing champion, chose Gwrych Castle as the training ground for his world title fight with America's Lee Savold. One night in mid-May, Woodcock, while out walking in the ground, with a sparring partner, encountered the Gwrych Lady. This is how his companion, Ted Greenslade, described the incident at the time, fully vouched for by Woodcock:

"Bruce had a bit of supper. Normally he doesn't eat before turning in at ten o'clock, so we decided to take a stroll to walk the meal down a bit. It was about eleven o'clock. We had walked right round the castle when we came to a lonely path and saw the bent-up figure of a young woman sitting on a fallen tree tunk. She had a very pale face and wore a long, dark velvet gown.

"It looked as though she might be in difficulties, so we went up to her. When we got about six yards away she just disappeared. Bruce and I just turned and ran for it; it was the fastest bit of road work we have ever done together."

Mr Salts, after this incident, disclosed that he had been told of the ghost being seen three times in the past eighteen months, always by the old tree trunk.

Others among the several people said to have seen the Gwrych Lady in the early 1950s include Randolph Turpin, who trained there for three months of 1951, and Carroll Levis. Investigators of the Birmingham Society for Psychic Research held a vigil there and, according to their vice-chairman, Mr J. Rowland, in the early morning the watchers saw a luminous form which looked like swirling mist, cross the grass and appear to pass through the castle walls. The phenomenon was accompanied by a sudden rush of cold wind. No natural explanation was found.

Mr Salts tells me that neither he nor any member of his family saw the Gwrych Lady while they lived in the castle, though her various appearances were reported to him in good faith.

Tradition ascribes several other ghosts to Gwrych Castle, which, straggling round the side of a pine-clad hill, looks down on the Irish Sea as well as ancient battlegrounds. These additional spectres are said to be a knight in armour who haunts the battlements and a room in the round tower, a "panting dog", and the ghost of an old Welsh chieftain. They all seem to have their roots in the earlier turbulent history of the locality, where the battles once fought are remembered by such landmarks as one field known as Cae Gerail—"The Field of Corpses". A plaque at the castle states: "On no spot in the Principality has more blood been shed than in this defile."

Another phantom lady who must not be overlooked is one that reputedly haunted a ship, both at sea and in port. The ghost was that of the square-rigged sailing ship, The Lady of Avenel, in the late 1920s the only brigantine left flying the British flag.

The Lady of Avenel, when she lay idle in Leith Harbour during the winter of 1933, had been haunted continuously for seven years. She had a strange history. Built at Falmouth some sixty years before, she had sailed every sea with different cargoes and was at one time used in running slaves from Africa. She had been twice round the Horn, carrying hides, and had sailed on two Arctic expeditions, the last in 1925 with Commander F. A. Worsley, when she was almost crushed in the ice. It was after this trip, for which she was rechristened The Island, that the hauntings began, a female apparition being claimed to haunt her decks. To appease the crew her name was changed again to The Virgo, but this did not stop the ghostly incidents; if anything it intensified them.

On the last voyage of The Virgo the crew spent a very anxious time. A sailor who had never heard of the ghost was reading in his bunk one day when the bunk next to him began to shake violently. There was no apparent explanation. Another time the bosun was reading in his bunk at night when the oil lamp went dim. It seemed probable that the oil reservoir was empty, but on inspection it was found to be full. The wick was turned up again, but time after time the light went dim. Then the bosun kept watch, and was appalled to see a ghostly form "stretch out a long white arm and turn down the lamp".

Another sailor went to sleep with an electric torch under his pillow, and woke with a start when the light from it began to shine in his face. He vowed the torch could not have been switched on accidentally. The same thing happened several times, and he got so scared that he eventually left the ship.

One day at dinner-time the steward heard footsteps on the deck. There should not have been anyone about then, and he went up to check. There was not a soul there. Once at 4 am., said the same steward, he heard a woman's voice on the poop deck, though there was no woman on board.

It was not thought that the haunting would continue when the ship lay idle and up for sale at Leith, but it did. One night the watchman, who was on board alone, could not sleep and sat up reading. Suddenly he saw the ghost of a woman come through a bulkhead and go out again through the cabin door. He would not sleep aboard again, nor would any other nightwatchman stay alone.

The old ship was then bought by Mr F. S. Jackson of Ilkley, a member of the Royal Yorkshire Yacht Club, who took her to Bridlington to be converted into a comfortable cruising yacht. The first thing he did was to give the ship back her old name of The Lady of Avenel.

This seemed to satisfy the mysterious ghost, for the hauntings immediately ceased.

THE MYSTERY OF THE MUSEUM

It was on a Sunday evening in September, 1953 that the drama of York Museum began. A perfectly normal, quiet Sunday. There was a meeting on in the museum and Mr George Jonas, its 44-year-old caretaker, was waiting downstairs with his wife to lock up afterwards. When everyone appeared to have gone, he made a cup of tea before going upstairs to have a last look round and make all secure.

But his wife suddenly asked, *had* everyone gone? Then who was it tramping about upstairs?

Mr Jonas listened, and sure enough heard footsteps. Thinking it must be the curator, he went up to warn him he would be turning out the lights soon. He walked upstairs expecting to see the curator in his office; instead, he found in there an elderly stranger. This is Mr Jonas's account of what followed:

"He was bent over in the far corner of the room. He straightened up as I walked in, turned round, walked past me, and I respectfully drew back. I naturally thought it was some person who had stayed behind. I asked him politely if he was looking for somebody, but he didn't answer. I followed him out of the room, keeping a few steps behind.

"He was dressed, I noticed, in a frock coat with drainpipe trousers, like a professor, and wore elastic-sided boots. I noticed this distinctly as there were no turnups to his trousers. He went straight across into the library, the door of which was open, and I followed him in, turning on the lights as I entered. I heard him exclaim, 'I must find it—I must find it!' He spoke slowly, as if talking to himself.

"He went to a bookshelf and started rummaging among the volumes. By this time I was feeling a bit fed up at being ignored. I thought he must be deaf, so I went up close to him and said, 'If you want to see Mr Willmot (the curator) I'll escort you across to his house.' As I spoke I reached out to touch his shoulder, but when I touched him he vanished . . . just vanished."

It gave the caretaker a terrible shock and he stood transfixed for a minute or two before running to his wife and telling her it was time for them to go. They left for their cottage home in Copman-thorpe, just outside York, not knowing what to make of the extraordinary incident.

Just before the ghost vanished it dropped a book on the floor. Mr Jonas found the volume still lying there the next morning when he looked into the library, and he then told the whole story to the curator.

Four Sundays later Mr Jonas encountered the ghost again. It looked as solid as before—"a very real person"—yet as he watched, the old man in Edwardian dress went through a hall to the library and shuffled *through the locked door*. After this weird episode the caretaker ensured that he had a friend with him on Sundays, so that when, on the next fourth Sunday, the ghost returned yet again, he had a young ex-Guardsman as witness. As they went together into the library, Mr Jonas and his friend heard the pages of a book being turned over, and on walking in they saw a book drop down on to the floor. It was the very same book the ghost had disturbed before.

Mr Jonas was not a nervous man. He had served eleven years in the Army, reaching the rank of sergeant. Before these uncanny incidents he had not believed in ghosts and always classed such things as ridiculous. Now, however, with few people believing his story, he went to his doctor and asked if he could possibly have imagined it all. More than that, he asked the doctor if he would come along to the museum and see for himself. The doctor agreed.

So it happened that on a night of December, 1953 when the ghost was due to appear again—it seemed to be following a regular monthly cycle—a group of six people sat tensely waiting with Mr Jonas in the dimly-lit museum library. They included the doctor and a solicitor friend, also the caretaker's brother, Mr James Jonas —who was among those people strongly sceptical of the haunting —and a representative of the *Yorkshire Evening Press*.

The spacious room with its tall bookshelves had been thoroughly examined beforehand and the blue-backed book which the ghost seemed to make for was inspected by everyone present before be-ing pushed back firmly into place on the shelf. It was an innocuous volume entitled *Antiquities and Curiosities of the Church* and had once belonged to Alderman Edward Wooller, a Darlington solicitor and antiquary, who collapsed and died at a meeting nearly thirty years ago. His business card was pasted inside the book.

The ghostly visitor had always arrived at about 7.40 pm. and shortly before then the watchers took their places. The long minutes ticked by. Then, at exactly eighteen minutes to the hour, the intense silence was broken by a rasping noise as the book was drawn slowly from the tightly packed shelf by an unseen hand and then dropped gently to the floor, coming to rest the right way up and slightly open, close to the rack.

The watchers were overcome with astonishment, all except Mr George Jonas, now greatly relieved at this corroboration of his unnerving experiences. The doctor, who was one of the people nearest to the book, said that a second before it moved his legs had gone strangely cold up to the knees. After the incident he again examined the bookshelf with a torch, removing every book from the shelf, but there was nothing there but a plain wooden shelf and the group were perfectly convinced that there was no natural explanation for what they had just seen. In the words of the doctor, "Without a doubt that book was taken from the shelf by something that is not of this world."

Was the frock-coated ghost of Alderman Wooller walking the museum? Among many letters received by Mr Jonas was one from Miss D. M. Willis, a niece of the alderman living in London. She said that shortly before the apparition made its first appearance she had visited the family grave in a Darlington cemetery; it was her first visit for many years and, she thought, might be responsible for the haunting.

The puzzle of the ghost's identity was, however, the least of it. There was vigorous disagreement within the museum's controlling body, the Yorkshire Philosophical Society, over whether or not the ghostly incidents should be further investigated. The museum's curator for the past four years, Mr F. G. Willmot, maintained an open mind about the various manifestations, now witnessed by a total of nine people, and believed there should be a proper investigation. The Society's chairman did not. He was reported as saying, "It is too silly for words. There will be no investigation. I would not let the subject be brought before the council of the Society. I would not waste time on such tripe."

The clash of opinion led to Mr Willmot handing in notice of his resignation; in the meantime the investigation he had supported went ahead. There could be no January "sitting" because Mr Jonas fell ill, but on the evening of February 7, 1954, the next "fourth Sunday" in the ghostly cycle, twelve investigators waited silently in the museum's shuttered library, its only door locked and elaborate precautions being taken to ensure that no outsiders were near the 100-year-old museum. The watchers included members of the Society for Psychical Research, led by Professor J. W. Harvey of Leeds University, together with two representatives of the Magic Circle, and Mr Jonas himself. They took up their positions at 7.15 pm., twenty-five minutes before the ghost was expected. But although there was a moment when two of the watchers sensed that something was about to happen, both experiencing a sudden feeling of coldness, nothing in fact did; the book which had been disturbed on previous occasions remained wedged in its place. At 8 pm. the ghost-hunters decided to call it a day.

On the next "fourth Sunday", March 7, Professor Harvey led another vigil in the library, with Press and public locked out of the museum grounds as before. Among the six observers who this time sat for forty minutes in the darkened library were the doctor and solicitor present at the original unofficial "sitting", together with Mr Jonas. But again nothing was seen. As one of the observers afterwards said, "Contact with whatever manifestation there might have been in the museum in the past now appears to have been lost."

While all this was going on, strong feeling had been aroused among some members of the Yorkshire Philosophical Society regarding the curator's resignation. It culminated in a special meeting being held to inquire into the circumstances of his going. At this meeting, held the day after the second library vigil, there were, it was reported, "some bitter attacks and some strong defence", and the result was that members, by an overwhelming vote of seventy-seven to twenty-two, decided to ask the curator to withdraw his resignation. Mr Willmot, who had been about to leave for another appointment, agreed to stay, and a crop of resignations came instead from other quarters, the sequel being that at its annual meeting two months later the Yorkshire Philosophical Society emerged with a completely new twelve-member council.

With the ghost retreated and differences over it settled, all was thankfully back to normal at York Museum. The one person, it seemed, to be regretful of this was a grandson of Alderman Wooller in Somerset, who, confirming that the description of the Edwardian ghost tallied exactly with that of his grandfather, expressed himself as being quite thrilled at having a ghost in the family.

THE NIGHT HORSE

The old Royal Ascot Hotel, near the racecourse, once a favourite with the Berkshire race crowds, was put up for auction in the spring of 1964. At the end of the year the demolition men moved in to knock down the old building where the fashionable life had once flourished and guests were met at the railway station by an immaculate coach and pair.

Some of the demolition men made up temporary sleeping quarters in part of the forty-roomed hotel, but work had not long started on the building and its numerous stables, before it became evident to them that something was wrong. There were rumours of "strange goings-on" in the building. Then, shortly after Christmas, the old nightwatchman quit the site hurriedly and vanished without even stopping to collect the two or three days' pay owing to him. He said he had seen and heard a ghostly horse whinnying and stamping late at night in a doorway, and had heard ghostly footsteps.

Other workers then spoke of seeing the phantom white or grey horse, and hearing stamping and snorting in the empty corridors of the derelict hotel; they had also heard the ghostly footsteps. One demolition man, Mr Thomas Murphy, claimed to have seen the ghost horse standing under an arch, while a workmate, Mr Pat Bradshaw, said that sometimes when doing his rounds at night, in the absence of the watchman, he had heard an eerie stamping and snorting in the building which made his hair stand on end. The noises, he said, seemed to start from a small box-room upstairs.

There were other odd occurrences. One night as the men went back to the hotel after finishing work they found themselves unable to open the door; yet it had been left open only minutes before.

The six men then sleeping in the building grew more and more uneasy at night and the site foreman began to find it difficult to get men to work there.

One theory among older residents in the locality was that the ghost grey horse was one of the horses used to drag the bricks up from the kilns to the site when the hotel was built; the unfortunate animal had collapsed from overwork and had to be destroyed. Perhaps, it was thought, after working so hard to help put up the building, it had returned to haunt those who were now pulling it down.

It was a case, however, in which speedy demolition work appeared to bring its own end to the haunting.

A demolition firm of three brothers who contracted to knock down an old country mansion in the Leicestershire village of Bushby, met something more than noises and an apparition, two of them apparently being struck by the ghost or ghosts that lingered on there.

Mr Fred Lunn and his brothers Patrick and Peter, started knocking down the mansion, Bushby Old Hall, in March, 1965. It was a substantial thirty-roomed property built in 1823, and was being demolished to make way for a new housing estate. Its last owner, a tobacco importer with a business in Leicester, had died only months before, and the house was littered with thousands of empty cigar packets.

Trouble began as soon as the demolition work got under way. A strange tapping noise was heard coming from the walls, and ghostly footsteps sounded along a corridor. Then Mr Patrick Lunn, aged thirty-eight, when working in the corridor by himself one evening, was struck by an unseen force. He described the incident:

"I opened six doors in the corridor and walked away from them, and they all slammed shut. There was no breeze or anything that could have caused it. I thought my brothers had crept up on me and were larking about, but I had a look round and could find nobody. I went out on to the roof to look around, and then went back into the corridor, and something hit me between the eyes. I did not see what it was, and it was not so dark that I wouldn't have seen it if there had been anything to see. I did not hang around— I was off like a shot."

He carried the bruise on his face for weeks.

On a later occasion the unseen force attacked Peter Lunn, aged twenty. He said, "I was just getting brass stair clips out of the stairs when I smelt cigar smoke. I knew there was nobody else in the house and I looked up. As I did so, something I could not see hit me in the face and split my lip. I was bowled downstairs by the blow. I got up and searched around, but there was nowhere anybody could have hidden, and there was certainly nobody there."

The brothers made inquiries in the village and learned that the house was reputed to be haunted by the ghost of an old woman who was housekeeper there many years ago, and who had lost her mind and committed suicide by jumping off the roof. A former butler at the mansion told them that the corridor in which Patrick Lunn was struck was in his day haunted by the ghost, which was known as "Mary"; she often walked the corridor and banged the doors shut all at once. But, said the old servant, "Mary" had never harmed anyone before. This gave rise to a belief that there might now be two ghosts active in the building.

There were other incidents. One day as eight of the demolition workers were sitting talking about the mysterious haunting, an upstairs window came hurtling down of its own accord, narrowly missing them. Another time, Patrick Lunn was standing on a low parapet when it suddenly and unaccountably crumbled, sending him crashing to the ground.

One worker stayed only two days at the haunted mansion. He was working in one of the older parts of the building when he suddenly raced down the stairs and out into the garden. He said something about "the old lady" as he went, and that was the last that was seen or heard of him; the frightened man did not return to collect his pay. Two other men after hearing strange noises refused to work on the mansion and had to be drafted to the firm's other sites; another refused to go inside the building. The demolition chief, Mr Fred Lunn, had to search for new workers.

Once again, however, the ghost or ghosts seemed to vanish with the removal of the last brick of the old building, as they did also at Leamington, Warwickshire, in 1960, after demolition men there had narrowly escaped an attack by a seemingly invisible force. The men were knocking down Brookhurst, a hundred-year-old building formerly the clubhouse of Leamington Golf Club, to make way for a block of flats. A gang of four were working on the joists of a top-storey window when suddenly three bricks came crashing through the panes. Glass flew in all directions as the men dived for safety. When they looked to see who or what was responsible for the incident there was no one in sight. It was impossible for children to have thrown the bricks as they were far too heavy for them to handle.

It was, the men said afterwards, a terrifying experience, as if someone was trying to scare them away. One workman refused to go on working alone on the roof. He said he had the strong feeling that there was someone by his side all the time.

The big difference between the Leicestershire and Leamington incidents is that the men at Brookhurst had been warned what to

expect when they started the job—that "George" might be busy—
but no one had believed the story. They did afterwards, as had
many before them who encountered the Brookhurst ghost and
reported its strange activities. Dozens of men and women in
earlier years had claimed to have heard the ghost. Echoing footsteps which passed through locked doors were heard by groups of
people on many different occasions. Doors opened and unlocked
themselves, though the keys were always in the safekeeping of one
man; lights were switched on and off and the front doorbell rang
of its own accord, swift and thorough searches always revealing
that mischievous children, burglars or practical jokers could not
possibly have been responsible.

Several people claimed that the ghost actually "combed their
hair" as they walked down a certain passage. Others who heard
something fly past them in the house had each compared the
noise with that of a huge bird flapping its wings.

The *Leamington Spa Courier* was able to gather many authentic
stories of the ghost from eye-witnesses. Mrs Hilda Heffer, who in
the early 1950s was manageress of the golf club and lived on the
premises, said that her son, aged twelve at the time, once woke her
up in the middle of the night saying he had seen a shadowy object
fly across the room, making a great flapping noise as if it had
wings, and that it had flown out through the *closed* window. She
could not leave the terrified boy alone at night for a long time
afterwards.

Mr Granville Gulliman, a Leamington businessman, said he had
first become aware of strange things at Brookhurst when he took
it over in 1935. He often heard footsteps and sensed that he was
being followed, only to find that there was no one there. Sometimes the uncanny presence made a flapping noise which he
described as "like a mackintosh blowing in the wind".

Several people recalled when, four times in succession, the front
door opened and footsteps passed through the house. No one was
found, and though there was deep snow outside there were no
footprints.

Mr Gulliman said that on many occasions the police came to
lock up for him late at night, only to return first thing in the
morning to find the place unlocked. On one occasion in 1948 when
a constable called at the club they both heard the sound of someone groaning. They searched the building but could find no one,
and the constable was so unnerved that he jumped on his bicycle
and pedalled off as fast as he was able.

Mr and Mrs E. T. Gulliman and their young son, who lived at
Brookhurst prior to its demolition, said they heard "George"

frequently and, although coming in time to accept him as one of the family, tired of answering the doorbell and finding no one there, and of going to meet footsteps which did not have an owner. Mrs Gulliman heard "the wings" at times, while her mother, who also lived on the premises, saw "a winged object" float down the passage.

But the ghost seemed quite harmless, which made its apparent attack on the demolition men so unusual, and perhaps, many thought, a sign of its resentment as being finally deprived of its home.

One of the strangest shocks to any workman in recent years must be that received by Mr Harry Myerthall, a painter's labourer, at Rosyth Dockyard, Fife, in 1955. It happened early one morning when he went to work alone on the aircraft carrier Glory, then undergoing a refit. Mr Myerthall, of Edinburgh, tells his own story:

"A few days after Christmas I left the dining hut near Glory at half-past seven in the morning and went aboard the ship. I went to Cabin 8 on the galley deck where I kept my working clothes. By the time I reached the cabin it was about a quarter to eight. Outside the cabin there was a locker in which I kept my lamp needed for working in the passageways. It was a double lamp that would light both the cabin and the corridor, and I stepped inside the cabin to plug in the cable.

"When the light was switched on I saw a man standing by the dressing-table near the door of the cabin. He was quite tall, about 5 ft 9 in., and was dressed in tropical flying kit. He wore a pair of blue shorts and a leather flying jacket with a fur collar, the jacket hanging open. On the right-hand side of the jacket a row of small bombs was painted in red, and on the left-hand side were pilot's wings. The man had a flying helmet on the back of his head and a wave of blond hair stuck out from under it in the front. On the right side of his neck he had a long red scar. I did not notice if he was wearing flying boots or if the helmet had goggles attached.

"After staring at the man for a moment, I concluded that he was one of the small maintenance staff of naval men aboard the carrier and said, 'Good morning. Did you enjoy your Christmas?' There was no reply to this. I stepped out of the cabin again to get a leather jerkin from the locker, then I suddenly realised it was odd that a man should be in Cabin 8 in full flying kit. I turned round to ask the man who he was, but there was no one in the room.

"I grabbed the lamp which I had hung above the door and rushed into the cabin to search it. There was only a bunk, a dressing-table and an open locker; there was nothing in any of them and no sign of anyone in the room."

He dropped the lamp and rushed along the passage, shouting.
As he was plunging down the stairs he was stopped by a workmate
who saw his distressed state, and together they returned to the
cabin and examined it again, but found nothing and no one.

When the naval commander came aboard, Mr Myerthall and
his colleague told the officer about the man with the scarred neck
and once again the cabin was searched thoroughly but nothing
found.

Mr Myerthall was taken from the ship in a state of shock.
Rumour spread through the dockyard that the apparition he had
seen was that of an officer who was killed in a crash-landing on the
Glory after returning from an operational flight over Korea,
shortly before a Christmas during the Korean War. The ghostly
airman, it was said, had appeared before, in each case after
Christmas and always in Cabin 8, which he was believed to have
occupied.

The naval commander, however, said there was no record of a
previous manifestation aboard the ship. There had certainly been
considerable loss of life among the flying officers of the Glory
during her Korean service; in all, twenty-five men had died, but
none as a result of a crash-landing on the ship's deck. Nor was it
likely that the apparition was that of an RAF officer who was
killed, as it was not thought that any RAF personnel had ever
served aboard the ship.

So the red scarred ghost of the Glory remains a complete
mystery.

THE HAUNTED WARDROBE

On the morning of Thursday, August 19, 1937 the main news of
the day was of 300,000 Chinese troops marching to counter a
Japanese invasion, Sir Malcolm Campbell all set to capture the
world speedboat record, and Tommy Farr besieged while training
in America for his heavyweight contest with Joe Louis. What
attracted many readers of the *Morning Post*, however, was the
following heart-cry tucked away in the Personal Column:

> FOR SALE.—Haunted wardrobe.—Advertiser will be glad to
> deliver same to anybody interested, complete with ghost, which
> would also no doubt feel more at home if welcomed.—Write Mrs
> Barclay, Carterton Manor, Oxon.

Within a few hours of publication more than thirty offers were
received by telegram and telephone from many parts of the country.
Then the letters started arriving, scores of them.

The strange chain of events which led to Mrs Barclay in
desperation placing her advertisement in the national newspaper
had begun, innocently enough, three years before, when she
looked in at a sale of effects at a private house near Streatley,
Berkshire. There she saw the wardrobe in question, a perfectly
ordinary piece of Victorian furniture in walnut, seven-foot high
and seven-foot six inches wide, with four drawers and mirrors.
She paid only £10 for it, for although she was in need of a spacious
wardrobe and it took her fancy, there was little of artistic merit in
it. She put it in a guest room in her house and thought nothing
more of it. There it remained for over two years.

Early in the spring of 1937, Mrs Barclay and the household staff
began to hear strange rattling and banging noises in the house,
but could not understand where they came from. Then, several
friends who at various times came to stay for the weekend asked
Mrs Barclay if there was anything odd about the wardrobe. When
she expressed her surprise they did not care to explain any more
about it; but eventually some guests who slept in the room asked
her frankly if she could account for the strange opening and

shutting of the wardrobe doors. It had, they said, kept them awake all night.

After her friends' departure, when the weird banging noises continued, Mrs Barclay kept observation and found that the wardrobe doors did seem to be opening and shutting of their own accord. But still she was only half convinced of the wardrobe having any strange properties, and she and her secretary, Mr East, an ex-RAF officer, were inclined to joke about the whole affair. In this mood they decided to investigate the wardrobe for a hidden panel. They went upstairs and walked towards the wardrobe, but before they could touch it, the centre door jumped off of its own accord and smashed the mirror on the door opposite. They were so startled that they decided not to touch the wardrobe at all.

The banging and rattling noises, which could be heard all over the house, now continued almost every night; but that was not all. One night there appeared from the wardrobe the figure of a somewhat bent and wizened man, dressed in old-fashioned clothes and wearing a kind of deerstalker's cap, which walked downstairs and straight out of the front door. Mrs Barclay saw the strange figure when the electric lights were full on. It appeared again on another night, and after the first shock she tried to touch it, but it vanished in her fingers. The ghost continued to make its nightly excursions and she saw it several times. So did her secretary, and her brother. To the three of them together it was its procedure to appear for half a minute or more, then vanish.

Mrs Barclay again tried to touch the ghost, but it slipped from her fingers. On one occasion it stopped and looked at her for a full minute, before turning to the door and walking out, banging the door behind it.

From a chilling phenomenon the ghost now became an out and out nuisance. Mrs Barclay explained at the time, "I am not psychic, nor am I nervous, but this wretched ghost will make such a noise. He clatters across the landing, and shuffles down the stairs, and the noise is often exasperatingly loud."

None of her friends could be induced to spend a weekend at Carterton Manor so long as the wardrobe remained, and her staff threatened to give notice. A friend, Mr E. Rundle, landlord of the Plough Inn at Clanfield, not far away, one night tried lashing the wardrobe up with string, securely fastening it round the doors and drawers. But in the morning the string lay on the floor. The noises continued, the wardrobe drawers opening and shutting all night, and Mrs Barclay had to move her bed out on to the sunshine roof in order to get some sleep.

The ghost seemed to take a dislike to the butler, whom it kicked roundly on the shins. It finally made the life of both butler and maid so unbearable that they gave notice and left hurriedly. It was now clear to Mrs Barclay that she would never be able to get anyone to work for her until the haunted piece of furniture was out of the house. So, just as the cook gave notice that she would not sleep in the house another night, and removed all her belongings to the village, Mrs Barclay decided to put her advertisement in the *Morning Post*, in the hope that someone who could understand ghostly phenomena would take the wardrobe off her hands.

On the day of publication the telephone at Carterton Manor rang incessantly and the rustic calm of the hamlet of Carterton was shattered by the intrusion of eager ghost-hunters, several American visitors calling in their cars to see the ghostly wardrobe. Other offers were for the immediate transport of the wardrobe to country houses hundreds of miles away, while yet others asked Mrs Barclay to name any cash figure she liked.

The ghost apparently did not take very kindly to all this. Mrs Barclay later described how she was just sitting down to lunch, after dealing with the rush of inquiries since breakfast time, when another telegram arrived. It was from Chobham, Surrey, and the sender, in making an offer for the wardrobe, asked, "Can you guarantee ghosts?" Mrs Barclay, by her own account, had a good laugh at this and was about to start her lunch when she heard a noise behind her; and there was the ghost itself, standing in front of the mantelpiece, wearing its deer-stalker cap. It vanished again without a word.

The inquiries and callers came all that day, and there was also the Press to contend with. Mrs Barclay and her secretary agreed to keep a vigil that night with two newspapermen. For an hour nothing happened, then inside the wardrobe there was a noise which one of the witnesses likened to the sound of berries falling off trees. The peculiar noise gradually increased. One of the party, shining his torch, then saw on the floor in front of the wardrobe a button that had not been there before. Suddenly Mrs Barclay screamed, "He is there!" None of the others then glimpsed the ghost, but Mrs Barclay said she had seen it quickly leave the room, wearing as usual its deer-stalker hat.

Not long afterwards there was a loud cry from outside the house and a six-foot figure in white could be seen bobbing about in the vicinity; the practical jokers were now at work. The intruder was chased off the grounds by Mr East.

Mrs Barclay and her secretary then decided to have the wardrobe moved out into the garden, so that all could get some rest.

Next day the stream of letters and telegrams continued to pour in from places throughout the country; making offers, giving advice, and including even a proposal of marriage. Telegram after telegram asked for the wardrobe to be reserved. A college of astrology wanted it; so did four spinsters, who asked to be allowed to have the ghost to protect them as they lived alone in a large house; while another letter asked, "Do you think the ghost would be happy in a small modern house?"

Then there was the flood of advice. "I should say it's doubtful if the ghost will go with the wardrobe. He shows himself to you as you are sympathetic, but he may not do so to others. . . . Don't lock the wardrobe, you should never lock a door on a corpse or a ghost. . . . Leave the door open at night so that he can come in and out, and put a nice comfortable chair beside it for him, as he clings so to the wardrobe. . . . I should say his treasure is concealed somewhere inside it. I should search until you find out what it is. . . . Never mind the cook, cooks are plentiful, but you can never get another wardrobe like this."

Mrs Barclay's one fear was that the ghost would not agree to its enforced removal and depart with the wardrobe, but would stay on in the house, in which case she herself would have to leave. Resolute to have the wardrobe off the premises at the earliest moment, she accepted an offer of £50 from her friend Mr Rundle at Clanfield—it was the highest of a number of early bids she received—and the wardrobe was transported the few miles south to its new home at once.

Mr Rundle put the wardrobe in an outhouse in the garden of his inn. The Plough was then being rebuilt and there was as yet no room large enough for the wardrobe. But, said Mr Rundle, an ex-RAF officer, he would have his own bedroom enlarged and put the wardrobe in it, then anyone who would like to sleep in the room would be free to do so. He emphasised, however, that he personally had no belief in ghosts.

Nor, unfortunately, had the more boisterous elements in the neighbourhood, for no sooner did peace come to Carterton, with an end to the jokers in white sheets running about firing pistols near the manor, than pandemonium reigned in the village of Clanfield. News of the wardrobe's arrival soon spread and all the lads from miles around gathered round the outhouse and began catcalling and throwing bricks on to the iron roof. It was impossible for a long time for the residents of the Plough even to hear themselves. One or two of the village youths in all seriousness asked to be allowed to sit round the wardrobe and keep watch, and they were given peace for a few minutes, but then the majority outside restarted catcalling, wailing and throwing brick-bats, and the "sitting" was a failure.

Mr Rundle, though still stressing his scepticism, testified that during one of the quiet spells on this first night one of the wardrobe's doors started trembling considerably; and there was no question of vibration coming from anywhere as the outhouse walls were of two-feet thick Cotswold stone. His wife, too, heard curious rattlings and a "noise like an aeroplane" coming from the wardrobe.

On the next night the row from the villagers was worse than ever, so in the morning Mr Rundle had the wardrobe brought into the hotel and put into the one available room. As it had been strongly suggested that the ghost was seeking something in the wardrobe, he took it to pieces. He found nothing abnormal—and certainly no bloodstains, as had also been claimed. A furniture expert also examined the wardrobe, finding nothing except some signs of alteration inside.

From that day on the wardrobe remained silent. Mr Rundle was left with an ordinary utilitarian piece of Victorian furniture; and wherever the unknown figure in the deer-stalker hat might have departed to, it never again visited Carterton Manor or bothered anyone at the Plough.

THE SAD CAVALIER

Soon after taking over the Ring o' Bells, a very old public-house in Middleton, near Oldham, in December 1966, Mrs May Penneyston began to hear footsteps in the passage, though when she went to look there was never anyone there. Frequently on hearing the footsteps she would think it was a customer, but on going into the bar would find it empty.

There were other puzzling incidents. Mrs Penneyston was often woken up in the night by bumping sounds, as if someone was trying to get in, but when the premises were searched everything was found to be in perfect order. One night she was woken by a big crash like the sound of windows breaking, but again, on a search downstairs, there was no one there and nothing to account for the noises. On yet another night she heard strange rustling sounds, which she thought at first might be her son moving about, but it was not, and once again there was nothing to explain the disturbance.

Meanwhile the mysterious footsteps continued their wandering at all times of the day and night; as they still do.

Mrs Penneyston is now firmly convinced, as others before her have been, that the centuries-old public-house is haunted by the ghost of the "Sad Cavalier", a local Royalist who is believed to have been murdered and buried in the cellar there in the days of Cromwell.

The Ring o' Bells goes much farther back into history than the time of the Civil Wars. Its foundations, like those of the church nearby, are believed to date from Saxon times, and a Druid's temple is thought to have once stood on the site. Later, and until the dissolution by Henry VIII, the Bells served as the refectory to the church and monks brewed their beer there. In Cromwell's day there still existed a secret passage from the cellar to the church, and it was this passage that played a prominent part in the fate of the Sad Cavalier.

The cavalier, tradition says, was the son of Lord Stannycliffe of Stannycliffe Hall, near Middleton. Father and son were staunchly

Royalist, whereas Middleton was a powerful stronghold of the Roundheads. Cromwell's men used as their headquarters the Old Boar's Head, which still stands not far away on the main road to Rochdale. The Royalists were obliged to meet secretly in the Ring o' Bells cellar, which then formed the public-house itself.

One day while the cavalier was in the cellar someone betrayed him to the Roundheads. He escaped hurriedly through the secret passage to the church, but the Roundheads, who, some say, made their own way to the church through another passage from the Old Boar's Head, intercepted him at the church and cut him down. It seems uncertain whether the cavalier was actually killed inside the church or whether, left for dead, he managed to drag himself back through the passage to the Ring o' Bells' cellar, where he died; but at any rate tradition is firm that he was buried by his friends under a flagstone in the cellar.

Today, in a little "snug" above the cellar where the cavalier is supposed to lie buried is what is known as the Cavalier's seat. Mrs Penneyston tells me, "Some people who had not heard about the ghost have complained about feeling cold and having the shivers when they sit there, though it is warm everywhere else and there is no draught." Other customers, she adds, have refused to sit there at all, including one man who said he would not do so for £100. The ghosts of the Royalists are supposed to sit around the table at this spot at night; it is referred to as "the ghosts' table".

Other occupants of the Ring o' Bells have, over the years, reported seeing the cavalier, dressed in a wide-brimmed plumed hat, lace collar and cloak, and carrying a sword. Mrs Penneyston has not seen the apparition but she has a strong feeling that the ghost is there always. She describes him as "friendly but terribly sad", and says she thinks he likes to mix with the customers. There have been many instances of this. Once, when a customer went to the bar for a drink, he made way for someone apparently trying to pass him, yet on looking round found there was no one there. Another time a customer heard someone laughing at the back of Mrs Penneyston, a hearty "Ha, ha, ha," but again there was nobody there.

Mrs Penneyston's husband, Duncan, keeps an open mind about the ghost but he admits to once hearing a voice in the cellar that he could not explain. He was in the cellar when he heard footsteps coming downstairs and a voice, very deep, saying "'Ow do you do?" apparently behind him. Mr Penneyston replied "I'll be with you in a minute", and continued for a moment looking for something in an old cupboard. When he looked round there was no one there, nor was there anybody in the public-house at all.

This occurred on one of the nights that Mrs Penneyston heard the ghostly footsteps in the passage.

Mrs Penneyston considered having the cellar flagstone lifted and the floor dug up in a search for the cavalier's grave. She thought that on the one hand it would show if there was any truth in the legend, which seemed well supported by the discovery in recent years of at least one secret tunnel and helmets, pikes, and other weapons; while on the other hand it might give rest to the cavalier if, should his bones be found, they were given a proper burial in the churchyard.

But on second thoughts she decided against having the cellar floor disturbed. The cavalier, she now believes, might prefer to remain in peace in the place where he was buried. She looks upon him as a friendly sort of ghost and says he does not frighten her at all.

"The tune of 'Greensleeves' is supposed to have been the sort of theme of the cavaliers," she told me. "Apparently they used to whistle the tune to identify themselves. One day I was sitting at the piano and found myself playing it. It just happened. I often play it now; I think he likes it."

The only person now in the locality who is said to have actually seen the cavalier's ghost is Mrs E. Peacock, who lives in an old cottage nearby. She had to be up very early one morning to deliver papers and suddenly came upon a man in a slouch hat and dress of the cavalier period. His dark brown hair was in ringlets and he had a very sad face and was crying, she says. He came towards her, and then vanished just as suddenly as he had appeared.

Another case of encountering a ghost almost immediately on moving into the premises occurred at Kidderminster in 1963, although here there was no local tradition to explain the sudden haunting.

Within weeks of taking over as bar manager at the licensed premises in Swan Street of Charles Harvey and Co, more popularly known as Harvey's wine vaults, Mr Bert Pye began to hear footsteps when there was no one but himself in the building. Then there were several other uncanny incidents, including mysterious bangings and doors opening and shutting of their own accord, which prompted Mr Pye to stay no longer than necessary after closing the bar each night.

On one alarming occasion a customer was sitting alone in a room at the back of the premises when one of the doors suddenly opened and closed; then the latch on another door which led out to the street was raised and the door opened by itself *against a spring*. It just seemed, Mr Pye told me, as if someone had walked across the room from the one door to the other. The startled customer left his drink and the premises rather hurriedly.

Shortly afterwards one of the barmaids, Mrs Winifred Mac-Donough, saw the ghost. One afternoon after closing time she was clearing up on one side of the bar when she heard footsteps. Thinking someone had been accidentally locked in, she went to check around. There was nobody there, but as she turned to go back she was surprised to see the figure of a woman suddenly coming towards her round the bar.

Mrs MacDonough described the woman as being tall, young, and smartly dressed. "She was wearing a long brown dress with ruffled collar, pulled in tightly at the waist, and a straw hat. I still thought she was a customer and then I realised she was wearing clothes from another century. She had a friendly face and I wasn't frightened. She seemed to float past and then disappeared through the side door."

A second barmaid also experienced a visit from the mysterious Lady in Brown. The big puzzle was, who *was* the restless phantom?

It seemed that the cellar at Harvey's, which was used for wine and spirit storage, might provide a clue. The *Kidderminster Times* recalled the surprise discovery of this cellar in 1851. The Harvey's building was rebuilt on the site of the former Clarence Inn, and in 1851, when this inn's stable flooring was being repaired, it gave way to disclose a great vault below containing a two-foot deep layer of decayed animal matter and human bones. It seemed that the vault had been filled with the human remains and then arched over, for the bricks of the arch were of much later date. Finds among the rubbish included a small black bottle, an old drinking glass, a clumsy pick-axe and some heavy tobacco pipes of an unusual shape.

Historians believed that the vault, which had a pointed roof and gothic windows with mullions of the sixteenth century, was at one time a chapel belonging to an old gild, or perhaps the chapel to a private manor house nearby. Whether there was any connection between the chapel and the Lady in Brown it was impossible to say, but the report of the haunting brought word from Mr Arthur James, who years ago had lived over a shop adjoining Harvey's premises. Mr James said his family then had use of the vault, which had been adapted as cellars, and often the atmosphere in there felt rather strange; his sister was afraid even to go past the entrance. But although he lived there for about six years, Mr James never heard or saw anything of the ghost.

Unlike the Lady in Brown, whose appearance seemed short-lived, a crinolined ghost that walked the old Volunteer Inn at Frenchgate, Doncaster, in the 1950s was very consistent in her haunting. Nor was she entirely unknown, local belief being that she was the spirit of a young woman who had died in the inn after a fall from her horse in the courtyard 200 years ago.

The licensee, Mr George Greetham, and his wife did not believe in ghosts when they first moved into the inn; until they saw what they described as a "crinolined shadow" moving about the corridors and bedrooms. Mr Greetham said the ghost's features were so delicate that he and his wife were not a bit scared, and in time, like Mrs Penneyston with the Sad Cavalier, they grew rather attached to the wraith; so much so that when the Volunteer Inn was due for demolition to make way for a road scheme, they became anxious to find her another "home", and seriously considered whether the ghost, whom they called "Cynthia", could be transferred somewhere else by clairvoyance; preferably to a public-house, as the ghost seemed to like mixing with the customers.

Mrs Greetham described her as "such a sweet ghost. She wanders about and never bothers anyone."

Many ghosts can be just like that.

THE PHOTOGRAPHIC GHOST

In the little mid-Devon village of Spreyton, on a pleasant sunny day in 1932, the vicar, together with a friend, walked out on to the vicarage lawn, the vicar carrying his inexpensive box camera. In turn each took a snapshot towards the vicarage; and the resultant pictures began arguments that went on for years afterwards.

In each case there appeared in the photograph the shadow of what seemed to be a monk, kneeling some five or six feet from the photographer, apparently in prayer, and wearing a flowing robe and cowl.

At the time of day the pictures were taken, and from the standing position of each photographer, it would have been impossible for the sun to cast a shadow in front of them. Yet the "manifestation" was quite clear in both pictures, the cowled head being perfectly distinct. In the picture taken by his friend, the vicar, the Rev W. R. Dunstan, was seen standing in front of the house. Any possibility of the monk being Mr Dunstan's shadow was disposed of by the fact that Mr Dunstan was wearing jacket and trousers, while the mysterious shadow was undoubtedly that of someone in a long robe. In addition the vicar was a small man, while the strange figure whose shadow appeared in both photographs was of unusually large build.

The pictures were carefully examined by experts, who could offer no explanation for the ghostly monk. The developers, too, could detect nothing abnormal about the film or the camera, which were both perfectly ordinary.

It was an eerie shock for the vicar and his friend, but stranger things were witnessed inside Spreyton vicarage, a building centuries old. Mr Dunstan described them:

"One evening I called in my sexton on some business or other, which we were attending to in an upstairs room. Suddenly, heavy footsteps crossed the hall, directly below us. They were calm, unhurried and deliberate, and we sat amazed, for we knew there could be no other human being in the house. The moment they ceased we leapt up and ran downstairs, but there was no one there. The poor sexton was very puzzled. He had heard rumour of such things in the village but had been sceptical about their veracity; now he is prepared to swear that he heard the footsteps.

"On another occasion my wife and I had retired for the night and I had gone soundly to sleep, when the phantom footsteps manifested themselves. My wife tells me that she plainly heard the footsteps cross the hall, mount the stairs, pass the bedroom door, and enter the next room, where some clothes were drying on a clothes horse. At this point there was a report, exactly as if the clothes horse had gone over. The noise awakened me, and after my wife told me what she had heard, we both went into the next room to see what was there. But as usual, there was nothing—and the clothes were just where they had been.

"These things never startle us, however; on the contrary, we are quite used to them, and at each incident wonder interestedly what the next will be. Often we will hear a chair or something fall in another room. We will know by the sound exactly what has fallen over, and yet never, on inspection, have we found anything out of its place.

"Once I was sitting reading when I heard the letter-box bang, as it always does with the post, and I heard something fall flat on the floor. I went straight to the hall, a couple of steps, but there was nothing there—absolutely nothing."

Though the ghostly footsteps and other strange noises continued at the vicarage for some time, no apparition was seen apart from that apparently captured by the box camera. Nor was there a conclusive explanation for the haunting, despite lingering memories in the village of similar disturbances at the vicarage reported by a vicar many years before. Mr Dunstan's two immediate predecessors had heard nothing beyond the scurry of rats, the flutter of nesting bats in the roof timbers, and the activity of bees settled in the corridor walls. The only slender clue to the haunting provided by history was that in 1445 the priest of the parish was Henry Le Mayne, a Norman, whose name was supposed to be a corruption of *le moine*, which meant "the monk".

Spreyton vicarage, however, was not alone with its ghost. Close by stood rambling Bush House, the biggest house in the village, with no fewer than four staircases leading to its upper rooms. Attached to this building, which was at least 400 years old, was a legend that if one followed the ghost of a woman in a black silk dress, she would lead the way to a vast sum of money stowed away in one of the nooks and crannies that abounded in the place. No one as yet had had the courage to test the truth of the legend, though the Black Lady was by no means as elusive as the spirit of the vicarage and appeared fleetingly at intervals. She had last been seen only two years before, in 1930, by two girls staying in the house, and her practice seemed to be first to attract attention by the loud rustling of her dress, and then to emerge from an old cupboard in a corner of a room in which stood an old style four-poster bed.

There was, however, nothing to suggest that the Black Lady had transferred her attention to the vicarage, and certainly her apparition bore not the slightest resemblance to the monkish figure in the vicar's photographs.

About this same time another vicar told of how he had witnessed the activities of a spectral nun. This was at the old village of Monkton, in Pembrokeshire. The vicar, the Rev Tudor Evans, and his family had to live for a time in the Old Hall, which was believed to be part of an ancient priory; some of the rooms had been cells, and there was a large groined crypt under it. Mr Evans said that for some time he heard a heavy knocking on his bedroom door regularly at four o'clock every morning and it could not be traced to any normal cause. There was one room into which the family's dog refused to go; one day his daughter saw a glow in this room and the distinctly outlined head and shoulders of what looked like a cowled figure, leaning out of the window and apparently waving to her. On another occasion, said the vicar, a friend who slept the night in the haunted room heard the rustling of garments round his bed all night, and when he tried to light candles they were mysteriously snuffed out.

Evidence in support of this haunting was the discovery of the kneeling body of a woman walled up in the priest's room of Monkton Church. The vicar believed she was a nun who had committed some sin that had kept her spirit earthbound. It had been, perhaps, her task to wake the other nuns for a four o'clock service, and this her wraith was still continuing to do.

The ghost of a nun seen in the 600-year-old rectory at South-fleet, near Gravesend, was also believed by the rector, the Rev William Falloon, to be that of a woman who had sinned. This ghost had actually been exorcised by the Bishop of Rochester many years before, in 1874, but apparently with little success, for during his twenty-one years at Southfleet until retirement in 1953, Mr Falloon several times saw the nun in her brown habit walk from the monk's room of the rambling old rectory. Mr. Falloon, who described the nun as having the red face of a country-woman, thought it possible that she had associated with a monk whose gravestone had been uncovered near the church nearly a century before; the monk had been excommunicated, obviously for some terrible sin.

In the fine old Queen Anne rectory at Ash, near Aldershot, a shock for the rector, one night of 1938, was not the sight or sound of a wandering figure but the noisy appearance of a phantom vehicle which passed right through his bedroom. The Rev W. J. Blaikie told in his parish magazine how he was suddenly woken from his sleep by the noise of a post horn and galloping horses; next thing, wide awake, he saw a stage coach and four rush up and clatter through his bedroom in the direction of St Peter's Church.

"No one," he said, "was more surprised than I at being awakened by the noise of a horn and the thud of horses and seeing this strange apparition canter through the house. I both saw it and heard it quite distinctly—it was most realistic."

Ash Rectory, with its old cobbled coaching yard attached, was built on the site of an old coaching road and, Mr Blaikie thought, the coach-and-four, apparently resenting this intrusion on its right of way continued to drive through the rectory as if it did not exist. On making inquiries Mr Blaikie discovered that the previous rector had witnessed the very same noisy passage of the spectral coach.

As might be expected, vicarages have many times been thought to be haunted by their late incumbents. A recent case was at Deddington, Oxfordshire, in 1962 when mysterious happenings at the vicarage were attributed to the restless spirit of the late vicar, the Rev Maurice Frost, who had died on the Christmas Day previously, aged seventy-three. Mr Frost, who had been vicar of Deddington for thirty-five years, was a collector of antique clocks and kept about a dozen of them at the vicarage, always making sure that they all chimed together. When Mr H. Campbell-Jarratt moved into the vicarage nearly four months after the vicar's death, to settle his cousin's affairs, he decided to sell the clocks. They then all began striking at 4 am., though they had not been wound since the vicar's death.

The chimings stopped when the clocks were taken away to be sold in London. But there were other odd happenings. Strange noises were heard in the ground floor rooms of the vicarage, especially in the study, usually between 3.30 am. and 9.30 am. Mr Campbell-Jarratt never saw the ghost but, he said, for a long period the feeling was always there that someone was in the place all the time. Once when he was leaving a room carrying an antique handle, the handle was suddenly wrenched back in his hand. He tried to walk on but was pulled backwards; he was forced to drop the handle and walk away. On other occasions beds were pressed down as if someone was sitting on them beside his wife and himself; he heard footsteps in the vicar's study when no one was there; domestic staff heard coughing in the empty study, and gave notice. This coughing was also heard in the drawing-room, and the late vicar had been a chain smoker. Then there were instances of pictures being disturbed; once, while a visitor was being shown round the vicarage, a picture which was in its proper position was later seen to have been turned round.

The incidents stopped shortly before the auction sale at the vicarage, but so often in these cases a service becomes necessary.

In 1931 a Roman Catholic priest in Eccles, Lancashire, decided to offer prayers and sprinkle holy water in a house claimed to have been haunted for four years by one of his predecessors. The Lees family had spent two uneventful years in the house in Liverpool Road, Eccles, before the ghostly incidents began. First Mrs Lees herself became aware of them, then other members of the family, and friends. There were strange noises in the night, and members of the family wakened in the early hours to find their beds moved from the positions in which they had been when they went to sleep. Then there came, at intervals, a figure in priest's clothing which was seen to move down the stairs and disappear through a wall. The ghost's appearance was usually followed by more odd noises.

The family eventually had to move out of the rooms in which the phenomena was most pronounced, though the apparition continued to visit all rooms of the house at night, dissolving into nothing when challenged. Two girls sprinkled holy water in an attempt to lay the ghost, but the disturbances continued and frightened visitors to the house, one at least of whom clearly saw the ghost walk through the wall at the bottom of the stairs.

Neighbours were convinced that the apparition was that of Father Sharrock, the first Catholic parish priest of Eccles, who had died at the house, then the presbytery, forty years previously. This fact of the ghost's probable identity made the Lees family all the more reluctant to take action and it was a friend who finally approached Father J. Drescher, the parish priest of St Mary's, and told him the whole story. Father Drescher decided the Lees needed help. So, on an October afternoon of 1931, he went into each room of the house, sprinkling holy water and murmuring blessings to allay the fears of the occupants; and prayers for the family and the dead priest were also said in the old church.

This seemed to give the ghost of Father Sharrock release at last.

THE HOUSE OF SPOOK WATER

Mr Samuel Long and his wife had lived quietly for thirteen years in their house in Bell Lane, Leicester. It was a comfortable enough house and certainly had no signs of damp; in fact it was commonly acknowledged to be the driest of all of the properties in the road.

There had been just one spot of bother for the Longs, in the twelfth year of their tenancy. This was when a new floor was laid in the kitchen and soon afterwards began to flood with water. At first the sink outlet was thought to be at fault, but it was found to be quite sound. A plumber eventually cured the flooding by putting an air brick under the floor; he said he believed there was a hidden spring below the house.

There was no more trouble and the incident was soon forgotten. Some eighteen months later, however, in the long hot summer of 1933, the peace of the neat house in Bell Lane was disturbed in the most distressing manner.

Mr Long was a retired hotel barman of seventy-four, in such perfect health and vigour that he looked at least ten years younger; his wife Annie, an active woman in middle-age, went out daily to work, and they had an adopted daughter aged thirteen. They also let one of the rooms to a lodger.

One August day, during one of the worst droughts in Leicester for years, Mr Long was startled to find water coming unaccountably from a bedroom ceiling. He thought it must be due to a leak in the roof, though with no heavy rain having fallen in weeks it was very puzzling. The water stopped as mysteriously as it began, but then came another inrush in the front bedroom, which saturated the bedclothes and flooded the floor to such an extent that he had to double up the linoleum like a trough and run off the collected water from it into a tin bath. Again the water abruptly stopped, and the ceiling where it had come through was immediately dry and perfectly unmarked.

Then came an outbreak in the back bedroom, over the landing. Hearing a hissing noise, Mr Long rushed in and found his young daughter playfully enjoying a light shower bath in a spray of water which was issuing from the wall. Water then began pouring from the bedroom ceiling, in such volume that it overflowed from the floor and cascaded down the stairs; it also spouted from the wall over the fireplace in the living room downstairs, as well as from the wall opposite; and always it stopped as suddenly as it began and the points on the ceilings and walls from which it had poured were quickly dry and the wallpaper absolutely unmarked.

Everything the water fell on, however, did not dry instantly in the same remarkable fashion. As Mr Long went on to collect more than ninety bucketsful of water from the various outpourings all manner of the family's belongings, including the piano, were damaged; kindly neighbours stored some of their furniture and the rest they tried to protect with brown paper, but with all of the bedding in the house saturated Mr Long's wife and daughter had to go to neighbours' houses to sleep, while he and the lodger stayed up for three nights to deal with any fresh outbreaks. There were none, but then Mr Long and the lodger also left the house while the corporation's experts examined it.

Earlier, the reaction of one water inspector to Mr Long's urgent call had been that the flooding must be due to a burst pipe to the bathroom, or a leaking tank. But when he got to the house he found it had no bathroom and no tank, neither was there any trace of water pipes in the wall of the roof space. Water erupted from a wall as he made his survey, but still he could not trace the source of it. Another water inspector then came to question the family and examine the premises, and he was nearly knocked down by a sudden stream of water when he tried to mount the stairs.

The mystified water men now sought the help of the city's health and building departments, and while the family lodged with neighbours a group of experts searched the house. The most curious aspect of it all was that some of the water had been claimed by the Longs to have come from a wall only $4\frac{1}{2}$ inches thick, a single brick wall. Mr Long scorned all the suggestions of ghosts or other psychic phenomena which were put forward and maintained his belief that a hidden spring, as mentioned by the plumber, was the possible cause—it was, he thought, forcing its way up the walls to find an outlet. But against this a city water engineer said that if such was the case, why was not water forced out into rooms of the adjoining houses?

The corporation officials did a thorough job. Bricks were loosened from the walls and found to be quite dry and the walls perfectly sound. Skirting boards were removed and floors tested. But there were no signs of water anywhere, not even in the cellar, though here it was seen that the pressure of water from the flooded floors above had broken down plaster from the cellar ceiling.

A city engineer now blamed the house sparrows. He suggested that the spouting of the house had possibly been blocked up by the nests of sparrows, and that half an inch of rain which had fallen in two days recently had accumulated in the roof space. It had probably overflowed down the walls and, finding the weakest places, spurted out into the rooms.

The truth was, however, that no one really knew how the water had got into the walls and mysteriously poured out of them, gallon after gallon of it, in the middle of a serious drought.

So the Longs returned to their home. Not once in their absence had the "spook water" been seen to flow, but now, immediately they moved in, it began again. A reporter of the *Leicester Evening Mail*, as he entered the house, was astonished to see water streaming down the walls of the living room. The piano was saturated, and the water had penetrated into cupboards.

"The floor was flooded, and Mr and Mrs Long were unable to sit down to a meal because of the water which streamed down upon them. I was taken upstairs and only just dodged a shower of water which fell from the ceiling of the landing. All the beds have had to be covered with waterproofs, which hold pools of water. Amid the scene of desolation, Mrs Long's young daughter tried vainly to eat her meal in comfort, but was continually disturbed by water falling on her food and drenching the table. Mr Long said that the water generally stopped flowing about nine o'clock in the evening, and the walls were soon perfectly dry, without any signs of disturbance."

Among other visitors to the house that day were detectives of the Leicester City Police. Mr Long had kept a diary of the outbreaks, which on some days had occurred nearly every half hour, and they examined this and made a thorough search of the house but, like the building experts, failed to suggest a solution. The jets of water began to play again after the police had left, as they did after a further visit by the architect, who re-examined the property without result.

Some people now firmly believed that the unfortunate family— or one among them at least—were attracting uncommon psychic phenomena, though the more general opinion was that there must be a rational explanation, if the only way of deciding it was to demolish the house.

The Longs continued to live a hand-to-mouth existence trying to dodge the frequent spouting. Two days after the visit from the police the water was more active than ever, seemingly following

Mr Long about the house all day. As soon as he went into a room, water would pour from the ceiling and out of the walls, all over the floor. Several times he was drenched, while every article of furniture was thoroughly soaked. In desperation he went out into the garden and sat on a stool near the house, but in seconds he was soaked again as water shot from the *outside* wall down his neck. When he jumped up and stepped back the water spouted again all over him.

Unable to endure it any longer Mr Long and his wife made arrangements to move out and stay temporarily at the house next door, occupied by Mr and Mrs J. Worrald and Miss Evelyn Law; and the following day they shifted their belongings in. But in less than an hour the Worrald home was also visited by the water. An *Evening Mail* photographer happened to be in the house at the time and to his amazement saw a jet of water issue through the wallpaper, pour over a picture and splash on to the fire. At the same time Miss Law ran downstairs shouting that water was pouring into the upstairs rooms. The water, reported the photographer, soaked through the roof, poured down the wall and on to the floor "like a cascade coming out of nowhere".

Miss Law was in a bedroom when the water first spurted out at her. She said, "I jumped away but the bed was covered. The walls were quite dry a minute after. I went on to the landing and the water had come through the ceiling there. It ran down the walls and left them dry, but gathered in a pool on the floor".

All this happened just after Mr Long had finished putting his furniture into a room—the water spouted from the walls the precise moment he took a seat in his neighbours' kitchen. Happily, no more water came after this surprise upset, and, next door in the Longs' house, there was only one more outbreak, which occurred when Mr Long visited it to get some belongings. After that all was quiet. The brewery which owned the house now took a hand and sent officials to lock it up so that the premises could be thoroughly searched and inspected again. The doors and windows of the deserted building were carefully sealed pending the investigation.

It had now been suggested that someone was throwing buckets of water over the walls, but, said Mr Long, that was ridiculous. Nobody bore them any malice and certainly no member of his family wished to break up the home. Besides, all the many other witnesses of the phenomenon could not have been fooled. It now seemed possible that there was a spirit loose in the house but he did not know what to think; the one thing certain was that he and his family had been driven out of their home.

For some three weeks the troubled house in Bell Lane was kept under observation by experts called in by the brewery. An inspection was carried out each day, but there was no sight or sign of the "spook water". Mr and Mrs Long were told that the phenomenon had definitely ceased, and so on an October day they moved their belongings in again.

All was peaceful in the kitchen after the furniture had been carried in, and Mr Long was making some tea, when suddenly a powerful jet of water shot from the ceiling, drenching the floor, the table, the tea things, and the opposite wall. This was the start of yet another onslaught. Mr Long was soaked by water which frequently shot across the room from the ceiling—the force of it broke four gas mantles; three times his wife came home from work to find the kitchen so full of water that she could not have her dinner. Again there were several other witnesses to the inexplicable outbreaks. One was a workman who was taking the top off a wardrobe in a bedroom when water suddenly spurted from the wall and hit him in the face; another was a newspaper reporter seeking the latest developments, who arrived to find Mr and Mrs Long standing gloomily in the kitchen with the floor drenched with water, and the table and a mirror on the wall heavily splashed; while still on the ceiling was the wet patch, rapidly drying, from which the water had poured not long before he entered the house. Walls, floors and ceilings were always very quickly dry and at the start of every day the house was bone dry from top to bottom.

It seemed clear that the family could not go on living in the house and Mrs Long insisted that they should move, though it was difficult to find comparable rented accommodation in such a hurry. As Mr Long made efforts to do so, however, the water mysteriously stopped and the family experienced an uneasy peace. The lull lasted just eleven days. Then, one Sunday, Mrs Long was sitting in her living room when water suddenly began to pour from the ceiling, thoroughly soaking her. It flooded the living room and the kitchen and then spouted in further jets from the ceiling and walls, and she had to cook the dinner wearing her mackintosh and rainhat.

Police called at the house again and searched every inch of it, but left no wiser than before. It was now nearly mid-November and the distressed family had been battling against the "spook water" since August.

Mr Long said plaintively, "People are saying that we have done it ourselves because we want to get a council house, but that is not true. Why should we wilfully ruin our home? We had just had part of the house redecorated and we should not have done that if we had wanted to leave. I have tried everywhere to get another house, but I cannot find one. I wish someone could get one for us. This thing is driving us mad."

It was at this point, with the family prepared almost to walk the streets rather than endure the constant showers, that the outbreaks of the "spook water" began to lessen. Days passed without a single flooding, and when the water did come, at intervals, the jets seemed very much weaker. Finally, during the winter months the showers stopped completely, as mysteriously as they had begun. The house became perfectly dry again, and remained so up to Mr Long's death in 1936, and after.

THE GHOST BUS OF KENSINGTON

It was in the summer of 1933 that talk of a mysterious "ghost bus" seen hurtling by in the early hours first began to spread among the residents of North Kensington, London. People who had, until then, kept secret their own glimpse of the strange vehicle, for fear of ridicule and their own sanity, were relieved to find, as the matter came out into the open, that they were among at least a dozen positive witnesses of the phenomenon.

The phantom bus was invariably seen driving fast at the dangerous junction of St Mark's Road and Cambridge Gardens, where there had been many fatal accidents. The borough council had recently removed the corner of a garden to give motorists better visibility. At normal times of the day drivers travelling along Cambridge Gardens, a quiet residential road leading out of Ladbroke Grove, unless familiar with the district were totally unprepared for the number seven buses that turned quickly out of St Mark's Road into Cambridge Gardens, and there had been many near shaves.

At night the junction took on a chilling aspect as drivers began to tell of their surprise at seeing a bus travelling fast down St Mark's Road at one in the morning, and how, on swerving violently to avoid it, they had looked round to find no bus there at all. At that time of night all the regular buses had stopped running.

Further evidence of the phantom came when a car crashed into the wall of a house on the corner of Cambridge Gardens. Again this occurred at about one in the morning, the dazed driver telling those who rushed out to his aid that he had been travelling along Cambridge Gardens when he suddenly saw a bus drive fast round the corner. He swerved to avoid it, hitting the wall, yet when he turned to look after the bus there was no vehicle to be seen.

A mechanic at nearby St Andrew's Garage then disclosed that several puzzled motorists had told him of their personal encounters with the phantom bus. He added that one night the foreman and an assistant were on duty at the garage when the foreman saw a bus out in front, evidently wanting petrol, and called to the assistant to attend to it. But the mystified assistant came back to say that the bus had gone.

During the next few months several more people reported seeing the ghost bus. Then in June the following year, at a Paddington inquest, it was strongly suggested that the apparition was the cause of a night collision between two cars at the junction. One of the drivers involved, not an inexperienced road user, died in the crash; the other driver, and a pedestrian who had paused at the junction and saw the crash, both said that the dead man, driving a small car, had suddenly and for no apparent reason accelerated as if wanting to get quickly across the junction; the larger car was unable to avoid him and they struck bumpers, after which the small car veered off, crashed into a lamp-post, overturned and burst into flames. There was no other traffic about at the time.

The inquest court now heard how the dangerous junction was firmly believed to be haunted by the phantom bus; how hundreds of people in North Kensington talked about the apparition and dozens claimed to have seen it; how on nights after the regular bus service had stopped, people living there had been awakened by the roar of a bus coming down the street and rushed to the window to see a brilliantly lighted double-decker bus approaching with no visible driver or passengers. According to all the witnesses, the bus went careering to the corner of Cambridge Gardens and St Mark's Road, then vanished completely.

Was it a late staff bus? A glistening reflection of car headlamps from a pillar box on rainy nights? These and many other explanations were put forward, but none was sound. The phantom, according to witnesses, appeared a few more times before stopping its one o'clock run, by which time it had proved beneficial in one respect at least, drawing the serious attention of the authorities to a road blackspot.

Only three years earlier a strange, ghostly motor coach had been said to make an appearance in the East Riding of Yorkshire, though this seemed to be linked with a recent tragic holiday crash. This occurred on Garrowby Hill in August 1931, when a coach travelling from Bridlington to Liverpool collided with a car and crashed into a tree; two people were killed and twenty injured. During the late autumn rumours spread that the lonely road was haunted by a spectral vehicle which appeared out of the darkness travelling silently at enormous speed. It seemed by all accounts to appear only on moonless nights or when there was fog over the countryside, though the motorists who encountered it were in no doubt about its ghostly reality and strongly rejected the theory that it could be a trick of the mists. A series of incidents on the road was attributed to the alarming passage of the phantom coach and villagers were afraid to venture along the road at night. The following statement by one motorist who saw the phantom is typical of others:

"Last night, driving towards Bridlington, I saw what appeared to me to be a huge vehicle silently approaching. Thinking it was a bus or lorry, I felt no fear. But when the vehicle drew nearer I noticed that it made no sound in its progress. It rushed towards me at a great speed and I turned the wheel sharply. When I looked again the mystery bus had disappeared and I had to concentrate on preventing my car from rushing into the ditch."

All appearances of the spectral coach were made near the scene of the accident the previous August. Here at the roadside Lord Irwin, through whose Garrowby Estate that part of the road ran, had erected a five-foot high cross fixed on a wooden base, in memory of the two people who lost their lives.

Accidents are held to account for much road phenomena. In the West Riding in 1937 a stretch of the Ingleton-Lancaster road was haunted for some weeks by the figure of a man in a blue suit who had been knocked down and killed. A reliable account of their uncanny experience was given at the time by Mr Walter Holdsworth of Whitley Bay, a passenger in a car driven by Mr J. Harrison, a quarry manager described as "one of the most level-headed men living". Mr Holdsworth testified:

"We had just left Ingleton when I saw a man wearing a navy blue suit start to cross the road in front of us. I realised that Mr Harrison could not avoid hitting him and jerked myself back ready for the shock. Then the man disappeared. There was no bumping of the car to indicate we had hit anything.

"I said nothing for a moment and Mr Harrison asked me, 'Did you see that man?' I replied that I had seen the man three times on the road since a pedestrian was killed at that point three weeks ago, and that he must be a ghost."

The ghosts in these cases, and there are many, are not only seen shortly after a fatal accident but linger on sometimes for a very long period. For instance, in an incident reported from Berkshire in late 1964 the ghost seen was believed to be that of a man who had died in a village road accident nearly three years before. Two sisters, Mrs Margaret Prior and Mrs Marcia Colling-Hill were driving through the village of West Hendred, near Wantage, when in the dark they saw a man in cap and overcoat dash in front of their car. Mrs Prior, who was driving, said, "I could not possibly have avoided hitting him. I braked instantly and prepared myself for the bump, but nothing happened. I was shocked.

My sister and I turned round but could see nothing or nobody."
It was afterwards that they learned that an old man had been
killed in a car accident near the spot.

Motorists on a lonely stretch of the main Lanchester-Durham
road in 1931 were troubled by a similar darting apparition, though
in this case with nothing to explain it. There was many a shriek of
brakes in the woodland quiet as cars were brought hastily to a
stop. Bewildered drivers said afterwards they had seen the
mysterious figure of a man dive into the roadway almost under
their wheels, but on walking back expecting to find a body, they
had found nothing.

Similarly there was nothing to explain the road haunting near
South Mimms, Hertfordshire, during the spring of 1935 which
was witnessed by motorists and residents. Drivers who saw a figure
suddenly appear in the road and hold up its hand stopped, thinking there had been an accident, but the ghost vanished immediately, as mysteriously as it had appeared. The then vicar of South
Mimms, the Rev Allan Hay, confessed that when he first saw the
spectre while cycling he was so alarmed that he pedalled for all
his worth to the vicarage.

This haunted road was once the main route to the North and
was notorious for the number of highwaymen who infested it;
several of the brigands were believed to lie buried in the old, grey
churchyard of South Mimms. A popular theory was that the
ghost was the shade of one of them returned.

An extraordinary case in which a road haunting was, to the
majority of people successfully explained away, only to recur
within months, happened at Leatherhead, Surrey, in 1930-31.
Swan Corner in 1930 was known among motorists as one of the
worst crossroads in England, its corners, difficult inclines and blind
approaches forming a dangerous trap for the unwary. Late that
year it achieved fresh notoriety when motorists reported that at
dusk, on approaching the corner from the south, they were "held
up" by the tall figure of a woman standing some 200 yards south
of the crossroads. In most cases the ghostly figure disappeared as
soon as the alarmed motorist stopped. In one instance the driver
of a heavily laden lorry saw the figure in the gleam of his headlights too late to pull up, and thought a serious accident had
occurred. He was relieved, though puzzled, when a search failed
to reveal the victim or any evidence of an impact.

A local investigator then examined the road carefully and found
that as a result of an accident, a quantity of corrosive acid had
been dropped on the road. The fluid had run into a shallow dip
and been absorbed, but the vapour was now inclined to rise from

the road, and this could only be seen after dark in the gleam of bright headlights. It rose up in a thin column, which, it was suggested, might with a little imagination be taken as a ghostly form. This very feasible solution to the "haunting" was accepted by almost everyone except a number of drivers who had seen the figure and swore that it was more than simply vapour. Reports of the ghost, however, grew fewer. Then, in the late summer of the following year, there came disturbing reports of a new and different haunting at Swan Corner. Motorists and residents both plainly saw the still figure of a woman in nurse's dress lying across the road. Motorists had narrow escapes trying to avoid running over it, and not only they but passers-by as well clearly saw the figure, which disappeared quickly after every sighting. There was nothing vaporous about it and it was far too clearly defined to be explained away as odd reflections of light, many points of the nurse's dress, such as the bow and cap, being clear and correct to the smallest detail. The ghost, which some people took to be a warning of an approaching accident, made several more distinct appearances before vanishing with the onset of winter.

Perhaps of all the road ghosts it is the one seen in broad daylight that produces the keenest sense of shock. A striking example of this is the following experience told to me by Miss Nesta Howard, of Malvern Wells:

"In the summer of 1936 or 1937 I was driving southwards along a straight country road near Minety in Wiltshire, about noon on a fine sunny day. The road was a moderately wide one, with high banks on each side, and on my right the bank was topped with a thick hedge. I was in a cheerful and unreflective state of mind.

"Presently in the distance I saw a man coming towards me, dressed in a cassock and biretta; I knew that there was a village not far off and subconsciously assumed that he had just taken a service. Behind him, also walking towards me, I then saw a nun; and I remember idly thinking it a pity that they could not walk side by side, as they should have had much to discuss! This was really the only reason that I consciously observed them.

"Before we met they turned to their left and, as I thought, went down a lane at right angles; but when I reached the spot there was no break in the high bank—no lane, no path, no way up to a stile or anything at all. Puzzled, I drove on until I came to the first gate on that side of the road and walked across to look through it. The field was flat and open and stretched back much farther than the place where the two people had been, but there was no sign of them on either side of the bank.

"They had vanished completely."

HANNAH OF BUNTINGFORD

Queen Victoria stayed there; twice. In the late 1940s this was one of the few remembered fragments of history attached to an old building standing hard on the narrow pavement in the village of Buntingford, Hertfordshire. Queen Victoria had stayed there on the way to Cambridge to see her son, the Prince of Wales, and now the former inn, tightly sandwiched among other buildings in the little high street, felt the tremors of modern traffic rushing past its ancient coach entrance, bound for Cambridge and Huntingdon.

Bell House, or the Old Bell Coaching House as it was once known, was an architectural puzzle. Built about 1450, its rooms, staircases and passages all rambled together to make a roughly T-shaped dwelling. There were wide cavities between the walls and unaccountable depths between the stairs. Two channels having no apparent use ran up parallel with one of the chimneys, which was topped by a hip-roof. This chimney was the outlet for a huge Tudor fireplace with a priest's hole in it.

The fireplace was about twelve feet high and four feet square, and it appeared to be one of the main sources of the hauntings that began after Mr John Kewley bought the property.

Mr Kewley let part of the building, which, as a few alterations were made to it, yielded some very old coins which he gave away to the local children, whose delight it was to "help" him. He was a very likeable, good humoured man, and as an officer in the Salvation Army had seen life in many facets, but he had certainly given no thought before to ghosts, no more had his handful of tenants.

Shortly after the Parker family came to live at Bell House, footsteps heard early in the morning caused comment at the breakfast table. "Oh," said Mrs Parker's ten-year-old son, "I saw that man going downstairs. He was dressed in black."

But there was no one else in the building at that time except the family.

The Parkers then began to hear footsteps walking along the landing and up and down the stairs, some of the steps having a dragging sound; and "something" would knock or scratch at the door, but on opening it they would find nothing there. These incidents happened at all times during the day as well as at night; as Mrs Parker said, "We've heard them at seven in the morning and at tea time."

The elder of her three sons, who was in his twenties, had a frightening experience in one of the rooms. He said afterwards, "I woke up during the night and could not move. I knew I was awake because I could see the room and the window, but it seemed as if there was a great weight pressing on me. I struggled to get up, but couldn't. At last I had the idea of trying to roll from under the weight, and after what seemed like hours I managed to do it."

He was found next morning fast asleep, lying half out of the window.

On another occasion Mrs Parker's teenage son, who was over six feet tall, was found crouching in the fireplace the length of the room away from his bed. He did not remember anything during the night or how he got there, and he had never before walked in his sleep.

Another tenant, Mr Leslie Wells, who lived at the other end of the building, often heard footsteps going up and down the stairs leading to his room. One night he heard a sound which he described as "like an old woman crying softly".

Once, too, a visitor to Mr Wells' room left it suddenly, saying he could "feel something".

The other tenant of Bell House, Mr Tony Fruin, awoke one night with the sensation of hands round his neck, and sat up on the bed fighting to get his breath.

A Canadian friend of Mr Fruin's, described as "a real tough guy", went to sleep one night in the room containing the huge fireplace with its priest's hole. Next morning the room was empty and the friend was found in another room. He would give no explanation for his behaviour but refused to sleep in the room with the fireplace again.

Another time when a friend of Mr Kewley's called to see him, Mr Kewley asked his caller to stay on while he went out, but he returned to find to his surprise that the friend had vanished. When he met the friend again some time later, the man said he had had to leave as he could not stay on any longer in the house alone because of the clanking of chains and other uncanny noises.

On investigation it was found that some of the noises from the chimney were due to a chain, possibly used for turning a spit or giving access to the priest's hole, rattling when the wind blew, but this did not account for the other strange noises and footsteps which continued to sound throughout the old building, and other frightening incidents. Such as when Mrs Parker and her daughter, alone in their big living room, heard feet coming down the passage and saw the door handle turn. When they threw open the door there was nothing there as usual.

In early June, 1949, when the *Hertfordshire Mercury* investigated the ghosts of Bell House, the hauntings had been going on for nearly two years. A writer for the newspaper and his colleague persuaded Mrs Parker and her elder son, together with Mr Wells and Mr Fruin, to join them in experimenting with the upturned glass. As the writer explained, "We did not enter into it frivolously, but neither were we in dead earnestness. Our one concession to ghost etiquette was candlelight; otherwise we were just a group of ordinary, curious people."

The story the glass told them was a strange one. It began moving almost immediately, and the first "spirit" to give a message, calling itself "Hugh," stayed long enough to tell the sitters that many spirits wandered through the old house. Then the glass spelled out the name of "Hannah Bedwell". The house, said "Hannah", had once been the Bell Inn, and she had worked there. In reply to questions she said she haunted the house and "was there always". The sitters questioned her closely.

"Why do you haunt the house?"
"I am not free to do else."
"Why are you not free?"
"I search."
"For whom do you search?"
"For myself and another."
"Who is the other?"
"My littling."

The sitters could not understand this and asked "Hannah" for its meaning. She answered "My child".

"Do you search for your child in this house?"
"Yes, with lamenting."
"Did your child die?"
"Woefully."
"How?"
"I lay upon her."
"Why?"
"I was afraid."

"Of whom were you afraid?"

"My mistress."

"Why?"

"Because she would turn me off."

"Hannah" went on to say that she lay on her child in the end room in the west; apparently Mr Wells's room, in which he had heard a woman sobbing. "Hannah" said she was born at Reed, some four miles north of Buntingford, and when asked if the house was still there, she replied "field". Her father was an ostler at the inn, and the innkeeper's name was White. Asked what sort of people came to the inn, she replied, "Bawds and cutpurses".

"Who was your child's father?"

"John Price, porter here."

"How old were you?"

"Fifteen summers."

"What happened to Price?"

"Killed."

"Where?"

"Leyston fields."

"By whom?"

"Lame Robert."

At first the sitters thought she said "Lane Robert", giving the name the wrong way round. They pressed the point and she said, "Twist leg". Lame Robert, she said, was a footpad.

"How did you die, Hannah?"

"The noose."

"Where?"

"At Newgate."

"Were you imprisoned?"

"Bedford gaol."

"How long?"

"Months."

"Are there other spirits in the house?"

"Many."

"Are they happy?"

"No, all unquiet."

As a result of this report a group of interested people checked back on "Hannah Bedwell" in old parish records and found mention of her baby's birth, also a record of her conviction for infanticide.

As in many cases where a haunting is established, Mr Kewley was approached by several people wanting to buy Bell House and its ghosts, and, he told me before his recent death, he eventually sold it "to a lady who was delighted with it".

Another instance of the upturned glass being used to try and identify a ghost occurred in Ludlow in 1954, and again it was a building more than 400 years old that was the scene of the hauntings. This was the Globe Hotel, standing in the oldest quarter of the Shropshire town, within a few hundred yards of Ludlow Castle.

Airman John Stokes and his wife moved into a flat above the hotel in Market Street in January, 1954 and the first strange incident occurred only a month afterwards. One night the couple had gone to bed when they heard a noise in a bedroom on the floor above. On making inquiries next day they discovered that the room was unoccupied. But the same noise from it occurred on another night, and then again on the staircase outside their room, yet each time when they investigated they could find no one, nor anything capable of creating such a disturbance.

Later that year another RAF man, David Thomas, with his wife and child moved into an adjoining flat. Immediately, the new couple experienced similar happenings, and the hauntings intensified. One evening while their husbands were on duty at the nearby RAF camp, Mrs Stokes and Mrs Thomas were sitting together in the living room of one of the flats, when they had a sudden presentiment of fear. A chill seemed to come into the room, though the fire was burning in the hearth, and when Mrs Thomas looked towards the door she saw the figure of a man standing there. He had a cloak flung around his body and wore a wig, his features indistinguishable.

Mrs Thomas was petrified with horror and fear, while her companion was so scared that she dared not look round. After a minute or two the figure vanished.

When the husbands returned that evening the two wives told them of their frightening experience, at which the men decided they would all spend the evening together. Shortly after ten o'clock all four heard a knocking on the staircase and turned to look at the doorway. A light knock was heard on the door, and Mr Thomas opened it. Although he could see there was no one there, *the knocking on the door continued*, and as he stepped back into the room the others saw something pass by the aperture in the doorway.

In the following days the two couples continued to hear strange noises and there were instances of articles being moved from one side of the room to another by some unseen hand. The couples did not say much about the unusual happenings as they were afraid of ridicule, but on making tentative inquiries they found that former tenants above the Globe had experienced similar things. One woman who had occupied the Stokes' flat told the young couple that when living there she had the frightening experience of

waking up and seeing a figure standing near her bed. It disappeared as she looked.

It was then that the two RAF families decided to try the upturned glass. It spelt out several messages and when they asked the
ghost's name, the reply came that it was "Edward Dobsod", and
that he was a soldier at Ludlow Castle who had died in a room on
the other side of the landing to the flats in 1513.

Both couples now tried not to allow the experiences to affect
their nerves, but they looked for other accommodation.

A few years later, in 1959, the ghost of the Globe was reported
again, this time in the hotel lounge. A Birmingham woman on
holiday told how she was sitting alone in the lounge when she
suddenly felt someone breathing down her neck. She turned
quickly, fully expecting to see someone behind the chair, but there
was no one else in the room.

Other odd things happened. Doors locked themselves of their
own accord, and lights were switched on and off by unseen hands.

The hotel's regular customers were not unduly concerned.
Accepting that some uncanny presence was active, they simply
called the ghost "Joe" and blamed the slightest mishap on him.

THE NAMELESS ONES

It was ten minutes to noon on January 28, 1954. Miss Julie Groves, aged seventeen, typist for a firm of beer, wine and spirits wholesalers in Bridlington, Yorkshire, was working alone in the office when she chanced to look out of the window. Her glance fell on the door of the warehouse across the yard. It was padlocked, but from it, as she watched in rising fear, there came a very strange figure. Miss Groves tells her story:

"I saw a man come out of the warehouse, melting through the door. He walked across the yard, then into the house opposite my window, walking half through the closed door and half through the brick wall. I was afraid and could not stop looking at the place where he had gone through. A minute or two later he came out by the same way, with a saddle under his arm, just walking through the wall. He then disappeared through the closed door of the warehouse.

"He was dressed in riding breeches, with leather leggings, and was wearing a light-coloured jacket. He was slightly-built, and somewhat hunch-backed."

Miss Groves, now really frightened, telephoned her mother, who sent a taxi to bring her home. In the afternoon the girl returned to the office with her dog for company, and told the area manager what she had seen. All she knew about the premises was that years ago they had been in use as stables. The area manager, Mr J. H. Rodger, telephoned a former occupier of the premises in Wycliffe Lane, repeating Miss Groves' description of the strange man, and was told at once that it fitted completely that of William Robson, who had formerly worked there as a groom. At that time the warehouse was a stables and the building opposite the office was the coach-house, through which entry was gained to the saddle room. But this was years ago and Robson had been dead more than ten years and was buried miles away, near Hull.

Such ghostly happenings are not uncommon but the incident does show that apparitions are not only to be seen at night, and that the shades of the dead, if that is what they are, certainly are not restricted to the locality of their last resting place. It also examples the way in which many apparitions are very swiftly identified, so corroborating the story of an unknowing witness. In a great number of other cases, however, the ghosts remain nameless.

For months mysterious footsteps, the clicking of electric switches and other strange noises were heard at night in the house and grounds of Park Farm, the home in Lambourn, Berkshire of Mr Harry Whiteman, the racehorse trainer. They greatly disturbed Mr and Mrs Whiteman and the household staff, also the stable lads living in a cottage nearby. Then, on a bright moonlight night of November, 1951, an apparition was seen in the house by Mr Hoodless, secretary to Mr Whiteman.

Mr Hoodless had been reading in bed and had just put out the light when the figure of a man entered his room. "Moonlight was flooding into the room and I could see him quite distinctly. He was wearing an overcoat and a hat, but I could not see his face as he had his back partly turned to me. He came in through the door, which appeared to burst open in a way hard to describe, and walked to my dressing table. I shouted and he simply disappeared."

There was no ghostly history attached to Park Farm and therefore no explanation for the haunting, which finally had to be dealt with by the vicar of Lambourn. Expressing himself as satisfied that evil spirits were troubling the household, the Rev Ernest Rumens, assisted by a neighbouring rector, the Rev Harold Mansbridge, toured the farmhouse saying prayers, sprinkling holy water on the floors and making the sign of the Cross. They afterwards went into the other buildings, including each of the many horseboxes, repeating the traditional form of service for blessing a house, the vicar intoning, "I command all evil spirits to depart from this place, in the name of the Father, the Son and the Holy ghost."

This service seemed to bring peace to Park Farm.

Often when newspapermen and investigators hurry to the scene ghosts not surprisingly either cease or suspend their activities; but not so the nameless ghost or ghosts that walked a house at Woodmansterne, Surrey in 1948. A *Daily Herald* reporter could write, "Yesterday I did not believe in ghosts, but I heard these things during last night in the stables of Fairlawns, an old house yards off Croydon Lane here:

12.14 am. We are sitting, three of us, in a small, barely furnished bedroom when suddenly there is the loud ticking of an unseen clock.
1.30 Light footsteps pace up and down the passage for twenty minutes.
2.27 Above our heads, where the distance between ceiling and roof

timbers is only three feet, we hear the leisurely tread of what might be a heavily built man—eight paces one way, seven back.
3.14 Urgent rapping on the outside wall, twenty feet from the ground.
3.53 Dogs in the kennels outside whine as footsteps march briskly across the cobbles; nobody can be seen from the window.
4.21 An owl screeches and heavy footsteps again pound the ceiling, this time for twenty-three minutes without stopping.

"That is an exact record of what occurred when we sought the explanation of reports of supernatural happenings at the home of Mrs A. E. Lipsham, a breeder of pedigree dogs. . . ."

It was not only strange noises which troubled Fairlawns. Sceptics, including Mrs Lipsham, had laughed when the young twin son and daughter of Mrs Ada Brinkworth, the housekeeper, said they saw a tall man in medieval clothes prowling about the house. Then Mrs Lipsham herself saw the figure in the drive; and Mr George Dale, her partner, also no believer in ghosts, saw and heard things he could not explain.

Three ghosts in all came to be seen at the house and were adjudged responsible for the loud footsteps, rappings, opening and closing of doors, and the loud insistent ticking of an unseen clock. They were the phantom figures of two men and a woman wearing a centuries-old dress; and between the male ghosts, according to Mrs Brinkworth, there seemed to exist a feeling of intense hatred.

The stables dated back to 1780 and it was believed that the haunting spirits were those of one-time employees on the estate, which was originally owned by the 12th Earl of Derby, founder of the Epsom classic. Seances were held in the stables with the object of trying to give the unhappy trio of spirits their release, and these seemed to be effective.

There was no such fortunate conclusion to the activities of an unknown "black ghost" which terrified the occupants of an old Victorian house in the Camp Road district of Leeds, in 1932. Mrs Annie Halliday, who moved into the big house in Fieldhead Terrace in April of that year, at first did not suspect a ghost when she heard strange knockings on the attic floor at night, though these quickly assumed a regular pattern. They seemed to start with a muffled thud on the attic floor, followed by two more similar noises, then a kind of shuffling sound on the stairs and landing. For a long time there occurred only these puzzling sounds, then the apparition appeared. Mrs Halliday first saw it early one morning, a strange man six feet tall, dressed in a long black coat reaching down to his ankles. He did not speak, and, quite unafraid, she went forward to him, thinking him to be a friend of one of the lodgers, but as she put out a hand she received

a shock when he suddenly vanished. Shortly after this the knocking sounded every night and the apparition made regular appearances, terrifying all the other thirteen occupants of the big house
in which Mrs Halliday had sub-let rooms. First would come the
three loud knocks from the top of the house, and finally the black
ghost would appear standing on the landing, one hand clutching
the banister.

Mrs Halliday's sub-tenants consisted of two families and three
single men, including an artist and a soldier, so that there were
eight adults and six children all affected by the activities of the
nameless ghost. Mrs Halliday said at the time, "We are terrified
out of our wits, but when we hear the knocks we cannot resist
going to the stairs to see him." The neighbours, too, were in a state
of fright and the whole matter was brought out into the open by
the last of Mrs Halliday's lodgers to arrive at the house. This was
Mr Thomas O'Donoghue, a young, powerfully-built labourer. He
heard the knockings during the night but took little notice of them
until, early one morning, he also saw the ghost. . . .

"There he was, a huge man, looking about 45 or 50 years old. I
did not know what to do. I could feel my hair prickling me at the
back and just made a mad rush past him into the nearest room
and locked myself in."

Mr O'Donoghue went for a priest, and Father Mawson, curate
at St Anne's Cathedral, came and blessed the house, sprinkling the
walls with holy water. But it did no good. The following night the
sounds from the attic came again and were heard by a group of
people keeping vigil: first the three loud, uncanny thuds on the
attic floor, with long intervals between, and after the third noise,
the loudest of all, the sound of someone or something stumbling
across the floor of the attic. Although some of the observers
immediately rushed upstairs there was nothing to be seen and the
apparition did not appear. Floorboards, roof, cisterns and man-
holes were examined but nothing was found that could in any way
account for the noises.

In the ceiling of the attic was a large hook, and some of the
tenants began to wonder if a man had ended his life from it; but
there was nothing positive to account for the black ghost, though
Mrs Halliday now learned from neighbours that curious things
had been heard and seen in the house before she came to it. Father
Mawson checked the Leeds police records to see if there had been
any tragedy in the house, but nothing came to light. Again, a
thorough inspection was made of the house—walls were tested,
floorboards pulled up and chimneys searched, but nothing was
revealed.

A further shock came one afternoon when one of the young children in the house, who had gone down from the first floor to the ground floor to get some sweets from a shop kept by Mrs Halliday, was heard to give a terrified scream. Mrs Halliday rushed up to the first floor landing at the same time as the child's mother ran out of her room to find the girl standing petrified. She told them she had seen a tall man whom she had at first thought to be her father, but then he had come to her with his hands up to his face and fingers outstretched, as if they were claws. At her shriek the figure vanished.

There was no rest now for Mrs Halliday and her tenants as the thuds from the attic went on, together with opening and closing of doors and the nightly shuffling on the stairs. Two weeks later all fourteen people moved out of the haunted house and went to live in other parts of Leeds. On a bleak November day in 1932 the house stood locked, bolted, empty and silent, and for the first time for weeks, people living near it were able to look forward to a good night's sleep. The neighbours next door to the deserted house, who had suffered most, stayed up till the early hours listening, but to their relief there was not a murmur. After forcing out the tenants the ghost itself seemed to have finally taken its leave.

At Caepantywyll, Merthyr Tydfil, in 1938 the unknown apparition of a "woman in white" forced a young couple to leave their rented home after they had lived there only eighteen months. The first sign of any disturbance came three months after they moved in, when one night Mr David Jones and his wife heard mysterious tappings on the fireplace wall.

"A couple of nights later we saw her for the first time. We were in bed. My wife woke me, and motioned to the foot of the bed. We both saw quiet plainly the figure of a woman in white—she had long hair and wore beads. When she moved I got out of bed and followed her down the stairs. In front of the fireplace she vanished."

More mysterious happenings occurred from time to time. Sums of money and a watch disappeared from the house at night when all the doors and windows were locked; water started running from a tap in the back kitchen when the control tap in the front kitchen was turned off. The climax was reached when a friend and his wife spent two evenings with the couple.

"On the first night," Mr Jones testified, "we were all sitting in this room when we heard a tapping at the back door, or so it seemed. My wife got up and went to the entrance to the back kitchen. She called me and my friend, and there, standing by the fireplace in the back room, was the woman in white. The three of us saw her for a few seconds.

"Next night all four of us were sitting there again joking and laughing. My wife went into the back kitchen for something, and we heard her scream. We rushed in and she told us she had seen a woman in white standing on the table. We left the house that night with our baby."

They went to stay with their friends, Mr and Mrs Rees, who corroborated their story. It appeared, however, that there were in fact two ghosts in the house, for the "woman in white" seen by the three witnesses together was described as being tall and slim, with a beautiful face, while Mrs Jones described the apparition which she alone had seen in the back kitchen as "elderly and stern-faced". A child's red slipper also played a part in the mystery. It did not belong to the Jones baby but had been found in the house by the couple. When, after Mr Jones and his wife had left, a policeman and others visited the house, the slipper was placed in a certain position on the kitchen floor; the following night when they returned, the slipper was found underneath the pantry shelf, though no one could have gained entry to the locked house in the meantime.

The house and roof space were thoroughly searched but nothing was found, and it was checked that there was no other means of entry to the property. An evening's ghost vigil produced no result, nor did a seance which plain clothes police attended, except that sitters heard the noise of dragging footsteps. When Mr Jones and his wife left the house so, apparently, did the mysterious woman—or women—in white.

Also frightened by an inexplicable presence in their homes were three families at the Welsh border town of Chirk, Denbighshire in 1955. The strange happenings occurred in their wooden flats at a former prisoner-of-war camp, which had been converted to ease the housing shortage. The trouble here seemed to emanate from a small back bedroom in the flat occupied by one of the families; it was a room where many people had tried to sleep at various times, and emerged in the middle of the night trembling with fear. Mrs Rose Vershuren, a young mother with three children, told of the feeling when lying in bed there, that a weight was being placed across her feet, and of the cold numbness and oppression that would grip her from time to time. The former residents of her flat, who had since moved to a new council house, now disclosed that they also had experienced strange happenings in the bedroom. There had been odd noises, and white faces had seemed to peer into the room; and the water had played strange tricks, a tap being turned on when no one in the flat could have been near it. They had also been troubled by a peculiar smell which was now experienced again by the Vershurens.

One man told of how, in the strange atmosphere of the bedroom, he lit a cigarette to calm his nerves and was stunned to hear a voice begging him for a stub, though there was no other physical presence in the room. A young wife in one of the three flats said she was afraid of being alone at home because of invisible eyes that seemed to follow her every movement; she and her husband moved out.

It was an oppressive, disturbing haunting at the former camp with nothing to account for it. Eventually a seance was held in the bedroom at which the gathering deduced that the ghost was that of a morose Italian prisoner-of-war who had died of pneumonia in the back bedroom, lying on a bed near the window. There seemed also to be another ghost involved, that of an emaciated woman with black hair to her shoulders, who communicated her story, telling how she had provided all the extra food she could for the prisoners during the war and kept her own hunger away by cigarette smoking.

Further seances were held, which seemed to have some effect.

Another apparition which still remains nameless, though seen very strongly and distinctly at the same time by three people, is a figure which, in 1949, manifested itself in the austere surroundings of Nottingham's Public Health Laboratory. The laboratory, in Cumberland Place, was housed in what was formerly a part of the old Nottingham Children's Hospital, and what had been a mortuary now housed the guinea-pigs used in laboratory experiments.

At 9.30 pm. on a dark Saturday night of January, when the building was deserted, two young girl technicians, one accompanied by her sister, went out down a yard behind the laboratory to the guinea-pig house to feed the guinea-pigs and a pet cat. The girls had just given the guinea-pigs some cabbage leaves when, quite suddenly, the animals all stopped squealing. There was absolute silence, and the atmosphere went cold. Then the girls were startled to see the figure of a nurse in rather old-fashioned uniform appear at the door. The eldest girl of the three, whose ages were sixteen, nineteen and twenty, describes the scene:

"First the nurse seemed to put her left hand through the slightly open door. It was holding what looked like an instrument or knife. Then she glided before us and, after a few moments, vanished. We left the house as quickly as we could. But I had a clear vision of her and could identify her in a minute. She was about twenty-seven years of age, had a very pretty face with a very intent expression about it, and golden-brown hair."

The girls separately described to the doctor in charge of the laboratory what they had seen. One of them shortly afterwards found herself affected by a strange influence in other rooms of the building, and the result was that a woman medium was asked to investigate the laboratory, being told only that there seemed to be an unusual atmosphere present in the buildings.

In a room on the top floor the medium said she felt an air of "great distress", while in the guinea-pig house she immediately felt "as if all my physical power drained out of me, and left me helpless"; she was convinced, she said, that something tragic had happened in the place. When, for the first time, she was told what the girls had seen, the medium said that whoever it was they saw had been hurt very badly, but was not dead when she entered the building. The medium believed that a great tragedy had happened, probably in the room upstairs, and the person involved had been brought or came down to the former mortuary in great distress, and died there.

Was it the pretty nurse who had died tragically, some time in the past? A search of the hospital records was an impossible task with such little evidence to go on, and so the golden-haired apparition remains unidentified, just one more among the many nameless ones.

LOCKED UP TO DIE

In 1944 a young London girl was evacuated to a big old house near the village of Woburn Sands, on the Buckinghamshire-Bedfordshire border. On her arrival a temporary bed was put up for her in the drawing room. What happened next is best described from a statement she made three years afterwards.

"In the night I awoke and saw hands and arms coming out of the wall above my head. I felt somewhat aghast. However, I must have dropped off to sleep, but some time later I again woke up and saw the hands and arms once more coming out of the wall.

"Afterwards I felt much more disturbed by what I had seen than I did at the time. I felt that I could not possibly sleep in that room again. I moved to another room and I never again saw anything uncanny."

The girl's ghostly experience might have remained one of those isolated incidents that occur so frequently but are seldom told outside the family circle, had not the owner of the house in 1947 claimed a reduction in its rateable value, on the ground, among others, that it was haunted.

The owner of the house, "Woodfield", in Weathercock Lane was Mr B. Key of Twickenham, who told the Luton Area Assessment Committee that the house had fallen in value because it was said to be haunted by the ghosts of two lovers who were locked in a cupboard and left to die by the girl's angry father some 250 years ago. Their skeletons, he said, were claimed to have been discovered by Dick Turpin when seeking refuge there, and the highwayman had agreed to keep silent at the promise of sanctuary at "Woodfield" whenever he needed it. The house had stood empty for many years before World War II because no one would buy or occupy a property with its reputation.

Mr Key's case was listened to with particular interest by Mr H. W. M. Richards, a member of the assessment committee and also a Dunstable borough councillor. In the general air of high scepticism which greeted the owner's claim, Mr Richards suggested to his committee colleagues that the fairest way to settle the matter would be to visit the house and test the validity of the supposed haunting. He undertook to arrange such an investigation entirely on his own responsibility and report his findings to the committee. This was agreed.

Mr Richards planned his investigation with care and at no cost to the ratepayers. A medium approved by the Psychic Research Board was chosen for a seance at "Woodfield", and at midnight on a Friday in September, 1947 eight people sat with linked hands in the darkened room where the young evacuee had seen the groping hands emerge from the wall. They included, along with Mr Richards, Mrs Florence Thompson, a London medium, Mr Peter Craven, her assistant, and several newspapermen.

The night passed uneventfully except for one brief interlude when the medium went into a trance. In a distressed voice she then began repeating, "You're killing me . . . stop tying me up . . . let me go . . . I want to go away . . . ." For some minutes the others sat in silence while the medium moved her arms agitatedly and could be heard sobbing, saying she had been shot in the head. After regaining control she complained of violent pains in one side of her head and, pointing to one corner of the room, said she felt sure that a terrible love tragedy had taken place there. There were indications of two spirits who were in need of help, one of them a girl of about twenty-two, and she thought that a seance by a "rescue circle" would release them.

During the seance the sole occupier of the house, Miss Amy Dickinson, who had put up the young evacuee, sat awake in her room. She dismissed newspapermen's questions about the ghosts, saying she had heard tales but was not the nervous type.

Mr Richards felt that the seance had shown there was some influence present, but he was not fully satisfied and decided to hold another seance, before reporting back to his committee. This was held a fortnight later, again on a Friday night, and besides Mrs Thompson and her assistant Mr Craven, another approved medium, Mr George Kenneth, was present; also Dr Donald West, of the Society for Psychical Research.

This second seance produced much more result, two of the sitters claiming to have seen the ghostly face of an old man moving about the darkened room. One of them, Mr Craven, said the face was "an awful greyish colour"; the old man appeared at the side of Mr Kenneth and seemed to be trying to whisper in the medium's ear. Mr Kenneth afterwards told the circle that he saw a tremendous black horse in the room, and heard screams at the beginning of the seance. He also saw an elderly man with a long beard, who looked like a farmer.

Mrs Thompson, while under trance, "contacted" a young girl

who said her name was Bessie and gave the name of her lover as John. Mrs Thompson said the girl was about twenty and very beautiful; her lover was gaunt and dark. The girl told her, "We were going away together, but my father knew, and hurt my head. We have been shut away a long time . . . help John for me . . . help us to rest." The medium said she had the impression of being bound and helpless, and she was certain there had been a double tragedy in the room.

There was some disappointment that nothing had come through the seances that could be firmly checked, or that was over and above what was already known. Mr Richards had hoped they might be given some indication of the burial place of the lovers' skeletons after their discovery in the cupboard by Turpin. But he was now fairly satisfied that the house was haunted and told the assessment committee as much at their next meeting, when he described his investigations at "Woodfield" in full. He then stood down while his colleagues considered their decision. After little deliberation they rejected the owner's claim.

The events at "Woodfield" had by now created such interest that requests were received from people all over the country asking to be allowed to attend a seance. Their requests could not be entertained, but Mr Richards, undaunted by the committee's verdict, decided to hold a third and final seance, and at this the spirit girl "Bessie" again controlled the medium, Mrs Thompson, asserting that she had been killed by her father, and that "John" was with her. Two of the sitters claimed to see manifestations clairvoyantly.

"Woodfield's" owner, Mr Key, lodged an appeal against the assessment committee's ruling. But this went through for consideration on other grounds than that of the ghosts; and so one of the few semi-official investigations into a haunting remained, as far as the local authority's records were concerned, "not proven".

More than ten years earlier, in 1936, ghosts had brought another house owner to court over her rates, though on this occasion not to claim depreciation of the property but absolute financial ruin because of the hauntings.

Mrs Florence Hilda Loury bought Enborne House, an isolated, tree-girt property two miles from Newbury, Berkshire, through a mortgage with a building society, and without any capital except a small grant from a relative, set out to establish it as a guest house. The big old Victorian building was built on the site of a much older mansion dating from the days of Cromwell, parts of which remained. It was not without a certain appeal, especially to the visitor from town, but Mrs Loury had not been there long before she found the house was always full of noises, some explainable but others not. Soon her guests began to complain of hearing strange clanking sounds in the night; some were so frightened that they had to leave. One girl was so upset by the weird noises that she quit the house at once, on the verge of a nervous breakdown.

Mrs Loury herself saw the noisy ghost, that of an old man bent almost double with age, with his hands and feet shackled, walking slowly down a dark corridor. He vanished in a moment. A kennel boy left alone in the house for a time also saw the old man shuffling down a passage. When the other occupants returned they found the boy sitting huddled up, petrified with fright; all he could do was gasp "I have seen a ghost . . .".

It seemed clear that the noises were being caused by the old man moving through the bedrooms in his chains. Mrs Loury herself was not afraid of the ghost as she had been in a haunted house before, but the reputation of Enborne House quickly spread and soon no guests came at all. Mrs Loury's venture failed and on a day in September, 1936 she found herself at Newbury police court, summoned for non-payment of rates. It was then she told the magistrates the full story of her ruination by the ghost.

By this time the house had been resold, soon to be taken over by its new owner, a Southampton surgeon, and Mrs Loury, all her money gone, had had to take a post elsewhere as a housekeeper.

Just who the ghost was who had brought about her failure nobody knew. There was a tradition in the locality that a beautiful Newbury girl was murdered at Enborne House by her lover in a fit of jealousy 200 years ago, but the identity of the old man remained a mystery. Further evidence of the hauntings came from several people including Lady Hewett, a friend of Mrs Loury's, who told of how she had talked to people who had heard the ghostly noises in the night—chains clanking and doors banging—and had no doubt they were genuinely frightened. An alert reporter of the *Sunday Referee* who kept watch all night for a sight of the old man in chains had a fright himself when he saw something for which he had not been looking. At about 4.15 am., when glancing from an upstairs window at the silent lawn and hedges probably little changed since the murder two centuries before, he saw a bush tremble, and for a fleeting instant a slim, shadowy form seemed to come into view. He could not see a face but had an impression of a wide skirt and two hands. The lonely figure turned a corner of the house and vanished in the direction of the stables.

The presence of one more ghost did not deter the new owner, who said he would not lose any sleep over them; and in fact no more visitations were reported once the guest house was re-occupied as a private home.

And Mrs Loury? After establishing that she had not received a penny profit from the resale of the house, the sympathetic magistrates decided that if she paid off the rates by weekly instalments, they would reduce the £40 she owed by half.

The sympathy of a court of a different nature was asked for in 1933, when, during the days of depression and high unemployment, a man who abruptly left a job found for him in South Wales had to show cause why his dole money should not be stopped.

The events leading up to this unusual case began when the man, an unemployed baker of Llangollen, Denbighshire, obtained through the local employment exchange a job in the mining village of Glyncorrwg, a hundred-odd miles to the south, near Port Talbot. He made his way there as instructed and began work at the old Glyncorrwg Bakery on the night of his arrival. Nothing unusual happened then, but on the second night, shortly after midnight, he heard weird tappings on the bakehouse window, and on the third night he felt a sudden draught as if someone was passing him hurriedly.

The climax came on the fourth night. While busy kneading he heard strange noises in the room next to the bakery and, looking up, saw the door open and an elderly woman wearing a black dress "waft in". She looked him straight in the face and then vanished. He was so shocked that he staggered back, nearly knocking over his mate, who, though he had not seen the ghost, had felt the draught.

The baker packed up at once and returned to North Wales, where he was threatened with stoppage of his unemployment pay for walking out of his job without good reason. He appeared before the Court of Referees at Wrexham, who listened to the detailed explanation of his ghostly experience, his testimony being supported by a statement written out for him by the owner of the Glyncorrwg Bakery, who admitted that many journeymen who worked there in the past had claimed to have seen the unknown lady in black, though he himself had never encountered her.

The baker's obvious sincerity impressed the court, who directed that his unemployment pay should be suspended for one week only. Meantime, at Glyncorrwg a night's vigil in the old bakery proved fruitless. But older villagers recalled a sensation of thirty years ago when a ghost was seen several times in the village, in the churchyard, and in a cottage on the hillside. This, too, was an unknown "lady in black" who vanished as mysteriously as she came.

THE TEN OF DIAMONDS

There are some strange incidents that are unique in their circumstances and do not fall readily into any ghostly category. Such are the following three stories which involve respectively a playing card, a common kitchen chair, and a used food tin.

The first incident comes from Dorset in the 1920s.

In the little village of Leigh lived Mr Herbert Faulkener, a man who had given up the ambition of becoming a surgeon and taken to a country life. His wife came from Frome, in Somerset. She was the only child of Mr Percy Benjamin Newport, a butcher in Frome for many years, who eventually came to live with the couple at Leigh. Mr Newport was in indifferent health, and though still only in his fifties had to spend his mornings in bed.

One morning in the first week of January, 1927, while busy with her housework, Mrs Faulkener heard her father cry out upstairs. She hurried up to find him sitting up in bed, gazing intently before him.

"Look, look!" he cried. "That nurse! She has a black pot with hot, steaming stuff in it. And a card, the ten of diamonds. Take it away from her—take it away. She is threatening me—she'll empty the boiling stuff over my head if you don't take the card away."

Mrs Faulkener was unable to see either the nurse or the ten of diamonds. She tried to soothe her father but he persisted for some time, moaning "Take the card away from her and that will save me."

Eventually Mrs Faulkener managed to coax her father round to a calmer state of mind, and later on he dressed and came downstairs.

He then said to her, "Don't think I'm silly, but"—pointing to a pack of cards on the table—"I wish you would take the ten of diamonds out and burn it. I can't get it away from my eyes."

His daughter laughed away his fears and said she would not do anything so silly.

Next day Mr Newport returned to Frome to enter the Victoria Hospital for an operation. He died in the hospital exactly ten days afterwards.

The funeral took place from his brother's house in Frome. The coffin was carried out of the house and placed on a bier on the garden path; it was a walking funeral, and the chief mourners filed out of the house to take their places in the cortege. They were led by Mr Faulkener, the son-in-law, and the dead man's brother. As the two men took their places next to the bier Mr Faulkener happened to look down at the ground, and there, beneath the head of the coffin, lay a playing card. It was the ten of diamonds.

Mr Faulkener, greatly surprised, nudged the elbow of his companion—who knew nothing of the dead man's sight of the nurse with her black pot—and he, too, plainly saw the card lying on the path. Neither man wanting to disturb the funeral procession they left the card where it was, but when they searched for it shortly afterwards it had vanished. Yet during the interval no one had been in the garden.

The extraordinary sequel came at the Faulkeners' home at Leigh soon afterwards, when the couple were visited by the dead man's brother. A game of cards was suggested, and it was decided to open a new pack. On the seal being broken and the cards checked, one was found to be missing. The ten of diamonds.

The Faulkeners could give no clue to the mystery, which coincidence alone could scarcely explain. The dead man had been very fond of playing cards at home, but he had had no belief at all in psychic phenomena.

The second unusual story comes from the West Riding of Yorkshire in 1933. Following a rumour in the locality of Wharfedale, on the edge of the wind-swept moors, a reporter of the *Sunday Referee* traced a woman who kept a small farm single-handed, and who admitted to a strange haunting that had troubled her, giving the circumstances of it on condition that, to preserve her solitude, her name should not be disclosed.

The land and buildings of the farm had been in the woman's family for 400 years, and on the bare stone floor of the kitchen, the style of which had not changed since the days of the Brontes, the reporter was shown the object of the haunting, a wooden chair.

The woman told him that when her father was alive they both frequently heard a strange noise shortly after midnight, as of a blow being struck against wood. Next morning they would find the chair turned round, with its seat to the wall. Since the death of her father she had caught the chair performing its weird and frightening trick in broad daylight.

"My brother paid me a visit one day," she said, "and in the afternoon while sitting in the kitchen, we heard a scraping noise.

Suddenly we saw the chair begin to turn. It was horrible. My brother had long hair; it rose on his head like the bristles on a new broom. I never believed human hair did stand on end until I saw him.

"I was stiff with fright by the time the chair had stopped, with its seat to the wall. But my brother seized it and flung it out into the lane. 'We're not having that horrible thing in here', he shouted, and went for the axe. But I stopped him. I live alone, and was afraid of what might happen if he broke it."

So the old chair stood again in its corner, sharing the lonely life of the woman whose only living companions were her dogs and cattle.

The third odd story comes from South Devon and concerns what must be one of the queerest ghosts on record: a "bewitched" tin. Its strange and frightening behaviour brought near chaos to a little cottage in the village of Malborough occupied by Mr F. H. Bridle, a labourer, together with his wife and their seven-year-old adopted daughter.

It was just an ordinary Ovaltine tin in which Mr Bridle used to keep his tobacco, and he had had it for a long time, which made its sudden weird antics all the more distressing.

The incidents began one day in February, 1934, as the family were sitting quietly in their old cottage. After taking some tobacco out of the tin Mr Bridle replaced it on the kitchen table, but as he turned his back he heard a crash and, looking round, saw the tin on the floor. Puzzled, he put it back on the table, this time behind several other articles, but it jumped over these and crashed again to the floor. Once more, still unbelieving, he replaced the tin on the table, but again it leapt over the other articles and dropped to the floor.

This unnerved him and he gingerly looked inside the tin, but saw only tobacco. He cautiously placed the tin inside another, larger tin and stood this in the centre of another table in the room, but he had scarcely turned away before there was a loud crash and the big tin was on the floor with the Ovaltine tin rolling out of it.

Now quite distressed, Mr Bridle and his wife decided to put the tin away out of sight in a cupboard, fastening the cupboard door on its button catch. But to their amazement the door burst open and the tin came sailing through the air. So violently did the cupboard door open that it crashed against the chair on which Mrs Bridle was sitting, striking her on the ribs with such force that she cried out. Her husband quickly seized the Ovaltine tin and thrust it into a drawer which he slammed shut—but the drawer was forced open as if by unseen hands and out jumped the tin again.

"Uncanny and terrible" was how the bewildered couple afterwards described this fantastic episode, but there was much more to come.

Mr Bridle grabbed the tin and took it to an outhouse some yards from the cottage, where he put it inside and securely fastened the door. The relieved couple now thought themselves to be safely rid of the tin, but when Mr Bridle had been back in the cottage only a short time they heard a noise at the door. Their small daughter opened it to greet the unexpected caller, and in a flash the tin came in through the doorway "like a bird going through the air" and, turning to the right into the kitchen, moved across the floor towards Mr Bridle.

In order to get to the front door the tin had had to go right round the outside of the cottage. When the couple ran out and examined the outhouse door they found it still securely fastened.

With the tin now quiet, Mrs Bridle and her daughter went up to undress. But no sooner had they got to the bedroom than the tin came flying up the stairs to stop with a crash on a small table. When they left the bedroom it came down the stairs after them; then again it was quiet.

All that night the uneasy couple heard the tin rattling as it moved about downstairs. Mrs Bridle, thoroughly frightened, suspected that her family were "ill-wished" by someone in the village and the tin's antics were the result. She told her husband she would not have the tin in the house any longer, so in the morning he took it with him to work, placing it on a hedge in view of himself and his workmates. It did not move an inch all day. However, as he could not take it home again he gave it to another of the workmen. This man, when the tin still did not move, lost interest and gave it to someone else, and it was this third party whom a reporter of the *Western Evening Herald* finally tracked down to get possession of the Ovaltine tin, whose behaviour had now attracted the attention of a wider public. The reporter took the tin home and slept with it by his bedside, but it never once moved from its position during the night.

The tin's short, hectic career remained a mystery, though as some people suggested, probably the tin itself was not to blame but was made to perform the frightening tricks by some ghostly presence or poltergeist in the Bridles' 200-year-old cottage. Whatever the cause, with the tin out of the house the family were not troubled again.

LIVING WITH A GHOST

One evening in 1933 Mr Allan Hall glanced out of the window of his large house in the mining village of Forest Hall, near New-castle-on-Tyne, and to his surprise, as there were no callers expected, saw a "man in grey" emerge from the semi-darkness and walk up the drive leading to the house. Mr Hall went immediately to the front door, but on opening it found no one there.

A few days later the same mysterious grey figure reappeared, this time in daylight. And so began the long haunting of Rose Villa, which had been built on the site of a former mansion, Forest Hall, from which the village took its name.

During the next three years Mr Hall, his wife and daughter, and friends of the family all saw the ghostly man in grey walk up the driveway of the house at various times. The figure always came the same way, walking to the house and disappearing behind it, and the family eventually became quite accustomed to it and began to refer to it as "Our friend"; it seemed to be quite a friendly ghost and never frightened anyone. Mr Hall, an undertaker, often used to stand at the window and watch for the spectre to make its appearance.

The Halls lived quite happily with their ghost for three years until December, 1936 when news of the apparition finally leaked out and was published in various newspapers. Then, so many sight-seers swarmed to Rose Villa and stood outside it day and night, watching for the apparition, that police had to be called to control them. The ghost, hardly surprisingly, chose not to appear for the crowds.

Local tradition was that a subterranean passage once connected the old Forest Hall mansion with Seaton Delaval Hall, some three miles away, and this inspired the suggestion that the "man in grey" might be the spirit of the famous Delaval monk of Tyne-mouth Priory, who, centuries ago, calling at Seaton Delaval Hall for food to feed the poor, carried away a boar's head ready to be served and was slain by Lord Delaval for the theft. Alternatively it was suggested the ghost was some other uneasy spirit from the subterranean passage, or a vault, the entrance to which was believed to lie under a huge moss covered stone slab in the grounds of Rose Villa. The slab was only a few feet from the drive where the "man in grey" was regularly seen to walk. Excitement ran so high that police had to restrain over eager sightseers who ran into the grounds to examine the mysterious stone slab.

Mr Hall had never attempted to raise this stone and he now made it quite clear that he had no intention of disturbing it in any way; in fact he had no desire to lay the ghost. So the numbers of sightseers and visitors gradually dwindled until all became quiet again at Rose Villa, leaving the family in peace with their friendly spectre.

A ghost outside the house is one thing, having it permanently about inside the building is another, as Mr Edwin Tugwood and his wife found on taking over the grocery store in the tiny Wiltshire village of Steeple Ashton. Yet after the first shocks they also managed to live with their spectre quite well.

Mr Tugwood and his wife, having spent most of their lives farming in Kent, bought the store at Steeple Ashton in 1944. The little shop formed part of a fine old timbered cottage with dark oak beams and heavy iron-latched doors, which in the reign of James II (1685-9) had been used as the village courthouse.

Mr and Mrs Tugwood were told of rumours concerning the centuries-old building immediately they moved into it. Customers spoke of how it was reputed to be haunted by a ghost in an upstairs cupboard; it was believed to be the ghost of "Bloody" Judge Jeffreys, who had held circuit courts in a large upstairs room.

The Tugwoods, who had no belief in ghosts, dismissed the stories. They heard creaking at night and doors opened and banged, but they expected such noises in a building of that great age. As for the former courtroom, Mrs Tugwood used it as a sitting room and kept the four oaken cupboards in it closed, because she had seen black spiders in them and she had a horror of spiders. She did notice one odd thing, however. The corner cupboard, a pigeon-holed one, was often found open in the morning.

They had been two years in the store when Mrs Tugwood decided to change their living arrangements and turn the old courtroom into a bedroom. It was immediately after this that the ghostly incidents began.

One night as she was standing by the window side of the room, preparing for bed, with her husband already asleep, she heard footsteps on the landing outside. Then the iron latch of the bedroom door was lifted, the door pushed open, and the latch released again, as though by a human hand. She waited, expecting her daughter to appear, but instead to her horror saw a "cloaked shadow" pass from the door across to the corner cupboard, making a heavy tread as it walked, and open the cupboard door and search the pigeon-holes, as though for missing papers. As soon as the thing's back was turned she dived into bed and under the clothes, too frightened even to wake her husband. She remembered how it was said that Judge Jeffreys had used this cupboard for filing his papers.

Her husband, when she told him next day of her experience, was sceptical but sympathetic, believing she had perhaps been working too hard. But three months later Mr Tugwood both saw and heard the ghost himself, so clearly that he flung a heavy shoe at it; but the shoe passed right through the cloaked figure and only succeeded in cutting a piece of plaster from the wall, the ghost continuing uninterrupted on its way to the cupboard.

After this the ghost paid frequent, if irregular, visits in which it climbed the stairs, walked along the passage, lifted the heavy latch on the door and, walking across the bedroom to the old oak cupboard, searched among the pigeon-holes. Relatives who came to scoff at the spectre stayed, saw it, and left convinced of its existence. One evening a nephew of the couple in his twenties, who had been more sceptical than most, rushed downstairs "with his hair on end", shouting hysterically that he had seen the ghost. He said he had heard it walk the passage and seen the door open as it entered the old courtroom.

The Tugwoods had to decide whether to give in to the ghost and quit the cottage, or to stay and put up with it. Mr Tugwood reasoned that it seemed harmless enough and appeared to have no objection to their presence, so they would stay. The couple made one change. As Mrs Tugwood could not stand the noisy way in which the ghost opened the bedroom door, with a sudden clang of the latch, they slept in future with the door open to allow it easy admittance.

Several tenants of a farm near Watford, Hertfordshire, were driven away by its ghost before a couple arrived who learned to live with it. The ghost was said to be that of a little old woman in a black gown with white lace, who was seen wandering around the ancient buildings of Green End Farm. She was never threatening, but was apparently responsible for waking people in the night by pulling off the bedclothes.

Strange noises, too, were heard at the farm: the sound of a whining dog, the jingle of harness, and hurried footsteps, seemingly clattering over cobbles outside. The history of the sound of horses was believed to go back to 1642, when Cromwell quartered some of his Roundheads in the attic.

Local villagers, as well as the farmhouse occupants, heard the various noises right up to the late 1940s, though the cobbles had been removed some twenty years before.

There was no explanation for the lady in black. No one knew who she was; no bones had been found, and there was no record of any person dying violently at the farm. Some people believed that to see the ghost was a warning of disaster. Mr Herbert Simmonds, a former tenant, told how his brother was awakened night after night by the old lady who beckoned him to follow her, but he never did. Soon afterwards he was drowned. A woman visitor to the farm also saw the lady in black just before her husband was killed.

But Mr and Mrs David Keeble, on moving in, believed the ghost to be perfectly harmless and they liked her happy smile. The first night was a shock for Mrs Keeble. "I shall never forget it—it was horrible, especially the sounds outside," she told the *Empire News* in September, 1950. "But now I don't mind. The old lady seems happy with us. She not only appears at night; during the day I meet her on the stairs or when I am cooking. Sometimes I feel she is the rightful owner and I am only the guest."

An unusual haunting has gone on for some years in a house at West Tisted, Hampshire. Commander John F. Baird, a retired naval commander and his family, call the ghost "George". They have never seen "him", but he smokes foul tobacco, which the family usually smell in the kitchen or on the stairs. A cloud of tobacco smoke is also seen on occasions. Mrs Baird had an early shock when, on seeing it blowing about in the garden, she realised suddenly that the smoke was blowing in the opposite direction to the wind. At other times the mysterious smoke has inexplicably blown in her face.

But, she tells me, "There is nothing sinister about 'George'. He seems a very benign and well intentioned presence."

The family believe "George" to be the ghost of a French prisoner, as apparently some prisoners were kept there during the Napoleonic wars. Part of the house is some 400 years old, and at least one old French coin has been unearthed there.

THE GHOST OF WOOKEY HOLE

Wookey Hole Caves, a series of underground caverns at the foot of the Mendip Hills in Somerset, are the oldest known home of man in Britain. They were also, according to local legend, the home a thousand years ago of the Witch of Wookey, an evil woman whose activities put a blight on the district. A monk of Glastonbury had to be called to exorcise her, and for her persistent wickedness he turned her into stone. A black stalagmite formation which rises in striking profile beside the underground river in Wookey Hole is said to be the witch's frozen effigy.

So much for the legend, which has been passed down through generations in the nearby village of Wookey Hole and surrounds. In this century, just as numerous excavations have proved the existence in the caves of early British tribes, so they would seem in addition to give added strength to the legend of the witch. For during excavations in 1912 there was found, at a depth of ten feet, the skeleton of a young woman, together with a dagger, knife, weaving comb and ball of white stalagmite resembling a witch's crystal; and beside her, the bones of two goats.

Fifteen years later, in 1927, Wing Commander Gerard Hodgkinson, whose family had owned Wookey Hole and the land round about for hundreds of years, began to develop the witch's "lair" as a public attraction. Gardens leading up to the caves were created, and a museum, shops and restaurant added as the enterprise was gradually built up into the showplace of the Mendips it is today, with the legendary Witch of Wookey becoming known throughout the world.

With this evocative background it is not to be wondered at that in the late 1940s, when uncanny incidents began to occur in a cottage on the Wookey Hole estate, some people thought it might be due to the witch having returned to start her strange tricks again. Certainly there were few places more suggestive of the darkly supernatural where a ghost could have chosen to appear.

The haunted cottage itself had no previous ghostly history. Built in the 1870s, it had been lived in for almost the whole of her life by a woman who died there in 1947, aged over eighty. She had declined to have electricity installed in the cottage, so this work was done after her death. It was then the hauntings began.

A couple with a young son took over the tenancy of the cottage temporarily. One evening the eight-year-old boy, who had gone upstairs, came down looking very frightened and asked his mother, "Who is that old lady in the white apron upstairs?" His puzzled mother went back upstairs with him to investigate and was shocked to see the ghost of an old woman walk across the landing. After this upsetting incident the family repeatedly heard phantom footsteps going up and down the stairs, and saw the old woman's ghost several more times. It was too much for them and they moved out.

But the hauntings did not stop with the family's departure. Instead, over the next few years it got progressively worse, until it became impossible to get people to stay in the cottage. The footsteps continued their eerie tread, as if someone was walking about upstairs, though whenever anyone went up to look there was no one there. Doors bulged with pressure and flew open and shut, electric lights switched themselves on and off in the middle of the night, and things moved from place to place. The ghost, in a mob cap and white apron, continued to walk, accompanied always by a wave of intense cold and a dead, dank smell.

When the cottage, together with the one adjoining, was taken over for use by catering staff at the Cave Restaurant, a terrified woman employee who slept there saw the ghost step through the wall into her bedroom.

The restaurant manageress at the time, who had no belief in ghosts, then agreed to sleep in the cottage; but after only a short time in the building she felt very uneasy and could not sleep. She went for the assistant manageress and together the two women searched the cottage but found nothing wrong. The manageress went back to bed. At 2 am., however, she awoke with the chilling sensation of a cold hand on her shoulder, and, sitting up in bed, was horrified to see the ghost walk through the doorway. As on previous occasions the old woman's apparition was accompanied by "a smell like death itself".

By the summer of 1952 the hauntings in the cottage had continued at intervals for nearly five years, and Mrs Olive Hodgkinson, wife of Wookey Hole's owner, had evidence from a total of twenty-three people who had experienced the ghost, seven of whom had actually seen it. She decided that something would have to be done about it.

A psychical research investigator held a vigil in the cottage. This proved fruitless; nevertheless the incidents still went on. The help of the vicar of Wookey Hole was then sought, and in 1954 a service of blessing and prayers was held in the building.

The vicar's service was entirely successful. Mrs Hodgkinson tells me that there were no further disturbances and staff have lived in the cottage quite happily since.

So a thousand years after the sudden end of the Witch of Wookey, a second alarming spectre had been laid.

THE CRIME OF JOHN CARVER

The haunting of an old timbered cafe on the outskirts of Croydon, Surrey, in the 1940s brought echoes of a strange murder trial held nearly eighty years before; one which, because of its curious circumstances must be among the oddest cases in English criminal records.

The events leading up to the trial of John Carpenter Carver, in 1870, began early one day in May of that year.

Carver, an upholsterer and furniture dealer in his thirties, lived with his wife and their year-old baby in a house at South End, Croydon. The house was divided into two and had two small shops under the one roof. Carver rented his half of the premises from the house owner, William Morgan, a builder, who carried on business from one shop while Carver plied his trade in the other. Carver's share of the house consisted of the shop with a small parlour at the back, a bedroom on the first floor and an attic. He employed a young servant girl named Mary Ann Turner.

Carver had been married for ten years. His wife, Anne, was a small, lightly-built woman who apparently had to suffer a lot from her husband's bitter tongue. He was often heard to quarrel with her, using abusive language, and even to threaten her, and she was known to have fits of hysterical sobbing.

On this May morning Carver was heard once again abusing his wife, and in the early afternoon he quarrelled with her again. A man who happened to come to the shop door at about half-past two heard Carver swearing at his wife, while another witness (names were not given in the court reports) told of how he heard Carver suddenly shout in the parlour, "I'll knock your brains out!" This witness said that as he stood watching, Carver appeared to fall from one part of the room towards another. He then saw Carver raise his hands three or four times, as if striking at something violently; but as Carver had nothing in his hands he decided he had better mind his own business, and walked away.

A short time after this Carver went next door to the Morgans and asked them to send for a doctor, as he believed his wife was dead or dying. Mrs Morgan ran into the Carvers' parlour, where she saw Anne Carver lying on the floor quite still, with blood on the upper part of her dress. Mrs Morgan exclaimed to Carver, "Oh, you wretch!" He replied simply, "It was an accident."

The doctor found that a deep knife wound had penetrated Anne Carver's heart, killing her instantly. Carver went for a policeman on duty in South End and brought him to the house. Then, quite calmly, he gave his version of what had happened, during which time large groups of people gathered outside his house and in various streets round about, for the news had travelled quickly.

Carver swore that his wife's death was an accident—"and if I am hung for it I can't help it." He said that on coming home to a dinner of boiled bacon, he went out and cut some mustard and cress which he gave to his wife to wash. She did so, and then served it up to him on a plate from which the servant girl had just had her meal. This plate had lain on the top of two other plates, which were clean. Carver said he remonstrated with his wife for giving him his dinner on the dirty plate. They quarrelled and she aggravated him so much that he flung all three plates at the wall and smashed them. This made his wife "savage" and she flew at him with great violence, just as he was cutting some bacon. The impact knocked him over a chair with his back to the wall, and he was transfixed there with the knife and fork held forward in his hands. While he was in this position his wife again rushed at him and fell against the extended knife.

He said he did not realise at first what had happened. His wife turned round, walked across the little room and sat down in a chair, but then fell off it, as he thought in a fainting fit, into the fireplace. He lifted her out of the fireplace on to the floor, and only then discovered that she had been wounded and appeared to be dying. He went for the Morgans.

Carver was taken through the crowds to the police station where, when charged with the wilful murder of his wife, the *Croydon Times* noted "he exhibited great coolness. He made a statement with the utmost deliberation, and after it was read over to him, he dictated some verbal alterations."

The trial was held at Guildford Assizes that August. A doctor agreed that Anne Carver, small as she was, could have received the fatal wound just as described by the husband, even though it was inflicted by a common table knife with a rounded end and not one with a sharp point.

Carver's counsel then submitted there was no case for the jury to consider, but the judge, after a short deliberation, said he "thought" he ought not to stop the case. So Carver's counsel briefly addressed the jury, after which the judge summed up and the jury retired, though their verdict seemed to be a foregone conclusion. Carver's counsel endorsed his brief "Not Guilty", handed it to the prisoner's solicitor and left the court.

But the jury returned in half an hour to pronounce Carver "Guilty", though adding that they recommended him to mercy as they thought that his wife, in putting the dirty plate before him, had provoked him. When asked if he had anything to say before sentence of death was passed, Carver strongly challenged the evidence of the witness who claimed to have seen his hands raised, and said he would die happily as he knew he was innocent.

Carver's solicitor, Mr H. Parry, was thunderstruck at the jury's verdict. He wrote to the editor of the *Croydon Times* asking him to inform the public that, following the "extraordinary verdict" he had sent a copy of the depositions to the Home Secretary, urgently requesting him to have inquiries made "for the purpose of obtaining the only reparation that can now be made my unfortunate client—a pardon—which I feel the greatest confidence in obtaining".

Remarking on the trial scene, the solicitor wrote, "While the jury were being conducted by the officer of the court upstairs to the jury-room, a lady in the company of two other ladies of the high-sheriff (all of whom sat on the Bench during the trial), exclaimed audibly, 'Poor fellow, I hope they will not keep him long in suspense.' In fact it was the universal feeling frequently expressed during the absence of the jury that the delay was unnecessary. The verdict caused quite a sensation in the town of Guildford, the universal expression being 'The prisoner ought to have been acquitted.' I don't think a single person in court (and there were several hundreds) excepting the twelve Cobham jurymen, agreed with the verdict."

Three weeks later Carver got his free pardon, and again his solicitor wrote in strong terms to the local newspaper.

"My anticipations have been realised; Carver has been pardoned, and was liberated on Wednesday morning at eleven o'clock. He is pardoned for what? For having the misfortune to be tried by a common jury for the most serious offence known to our criminal law—a jury devoid of common sense and by whom he was found guilty of an offence of which he was innocent."

Mr Parry charged in his letter that there had been prejudice against Carver from the start, from members of the inquest jury.

A month after his release from the condemned cell Carver returned to Croydon. He went first to the police court in the morning to claim some articles which had been taken from him on arrest, including his wife's wedding ring, afterwards saying that he intended to visit his wife's grave and then "look for a fresh place of business". News of his arrival soon spread and he was recognized in the street, carrying a loaded carpet-bag, at which, as *The Times* reported, "A number of women became violent in their demonstrations of disgust and he was pursued by a mob of seven or eight hundred people, who threatened to tear him to pieces."

The hostile crowd followed Carver wherever he went and tried several times to attack him. He was harried up and down the neighbourhood of South End, and on a number of occasions had to flee to a convenient house or hotel to escape assault, eventually being holed up by his increasingly violent pursuers in a house close to the Brighton Road, outside which a huge crowd gathered. The police arrived in force and had to run him out the back way, through the grounds, into the Brighton Road. Eventually, after finding himself still unable to throw off the crowds, he fled to the home of a relative in Purley.

There was no future in Croydon for John Carpenter Carver, the anger of the townsfolk made that plain. And so, slipping into anonymity, he quit the neighbourhood and, some say, the country.

Did his injured spirit return some eighty years later in the 1940s? Miss Hilda Steel, in her cafe on the Brighton Road, was convinced of it. Her cafe was in an old building that went back 200 years in time; massive oak beams supported walls and ceiling, floors were uneven with unexpected steps, and a narrow, twisting staircase led to the rooms above. It was when white-haired Miss Steel tried to sleep in the room immediately above the cafe that strange things occurred during the night. Baking tins rattled in the kitchen and the oven door slammed to and fro. Doors left locked were found wide open in the morning, with the keys hidden behind plates or under tables.

Miss Steel actually saw the ghost, which she described as being a tall, grey form without head or legs. Several of her kitchen staff saw it too. They said the ghost was invariably heralded by an icy blast of air, and that it glided in through the back door, climbed the stairs and hovered on the landing.

Why should Carver's ghost haunt the old cafe? Because it was thought that the cafe building had been one of his refuges when he had run from shelter to shelter in that area to hide from the mob. Added to this supposition was the fact that there was an additional ghostly disturbance in the cafe every year on the night of May 26, the date of his wife's death, when an unaccountable crash and tinkling of glass was heard "as if a heavy body had fallen through a plate glass window".

Yet no one at this time, after the long passage of years, could have known the exact circumstances of the Carvers' fatal quarrel; and certainly they had no knowledge of the incident (only recently brought to light by myself from old records) in which the husband had snatched up all the dinner plates and hurled them against the wall in his rage.

If the ghost, now gone, was Carver's, it would seem that he himself was haunted by the echo of his rash and unfortunate act.

THE ROMAN PATROL

Roman ghosts are not common and the one reported to have walked through the centuries at Mersea Island, Essex, has particular interest, appearing as it does only at times of heavy rains. The ghost is said to be that of a Roman warrior, fully clad in armour, who, when swamping rains threaten The Strood, the old Roman causeway to the mainland, is seen to walk in sorrowful patrol from Barrow Hill to The Strood, where he stands for a moment before gradually fading away.

During the last century and in the early 1900s the ghost, sometimes described by witnesses as having the appearance of a Roman general, was seen on several such stormy nights, with long intervals between. The warrior's last two recorded visits, however, were both made in July, 1939 during a week of heavy rains.

There were at this time many islanders who would not use the East Mersea Road after an appearance by the apparition, and some others who would not on any account use the road after nightfall for fear of meeting the ghostly figure. Among witnesses of th doleful spectre in earlier years was one woman who testified to both seeing and hearing the apparition on several occasions, and there were local historians who felt there was a firm basis for the stories of the haunting, though who the ghost could possibly be was lost in the island's eventful past.

Barrow Hill, the old burial ground from which the ghost was invariably seen to begin its walk was excavated at the turn of the century and Roman remains found; also, a burial chamber of Roman tiles, in which was found a glass urn containing bones, thought to be those of an Essex chieftain. The strong local belief has persisted that the remains of the sorrowing Roman patrol have yet to be discovered, although there have been no further sightings of the ghost since 1939.

Around this same time the sounds of ghostly soldiers of another early era were claimed to be heard close to the ancient moated mounds forming Thunderfield Castle, near Horley, Surrey. The castle is believed to have been a halting place of King Harold's army as it marched to Hastings to meet the invading soldiers of William of Normandy. For countless years there had existed a tradition that a ghostly army was sometimes to be heard marching along a road near the castle.

Early in 1937, some months after the first excavations had begun on the privately owned castle site, a local farmer, Mr F. Godden, and his wife, were surprised to hear at times the tramp of marching feet and the sound of a military voice giving orders, though there was nothing and no one in the vicinity. The noises seemed to issue from mid-air. Then early one night as Mr Godden was driving home in his car, he saw the tall figure of a strange-looking man suddenly appear standing before him in the middle of the road. The man seemed to be wearing a long red cloak and had unkempt fair hair. It was not yet dark and Mr Godden was driving with only his sidelights on. He immediately switched on his headlights and swerved, but the curious figure had vanished.

Other local residents now admitted to hearing the weird sound of tramping feet, as did a friend of Mr and Mrs Godden who came to visit them. The friend, Mr F. E. Jones, who was no believer in ghosts, afterwards described his odd experience while walking along Haroldslea Drive to Mr Godden's house:

"I heard coming towards me a faint, steady tramping of feet. Then as the sound became louder the atmosphere seemed to become icy cold. The sound of the marching became louder until I was in the middle of an invisible company of men. Round me there seemed to be a clink as of metal. Gradually the sound died away.

"It was not imagination; it was something I cannot explain. But it was something very real—yet unreal."

Other people who heard the eerie tramping described it in much the same terms. The burst of ghostly activity by the invisible army seemed to last over several months; then, as at Mersea, all was quiet once more.

ON CANDLEMAS EVE

It is often argued that people see what they want to see, and that impressionable people who have had hauntings described to them sometimes have a "vision" themselves, through imagination or self-suggestion. This is a perfectly valid argument and might perhaps apply in some unsubstantiated cases, but what of the person told of a reputed haunting who unexpectedly witnesses something entirely different?

Such was the experience of Miss Olive Gosden, of Castlemorton, Worcestershire. It happened on the night of February 1, 1940, just a few months after the start of World War II. Miss Gosden, a schoolteacher now retired, describes her uncanny experience:

"A few of us in the village of Colwall, on the Herefordshire side of the Malvern Hills, were running a small club mainly for the village girls and the soldiers camped on the local racecourse, and anyone else who cared to drop in. We were allowed extra rations to run a small canteen, which made it even more popular. I was more or less in charge, and that evening when I got to the club a little after half-past seven I remembered with dismay that extra work at the school nearby, where I taught, had made me forget to fetch our milk supply from a farm about a mile away. So while the others prepared the sandwiches, I seized my bicycle and a big enamelled jug and rode off as fast as I could in the half moonlight, the journey taking me across the village green and down a lonely bit of road which led to a very old sunken lane known as the 'haunted lane'.

"It was told locally how an unfortunate girl who had been turned from her home one snowy night by her brute of a husband had come up that lane with her baby in her arms to ask for shelter from her father, who lived in a house which then stood at the top of the lane. But on her father's orders she was turned away from the door by servants, and was found the next day, drowned in a small quarry pond at the bottom of the lane where the railway now went over a bridge. Her ghost was supposed to be 'seen' coming up the lane.

"Though not naturally nervous I did feel a bit creepy, but saying to myself firmly that my friends at the farm came down there every evening and were none the worse, and that I was not to be a fool, I sped on. There were in fact more earthly things to worry about. The troops had just put up posts with bundles of barbed wire attached beside the lane, and one of these made me jump because it looked like a man, and there was a rumour that German paratroops had been picked up a week before around there. Speeding on I got to the farm by the bridge and collected my milk. Then, feeling much better for a few jokes and their friendly faces, I set off on the return journey. I got back up the 'haunted lane', having to push my cycle most of the way as it was a gradual uphill now, and at the top drew a relieved breath, saying to myself, 'Well, here you are at the top—and it wasn't so bad after all, was it?' Then I gave a loud exclamation of astonishment, for slowly and clearly across the road in front of me I saw a strange small procession of black figures in sweeping black robes.

"I gathered they were cowled monks and got the vivid impression that in their midst they were carrying on a bier the body of a young man who had died away from home. It was all draped in flowing black, and I knew they were carrying him back to his home in the valley and that he had been greatly loved and there would be much sorrow because of his death. It was all quite vividly made known to me, just as if someone stood beside me wordlessly telling me the particulars—or as if I already knew them. I got the impression that the period was about 1400. The procession went slowly on and to my surprise it then seemed to go off down an old track towards the farms in the hollow below. But I had had enough. Terrified by now, I got on my cycle and rode off on the now mercifully downhill way back to the village.

"Then I realised to my horror that what appeared to be a horseman in a cloak and plumed hat was also riding hell for leather at my left hand, as if he, too, were riding away in terror from something he was afraid of. I then seemed to know that he was responsible for the death of the other man and was trying to escape from the knowledge of what had happened. When I looked round the figure did not seem to be there, but directly I looked to my front he was there again, and so we proceeded together all down that lane, round to the left, where he seemed less insistent, and right up the village green until we got to the railway bridge, when it all ceased. But as we came up the green, although the landscape on my left looked the same, in a way it appeared slightly different—at the bridge, where the impression left me, the old road (before the railway was built) led slightly left to an old posting house still standing.

"Feeling very shaken I got back to the club and my friends, more than thankful for the lights. One of them said, 'You *have* been quick.' I laughed and said, 'Yes, I did streak,' and then—'I think I have been haunted in the "haunted lane", but it wasn't where I expected it to be and it wasn't what I was afraid I might see,' describing the exact spot. My friend replied, 'Oh, but that *is* where the men about here say they see things.' I laughed and said, 'It must be an effect of the light there,' feeling quite sure, though, that it was not. It was only the next day, when the old school housekeeper who looked after me mentioned that it was Candlemas Day, that I realised my journey down the lane had been made on Candlemas Eve.

"Some time after I described the incident to an old friend in Malvern, and she told me there was a story that long ago, two young men had fought a duel and the son of the people who lived at a house in the valley had been killed; but whether there is any connection I do not know."

Corroboration can come, much to the relief of a witness, a long time after a ghostly incident. An example of this is the experience of Miss Margery Hookham, of Malvern Wells, who some years ago went with a friend on holiday to a farmhouse in a lonely valley in the north-west of Brecknockshire, in the vicinity of Llanwrtyd Wells.

"In this farmhouse," says Miss Hookham, "I had a large front bedroom, while my friend had a room at the back of the house. I used to wake in the night with my heart thumping, feeling terrified, and sometimes I could hear the sound of someone shuffling about outside my door, which I felt was an old man in slippers. This happened night after night until I quite dreaded going up to bed. Finally my room was changed to one at the back of the house and the feelings I had had, and the sounds I had heard, ceased. All this time my friend had felt and heard nothing.

"Some years afterwards, by the purest coincidence, I met a woman who told me that her sister had stayed at the same farmhouse and had exactly the same uncanny experience; a dog she had taken with her nearly went mad with fright and had to be sent away.

"She then told me the story of the house. It was said to be haunted by a horrible old man who used to keep a savage dog and set it to fight all the dogs of the neighbourhood, most of which it killed. The garden when dug up was found to be full of dogs' bones.

"The front bedroom which I had slept in was the haunted room."

Very often corroboration comes much sooner, as in a case at Streatham, London, in 1933. On Christmas night Mr Lewis Amis, of Clapham, a fireman at the newly-built Streatham Astoria had sole charge of the empty theatre, and this was his strange story:

"I was making my round through the darkened theatre shortly after midnight, and as I entered the tea lounge I saw a figure advancing towards me. Thinking it must be a burglar, I turned my torch full on to him and saw the figure of an old man, dressed in a long white gown with a hood over his head, gliding across the floor, his arms held stiffly at his side. I caught a glimpse of a wizened, wrinkled face and short beard, then he turned away from me and moved towards the stairs leading down to the vestibule.

"I followed, and as we reached the doors leading to the stalls they suddenly swung open. The doors are heavy, strongly fastened, and three men would have a job to get them open. The figure glided on down the centre aisle and then leapt, or rather floated, across the orchestra pit, landing behind the footlights in front of the curtain. It now turned and faced me, and, holding its hand aloft, cried in a weird, husky voice, 'I won't sell, I won't sell, I won't sell.' Then it vanished."

Mr Amis's fantastic story was received rather coolly, the kindliest of sceptics dismissing it as a dream. But then came firm evidence to explain the incident. It was discovered that four years before, on the site where the theatre now stood, had lived a Mr James, who, although constant pressure had been brought upon him to sell his pleasant, comfortable house, was loathe to leave it. Eventually he did agree to sell and moved to another part of Streatham, dying soon after. Mr Amis had never heard of Mr James, but the widow confirmed his description of her bearded husband and the fact that Mr James had been very strongly attached to the house and extremely reluctant to give it up so that the site could be developed.

The various ways in which corroboration of a haunting arrives, vouched for by totally independent witnesses, are often as fascinating as the ghostly incidents themselves. The following is a personal example.

In his book *The Midnight Hearse* which I edited, Elliott O'Donnell referred briefly to the spectre said to haunt the Church of St Bartholomew-the-Great in Smithfield, London. This is believed to be the spirit of the monk Rahere, who founded the church together with St Bartholomew's Hospital, the oldest hospital in London, in the twelfth century. Rahere in his early life, as a canon regular of the Order of St Augustine, was a story-teller in the houses of nobles and finally at the court of Henry I. Life at court seems suddenly to have palled, for he plunged himself into penance on a pilgrimage to Rome. On the journey he fell ill and made a vow to St Bartholomew that if he were spared he would devote the rest of his life to the service of the sick poor. He recovered, and returned to fulfil his vow. Granted a site in Smithfield by Henry I, he gathered about him young men and old labourers, and with his hands and theirs raised in 1123 on the site of the present hospital the first "Bart's".

Rahere's apparition is said by many to have been heard and sometimes seen walking along the aisles and ambulatories of St Bartholomew's Church. Elliott O'Donnell however, during a vigil there saw and heard nothing. Now Mrs Isobel Burke tells me from Salisbury, Rhodesia:

"After living in this country (Rhodesia) for some years my mother returned to England in 1928 for a short visit, during which time she saw many old friends. The two incidents I am about to describe happened there shortly before her arrival.

"My mother went first to see a friend who lived in the Midlands —a woman of the world, rich, unmarried and gay—who told my mother she had not been well of late and was full of desperate personal worries. This friend went on to say that one morning on a visit to London she was passing St Bartholomew's and by pure chance and on an impulse decided to go inside for a few minutes. She knelt down in a pew and prayed, her worries being very much on her mind, and was suddenly filled with a sense of peace, together with the feeling that a great burden was being lifted from her. She looked up, and in the pulpit was the figure of a monk in his robes. He looked straight at her and raised his hand in blessing, then slowly descended the steps of the pulpit and walked away. She was much uplifted and described this as a wonderful experience, maintaining that the monk—Rahere—haunted the premises to help people who were in trouble.

"The surprising coincidence came when my mother visited a second friend who lived, I think, in Brighton. She was a highly religious woman, very high church, and rather unworldly. She was in an advanced state of mental anguish and told my mother that her family thought she was—and had accused her of being— deranged, because after a trip to London she told them . . . and here she repeated an almost identical story of seeing the monk as that told to my mother by her other friend, saying also that the sight of the monk had lifted a tremendous burden from her shoulders.

"My mother was able to comfort this woman by telling her of the first friend's experience, so relieving her from the terrible doubt

that had been growing in her mind as to whether she had imagined
the whole thing. She had gone to the church seeking comfort, unlike the first woman who had acted on a sudden impulse. The two
women had never met or even heard of one another and there was
an interval of some months between the incidents."

The rector of St Bartholomew's at the time, and his wife, both
claimed to have seen the monk, the rector's wife several times.

Mrs Burke adds: "My mother spent the whole of one day there
praying, but nothing happened at all, a fact which comforted her
to some extent in the belief that her worries (which were of some
magnitude) were not so overwhelming that she needed help."

Finally, while considering the various ways in which ghostly
incidents are confirmed and explained, it should be noted how
very often the clue to an apparently meaningless haunting lies
buried in the past.

Many years ago there lived close to the hamlet of Barham, six
miles from Canterbury, an illiterate elderly woman who used to
wander off at times on walks across the Barham Downs. She knew
nothing of the history of the district but often described the things
and the people she "saw" during her wanderings. No one took
much notice of her fanciful talk, but when in later years her
stories came to be considered against the historical background of
the Downs they seemed to be very much more than the ramblings
of a queer old woman. She had once described how she had been
sitting at the back of the Black Mill, near what later was the road
to Aylesham, when she saw a body of men marching close together. They wore helmets and "kilts", and she saw the gleam of
metal on their uniforms. Yet she knew nothing of the fighting
between the Romans and the Britons near the spot.

Another time she told a friend that at a certain place she had
seen five ladies in silks and satins dancing with men, who had long
curls and feathered hats. Again she knew nothing of the gay life at
a camp on this part of the Downs at the time of the Restoration of
Charles II.

She also once described seeing a procession of white-robed
figures carrying "on a wattle-gate" a great golden image. They
passed her slowly, singing as they went, going down into the valley.
For this ghostly incident there is as yet no explanation, though
from what we have seen it is not unlikely that one will emerge.